PRAISE FOR T~~HE~~ ~~LIBRARY~~
OF J~~OHNNY~~

Plaster City

Winner of t

"Violent, hilarious, and to
brand of compassionate m~~a~~ ~~……~~ ~~…p ~~~~o~~ ~~Leonard stories,~~ ~~but~~
Anthony Award–winner Shaw does it extremely well, too."

—*Publishers Weekly* (starred review)

"Anthony Award–winner Shaw's second installment in the award-winning "Jimmy Veeder Fiasco" series hits the right note. Violent and ribald without being salacious, the novel maintains a tongue-in-cheek attitude that keeps the reader wholly entertained . . . Readers who enjoy mysteries and suspense novels with plenty of action and humor will delight in this series."

—*Library Journal*

"Mixing comedy with the ugly side of human experience is never an easy trick, but Shaw is well on his way to becoming a master at this difficult craft."

—*Booklist*

"Johnny Shaw has a way of making the ugliest, roughest, most insane misadventures feel honest and hilarious. Underneath all that vomit and blood is real affection, even tenderness, for a world that Shaw obviously knows well. His writing is brutal and profane and absolutely beautiful."
  —S.G. REDLING, bestselling author of *Flowertown* and *Redemption Key*

"If you do not love Johnny Shaw's new novel *Plaster City*, I will fight you."
  —CHRISTA FAUST, author of *Money Shot* and *Choke Hold*

"Johnny Shaw is a Scott Phillips of the American Southwest, like Phillips setting his novels in bleak, flat landscapes, and populating them with dangerous, violent characters who, call them bad or call them immoral, are almost always endearingly human. Oh, and, like Phillips's, his books will always make a reader laugh out loud while only rarely descending into jokiness."

—*Detectives Beyond Borders*

Big Maria

Winner of the 2013 Anthony Award for Best Paperback Original

"Comic thrillerdom has a new star."

—*Booklist Online* (starred review)

"This is one you'll soon be recommending to your friends. It's light-hearted but not lightweight, funny as hell but never frivolous. Shaw writes like the bastard son of Donald Westlake and Richard Stark: There's crime, and criminals, but there's also a deep vein of good humor that makes Shaw's writing sparkle. Combine that with his talent for creating memorable characters (the supporting cast, including a mute, severed head, often threatens to steal the show), and you get one of the best reads in recent memory, an adventure story that might just make you mist up every once and awhile, especially during the book's moving finale."

—*Mystery Scene* magazine

"Funny, fist-pumping, rockin', right-on, righteous fun."

—Barnes & Noble Mystery Blog

"Shaw has invented 'dust bowl' fiction for the twenty-first century. Funny, sad, madcap, compulsively readable, and ultimately, so very, very wise."

—Blake Crouch, author of *Pines*

"Johnny Shaw has an incredible talent for moving from darkness to hope, from heart-wrenching to humor, and from profane to sacred. His latest, *Big Maria*, is an adventure story that's equal parts Humphrey Bogart and Elmore Leonard, with just a little bit of the Hardy Boys thrown in. I loved every page."

—HILARY DAVIDSON, author of *Evil in All Its Disguises*

"I loved every page of *Big Maria*. You don't often read a gutbustingly funny book that manages to maintain its fundamental seriousness and bad-ass sense of plot. This proves what many of us suspected after *Dove Season*, that Johnny Shaw is one of the majors already."

—SCOTT PHILLIPS, author of *Rake*

Dove Season: A Jimmy Veeder Fiasco
Winner of the 2012 Spotted Owl Award for Debut Mystery

"[Johnny Shaw] is excellent at creating a sense of place with a few deft strokes . . . He moves effortlessly between dark comedy and moments that pack a real emotional punch, and he's got a knack for off-kilter characters who are completely at home in their own personal corners of oddballdom."

—TANA FRENCH, author of *Broken Harbor*

"Johnny Shaw calls *Dove Season* a Jimmy Veeder Fiasco, but I call it a whole new ball game; I enjoyed this damn book more than anything else I read this year!"

—CRAIG JOHNSON, author of *A Serpent's Tooth*

"*Dove Season* is dark and funny, graceful and profane, with beating-heart characters and a setting as vivid as a scorpion sting on a dusty wrist. Debut author Johnny Shaw is a welcome new voice. I'm already looking forward to Jimmy Veeder's next fiasco."

—SEAN DOOLITTLE, Thriller Award–winning author of *Lake Country*

ALSO BY JOHNNY SHAW

The Jimmy Veeder Fiasco Series

Dove Season

Plaster City

Stand-Alone Novels

Big Maria

FLOODGATE
JOHNNY SHAW

THOMAS & MERCER

Text copyright © 2016 Johnny Shaw

Published by Thomas & Mercer, Seattle

www.apub.com

Amazon, the Amazon logo, and Thomas & Mercer are trademarks of Amazon.com, Inc., or its affiliates.

ISBN-13: 9781503952195 (hardcover)
ISBN-10: 1503952193 (hardcover)
ISBN-13: 9781503950351 (paperback)
ISBN-10: 1503950352 (paperback)

Cover design by Cyanotype Book Architects

Printed in the United States of America

This one is for Mickey Batts.

1929

LONG PAST DAYS

It wasn't the stench I knew. Woke up coughing. Sat up in bed, board straight. A lungful of smoke. Throat seared. Different from the burnoff from the rubber factory. Acrid, black, thick. This was something else. A something else on fire. Wasn't until Sal showed that I learned it was the whole city.

"You got a gun?" Sal at the door. Jumpy. Maybe scared. A first for Sal.

If I had money for a gun, I wouldn't be a hood. A hood in training, at least. An errand boy. Drove. Collected. Backed Sal, maybe twice. Gun on loan both times. Sal knew this. He was wishing, grasping. I shook my head.

"Get dressed, kid. Grab the biggest knife in the kitchen."

"What's going on out there?"

"War."

❖ ❖ ❖

Sleep in my eyes. A late night working for Fat Jimmy. Still waking up. Threw on my clothes. Fingers shaking. Three tries to get my boots tied. Ma at my door. Me undoing a knot.

"What's going on, Rocky?"

"Nothing, Ma."

"Don't give me 'nothing.' That's Salvatore Carrelli."

"You smell the smoke, right?"

"What do you got to do with it?"

I didn't know. Walked past her to the kitchen. Dug through drawers. Big spoons and cooking wares. Copped an ice pick and a meat cleaver. Looped twine through the handle of the cleaver. Draped it around my neck. The ice pick slid in my boot. Ma and Sal watched me. Ma unnerved. Sal impatient.

"Fat Jimmy's waiting," Sal said.

"What about my ma?"

The look on her face. Like she'd drunk lemon juice with a castor oil chaser. Not intimidated by Sal or her hoodlum son.

"She'll be fine," Sal said, gave her a smile. She gave him a scowl. "She looks tougher than well-done horse meat. Besides, all the fighting is north of Cement Factory Road."

❖ ❖ ❖

Ma didn't let us leave right away, insisted we take food. God forbid we starve before we got killed. Hit the street armed with a sandwich and a piece of cheese wrapped in paper. The stink of not-so-fresh liverwurst, the burn of smoke.

Sal was wrong. The fires burnt below Cement Factory Road. In five, six, seven places. The whole Feldstein's Pianos block ablaze. The closest fires three blocks away. Smoke rose into the swelling gloom. Blackness hovered over the city. Midday, and the city dark as a moonless night.

People filled the streets. Fleeing south. Cars and wagons. Foot and horseback. Headed for the King Olaf Bridge. Trying to get out of the city. Away from the fires. Away from the warring gangs. The innocent of Auction in retreat. As the guilty built hell.

An old woman fell. Nobody helped. The surging crowd driven by fear and momentum. They trampled her underfoot. I took a step toward her. Sal had my shirt, threw me toward his Packard. Heard the woman's screams under the sound of the boots and shoes that killed her.

"You're going to see people die today," Sal said. "You'll kill yourself. But you ain't going to save a damn soul. You can't. Don't try."

4

The car crept upstream through the human current. The throng grew denser. The crunch of bone when Sal ran over some poor bastard's foot. People hit at the glass, kicked the fenders. The Packard clipped a horse-drawn wagon hauling birdcages. Brightly colored parrots and tropical birds squawking, feathers flying. The front bumper tied up in the wagon's spokes, locked together.

The wagon man jumped to the ground. Full of swearing and fight. Sal got out, drew his revolver. He won the argument. The man fled on foot. Absorbed into the crowd. His wagon and birds abandoned. The panicked birds violently flapped their wings.

"Somebody should let them go. Or shoot them," Sal said.

"The car's no good," I said, getting out. "Where we going?"

One last look at the birds. Sal said, "Turkish baths on 110th. Through Redling Park."

I turned to go on foot. Sal held my shoulder, stared me in the eye. As serious as I'd seen him. And he was a serious man. Seen him smile one time. When we found Ether Joe Poloni with a whore in Darktown. Ether Joe dressed like Laura La Plante. Had a string of pearls, but not around his neck. Sal got a kick out of that. He still beat Joe to death for stealing from Fat Jimmy. But with a smile.

"We're fighting everyone," Sal said. "The Tongs, the Wretches, the coppers, every bastard with a gun or knife or ax. It's a riot and a rampage. If you see a Negro or Chinaman or Irish, they're going to move to kill you. Kill the sons of bitches first."

I clutched the cleaver under my jacket. Hoped I'd have the backbone to use it. Hoped I wouldn't need to.

Took all of fifteen minutes to learn how worthless hope was.

❖ ❖ ❖

Redling Park was no safer than the streets. Tops of trees burning like struck match heads. Clusters of folk, lost and scared, trying to hide. We ran through the woods. Flaming leaves tumbling down on us. Out into the central pasture. The open field where people used to picnic. Now they wandered, dazed. No cover or safety. Eyes wide with fear. Ready to run or fight or die.

A company of Tongs appeared. Bloodred sashes. Stained hatchets. Four men and a woman. Only the Chinese could imagine a female assassin. A group crossed their path. Regular folk. Unarmed. Scared. Nowhere to run. The attack was a blur. Like wild dogs cornering a scurry of squirrels. Not a fight. A massacre. Screams turned silent. Bloodstained grass blades.

"Sal, we got to go." I pulled at him.

"To hell with these savages," Sal said. "They need a punish."

"You said it. We can't save no one."

"Does it look like them folks can be saved?"

Sal pulled his pistol. Aimed. Fired. One of the Tongs spun, fell to the ground. The butchery ceased. Blood-spattered faces searched for the shooter. We weren't hiding. I swear the Orientals smiled in unison. Charged the length of the field, hatchets in the air like Indian braves in a cowboy picture.

Sal stood his ground. Revolver ready. Waiting. Someone should erect a statue of Sal in that spot. A noble pose. Thug turned hero. I wanted to run. Couldn't. Ice pick in one hand, cleaver in the other. I got ready to die.

"I can't shoot them all. The she-devil is yours," Sal said.

"The girl?"

"She's the enemy. Not a person. It'll make stabbing her to death easier."

The Chinese ten yards away. Sal fired. And again. And again.

And on that day, I killed another human being for the first time. Fifteen years old. It happened quick. She fought ferociously. Her hatchet clipped me. On the shoulder. The skull. Fight ended with the Chinese girl slumping to the ground. Me clutching the ice pick lodged in her neck. She wasn't any older than me.

Before the sun set, more people would die by my hand. My life and Auction City changed forever.

❖ ❖ ❖

Sal was wrong. About a lot of things. Girl or she-devil, killing was not easy. And Ma wasn't fine. Annabella Colombo, like thousands of others, died on that December day. In a matter of hours, the city burnt out of control in the largest gang war in recorded American history. An unnatural disaster.

The papers called it the Flood.

1986

CHAPTER 1

I met me a girl. She was oh, so pretty.
Never shoulda took her to Auction City.
We had us some fun, but end of the night
She met her a rough man. Man wanted to fight.
Now I ain't no lily, no stranger to scuffles,
But I ain't done heard of no Auction City Shuffle.
The Auction City Shuffle.
A bloodthirsty dance them hooligans do.
The Auction City Shuffle.
One wrong step, that city'll kill you.
A jab and a hook and an uppercut later
Heard my girl laughing, knew then that I hate her.
And if bleeding and crying weren't even enough
Man had him a boot razor. That city play rough.
I got up and ran. From that town with no pity.
And I ain't never gone back to that damn Auction City.

—From the song "The Auction City Shuffle"
by Blind Willie Maxwell (1933)

Andy Destra liked complicated things, but that didn't mean he understood them. The more moving parts, the more fascinating. The more intricate the patterns, the stranger the connections. None of it necessarily led to any practical solutions. He liked the complexity for the sake of its complexity. The problem was that he got lost in the thing. Andy could not just see the forest for the trees. He would spend five days examining the bark of a particular cypress only to realize it was a birch. And upon the realization, he would become aware that he was lost and starving and dying of thirst and also missing his legs.

At the moment, that's where he found himself. In the metaphorical wilderness. Lost in the mechanism. A forest of circuits and wires and tubes. He stared and wondered what that red wire did. He could see where it attached to the rest of the device, but he couldn't discern its function. The green wire made sense. So did the black one. But that red one. It was screwing with him. He worked the process of elimination, searching for the answer in the absence. What did the other wires not do?

"I'm going to cut the red wire," Andy said.

"Don't cut anything," Champ said. "Your guesses aren't worth a tinker's damn."

"I can't not do something."

Andy closed the wire cutters, snipping the red wire. The television immediately lost its broadcast, and white noise loudly rushed through the room. He reached around to the front and turned the volume all the way down.

Champ crossed her arms in front of her chest, giving him a look that he had seen too many times during his childhood and teen years. "At least you figured out what the red wire does. It makes the TV work."

"Sorry, Champ," Andy said. "I'll fix it back."

"You got two minutes," she said. "Steve and Kayla are about to get down to business. It's been a long time coming, and I ain't missing it."

Days of Our Lives was sacrosanct. If Champ missed one second of the opening, Andy would catch hell. He quickly stripped the ends of the red wire and reattached them.

"How's the picture now?" Andy asked.

"It's a good thing you're a cop and don't need any real skills," Champ said.

Andy moved to the front of the television. He had picture and sound again, but the vertical hold sent the image scrolling up the screen only to reappear on the bottom. Like sands through a crappy hourglass. He played around with the dial and got the screen to hold. Just in time. The opening theme of *Days* filled the room.

"I'm not a cop anymore. Haven't been for over a year," Andy said. "You remember that, right?"

Champ shushed him, her eyes glued to the screen. "Come and watch with me. I'll cover your eyes if it gets too grown-up."

Andy moved to the couch, his eyes on the woman who had raised him. He never called her Mom. She was his Champ. It's what everyone called her. As the story went, she'd knocked out middleweight contender Max "Bruiser" Buchholz in a bar fight back in '44, and the name stuck.

In her seventies, she still had a youthful exuberance in voice and action, but her mind betrayed her. Mostly her memory. Andy didn't fully understand how it all worked. She could outline the genealogy of five generations of families in the fictional Salem but could lose the events of last month, last week, an hour ago.

The slow decay of her memory chipped at the thing that made Champ distinctly Champ. She and Andy may not have been blood, but it had been the two of them against the world for his whole life. Now she fought a losing battle on her own. Andy couldn't fathom her no longer in his life, fearing the day that she wouldn't recognize him. When she would be there and not be there at the same time.

"Worst decision you ever made," Champ said during the first commercial break.

"Which one?" Andy said.

"Signing up with those thugs."

"You mean the Auction City Police Department?"

"Most vicious gang in town," she said. "I got the scars to prove it."

"Wish I could argue," Andy said. "Seemed like the right thing. Should've listened."

"Quiet. Show's back on."

◆ ◆ ◆

The small room in the Michael R. Batty Senior Living Center consisted of a large living space, a bathroom, and a small kitchenette. About the size of a nice hotel room. It wasn't the house they both knew, but it had small touches that echoed home. Lace doilies on the small table, a few pictures on the bookcase, the "ashtray" that Andy had made at day camp. It looked more like a glittery dog turd, but you could put out a cigarette on it.

Andy wished she could have stayed at the old house, but not after her stroke and memory loss. He was glad that she had people looking after her. She retained a level of independence but acknowledged her limitations and allowed people to assist her. It wasn't easy for Champ. She was a scrapper, a fighter her whole life. But like any good brawler, she knew when she was in the late rounds.

"I'm going to take off," Andy said. "You need anything?"

"The body of a twenty-year-old and a functioning brain."

Andy laughed. "Your brain functions. The vertical hold just needs adjusting."

"You going to cut my red wire?"

"Hand me my pliers," Andy said.

"You could get me one thing," she said. "Real food. The meals here ain't bad, but I want the good stuff. Grease, fat, salt, fried. Cured meat, cheese, and gravies."

"Gravies, plural? More than one gravy?"

"I'll two-fist it."

◆ ◆ ◆

When Andy reached the first floor, the elevator doors opened to a woman who made him do a double take. Somewhere in her late fifties or early sixties, she still stunned. Red hair with a gray forelock. Mean but alluring eyes. She wore a red blazer over a white blouse, a red skirt, and red heels. The theme apparently being red. Most people would have looked like a real estate agent in that getup, but she wasn't supervising open houses.

Andy tried to be discreet as he tracked her curves. He failed at discretion. When he reached her face, Andy saw her smiling.

"Are you going to get out of the elevator?" she asked. "Or is this the best ride you could find?"

Andy snapped out of it, sure he was blushing. He mumbled incoherence as he passed. She smelled great, like flowers. Walking through the lobby, he turned in time to see the elevator doors close and the woman giving him a fingery wave. Like an idiot, he waved to the closed doors.

Andy handed a check to the receptionist. "Is there any way you can deposit this on Monday?"

The receptionist gave him a look and thumbed through a binder. "This month has already been paid."

He almost protested, knowing that she was mistaken. Considering his paltry bank account, Andy decided to accept a clerical error that was to his advantage. Lottery tickets sometimes came in strange shapes.

"That's right. Yeah. I forgot," Andy rambled. "Yeah. I paid that bill. Got it confused with the slip fees for the catamaran."

Realizing he was overdoing it, Andy stopped talking. To avoid eye contact, he glanced at the sign-in sheet and the most recent name written in hard, slanted cursive. Kate Girard. The name meant nothing to him.

◆ ◆ ◆

A block toward the Hampshire Court subway stop, he spotted Benny Gianfranco's Italian beef stand. Those salty, sweet sandwiches were Champ's favorite. He bought her the Italian beef deluxe with a fried egg, extra peppers, and mustard. The grease made the bag see-through within fifteen seconds.

"Going to run back up. Need to drop this off," Andy said to the woman at the reception desk, who didn't care. Not one bit.

Andy didn't knock. He walked in on Champ and the woman in red on the couch together, sitting close, knees touching. Champ held the woman's hand with both of her own. Heads leaning in like teenagers telling secrets. They turned to Andy. For a brief moment, Champ looked completely lucid, a light in her eyes.

"You have company," Andy said. "I didn't know. Um. Just came back to—" He held up the bag in his hand. A drop of grease landed on the carpet.

Andy glanced at the television. It was turned off, which was unprecedented. Champ was missing *Days*.

Neither Champ nor the woman offered an introduction. The woman crossed her long legs. Andy admired them, which he knew was the point.

Champ looked back and forth between the two of them, confusion clouding her once-clear vision. She contemplated the two people who didn't belong in the same room together.

"Claudia and I are old friends," the woman said.

"And you know each other from?" Andy asked.

"The past," the woman said.

"You okay, Champ?" Andy asked.

She snapped out of her daze. "I'm fine. Leave me and Katie be. We have things to talk about."

Andy leaned toward the woman. "I know Champ's friends. Why haven't I ever met you?"

"It's been a long while," the woman said. "How long has it been, Claudia?"

"A long while," Champ said.

"That long?" Andy said. "Who are you?"

"Andrea Salvatore Destra," Champ snapped, "you are being a rude brat. My life is my life. You don't get to know everything just because you want to know. Thanks for the sandwich."

Andy felt the blood rush to his face. When she said his full name, she meant business. He knew better than to argue. "It was nice meeting you. Kate, was it? Maybe we'll bump into each other again."

"I wouldn't be surprised. It's a small world."

As he left, Andy gave one last turn and met Kate Girard's eyes. Damned if she didn't wink.

CHAPTER 2

You don't tell a kid that his hero is a heel. Or a widow that
her husband was a philanderer. Some secrets should stay
secret.

—From a speech made by District Attorney Todhunter
Holbart after the conspiracy case against leaders in the
Furgele crime family was abruptly dropped. Speculation
rose that it would implicate too many city leaders (1939).

Andy sat on a bus stop bench with a good sight line to the front
entrance of the senior living facility. It wasn't the nicest place,
chipped plaster and scattered graffiti. While not officially in the Ruins,
it was Ruins adjacent. Andy wished he could afford more for Champ,
but since his shitcanning, money had been tight.

He never knew if he was stupid or diligent, but he couldn't let even
the smallest mystery go. He knew the people Champ knew. Their time
together spanned his entire life, decades, but he had never met or heard
mention of anyone named Kate Girard.

Andy should have stayed. Pressed harder for answers. Found out
who the hell she was. The way Champ dismissed him suggested that
Andy was never meant to meet her. Which made him want to know

even more. As ridiculous as it sounded to him, the idea kept floating past that Kate Girard was the right age to be his mother.

He had never met his parents. Didn't know their names. All Champ had ever told him was that they loved him, left Andy with her for his own good, and made her promise to keep their secret. After all this time, he would have thought that it would matter less. But with Champ's declining mental health, there was only a small window before her hidden knowledge disappeared forever.

Champ had never said a word about his mother. She had mentioned his father on two occasions, and all she had said was, "He was a criminal," and "He was a good man." Andy had analyzed every word and possible connotation in those two spare sentences, the contradiction and the past tense not lost on him.

Kate Girard was probably nobody of interest. A high school friend, someone Champ used to play mahjong with, a former coworker from the wartime artillery factory days. But he couldn't resist the possibility or the puzzle. Her appearance was just the kind of question that kept Andy up at night. Until he replaced the question mark with a period, he couldn't let it go. Andy didn't have hobbies—no ships in a bottle or crochet for him. He had fixations. He had obsessions. He connected things.

◆ ◆ ◆

Twenty minutes later Kate Girard exited the building. She stood on the curb and lit a cigarette. Andy leaned inside the bus shelter, out of view.

A late-seventies, faux-wood-paneled Chrysler station wagon pulled to the curb. It didn't really fit her veneer. He had expected town car, not Town & Country. Andy wrote down the license plate number on the back of a receipt for some AA batteries.

Kate Girard took one last inhale, flicked her smoke in a high arc, and got in the car. As it drove away, Andy walked into the open to catch a look at the driver. A man in a brimmed hat was all he made out. The car took a right at the first intersection and was gone.

With a pair of tweezers, Andy picked up the still-smoldering cigarette. Bright-red lipstick encircled the filter. He knocked off the burning cherry with his fingernail and put the cigarette in a small evidence bag. Besides tweezers and evidence bags, Andy carried a number of other essentials: roll of nickels, lock pick set, small magnifying glass, mini-tape recorder, Swiss Army knife, penlight, and a bag of salted almonds. Andy liked to be ready for anything.

The subway would have been quicker, but Andy chose to walk. It cleared his head. At the same time, he could disseminate more propaganda, stapling handbills to telephone poles and boarded-up windows. He had papered most of the city with the posters. Big letters with the heading: **WANTED: BAD COP**. A picture of Aloysius Gray, the deputy commissioner of the Auction City Police Department. The text below accused the department of numerous crimes committed on Gray's orders: testilying in court, bullying witnesses, graft, brutality, extortion, and even murder.

He had enough evidence to be sure himself, but not enough to do anything but anger the police. Since he'd started his crusade against police corruption, everyone saw him as a wingnut. It wasn't that people didn't believe him. It was that they knew that nothing could be done about it. It was difficult to gather hard evidence against the organization that collected the evidence.

He passed Cleo's Liquors and the tough guys loitering at the side of the building. A rotating cast of hardened, tired men. The cops constantly rousted them. The price of looking the part, even if no law had been broken. At the moment, a patrol car sat parked in the store lot around the corner. Two patrolmen had four of the toughs against the wall, emptying their pockets and throwing the contents on the ground. Loose bills, wallets, combs, pocket knives, gum. One of the men received a kidney punch for no apparent reason. Andy recognized the older of the two cops, Patrick Thornton.

There were at least a dozen Thorntons working in the Auction City Police Department. A savage cop family that went back generations. Goons with badges. Gray's key strong-arm men. Dangerous, cruel, and stupid. Patrick was no exception.

Andy strolled past, paying the matinee no mind. He turned the corner, walked to the back of the police car, and picked the trunk lock. Tucked under the spare tire, he found a paper sack with a few hundred dollars in mostly fives and tens, the day's protection money. He pocketed the dough and put the empty sack back where he'd found it.

By the time he came out of Cleo's with a box of merchandise, the patrol car was gone. Off to harass some other members of the taxpaying public. He wished he could've been there when the Thornton found the empty sack. He wondered if he would accuse his partner of stealing his stolen money.

Around the corner, the men shoved their belongings back in their pockets, cursing under their breath. One man chased a loose dollar bill caught in the wind. Andy set the box down. Inside, a case of beer, various Roscoe Peppercorn pepperoni snack products, two bags of Taterville potato chips, a half-dozen doughnuts, and copies of *Playboy*, *Penthouse*, and *Hustler*.

"Courtesy of the ACPD," Andy said. He walked away feeling like a sidewalk saint.

◆ ◆ ◆

Andy reached the fourth-floor landing of his apartment building. It wasn't the climb that left him out of breath. The excitement of a new—if dubious—case got his heart racing. His investigation of Gray and the police had stalled, idling until new evidence surfaced. Kate Girard was a welcome distraction.

Taking a breather outside his front door, he heard Mrs. Hammond's lock click. When he turned, he caught her peeking from behind the chain.

"It's me," Andy said, forcing a smile.

She stared at him for a moment, then screamed, "I see you, Crazy Andy," and slammed the door. Andy might have been insulted, but she'd called him that since he'd moved in. Even when he'd been a cop. If she'd called him "Sane Andy," he'd have worried.

It took Andy a full minute to unlock the series of deadbolts and mortise locks that secured his apartment. He had installed an extra-heavy door at his own cost, not even bothering to inform the super. Andy didn't consider himself paranoid. He preferred the word *cautious*.

He scoonched past a row of filing cabinets that lined the entry and created a narrow passage leading to what would have been the living room. Although no real living happened there. It looked like a hostage negotiator's temporary command post. More filing cabinets, stacked boxes, and the centerpiece—a hollow-core door on sawhorses with stacks of paper covering every inch.

When Andy had gotten rid of his bed, he knew he was one step away from buying tinfoil in bulk. Even as he saw it happen, he couldn't stop the momentum. He now slept in a sleeping bag underneath the makeshift desk. One small earthquake and they'd find him a week later when the smell of his flattened corpse alerted the neighbors.

Photos, maps, notes, string, pins, matchbooks, coasters, and fingerprint sheets completely covered the walls. The hodgepodge of ephemera created the core of Andy's investigation of the Auction City Police Department. Hundreds of officers marched lockstep to Deputy Commissioner Gray's commands regardless of law or civil rights. A praetorian system that stood broken and ruthless.

A map of the city covered one wall. Small pins and flags denoted locations cross-referenced in one of Andy's notebooks. From the old money of Gallows Terrace to the poverty-stricken housing of the Ruins, from the twisting alleys of Little Nagasaki to the disturbingly peaceful

Blackstreet Hollow, each neighborhood of Auction City represented a different class strata, a different atmosphere, and a different mystery. Separate but tied together by the money and corruption that ran the city.

What had started as a probe of the police department had extended far beyond, encompassing seemingly random aspects of Auction City, all the way down to the trash collectors and the river barges. Something was happening below the surface of the city, but it was like buying a thousand jigsaw puzzles and emptying all of them onto the floor at the same time. Occasionally he could fit two pieces together, the obvious matches, corners and sides. The problem was that the rest of the puzzle was all sky.

> KATE GIRARD
> Assistant to the District Attorney 1958–1966
> Major cases include: The City Vs. Horace Cavanaugh
> (see file #60-DA), The City Vs. the Auction City Seven
> (see file #64-DA), The City Vs. Nat Turner Shabazz
> (see file Shabazz-1)

That was all Andy had in his files on Kate Girard. He knew the Auction City Seven and Shabazz cases, but he hadn't remembered her name.

Kate Girard had been a lawyer who had left the DA's office in 1966. After that, no mention of her. Nothing. Gone. She had probably left the city. He would hit public records in the morning.

He dug through the scraps of paper in his pocket and found the receipt with the Chrysler's license plate on it. Now it was a matter of finding his phone. With all the mess, the telephone ended up in strange places. He went to the wall, found the jack, and ran his hand along the cord until it reached telephone. In the bottom drawer of a filing cabinet marked "Crime Stats—By District."

He pulled a file from another filing cabinet and dialed. He dropped his voice an octave, slurred a little, hint of a brogue. "Hi, Frank. Yeah,

Fergus Thornton. What? Christ." He consulted the file. "Badge number 872, like you don't know me. I need you to run a plate. Chrysler Town & Country, 1977 or 1978. Plate number is J4BX68." Andy listened. "No. I'm on a stakeout. I'll call you back."

An hour later, he learned that the car was registered to a John Dole, which might have been a real name but was more likely a bad joke. Either way, Dole had an address.

CHAPTER 3

As much a moral labyrinth as an American city. Irrecoverable, irretrievable, and irrevocable. A purgatory with no hope of heaven, only the promise of hell. They call the metropolis Auction City, but the bidding had closed years ago. Unfortunately, no one had informed the bright-eyed Twyla Tharn.

—From the National Book Award–nominated novel
Yearnings and Pig Iron, by Mason Caldwell (1984)

Andy regretted not bringing his beavertail. The powdered steel in his sap gloves froze his fingers and gave him a nasty chill. But when traversing Exposition Boulevard at night, it was a good idea to have something made of metal. Andy's simple roll of nickels had gotten him out of more than one pinch. The sap gloves remained the right tool, but he needed to invest in an all-weather version.

Little had changed in the thirty years he had known the Boulevard. Prostitutes offered their wares at every street corner, the outfits more revealing but the rented commodity the same. Bums camped in the doorways of closed businesses. Feverishly scratching at their arms and chests, ghoul-like addicts ducked in and out of vacant buildings.

Exposition Boulevard was as low-down as the city went. When you had reached the Boulevard, the only place lower was the sewer tunnels. And legend had it that the people who lived in the maze of the Underneath were damn near another species.

Members of the Wretches and Los Locos wore their colors, strutting with confidence, pedestrians parting to let them pass. It had been at least six years since the street gangs had consolidated, but Andy was still not used to it. He never thought it would stick. Thugs weren't really known for their peacekeeping skills. He wondered how they made it work.

Andy passed all the stalwart landmarks. Jerome Pinkfinger's EmPORNium II with its cartoony neon sign. A line of people queued outside Checks Cashed looking like a Soviet breadline. The narrow staircase leading to the second-story door of Panda Massage stood both mysterious and tempting. Candy Girls, Fantasy Arcade, All-American Billiards & Darts, Faust's Inferno, and Stogie's, the oldest bar in Auction City. Andy remembered the thick smell of beer and peanut breath from when he'd ventured in there as a kid to fetch Champ to tell her it was time for dinner.

Walking by the Apex Theater, Andy glanced at the marquee. A double bill: *Sploooosh!* and *Into Africa*. He cracked a smile. Except for the old-lady mystery novels that Champ read (*Parsley, Sage, Rosemary, Thyme & Punishment*, anyone?), Andy couldn't think of an industry that embraced wordplay more joyously than pornography did. If not for the rampant drug addiction, abhorrent history of exploitation, and the fluids, it would be quaint.

An old drunk stumbled toward Andy, the punge of alcohol engulfing him in a malodorous cloud. The man was clean shaven except for a gray mustache, but his face and body were filthy, smeared with mud. Andy hoped it was mud. As the drunk moved more side to side than straight ahead, his tattered trench coat made him the width of the sidewalk. Andy stepped off the curb, but the stumbling man still managed to bump into him.

The drunk grunted and staggered away. Andy grabbed his elbow.

"Pretty slick, Pops," Andy said, "but I ain't a tourist."

The man looked all over Andy's face, everywhere but his eyes. He said, "Hrrrghhfawll" or something equally incoherent. The only thing Andy caught was the man's spit.

"Give my wallet back and we'll call it a mistake," Andy said, squeezing the man's arm harder.

The drunk swayed, fell into Andy, and then abruptly stood upright, suddenly sober. "Fair enough, son. You got me," he said, holding up Andy's wallet. Andy made sure the contents were intact and returned it to his pocket.

"Nothing else to say?" Andy said. "No apology?"

"Just doing my job."

Andy released him. The two men stared at each other for a moment. Slowly the pickpocket's eyes went glassy again, his body slack. He shuffled away back in character, mumbling to himself, in search of his next mark.

Two blocks down the street, Andy realized his watch was gone. Now that he wasn't a cop anymore, maybe Andy was a tourist, after all.

◆ ◆ ◆

Andy pulled his notes from his pocket: scraps of paper; shredded napkins; a dollar bill with tiny ballpoint numbers on it; a matchbook with a name, phone number, and doodle of a werewolf. He reread the address, even though he had committed it to memory: 6243 Holt Avenue.

He turned onto Holt. Off the Boulevard, it got darker, the foot traffic more sparse. If someone asked for a light on one of these side streets, get ready to run, fight, or wake up wounded. The smell of garbage from a seafood restaurant almost overwhelmed Andy. It stank of salted fish, rotten cabbage, and a wrestler's gym locker.

Two blocks down, across the street from the Church of the Seven Martyrs, Andy found the address. There appeared to be nothing special about the six-story brick building. Classic art deco architecture. Like much of the city, it looked as if it was built in the early thirties after the Flood. Windows dark, no light inside.

There was no gap between 6243 Holt and the neighboring buildings. Every inch of real estate was used. Scoping the narrow alley that ran alongside the back of the building, he found the garbage bins empty and spotlessly clean. One still had a price tag stuck to the lid. There didn't appear to be any other way into the building other than the front door.

The buildings on either side were covered in graffiti, the familiar tags of Chaka, Lorenzo 15, and El Magnifico. In comparison, 6243 was clean, save a single piece of graffiti next to the door, an inverted isosceles trapezoid with five vertical lines in the center.

Andy recognized the glyph. It popped up randomly around the city. He had never learned its origin, probably something that tracked back to old hobo signs. Among the criminal class, it ostensibly meant "Keep Out." He made a quick sketch of the symbol on the back of an old gas bill to remind himself to research it again.

There was nothing distinctive about the building, other than the fact that it didn't exist. It was a ghost building.

◆ ◆ ◆

Everything looked more glamorous on TV and in the movies. In reality, sex on the beach was sandy and seaweedy, shooting two guns while jumping through the air was stupid and dangerous, and criminal investigations were paperwork and phone calls. If you were a cop or a doctor or a lawyer, the sad truth was that you didn't get laid nearly as often as on the tube. Andy might have been out in the field now, but it was the result of combing through volumes of documents in his apartment and in the records departments of the city and county.

The five hours downtown weren't exactly spellbinding drama, but after a thorough document search, Andy had found no deed of ownership or any other reference to the building. Other than John Dole's car registration, the entire lot didn't exist on paper, not on the zoning maps or in the city assessor's office. It wasn't that it was a foreclosure or city seizure or in some other real estate limbo. This was a building with no history or record of existence. Unless a person stood in front of it, there was no proof that it was.

He crossed the street and walked the grounds of the Church of the Seven Martyrs. He had been terrified of the church when he was a child. The angel with a sword that guarded the doors had an angry expression that made it seem poised to attack. Andy found some shadows and settled in, shoulder to the jagged bricks. He locked eyes on the doorway of 6243 Holt.

Andy hated waiting. When he'd been a policeman, he would lose his mind sitting in the front seat of a beige sedan, eating greasy lake trout and pissing in a Gatorade bottle. He knew impatience was stupid. It was literally doing nothing, but Andy would rather do something stupid than nothing at all.

Now that he was still, the cold found its way into his bones. He stomped his feet and pumped fists in his pockets, but the breeze off the Thief River blew icy. It was going to be an arctic winter. He focused on the door, trying to ignore his runny nose and uncontrollable shivering. After fifteen minutes he'd had enough.

Andy waited for an ice cream truck to pass and then jogged across the street and climbed the steps of the building, doing his best to act like he belonged. The street was empty of pedestrian traffic. He knocked and waited. Nothing. He reached in his pocket for his lock picks, but a quick turn of the knob revealed that the door was unlocked. Not the usual modus in this neighborhood. He'd seen what the dregs of Auction City could do to an abandoned building. It always felt as though the first thing a junkie did in an abandoned building was defecate. And never in a corner. Always in the middle of the room. He swung the door open and stepped into the building that wasn't really there.

Pulling out his penlight, Andy got a quick look around. There was no sign of vandalism. A bouquet of dead flowers in an oriental vase sat on an antique table in the center of the foyer. The fact that the vase had been neither stolen nor broken made Andy uneasy. He had expected graffiti, trash, destruction. This place was immaculate. He could make out the vacuum lines in the carpet.

Everything told him to leave. The cleanliness was chilling. The place was creepy, wrong. He shouldn't be there in the first place, but every piece of weirdness only made the question more intriguing. Might as well keep tugging at threads until the sweater was completely unraveled. After all, he wasn't tracking some villain, just poking around an abandoned building that some station wagon owner listed as his address.

Andy took tentative steps down a dark hallway, letting his barely effective flashlight illuminate the way. All doors appeared to have been removed. He poked his head from room to room, each fully furnished with antiques and at least one piece of taxidermy. The rooms were all strangely similar and equally functionless. Nothing practical. A series of sitting rooms. He couldn't tell if this was a business or a home.

He opened the empty drawers of a desk that smelled of artificial pine cleaner. No personal touches. The few photos on the wall were more than a hundred years old, and if they had any association to the building, he had no clue how to connect those dots.

Heading up to the second floor, Andy stopped abruptly when he heard a faint sound. A shuffle, maybe a human voice. With one toe frozen in space above the next step, he turned off his light and closed his eyes. A scuffling came from the floor above.

Andy slowly reached the second-floor landing. Through the blackness, he caught a flicker of light down the long hallway.

"Hello?" Andy said into the darkness.

The faint sound of a voice or animal drew him closer. He tripped on the edge of a rug but caught himself. His heartbeat boomed in his head. He silently counted to ten, waiting for the consequence of his clumsiness. When nobody ran at him with a chainsaw, he took that as a good omen.

The sounds developed into whispers, still unintelligible but definitely voices. Ghostly voices in the relative darkness. The unmistakable flit of candlelight projected into the hallway from one of the rooms.

Andy stopped next to the door frame. He expected to find anything from a satanic ritual to an underground poker game. Maybe Kate Girard taking a relaxing bath with some scented candles. That, he wouldn't mind seeing. He popped his head into the doorway.

Two naked teenagers rolled around on the ground, a candle illuminating their hairless bodies. School uniforms sat neatly folded next to them. Both wore headphones, listening to individual Walkmans. A couple of kids from the suburbs, slumming it down on the Boulevard and finding a place to bang. Outsiders that didn't know to heed the graffitied warning. Not smart like he was.

The girl caught sight of Andy and shrieked, horror-movie high. The boy didn't get it at first, thinking his skills had elicited the scream. It wasn't until the girl hit the boy in the face and pointed that he got the message. But the red-faced Andy was already halfway down the stairs.

When he reached the foyer, he turned his flashlight back on. He chuckled at the ridiculousness of it all. Kids these days.

His flashlight passed over the table in the center of the room. His smile vanished. A bouquet of fresh flowers sat in the oriental vase. The dead flowers that had been there minutes earlier were gone, replaced by red chrysanthemums with a note attached. His stolen watch sat next to the vase.

Andy picked up his watch, glanced around the darkness. He reached for the note. The handwritten message read:

We see you, Destra. This is a warning. Stop digging.

He turned to the long hallway, only seeing darkness but knowing he wasn't alone. From the shadows, someone whistled what might have been "Girl from Ipanema."

"I don't scare that easy," Andy said.

He rushed into the dark hallway, ready for a fight but not finding one. A search of all the rooms came up empty. Something strange was going on at 6243 Holt Avenue, but damn if Andy could figure out what it was.

CHAPTER 4

I ♥ Auction City. I Just Wish It ♥ed Me Back.

—Bumper sticker (circa 1978)

Andy stood in front of his wall map and stared at the address, trying to digest that note, the watch, those chrysanthemums, and that damn whistling. He didn't buy that the ghost building actually had ghosts.

Did the pickpocket know that's where he was going? Was he the whistler? What was his connection to the whole thing? It didn't make any sense.

The frantic walk back from Exposition Boulevard—looking over his shoulder at every turn—got his heart racing. He hadn't spotted anyone in his periphery, but his gut insisted that someone was watching him. He used his best evasive maneuvers, changed course three times, ducked into a few buildings, ran down deserted alleys, and got on and off a bus before grabbing the subway.

He slumped in his only chair, scanning his self-made chaos. If he chose to entertain, he'd be hard-pressed to find a comfortable place for another person to stand, let alone sit. Maybe Indian-style on the floor. On a stack of notebooks. It didn't matter. Nobody visited.

It was times like this when a drinking problem, a recent divorce, or an estranged child would have come in handy. Wasn't that every ex-cop's story? If he had one of those issues, his descent into conspiracy nut would have been socially accepted. There was nothing like a destructive past to give a man carte blanche to take a trip to Crazyville. But Andy didn't drink, hadn't had a serious girlfriend for years, and was childless. The only thing coplike about him was his love for baked goods, but even then he preferred a croissant to a doughnut. Maybe he had been meant to be a gendarme.

◆ ◆ ◆

In his teen years, the frustration of not knowing the identity of his parents led him down a path. Without any clues, his search transformed into a pursuit to learn everything about Auction City. The illogic being that if he examined everything, maybe he would inadvertently learn about his folks, even if he didn't know he was learning about them. From the politics to the architecture to its history and legends, Andy absorbed himself in the city's past. A pastime grew to an obsession, hours spent in the library or wandering the streets of the city.

When the structure of college didn't suit him, he found a new opportunity to feed his curiosity. Against Champ's urgings, Andy entered the police academy. As a kitchen-table historian, he knew the department's shady past and could guess its darker secrets. That didn't mean every cop became a part of the corruption. The police department fit his mind and allowed him to see inner workings that the public wasn't privy to.

Joining the ACPD was also a way of rebelling against a ghost. One of the only things he knew about his father was that he was a criminal. For all his desire to learn the man's identity, he was indifferent to him just the same. His father was the one who wasn't there. Andy wanted to be the opposite of the man who had abandoned him.

The ACPD became Andy's extended family. That's what indoctrination and a chain of command did. Not exactly everyone's brother-in-arms, he was at least their strange step-cousin-in-arms. Despite his weirdness, they accepted him. He belonged. He was good at his job. He didn't make his superiors' jobs harder. And he looked the other way, kept his mouth shut, and played the game. He might not have grabbed beers with the guys at the end of a shift, but they trusted him.

It surprised Andy how quickly he found ways to rationalize the side action. The political corruption, the protection rackets, the lost evidence. All in the name of keeping the city safe, is what he told himself. The truth was he was game for the corruption. He liked the loose moral latitude. And his lack of ambition didn't threaten anyone. It allowed him to investigate his personal matters without interference. He was all about the puzzles. As long as he had the challenge of a complex criminal investigation, a few kilos missing from evidence or a mysterious envelope full of cash didn't matter to him. After all, they were the good guys.

Then it all went to hell.

In the sixteen months since his retirement, Andy had gone from twice-decorated Detective Sergeant Andrea Destra, fourteen-year veteran of the ACPD, to Crazy Andy Destra, weirdo shut-in running in terror from whistlers in empty buildings to his cramped apartment full of conspiracy theories and canned soup. He could see himself falling, but he couldn't grab the sides.

It had started with the Chucho Montoya investigation. A run-of-the-mill case he had worked in Fraud and Pawnshops, one of the less noteworthy police divisions. Through some blind luck, he discovered a paper trail that linked Montoya, a known fence, to an enormous money-laundering operation. Andy had the structure of the network but was weeks away from attaching names and accounts to the scheme. When he submitted a request for more manpower, not only was it refused but Andy was taken off the case and transferred. The deputy commissioner had decided that the investigation was a waste of resources.

Andy wasn't an idiot. He knew that he had gotten too close to something. Something that threatened his brothers in blue. Andy was reassigned to Juvenile Booking. A promotion in rank, but he was no longer investigating anything. Which was the fun of the job. The whole point. He didn't become a cop to process forms and file them. Anybody who did was more insane than he was.

Andy could have let the corrupt cops have their corruption. If he was honest with himself, he didn't even care about justice. The problem was that he didn't know how to stop himself. He had eaten the cereal, and like hell he wasn't going to get the prize at the bottom. He was stupid like that.

A person doing a crossword puzzle had no good reason to fill in the last letter. Or even the last few. That person knew that he knew the correct answers. What did it prove? Who was it for? Why bother? Because it would be wrong not to.

With plenty of sitting-around time in Juvenile Booking, Andy idiotically continued to work the Montoya case, digging deeper into the deputy commissioner's connection. Ancillary schemes arose that sparked new threads. Strange names popped up. Police brass, politicians, bankers, known criminals, even clergy members.

Then it went tits up. Way up. All the way up. As high as tits could go.

Andy and six other cops were publicly arrested on charges of accepting bribes from a Japanese smuggling ring. Handcuffed at their desks and brought to holding cells one floor down—after they were taken outside to be photographed by the press and then brought back inside. The fact that the allegations were true made it less suspicious, but Andy knew it was retribution. He hadn't accepted money in five years, and even then it hadn't been more than a few hundred to look the other way when the restaurants smuggled in forbidden, nonnative fish. Payments from the Japanese and Chinese were historical, a tradition. Cops had been receiving the same payments for decades. There had never been one report on the matter, let alone an arrest, in the history of the city.

Those kinds of kickbacks were a part of police culture, an open secret. Even the good cops—which Andy considered himself to be—took money. In the case of the Japanese, it would have been an insult not to accept it. And how else were those old grandmothers going to enjoy their shark fin soup and moray eel mignon, or whatever they ate?

The kicker was what followed. After months of lawyer wrangling and pre-trial motions, Andy was released, all charges dropped. Even his union rep and lawyer were surprised. The decision came from the deputy commissioner. Only Andy's charges were dropped. The other six officers he had been arrested with were charged, convicted, and eventually put away, some for years. There had been no evidence against them that they didn't have on Andy. Yet they let him walk.

To every cop, it looked as if Andy had ratted out his brothers. He was the most hated man in the department when he went back to work that Monday.

He stuck it out. Kept his head down. Did the work. Within an organization that tight, it grew impossible. Between the threats, the silent treatment, and the actual punches thrown, it couldn't sustain. He could only find so many dead rats in his locker before he got the hint. (Thirteen, that was how many dead rats.) He struck a deal and took early retirement on a thirty percent pension. Left the only family, besides Champ, that he ever really loved. Dysfunctional as it was, it hurt.

He had been pushed out because he had gotten close to something big. Something to do with Montoya, the deputy commissioner and the other higher-ups, and a money-laundering operation. To make things more suspicious, Chucho Montoya died before his trial in a suspect fire at one of his pawnshops, all but ending that thread. Officially, the case was closed. And forgotten. At least by the police.

But give a man an enemy and you give him purpose. Once abandoned, a reformer was born. Andy didn't need to be in the police to investigate crime. All he needed was a target.

Andy's railroading strengthened his resolve. Before his arrest, he had only wanted to solve the puzzle. Now he wanted revenge. A punch-a-clock nine-to-five quickly turned into a vendetta. Take away an already-prone-to-obsession guy's reason for being and he'll find another one. He'll cover his apartment walls with photos and scraps of paper. He'll convert his living space into an active investigation.

The linchpin in the whole thing was Aloysius Gray. He ran the department. He was the one who had taken him off the case, spear-headed the bribery investigation, and eventually negotiated the deal that led to Andy's retirement. His hand was in everything. Andy would get that son of a bitch. One way or the other.

Kate Girard and the scary building were interesting, and he was going to pursue them, but Gray would always be his main target. Stalled for now, but Gray would screw up eventually.

Andy looked at his stolen-and-returned watch. Too late to go back to the senior living facility and talk to Champ about Kate Girard. Still early enough to start some trouble. He wondered how Gray would react to seeing him. At the least, it would remind the old man that cop or no cop, Andy Destra never quit.

CHAPTER 5

The police in Auction City have a reputation. We call twenty-dollar bills Get-Out-of-Jail-Free Cards. I got stopped for jaywalking one time. Usually a ticket, but this was one of the good cops. He let me off with an uppercut and his baton halfway up my toches. I saw a cop help a little old lady across the street. She was at gunpoint. Ninety years old. Four seconds flat.

—*From Johnny Schnitzel's live comedy album*
Meshuga Daddy *(1974)*

There was no way for Andy to be inconspicuous at Muldoon's. The mainstay downtown bar got no walk-in traffic, only regulars. All cops or retired cops. Andy fit the criteria, but he was persona non grata among local law enforcement. He was walking straight into the pig's den. The dozen handbills he posted outside wouldn't help his case.

Sometimes the best camouflage was standing out in the open. That's what Andy told himself as he entered. It sounded good, but Andy knew it was bull. The best camouflage was when you blended in, when you were out of sight. Because that's what the word *camouflage* meant.

Andy got surly looks and nonaccidental shoulder bumps on his way to the bar. Even more cold stares and muttered swearing. "Traitor."

"Judas." "Ratfuck." Considering that these epithets came from members of the most corrupt police department in the nation, their sanctimony seemed laughable. It was difficult to take insults seriously in a room full of hypocrites, liars, thugs, and bullies.

Andy had once considered these men his family. Now they were the kind of family that you dreaded seeing on holidays because Uncle Morris always got a little too drunk, insisted on teaching you some wrestling moves, and proceeded to get handsy around your thigh area.

He spotted Deputy Commissioner Gray in the corner with his right- and left-hand men: Colonel Hank Robinson of the Criminal Investigation Division and Captain Randall Ashley of the less than glamorous, but undeniably powerful, Fiscal Division. You could set your watch to their schedules. Every night after a long day of making the city safe, a series of backslaps and handshakes, then a tray of old-fashioneds to show that they were regular Joes. Gray reminded the men of his roots and in the process got a de facto debriefing.

Gray might have been deputy commissioner, but everyone knew that Commissioner Jenkins was a figurehead. The three men at that table controlled the department and subsequently much of the political machine in Auction City. In their early sixties, Gray, Robinson, and Ashley went all the way back to the Academy. A lot of history, even more secrets. They knew where the bodies were buried and who had hosed off the shovel.

Current scuttlebutt suggested that discord had surfaced between the three men. While Colonel Robinson was a loyal second and heir apparent to DC Gray, Captain Ashley no longer supported the direction that Gray was taking the city's police force. Some cops thought it was more than a policy disagreement. Some rift that went back decades but had only reared its head recently. Outranked, there was little that Ashley could do, but as the head of the Fiscal Division, he did control the purse strings.

Mike Muldoon, the ex-cop bartender and grandson of the original Muldoon, ignored Andy. Andy was fine with the indifference. It beat getting clocked with the cricket bat behind the bar. He hadn't come there to drink anyway. He found an empty stool and waited for Gray to spot him. See if he could shake the old man. Or whatever Andy's not-quite-a-plan was.

Of all the things that could have happened next, Kate Girard walking through the front door wouldn't have been on Andy's list. The men in the bar noticed, as well.

While the ACPD had a few women on the force, none of them wanted to socialize with the assholes they dealt with on their regular shifts. Besides the occasional badge bunny, that made Muldoon's a nightly sword fight. Any lady in the dump warranted attention. When you carried yourself like Kate Girard, you got more than that.

Walking with purpose and disdain, Kate Girard strutted though the corridor that the men created for her. Eyes stared. Jaws dropped. Mustaches got combed. Someone whistled. She spotted Andy, smirked a little, and walked toward him. She wore the same perfume as she had earlier in the day. It smelled like the flower shop on Fourteenth Street.

Muldoon wiped the bar in front of her. "Been a while, Girard. Can I get you?"

"You know how to make a martini, Muldoon?"

"I'm a bartender, ain't I?" Ever the charmer, and not really answering the question.

"Make it scotch and soda. And whatever Destra is having."

"He ain't having nothing," Muldoon said. "He was loitering. Now he's trespassing. On his way out."

"Does he know that?" She turned to Andy. "Were you leaving?"

"Not now I ain't," Andy said.

Muldoon exhaled loudly and walked to the other end of the bar, loudly banging bottles as he made Kate's drink.

"Twice in one day," Kate Girard said. "Do you believe in coincidences?"

"No," Andy said. "Absolutely not. You know Champ. Muldoon knows you. How come we haven't met until today?"

"I like to remain mysterious."

"What do you know about a building on Holt Avenue?"

"You'd have to be more specific. That's a long street."

"It's 6243. A friend of yours owns it. Someone probably not named John Dole."

She gave Andy a wide smile. Not quite fake but with little sincerity. "You need to stop. You're charging in blind and have no idea what's behind that door."

"Fill me in," Andy said. "You and Champ. What's the deal there?"

"Ask her."

"She won't tell me."

"Well, there you have it," Kate Girard said. "You need to back off Gray. That wanted poster crap. Does nothing but antagonize a dangerous man."

"How did you know I'd be here?"

"I didn't."

"Yeah, you come to drink in this dump all the time."

"From the guy not drinking in a bar that he's not welcome in." And on that, she waved at the booth where Deputy Commissioner Gray and his cronies sat. They didn't wave back. The three men stared at Andy. He mimed lifting a glass in toast.

"You're here to see Gray?" he asked.

Muldoon set down Kate Girard's drink. She picked it up, took a sip, and left a ten on the bar. She walked to the booth with every eye on her backside. Men are pigs, but in their defense it was a nice backside. He really hoped that Kate Girard wasn't his mother.

"I still have questions," Andy called after her, but he was ignored.

42

Kate Girard talked to Gray and his men for less than five minutes. At first Gray had a few angry words for Ms. Girard. But she wasn't having any. She countered. Andy wished he could have heard what she said. Gray took it, seething. He had never seen anyone talk to the DC that way. And in public. On his turf. Even more startling, he had never seen anything that resembled fear in Gray's demeanor until that moment. Only for a second, but it was there.

When the brief meeting adjourned, Kate Girard walked to the back door. As she reached for the knob, she turned to Andy for a moment. Then she was gone.

Andy rose to follow, but a monstrous hand pushed him back onto the stool.

Three large Irishmen stood in front of him. He knew them all too well. More Thorntons. With those ginger rhinos in his path, he could scratch his plans of catching up to Kate Girard. Andy's revised plan B consisted entirely of getting out of Muldoon's alive.

"It's going to be like that?" Andy asked the Thornton in the middle. He glanced toward the back booth. Deputy Commissioner Gray raised his glass in a toast, giving Andy as much smile as his evil allowed.

"It's going to be like that," the Thornton answered. The Thornton that Andy hit first.

◆ ◆ ◆

Cops liked to fight. The good ones and the rotten ones. Don't let them tell you different. Among the primary reasons men joined the force, a proclivity for violence trumped family tradition, good benefits, and sweet uniforms. You didn't hear about cops in it for the paperwork. They might frame it as "I like the action" or "I want to catch bad guys," but that was code for socially acceptable head stomping.

While Andy had joined the force in a weak act of defiance of a man he didn't know, government-sanctioned violence proved compelling.

When they first let him walk the streets with a loaded gun and a baton, he had wood most of the day. He wasn't proud of it, but he spent that first shift looking for a reason to bludgeon someone. It ended up being a purse snatcher, and it was as satisfying as he thought it would be. Dangerously addictive, too. A product of the power. His skill set might have been more suited to desk jockey, but that didn't mean he didn't have some thug in him. It probably came from his father's side.

As Andy hadn't seen any action in a while, a fight wasn't unwelcome. Who better than the Thorntons? They had beaten so many innocent suspects in their tenure, pressured so many store owners for their take, and terrorized so many citizens who happened to cross their path that Andy was sure that karmically they had a righteous thrashing coming.

If he didn't get knocked unconscious before getting a second punch in.

Fighting one against three, a congested space was preferable. While an open area gave avenues for escape, a crowded bar offered chaos. Alcohol plus violent men plus any excuse to punch a face equaled just-add-water bar brawl. It took two seconds for the proverbial breaking loose of all hell.

With the weight of the sap gloves assisting him, Andy's hook cracked the middle Thornton's jaw, sending him reeling into the table behind him. Spilled drinks, a ruined shirt, and before you could say, "Hold my beer," three mustaches joined the scuffle. They weren't on Andy's side. Or the Thorntons' side. They were their own side. A war fought on three fronts.

One of the other Thorntons slammed Andy's head against the bar and gave him a couple shots to the body. Since his ribs were mostly titanium plating from his last fracture, it would take more than that to bust them again. The upside of a life of violence revealed itself in strange ways.

Shaking the blur, he got hit again. He didn't know by whom. Andy ducked in time to avoid Muldoon getting in on the action with his cricket bat. The poor bastard sitting next to him got the brunt of that wood. The guy never knew what hit him.

From there it was punching, taking punches, a lot of shoving, grabbing lapels, hitting the ground, scrambling, kicking shins, crawling, inadequately hiding, hitting some more. Someone stepped on his hand. Someone bit his calf. Ground glass tore his pants and cut his knees. A chair flew past his head. If the bar had a piano player, he would have upped the tempo and pounded those keys. Among the grunting and slapping, Andy heard as much laughing. Wednesday night was gladiator night, drinks all over the house. The emergency room was going to be filled with stitches and stories.

◆ ◆ ◆

Bruised but not beaten, Andy slipped out the front door. The brawl continued. The sound of glass breaking, wood splintering, and dull thumping echoed down the cold, empty street. Someone with a sense of humor had put "Beat It" on the jukebox.

He'd glanced back at DC Gray on his way outside. Not afraid to get his hands dirty, the most powerful member of the Auction City PD was making quick work of some rookie who was either too afraid or too confused to hit back. Gray's eyes met Andy's as the man pummeled the poor subordinate. The death stare made Andy consider heeding Kate Girard's warning.

Holding a handful of dirty snow to his jaw, Andy tried to hail a cab. In his ripped, bloody clothes and disheveled state, he got no takers. All the better, as he didn't have any money. The walk in the cold air woke him and helped him think.

Andy strolled past downtown police headquarters, the First Precinct. It was a beautiful old edifice, but felt like a lie. He took a piss on the side of the building.

Most of the businesses on Benchley Boulevard operated past midnight. Not just the bars and restaurants. If you needed typewriter ribbon or cat food, stores were open to accommodate every late-night urge. Andy bought an ice cream cone from an Italian man whose name he knew but couldn't remember.

Then it hit him. He stopped abruptly, chucked his unfinished cone in the trash, and rushed down the street until he found what he was looking for.

He walked into the flower shop, past the small Asian man. Andy found the chrysanthemums and stuck his face into the bunches, taking a big whiff. They smelled just like Kate Girard's perfume.

The red chrysanthemums. The Holt address. Gray. And Kate Girard.

What the hell was going on?

1929

LONG PAST DAYS

Lost in Redling Park. Separated from Sal. Staying to the deepest trees, out of sight. Grasping the bloody ice pick, the cleaver, white-knuckle tight. Hands shaking. Body shivering. Nowhere to go. Every path leading to a new hell.

Screams. Dull thuds. Sharp cracks. Gunfire. An explosion in the distance. Sounded like thunder, definitely not. The trapped smoke from the burning trees like tule fog. Burning my eyes. Forced to mute my coughs. Crouching, looking for air. Not finding it.

Ducking behind a trunk at the sound of rustling leaves. Muted voices. Some scared. Some angry. Some laughing.

A group of Negroes. Just boys. None older than me. Poor. Ill-fitting clothes. No shoes. Unarmed. Running, arms flailing like they were swimming. Away from sharks.

Blue sharks. Four coppers. Tommy guns at their waists. One yeehawed. Another spat. They opened fire.

The teenagers cut down, backs arching. Dancing from the shots that followed. Hands stupidly reaching for the wounds. Spilling forward. Red mist mixed in the gray smoke. A wounded boy crawled through the brush. Insides trailing behind him. Crying. Nowhere to go. The cops stood over the boys. Laughed and fired their weapons until their magazines were empty.

The police reloaded. Shook hands. Slapped backs. They went through the kids' pockets, swore when they found nothing. One copper lit a cigar, inhaled. An arrow pierced his throat, puncturing his neck like a novelty item. Gray cigar smoke drifted from the wound. Body in spasm, he discharged his weapon, shooting the man next to him in the leg. That man returned fire. Shot the man wounded with the arrow. The other two froze. Looked at each other. Ran in opposite directions. Arrows found their backs, shoulders, chests before they got twenty feet.

I waited for my arrow. It never came.

I needed a plan. I could flee. I could hide. Find a corner. Put my back against it. Wait for it to end.

Sal had said the Turkish baths. Meeting Fat Jimmy. Sal came for me. Asked for my help. I would make my way there. Reunited, I would be told what to do. That's what I needed. Orders. A task. Survival wasn't a way to live. I needed purpose.

I had to get out of the park. Away from the killing. Get to somewhere I knew. Somewhere where fires didn't burn.

❖ ❖ ❖

The air in the sewer tunnel was cool. The water colder. Like a tomb. It was quiet. Dark as night. I could breathe. I didn't want to waste my matches. Those were for my cigarettes. I used the light from the sewer grates, a hazy glow. Nothing in focus.

Knee-deep in the water at the center of the passage. Slow but moving forward. The skritch of scurrying rats. Strange life in the water. The real monsters were above.

Younger, I had played down there on hot days. A dozen boys, a few brave girls, playing muckle under the city. Running wild through the dank maze, splashing through the runoff. Laughing. Screaming. Nobody cared. Until Vito Abatti drowned. Tripped, hit his head, sank in black water, woke up dead. Two hours to find him, floating facedown. I guess he won that game of hide-and-seek. Only the urchins played after that, no parents to forbid them. They had all the fun.

It hadn't been so long that I had forgotten my way. Headed toward the baths. Made good time. Thought I might get there before Sal. If Sal was alive. If anyone was.

A high-pitched scream. A woman or a girl or a child. Straight ahead. Not far. I gripped the cleaver. Inched closer through the water. Heard splashing. Another scream. A grunt. Voices.

The tunnel opened into a larger chamber where the water collected. Home base when we played. Where seekers counted. Where the flag to capture stood. Multiple tunnels in and out, water pouring from above, draining somewhere below. Slightly deeper. A faster current. A city delta. Faint light made the room churchlike.

One man watched as another held a girl. One hand around her waist. Another gripping her red hair. Fourteen or fifteen, she was small, but she fought. Nails across a face. Feet kicking, slowed by the water. A bearcat, but she had lost. The fight just hadn't left her.

"Shoot her—then screw her," the watcher said.

"Screwing dead things is a sin in the eyes of God," the other replied as he tore at the girl's clothes.

Sal told me not to try to save anyone. That no one could be saved.

This girl didn't need saving. From nowhere, a knife swung up, slashed her attacker's arm.

I helped anyway. Had the ice pick in the man's spine in seconds. Stuck. He fell in violent spasms, splashing and disappearing in the dark water.

The other man pulled the girl close, a shield. Not a smart man. She stabbed behind herself. The chunk of the knife as it sank into his leg. He clumsily reached into his coat. Before he could draw his revolver, the girl's thumb was in the man's eye socket. Digging behind his eyeball, forcing it forward. He pushed her away.

My cleaver landed where his neck and shoulder met, six inches deep. His collarbone cracked. The warmth of his blood ran over my hand and arm. I swung the cleaver again.

It took a lot of swings. Until my shoulder muscles ached. I turned to find the girl. She sat against a wall, the man's revolver pointed at me.

"You know how to use that?" I asked.

"I'm a quick study."

"I ain't going to hurt you."

She fired the pistol. Hit the man with the ice pick in his neck. He stood behind me. I hadn't seen him rise. The man fell back, sank, floated. Eyes open. Chest a bloody hash.

"I don't owe you," she said. "I don't owe you anything." Lowered the gun. Pulled her torn clothes to her body.

I nodded. Took off my wet coat. Held it out to her.

1986

CHAPTER 6

Some fires need to burn themselves out. That damn city is
beyond our control. Closest thing to a solution would be to
drop a bomb and level the son of a bitch.

—*From his private tape recordings, J. Edgar Hoover discussing
organized crime in Auction City with Mark Felt (1958)*

Andy had plenty of limitations, but his knowledge of the city, its history, and its citizens was not among them. As a kid, he had become a sponge. From books in the library or old newspapers, he absorbed every tidbit of city trivia. Not exclusive to book learning, he also walked the neighborhoods, letting the street educate him. Loose talk, sidewalk patter, barbershop bullshitting, Andy listened. He could name every comptroller the city ever had. He could tell you who owned the newsstand on Forty-Sixth and Parker in 1978 (Laszlo Fekete until he sold it to his cousin Zsigmond Farkas). Going back to the reconstruction after the Flood, Andy could name which architect designed which building in downtown, and every pimp operating on Exposition Boulevard. He knew the cops, the criminals, the politicians, and the moneymen. Or thought he did.

Kate Girard had come up in his files, but all he had was the DA job twenty-odd years ago. Considering the amount of information in his fourteen filing cabinets, this lack of data was data itself. Another clue made important by its omission. Kate Girard was tied to Champ, the Holt Avenue address, and Gray. She was an active participant. There were secrets out there, and people didn't keep secrets about unimportant things.

Andy may have left the ACPD, but he had maintained a few contacts. There was a whole subculture of people who traded information as a commodity like pork bellies or gold. People that considered him a friend or owed him a favor or were just flat-out scared of his perceived lunacy.

Then there were those who thought they could get something in return. The tit-for-tatters. The back-scratchers. The lowest of the low. The dregs. The journalists.

"How's Auction City's most hated ex-cop?" Rebane said, setting his newspaper aside and shoveling a fist-size knot of noodles into his mouth. A man of gigantic proportions, Kurt Rebane had passed three hundred pounds as a teenager and didn't stop growing. "With all the troubles you got in Auction, why not move somewhere else? California, maybe?"

"I love this damn city," Andy said. "Besides, palm trees don't give shade, I can't surf, and granola tastes like gravel. Wouldn't last a day on the West Coast. The people are too beautiful. Too much yogurt."

Andy sat next to Rebane at the counter in the Chinatown hole-in-the-wall Fu's Good Taste. While Chinatown struggled to survive, Fu's remained. As did the chain-smoking octogenarians who occupied all the tables. In the dozen times he'd been there, Andy had never heard one of them speak. They sat in silence, rhythmically smoking their cigarettes and nodding to themselves. The cloud of smoke that hovered at the ceiling made the paper lamps look magical.

"I hope you're not going to bore me with more bullshit about Gray," Rebane said. "Writing about police corruption in this town is like writing about why water is blue."

"Water isn't blue. It's clear."

"Who gives a damn?" Rebane said. "Nobody's going to print a bunch of unsubstantiated speculation. And that's all you ever have. It's not even salacious or perverted or fun. The guy's dirty, but where's the story?"

"Watergate wasn't salacious or perverted or fun," Andy said, defensive.

"What do you got?" Rebane sounded tired.

"Nothing," Andy said. "I need information from you."

Rebane laughed, coughing up a spherical clump of chewed noodles onto his plate. He picked up the tan foodwad, turned it in his fingers, and tossed it back in his mouth. Andy felt his stomach turn but said nothing. There's no upside in telling the guy you're asking a favor that he's disgusting to the point of near nausea.

Rebane picked at his teeth with his pinky. "What makes you think I'll help you with anything?"

"Old time's sake? I don't know," Andy said. "There may be a story in it. Who knows?"

"Can I get back to my lunch? I got dumplings coming."

"Kate Girard. I need to know what you know about her."

Rebane dropped his chopsticks and turned to Andy. His body shook, chins vibrating. He lowered his voice to a whisper. "How do you know that name? Where did you hear it? Forget you ever heard of Kate Girard, unless you want to tear this city down to its roots. And get us both killed in the process."

"Christ, Rebane." Andy glanced over his shoulder. The old men smoked indifferently. They had secrets of their own. "Who is she?"

Rebane whooped with laughter. "The proverbial fish in the proverbial barrel. You make it too easy for a jerk like me to screw with you."

He pointed at the front page of the *Auction City Intelligencer*. A photo of President Reagan. The headline: "Mistakes Were Made."

Rebane slapped Andy's back. "You're always looking for the big conspiracy. That's what you're wired to do, but history tells us that real conspiracies never stay secret. Look at this thing with Reagan and Iran and the Nicaraguans. Stuff like this and Watergate happen, sure. But some idiot always says something. It always leaks. Government scandals are about incompetence, not malevolence. Nicest thing I can say about conspiracy nuts like you is that they have an overly optimistic view of man's guile and cleverness. Realists like me see people for what they are: clumsy, selfish monkeys who try to grab all the bananas."

"Are you going to tell me about Kate Girard?" Andy asked.

"Just because you distrust one group doesn't mean you have to trust every piece of information that opposes that group. The government is bad, so obviously the moon landing was fake and fluoridation is mind control."

"Don't get me started on NASA," Andy said. "Kate Girard is someone. Used to work for the DA. I saw her last night, talking to Gray."

"Always Al Gray with you. Have something to do with the bruises on your face?"

"Ran into three Thorntons."

Rebane shook his head. "You might be a pariah, Destra, but the Thorntons are pure villainy. Smashed more cameras than I can count. My balls hurt from sense memory. There's nothing that justifies giving thugs like them badges."

"Other than their last name. Generations of Thorntons on the force."

"You give as good as you got?" Rebane asked.

"Pretty sure I broke a Thornton jaw."

The cook at the counter took Rebane's empty plate and put an order of steaming dumplings in front of him. He used his hands, eventually grabbing one of the slippery dumplings and sliding it in his mouth. It was like watching a hippopotamus swallow a seal whole, revolting but impossible to look away.

"For hurting a Thornton, I'm going to help you," Rebane said. "Only because I can do it sitting here."

"You'll be the first to get the story."

"I'll hold off cashing that check. You're also picking up the tab for my feast." Rebane corralled some more dumplings, racing to put them in his mouth. "You're going to be disappointed. Kate Girard was a bureaucrat. Maybe twenty, twenty-five years ago, a comer in the DA's office. Not many lady lawyers back then, and none with her traction. Big cases but always second chair. Hit a ceiling. It wasn't like she could run for district attorney. She's a woman, you know."

"I noticed."

"She quit abruptly. Scuttlebutt suggested she was recruited by another agency. Don't know which one, but she didn't leave town. Maybe a private group. Never got the complete record on it, mostly because I didn't care. What's the headline? 'Woman Leaves Job and Takes Different Job.' Film at ten."

"How would she know Champ?"

Rebane laughed. "I ever tell you the time I saw Champ arm wrestle three swabbies in a row? Shamed them. Made them walk back to their ship without any pants. Hell of a woman."

"Never heard that one," Andy said, having heard that one from Champ at least twenty times.

"I have no idea how those two broads would know each other. Auction is weird that way. Everyone's connected. We're probably cousins."

The cook took the empty plate and set down a bill with a fortune cookie. Rebane slid the bill to Andy and cracked the fortune cookie, throwing the pieces in his mouth. He glanced at the fortune, got off the stool, and tossed it on the counter in front of Andy. "Not everything is a big nefarious plot, Destra. Sometimes the world is a boring place with boring people."

Andy picked up the fortune. It read, "Society prepares the crime; the criminal commits it." Not a fortune at all. More of an observation. And a plagiarized one. In Auction City, crime found its way into everything, even dessert.

◆ ◆ ◆

The Japanese kid must have thought that to a round-eye like Andy all Asians looked the same. But Andy had worked Little Nagasaki as a cop. Setting that aside, the kid's sky-high, spiky mullet kept him from being inconspicuous.

As Andy walked out of the smoky Chinese restaurant, the kid pretended to look at the chopsticks and back-scratchers in front of a souvenir shop.

Andy headed south down Tyburn Boulevard. The kid kept pace, across the street and a block back. But Andy knew a thing or two about trailing someone. He looked forward to the chance to show today's youth that experience still had its place. Andy wasn't even going to break a sweat.

Andy walked around the next block. Right turn after right turn. Then he walked around the block again, circling the Fairmont Building. The kid followed from a distance, but with all the turns, he was forced to close the gap. Andy walked around the block again. By the third orbit, the kid knew he'd been made but kept following.

On his twelfth lap, Andy stopped and bent to tie the laces of his laceless loafers. On one knee, he glanced over his shoulder. The kid turned quickly, looking into the window of a women's shoe store. He had cut the distance to twenty yards.

Andy lifted into a sprinter's crouch, pushed off, and booked down the street away from the kid. At the end of the next block, he turned and waited. When the kid rounded the corner, Andy clotheslined him across the chest, knocking him to the ground.

A few pedestrians gave the violent moment a glance, but they went about their business. Getting involved wasn't protocol in Auction City.

With a foot on the kid's chest, Andy squatted and shouted, "Who are you? Why are you following me?"

"No English," the kid said.

Closer up, Andy saw that he was probably in his early twenties, not as young as he'd thought.

Andy coughed up some phlegm and spit on the ground near the kid's head. "Never going back to Fu's. Feels like I smoked a bag of briquettes."

"No English," the kid said, shaking his head.

"Anata wa dare?" Andy said, pretty sure that was close to right.

The kid looked at Andy as if he had three heads and one of those heads had a penis for a nose.

"Anata wa dare?" Andy repeated.

"Damn. Totally busted," the kid said in a West Auction accent. "You got me. Wasn't expecting you to know Japanese. That was Japanese, right?"

"Get up," Andy said, grabbing the kid's jacket collar. "Why are you following me?"

"How is my hair?" the kid said, tapping at the rigid spikes.

"Still ridiculous. Why are you following me?"

"Because I'm an asshole," the kid said.

"Did Gray put you up to this?"

"Waste of my afternoon. I canceled a mani-pedi."

"Kate Girard?"

"Dude, you are so far out of your league, you don't even know what game you're playing," the Japanese kid said. "Seriously, my hair better be okay."

"You're coming with me."

"I can still make my appointment." The kid twisted his body in a quick turn, like a dancer's pirouette. The result left Andy holding the kid's satin jacket but not the kid. By the time Andy realized what had happened, the kid was sprinting between the suit-and-ties on their lunch breaks.

CHAPTER 7

People keep acting like there's one truth to a story. Like the truth is a thing. Eventually—if you don't want to go crazy—you'll come to the conclusion that the choice is not about the truth, but which lie you prefer to believe.

—From former Auction City Superior Court Judge Joost Bakker's autobiography Joostice: Thirty Years on the Bench (1966)

The nurse at the front desk gave Andy a scolding look when she saw the Frank's Giant Franks bag in Andy's hand.

"Giving the gift of heartburn today, Mr. Destra?" the nurse said.

"The pleasure far outweighs the pain. Champ loves Frank's." Andy reached into the bag. "Does that mean you don't want the one I brought you? Mustard and relish, right?"

Andy held out the hot dog wrapped in greasy wax paper. The nurse looked over her shoulder and took the hot dog.

"How is she today?" Andy asked.

"Normal day. She told me to send up Tony, the new orderly, to help her with something. Nice kid. Muscles, no brains. He reported that after moving a table six inches, she pinched his butt and gave him a wink, and then pretended she thought he was her late husband, Manny. She's not a great actor, but it's a good sign when she's using her confusion as an excuse to cop a feel. Lucid enough to be grabby, at least."

"That's my Champ all right. She likes a beefy man ass."

◆ ◆ ◆

Champ flipped through the yellowing pages of one of three photo albums she owned. In an effort to slow the erosion of her memory, she kept a daily ritual of combing through the pictures and naming the people, places, and events that the images evoked. Even on her worst days, she maintained the routine, left to flip through images of strangers and strange places that she knew but didn't recognize.

Andy walked into the room and set the Frank's bag on the small table.

"Who is Kate Girard?" Andy asked. "You have to tell me."

"Be a dear and make me some tea," she said. "And put some whiskey in it."

Without lifting her eyes from the pages of the album, Champ reached into the Frank's bag, pulled out a hot dog, and stuffed half the thing in her mouth. Andy resisted the urge to lecture her on choking hazards. A part of him had always wanted to perform the Heimlich maneuver.

Andy went into the small kitchenette and put the kettle on to boil. "Kate Girard," he repeated.

With a finger tapping a photo, Champ mumbled through falling crumbs and meat bits. "Rory Connell. From the neighborhood. Funny ginger bastard. We're fifteen, sixteen here. Running some scheme or another. The two of us got beaten to hell after we conned one of Fat Jimmy's boys out of some coin. Worth it. We got the story. Crazy son of a bitch, but you could trust him, always had your back. Even if he was the one that usually started the trouble. Died young. Too young."

"I really need to know. I'm sure you have your reasons," Andy said, "but I'm in the middle of something and I need answers."

Champ flipped through a few pages silently.

Andy made Champ's tea and brought it to her. She took a sip and made a face.

"I can't taste the booze," she said.

"That's because I didn't put any in there."

Champ muttered to herself, but Andy couldn't pick out the words. Just when Andy thought he had gotten Champ on a good day, she squinted at him and asked, "Working any big cases?"

"I'm not a cop anymore," Andy said. "I'm pretty sure you know that."

"You finally come to your senses?"

"It was almost two years ago."

"Well, I just wanted to drop by and say hello. Got to be heading home." Champ stood but didn't move, eyeing her surroundings suspiciously.

"You are home, Champ," Andy said. "You live here now."

With frustration in her voice, she snapped, "I know."

"You had a visitor yesterday. A lady. Wore all red. Kate Girard."

"Katie." Champ shook her head, sitting back down. "It really was her. She was here."

"Who is she?"

"Doesn't matter."

"Yes, it does," Andy said.

"Tough shit for you, boy." Champ shrugged.

"Did she leave you some way of contacting her? A phone number? I need to talk to her."

Champ looked around the small table next to her. "I don't remember."

Andy reached in his pocket for a pen and something to write on. They both watched a flurry of paper scraps fall to the table. "You're not the only one with a bad memory."

But Champ wasn't listening. She had picked up the old gas bill, staring at the symbol drawn on it. The one graffitied on the front of the Holt Avenue building. The old woman's hands shook.

"Do you know what that symbol means?" Andy asked. He reached for the scrap of paper, but Champ knocked his hand away.

"Floodgate," Champ said.

"Like from back in the twenties?" Andy asked. "That Floodgate?"

"Was Katie here to talk to you or me?"

"Why would she be here for me? I don't know her," Andy said. "What's going on? Try to focus, Champ."

"You need to stop asking questions."

"If that symbol is from sixty years ago, why would it be painted on a building today?"

"You need to stop. You need to stop." Champ had grown visibly agitated, her hands shaking.

"This is important."

Champ threw her mug of tea across the room. "Every day, every goddamn day, I lose a little more. A name of someone I knew. A memory of a happy day. A kiss that meant everything. I see a picture but can only stare. I know the person, but I don't. Might as well be looking at an underwear model in the Sears catalog. I go to sleep every night afraid that I'm going to wake up and it'll all be gone. I won't remember anything. Not remember you."

Andy couldn't think of anything to say, so he said, "I'm sorry."

"Then there are memories that most people would be happy to say good-bye to. The pain and anger and even terror felt in the worst times. But I hold on to those just as tight, because, damn it, they're mine. I would rather keep them than my damn secrets. I would happily let go of all the secrets. Heavy weights I've carried for other people. Please don't ask me anymore."

"Okay," Andy said, eyes cast down, ashamed of himself.

"I love you. You know that, don't you, stupid?" Champ said.

Andy nodded. "You, too, Champ."

They spent the rest of the hour in silence. Champ drinking her tea and flipping through her albums. She went back inside herself, to wherever she lived most of the day. To the murky shadows of her long past days.

CHAPTER 8

During the Civil War, residents on the south side of the Thief River fought for the Confederacy, while those north fought for the Republic. River barges were considered neutral, converted to taverns, gambling halls, and brothels. There is no recorded account of violence on the river. A phenomenon that defines Auction City, a place that finds peace in its vice.

—From the PhD thesis "General Horton Harper and His Role
in the First Battle of Black Hand Hill: A Contradiction of
Power and Strategy within the Paradigm of the Leadership
Dynamic both Military and Social," by Stanton Pierce (1979)

Every kid in Auction City knew the stories of Floodgate. Andy could still remember his Big Little Books chronicling their adventures. At eight years old, he read them until the spines cracked and loose pages spilled out. Floodgate stood as part of the great American folklore tradition. Like Jesse James, Davy Crockett, and Al Capone. Part truth, part legend, and filled with American individualism and heroic derring-do.

The more academic books on the subject were not only dry but thin in terms of information. Most of Andy's knowledge of Floodgate came from those children's books. The overwritten prose and pen-and-ink illustrations replaced primary source material. According to *Floodgate:*

Criminal Justice, by Brace Godfrey, the Church brought together the police and the leaders of the warring criminal organizations for a parlay in an effort to end the Gang War of 1929. A truce was formed. The terms of which historians debated to this day. They didn't argue that it ended the fighting, but nobody but those involved ever knew the conditions of that agreement.

The generals could all agree that the war was over, but until the soldiers have been informed, the fighting continued. A citywide riot tended to chip at the concept of trust. People were shooting first and shooting second. Questions weren't being asked.

Volunteers from each faction were tasked with maintaining peace. Braving the fires and the fighting to stop the ground war. What formed was a vigilante force made up of members of the ACPD, the Chinese Tongs, the Wretches, the Italians, and the Church itself. One of Andy's favorite illustrations from that kid's book was a picture of a collared priest firing a tommy gun.

The volunteers temporarily set aside their allegiances. Divided into units that consisted of one member from each group. Armed with axes, guns, and knives in a show of solidarity and force, they spoke sense to those fighting. And if sense didn't work, their weapons did.

The group initially had no name. After the riots were dubbed the Flood, the group took the name Floodgate.

At least, that's what the Big Little Books said. According to the last chapter of the last book in the series, once the violence had ended and the city was rebuilt, the group disbanded. The members filtered back to their respective organizations. The police took back the role of keeping the peace. And their piece of the action.

But that didn't explain the graffiti he'd seen the day before. Had someone started using the name for its own purpose? And what did Gray and Kate Girard have to do with it?

◆ ◆ ◆

He would have to dig those children's books out of the bowels of his storage space. Maybe hit the stacks at the library. A fascinating foray into civic history, but it would have to wait. He had a lead in front of him. One that brought him to Little Nagasaki.

The Japanese kid's satin jacket advertised a restaurant on the back. An angry-looking fish held chopsticks in its fin. Puffy letters read **IKEJIME** at the top and **FRESH KILL** down below. It was a long shot, but Andy was low on clues.

Only ten blocks square, Little Nagasaki's density exuded the illusion of enormity. The labyrinthine alleys and narrow streets followed no logical grid, quickly absorbing a pedestrian within its high brick walls. No map fully captured every path. And with the rumors of tunnels and an extended system of catwalks and roof bridges, there was the sense that the layout changed. That the neighborhood was in constant motion.

Entering Little Nagasaki was like crossing a border into a different world. A threatening world, if you were the neighboring Chinatown. The entirety of Naga—as it was called by locals—was once part of Chinatown. But little by little, whole blocks had been absorbed. Every year, Little Nagasaki got a little bigger and Chinatown smaller. No love lost between the peoples of each community. A thousand-year history of spilled blood and claimed land will do that.

The short time Andy had worked Naga as a cop had been an adventure. The exotic smells, language, and people, full of distrust and secrecy. Where Chinatown embraced its role as a tourist destination, giving up any authenticity for General Tso's chicken, finger traps, and plastic Buddhas, Naga made no such diplomatic effort. Whenever the city put up a street sign in English, it disappeared that same evening.

Naga's low crime rate was misleading. There were few reported muggings and little street violence, but that was because there were never witnesses and often no victims. The residents of Naga didn't report crimes, and neither did the tourists, for the worst reasons possible.

People didn't get hurt in Naga. Like the street signs, they got disappeared. No body, no crime. Habeas corpus, Johnny Law.

A drab, gray community, understated storefronts were the norm. Local businesses rarely did anything to draw undue attention or give the impression that outsiders were welcome. Not Ikejime. The restaurant's exterior was bright and flashy, neon Japanese kana and giant plaster koi above the ornate front door. Somebody sure liked turquoise and pearl.

That kind of gaudy excess told Andy that it was owned by 893, Auction City's yakuza affiliate. In direct contrast to the reticent citizenry of Naga, 893 members were ostentatious. You could spot an 893 gangster by his Day-Glo clothes, expensive sports car, and the blue-green of his tattoo sleeves. It would be unwise to underestimate their clownlike garishness, though. 893 were a dangerous outfit. Deadly quick to retaliate and steeped in a distorted definition of honor, they radiated menace.

Andy stood out like a giraffe in a herd of shorter-necked animals, zebras maybe. Even the old lady wheeling groceries past him gave him the hairy eyeball. He backed against the brick wall, on the off chance that the passing octogenarian pulled a straight razor.

Asking questions in Naga was the equivalent of putting on pants made of meat and poking a tiger in the eye. Andy's stomach didn't care. He'd watched Rebane eat and had grabbed some dogs for Champ, but Andy hadn't eaten anything himself since breakfast. And that had been half a blueberry muffin that he'd picked the mold off. He didn't need a badge to grab a late lunch at a public restaurant. He hoped he could afford it.

◆ ◆ ◆

The inside was as gaudy as the exterior. Rather than traditional Nippon, it blindly stabbed at futuristic, giving up halfway through the effort. All white and black, severe corners and lines, clear plastic tables, and multicolored neon tubes like pick-up sticks on the wall. It looked like a 1970s movie set designer's vision of what a disco of the future looked like. He expected Michael York and Jenny Agutter to walk in any moment, or whoever their Japanese equivalents were.

Identical twin hostesses eyed Andy. Small Japanese women in slacks and suit jackets with nothing underneath. The two women turned toward a big guy in sunglasses and a lime-green suit. Leaning casually on the bar, he cracked his knuckles and nodded. The hostesses' neutral faces transformed to broad grins. Both women talked rapid-fire Japanese as if Andy were a long-lost friend. He didn't know what they were saying, but they seemed happy to see him. One of the women removed his coat as the other put a hand on his back and walked him to an empty table. Her foot brushed against his leg. They pulled out his chair, removed the extra place setting, and left him to make his meal selection, which was going to be a challenge as the menu was in Japanese. Andy wasn't even sure if he had it right side up.

He smiled at the twins, impressed by the most thorough and pleasurable weapons pat-down he'd ever received. Andy had to commend the security when even the hostesses were savvy enough to check for an ankle holster but made it feel like a game of footsy.

Only a few tables were occupied. Japanese patrons who spoke softly to one another, glancing at Andy when they thought he wasn't looking.

In the back corner, a Japanese man sat at a table that sat twelve. In his midsixties and dressed in a conservative suit, he took sips of cold sake, eyes on the front door. Behind him, four young men stood at attention. They appeared to be having a contest to see who could wear the most obnoxious suit. The guy with the pink cummerbund and matching fedora was the odds-on favorite.

When Andy accidentally made eye contact with the old man, he felt caught. The old man didn't avert his gaze, threateningly bored. Andy turned to his suddenly fascinating, yet still unreadable, menu. The sound of traffic on the street told him the front door had opened. He looked there instead.

"Now I'm completely lost," Andy said quietly to himself.

A priest walked into the Japanese restaurant. Andy couldn't imagine a stranger presence than his own in that foreign and pseudo-futuristic environment. It sounded like the start of a dirty joke, but there was no punch line. He would have known it was a joke if the priest had a parrot on his shoulder, but that would have been ridiculous.

Andy recognized the holy man right away. For years, Cardinal Macklin had been a magnetic religious and political figure. Some people liked the half that blessed orphans and built missions. Others because he drank and smoked and told bawdy stories of the old country that made you laugh until you pissed yourself. An improbable mix of piety and debauchery that tallied up to unequivocal charm.

The Cardinal walked past the two bowing hostesses, gave Andy a glance, and headed to the back table. He wasn't frisked. The bouncer in the green suit looked down. The rest of the patrons kept their eyes on their plates. When the Cardinal reached the back table, the Japanese man rose and bowed. They sat down together. Sake was poured. Nobody spoke. They waited for the rest of their party.

Their dinner companions turned out to be Kate Girard and an older man in a suit and hat.

"It keeps getting better," Andy said.

Kate Girard gave Andy a double take. But Andy's eyes were on the man with her. He was cleaned up, but Andy recognized the pickpocket who'd taken his watch on Exposition.

"What the hell?" he said, standing quickly. The bouncer in lime took a step toward his table. Kate Girard held up a hand. The bouncer stopped. She turned to Andy and shook her head. Stern enough for him to sit back down.

With his eyes on Andy, the old man whispered to Kate Girard and walked to the back table after a last, quick glance over his shoulder. He shook hands with the waiting men. Kate Girard sauntered to Andy's table.

"That guy stole my watch," Andy said, "then returned it. With a weird warning. In a weird place. At a weird time. Is that John Dole? What the hell is going on?"

"Move slow and keep it easy," Kate Girard said. "I am not joking. Even the other diners are assassins."

Andy glanced around. She may have been lying about the patrons, but he knew she was right about the danger. He took a deep breath. "The kid you hired to tail me was pathetic."

"Send a boy to do a slightly older boy's job. Ben is worthless. Been sending him out hoping he'd find a calling," Kate Girard said. "What are you expecting to find here?"

"I think I found it. Following leads. The Cardinal and 893 are an interesting pairing. Now you."

"This is not what it seems. Nothing is. You would be better off pretending you didn't see anything."

"Convince me that I'm not on the verge of uncovering something big," Andy said. "I'll buy you an appetizer of your choice. As long as it's less than three bucks. You can have the dim but not the sum."

"You've angered some powerful people," Kate Girard said. "Dangerous people."

"Means I'm onto something."

"Means you're going to get yourself killed."

"What do you care?" Andy asked.

She glanced toward the table in back. The old man talked to the Cardinal and the Japanese man, but they were both staring at Andy.

"Things are delicate right now. Negotiations in progress," she said. "If I have to, I'll sideline you before they do."

"You'll sideline me?" Andy said. "Do you work for Gray?"

"Do I look like a cop?"

"Floodgate?"

Kate Girard stood. "If you like ramen, I recommend the shoyu."

"I don't pay more than a quarter for ramen," Andy said.

She leaned in, her lips grazing his ear. "For your sake and Champ's, walk away. I'm sorry about what happens next."

"Was that a threat?" Andy asked. "What do you mean, 'what happens next'?"

Kate Girard walked toward the big table to join the others. As she passed, she said a few words to the bouncer in the green suit. He got off his stool and lumbered over to Andy, one hand in his jacket.

"You must rise and make to exit," the man said through a thick accent.

"I must?"

"Yes. Or I choose to assault and tote you. It is my mandate." He opened his jacket to give Andy a glimpse of his shoulder holster.

"Well, if it's your mandate." Andy stood and backed toward the front door, his eyes locked on the bouncer, who kept pace with him. When Andy reached the hostess counter, the twins slipped his jacket onto his arms.

He turned to leave, almost running into Deputy Commissioner Gray, who was entering the restaurant at the same time.

"Destra?" Gray said, surprised. "You're a persistent son of a bitch. I'll give you that."

"You can count on it," Andy said.

"Should've had you brought in after that fracas in Muldoon's. Thrown you a blanket party. To be honest, I had too much damn fun to bother. Nothing like a barroom rhubarb. Sad we were on the opposite ends of the place. I would've put on a boxing clinic."

"Anytime you want to go, old man," Andy said, squaring up. "I'll knock you right into senility."

"Speaking of which. How is Champ?" Gray smiled. "It's going to be a terrible blow when you lose that old lush."

"You don't get to say her name."

Gray let out a chuckle. "I could've used a tough guy like you. You got heart but unfortunately too much brains."

"I'm going to take you down, Al," Andy said, wishing he could have come up with something better. In the moment, you couldn't second-guess your one-liners.

Gray gave Andy a hard shove. "I look forward to drawing the chalk line around your body, Destra."

Andy took a step toward him, but the bouncer grabbed the back of his collar. As if to make clear his job title, he literally bounced Andy off the front door before he threw him outside. Andy heard Gray's laughter as he flew into the cold night.

◆ ◆ ◆

An hour later, Andy found himself standing in the cold watching the front door of the Japanese restaurant. There was nothing quite like anger to buoy one's capacity for patience. Every minute felt a degree colder, clouds of mist with each exhale. Andy didn't care. They could toss him out of a building, but they couldn't make him give up.

They could try to kill him, though. They could definitely do that.

When the man in the black trench coat turned the corner, Andy knew immediately that the guy was wrong. Trudging toward him with purpose, the monobrow Italian would have raised anyone's hackles. His stiff-legged walk told Andy that he was either happy to see him or the man carried a bat or rifle under his coat.

Andy casually reached a hand into his pocket. The man stutter-stepped. Andy charged him. The guy was definitely not happy to see him. It ended up being a shotgun he swung upward, not a rifle.

When you're unarmed and exposed, everything needs to be a weapon. Andy threw a handful of change at the man's face. Enough of a distraction to get the barrel of the shotgun under his arm. The gun fired. Andy felt the heat of the barrel, smelled the powder, and heard glass break.

76

With the shotgun pinned to his body, Andy threw right hooks into the gunman's ribs. The man headbutted Andy, almost knocking him off his feet. He gained his balance and gave the man a knee to the groin.

The blow did the trick, allowing Andy to pull the shotgun away. Like swinging too hard at a curveball, the momentum sent the shotgun flying through the air in a spinning arc. It landed in the middle of the street.

The man took a knee, one hand on his jewels. Andy didn't wait for an invitation. He kicked him in the head and took off down the street, turning the first corner. As he ran, he looked for Little Nagasaki landmarks, something he might remember from his cop days. No luck. Maybe if he lost himself in the maze, he could lose the shooter, too.

Every chance he got, Andy turned corners. He ran past curious pedestrians. He stuck to the alleys. He tried side doors, but they were locked. At one point, he dared to glance over his shoulder. The shooter was a block back. The gunman had retrieved the shotgun, brandishing it openly in one hand and a pistol in the other. Who was he trying to impress? He also appeared to be in better shape than Andy was, which was going to be a problem.

Andy turned into another alley and almost ran into a six-foot-tall bald black woman in a man's suit. Her tan suit was so crisp that the lapels looked like knife blades. Her lean body and high cheekbones made her slightly androgynous. She held a brick in each hand.

"Aw, crap," Andy said, wishing he had chosen better last words.

Then he saw the Japanese kid who had followed him standing behind her.

"What the hell?" Andy said.

"Get down," the kid said, pulling a pistol but staying shielded behind the tall woman's body.

The woman motioned for Andy to get down on the ground. Her ease convinced him. He dropped, lying as flat as he could on the wet and slimy alley floor. Some water got in his mouth. It tasted like month-old kitchen-drawer celery.

When the shooter turned the corner, the bald woman threw a brick. The sound it made when it hit the man's chest made Andy flinch. Lots of crack and slosh. The man kept running, but he had dropped the pistol and lost his balance. As he stumbled forward, the woman threw the other brick. It broke in half on the man's head. He crashed into the wall, bounced back, and fell on top of Andy.

Andy heaved the unconscious man off him. Blood oozed from the man's ear. Andy scrambled upright and turned to the woman and kid, ready to fight.

"Holy Christ in hell. What is going on? Who are you? Who is this? What the what?" Andy said, rapid-fire.

"No thank-you for saving your ass?" the Japanese kid said.

Andy looked at the man on the ground. "That guy was going to kill me. Someone sent him to kill me."

The bald woman walked to Andy. "What is the difference between a birthday cake and a punch in the face?" she asked, speaking with an accent that Andy guessed was West African.

"I don't understand. What are you talking about?" Andy said, frantic. "What does that mean? What could that possibly mean?"

"This is no birthday cake," she said and hit him with a sharp right cross. The shock, more than the force, dropped him back to the ground. He just missed landing on his would-be assassin.

"Okay, that's it," Andy said. "You want a fight? You got it, lady."

As he tried to get to his feet, he felt the hypodermic needle that the Japanese kid jabbed into his neck.

"I am so confused," Andy said.

Something warm flowed into his veins. It made his skin tingle and his body warm. It made him see an extra color. The world got swirly. He felt really weird but good. And then he felt nothing.

CHAPTER 9

Bad luck. Just bad luck.

—*Attributed to disgraced mortician Graham Berry after*
surviving a suicide leap from the King Olaf Bridge (1955)

It wasn't the first time that Andy had woken up underneath a bridge. Regained consciousness was more accurate. Those other times, he had been on undercover assignments or stakeouts. Getting assaulted, drugged, and transported to the bridge was a new one, something to tell his grandkids. If he lived long enough to have grandkids. Or kids, which were a prerequisite.

Groggy and half-awake, Andy deduced it was night from the darkness that surrounded him. That's the kind of astute observation that made Andy a crackerjack investigator. The painfulness of pain was another specialty of his. He was in some kind of tentlike structure, one that had seen better days. Through the gaping holes in the overhead tarp, he made out the bottom of the bridge above.

Andy's right eye felt swollen and tender to the touch. Dried blood caked his nostrils, but nothing felt broken and the bleeding had stopped. He rubbed his neck where the needle had gone in.

His pockets were empty. No wallet. No keys. No nothing. Even the scraps of paper with his random notes were gone. The most he could be happy for was that they hadn't taken his clothes. Naked under a bridge was a different level of trouble.

Kate Girard had tried to warn him. Someone had tried to kill him. Things had gone from curious to serious, but he couldn't stay in a stranger's lean-to and wait for it all to go away.

Crawling out of the tent, he recognized his surroundings. The unmistakable urban patchwork known as the Castles, an enormous tent town on the other side of the river that housed the undermost strata of Auction City's impoverished population. People who aspired to be lower class. On paper it was an illegal encampment, but it had existed as long as the city itself. If the system failed you, create your own system. Andy knew the Castles well. He had made enough arrests down there, carted off some bodies, and heard innumerable sad stories of what had led people to the outside.

While the residents changed, the community under the King Olaf Bridge dated back to the nineteenth century. The Castles had supported those affected by the Depression, the survivors of the Flood, war veterans forgotten by the people they defended, and those unfortunates for whom the American Dream had become a nightmare. Similar to the sovereignty of an Indian reservation, the Castles was autonomous. Forgotten and ignored long ago, it received little interference from the outside. With its own crude form of governance, the people of the Castles only reached out to the police when things got too big or weird for them to handle in-house. And if a politician required some extra votes, he would outright buy them rather than campaign down there. Cash trumped empty rhetoric every day.

A group of four women sat in front of the tent directly across from Andy. Each one of the women was Hispanic, in her midtwenties, and missing a limb. Andy gave them a weak smile. They stared back, indifferent.

Andy recognized them as members of the Broken. Victims from Auction City's worst days. A sad time when the world was reminded that man's capacity for cruelty had no limits. The pointless and cruel solution when the competition among the panhandlers had reached such a cutthroat peak that a few sadists borrowed a practice from India and started disfiguring young girls to up the sympathy factor. Hundreds of children had been maimed to make an extra nickel, their tiny limbs lost and buried in the city's landfill.

The ring of men who ran that racket were long gone, brought to justice by unknown vigilantes. They had been found hung by their necks from the very bridge that Andy found himself below. The police let the eleven men hang for a full day before cutting them down. Not a single resident complained.

Andy checked the time, but his watch was gone again. Of course it was. Now they were just screwing with him.

"It's around two," one of the women said. Like the others, she wore a tank top and camo pants. Shoulder-length hair framed a round face with penciled-on chola eyebrows. Her right arm was missing just below the elbow, a scarred cross dimpled the stump.

"Thanks," Andy said, trying not to stare. "Someone stole my watch. Twice."

One of the other women laughed. "Least you had a watch to steal?"

"Have you seen anyone suspicious?" Andy asked.

"You're in the Castles," the first woman said.

"Did you see how I got here?"

"The same as the rest of us, güero. Born poor. Bad luck. Lost your job or started drinking. Bad choices. Look inside yourself—maybe you learn some things."

"No, I mean literally. I got chased through Naga by a man with a shotgun. Then drugged by a Japanese kid and a bald African woman."

"How high are you?" one of the others said and laughed.

"Ain't going to get nowhere blaming other people, telling stories," the first woman said, as if to a child. "The first step is admitting you have a problem."

"Thanks. That helps," Andy said. "Can you give me directions to get back on the bridge, cross back into downtown?"

"If there's people out to get you, what's your hurry?" the first woman asked. "You're safe here."

"If someone is after me, they could be after my people," Andy said.

The woman nodded. "There are stairs at the bottom of the bridge, but you're going to have to pay the troll if you want to go that way, though."

Andy shook his head. "There had to be a damn troll."

"In a day or year, it ain't easy to get out of the Castles."

"I don't have money."

"There are all sorts of ways to pay."

◆ ◆ ◆

Andy headed down the "street." For a tent town, it was well organized, each of the paths and lanes between quick-and-dirty blocks named and labeled. How else could pizza, Chinese food, and mail get delivered? As Andy passed a couple of gang members, he recognized their colors. The Ghost Shadows patrolled the Castles, acting as security and ensuring that no deliverymen were accosted. People might live rough in the Castles, but commerce marched on.

"Troll" was the perfect one-word description for the behemoth at the bottom of the stairs. Wide enough to block the narrow pedestrian stairway, the brute stared indifferently as he tried to untie the knotted string of a yo-yo. The monster's bald head was lopsided and cratered, a planet that had seen too many meteors. The Planet Troll lazily held up a catcher's mitt of a hand.

"I'm going to make this easy. I ain't got no money," Andy said. "I got rolled. Left here."

"If I let you pass pro bono," the troll said, his voice as soft as a lullaby, "it sets a troublesome precedent for subsequent customers."

Andy reeled a little. He had expected caveman and got adjunct faculty member. "That doesn't change the fact that I have no money."

"No, but it establishes your negotiation leverage. Which is minimal to nonexistent."

"If you allow people to leave, you allow people in," Andy said. "Did you see how I got here? Who brought me?"

"I don't let people walk for free on a public staircase. How could you possibly infer that I would answer your inquiries?" The troll showed what was probably a smile but looked more like a crack in his face.

"Do you know anything about a bald black woman and a Japanese kid?"

"If you think this is a riddle-of-the-sphinx type of scenario, then I suggest you take a fresh perusal of your Greek mythology. The one blocking the path asks the questions," the troll said. "And the one blocking the path gets paid."

"I should have planned better before I got shot at, punched, and drugged. At least I'm wearing clean underwear," Andy said. "Can we cut to the chase? What do you want?"

"Are those Florsheims?" the giant said, pointing at his shoes.

◆ ◆ ◆

Every shadow held a new threat. Every change of light made Andy jump. That's what happened when a strange man tried to kill you. Especially when you were already a little paranoid. Andy prepared to defend himself from every pedestrian he passed, fists clenched, ready to go. Zigzagging through the city, he avoided people. When he reached a street with nonworking streetlights, he walked six blocks out of his way to find a well-lit route.

Nobody tried to kill him. Hurrah. When that was the best thing that happened in a day, you knew the kind of day you'd had.

Crossing the bridge, walking the fifty-plus blocks, and getting to his apartment took a little more than an hour. Walking barefoot through the city reminded Andy of how disgusting people were. The array of nastiness that Andy stepped in ranged from the mundane (dogshit and gum) to the dangerous (broken glass and a hypodermic needle) to the gross (a used condom, spaghetti in marinara that was probably vomit, and a single rain-soaked bread slice that texturally had been the worst).

When he got to his building, he circled the block three times looking for anything suspicious. Nobody in the alley. Nobody sitting in their car or smoking on the street. If there was someone watching, he couldn't find them.

It took fifteen minutes of pounding to get the super to answer his door. And another fifteen to convince the beboxered man to don some pants and let Andy into his apartment. He agreed to let him in, but he didn't budge on the pants.

On the fourth-floor landing, the super looked one flight away from needing CPR. No wonder he never made any repairs. The man took his life in his hands every time he changed a bulb.

The two men stared at Andy's apartment door, unlocked and ajar.

"I won't forget this," the super said through labored breathing. He headed back down the stairs, cursing at the enormous inconvenience he had suffered. For some people, doing their job was akin to torture.

Every instinct told Andy to run. To get out of town. To forget it all, find a cave, and become a guy who lived in a cave. Things had gotten too serious and weird.

He had his limits, though. He was tired, hungry, needed a shower, and if there was someone in his apartment waiting to kill him, so be it.

It was time to bring the fight to them. He had prepared for this moment a long time ago.

Using his thumbnail as a screwdriver, Andy removed the grate from the vent in the hall. He found the string and pulled out the go-bag that he'd stowed there. Digging through the duffel, he wished he'd had the foresight to throw some tennis shoes in there. On the plus side, there was some beef jerky in the bag. He shoved some in his mouth and quickly chewed it down. It made his jaw hurt, didn't take away his hunger, and made him thirsty.

He found his revolver, an unregistered throw-down piece he'd never had the need to use. The weight of it was comforting. He could see himself shooting someone that night. Pistol in one hand, bag in the other, Andy took the long, slow walk down the hall toward his apartment. And nearly jumped out of his skin when the door behind him opened.

CHAPTER 10

Here lies Anton Hansen Osborne. Born 1863. Died 1933.
Owes his brother Erik $28 for this tombstone. Plus interest.

—*Headstone discovered in the St. Dymphna Memorial
Cemetery*

Andy came within a nanosecond of shooting Mrs. Hammond. He held the gun inches from her face. Tears filled her eyes.

"Oh, hell." Andy lowered the gun, a glance over his shoulder at his own apartment door. "I didn't mean to scare you."

She didn't seem to notice the gun. Thick mascara poured dark lines down her cheeks. "You didn't tell me you were moving, Crazy Andy. I would have made you a Bundt cake."

"I don't understand."

"I'll miss you, you damn lunatic."

"I'm in the middle of something here." Another glance at his door.

"A fresh start. A new leaf. We all need it." Mrs. Hammond looked Andy up and down. "You're a ten, Crazy Andy."

"I'm flattered," Andy muttered, "but on my best day I'm maybe a six after a haircut and shave. To someone who is myopic."

She pointed at his feet. "Your shoes, you insane bastard. I still have Marvin's things. Are you a nine and a half or ten?"

"Oh. A nine and a half."

"Wait, Crazy Andy." She slammed the door. He heard about ten locks engage.

After thirty seconds, he wondered why he was standing there. If there was anyone in his apartment, that person surely knew he was there by now. He decided to call it strategy. He was icing them, like you would a field goal kicker. Making them nervous by making them wait. Throwing them off. If there even was a them.

The locks clicked, and the door opened again. Without leaving her apartment, she held out a pair of white wingtips that were in fashion never. The moment he took them, she screamed, "You're crazy, Crazy Andy," slammed the door, and engaged the locks.

The shoes looked considerably smaller than a nine and a half. He tried to wedge one onto his foot. Without a shoehorn and a lot of butter, it wasn't going to happen. He put the shoes in his duffel bag.

"Here goes nothing."

Andy kicked open his apartment door the rest of the way. The extra-heavy—yet apparently ineffective—door slammed against the wall inside, the knob digging into the cheap drywall. When he flipped on the lights, Andy's view of his apartment nearly knocked him over. The front room was empty. Completely empty. Gutted. No filing cabinets, no maps on the wall, no mini fridge, no dust bunnies in the corner. For some reason, they hadn't taken his telephone. It sat in the middle of the floor.

He glanced at the apartment number on the door. It was his apartment. He could see the former layout like a blueprint from the indentations in the carpet where his furniture had been. He walked through the space on the outside chance that his possessions had become invisible.

Andy ran his hand over the pinholes in the wall. Whoever had taken his things had literally taken everything down to the brass tacks. He was surprised they hadn't spackled and repainted.

He focused on the telephone, waiting for it to ring. Waiting for the person at the other end to give him an explanation. A deep, mysterious voice with a series of instructions. He had seen too many movies.

His anger boiled to the surface. He wanted to throw something, break something. Of course, there wasn't anything. Then he remembered the shoes. He took them out of the bag and threw them across the room. It was unsatisfying. He considered shooting a wall. Instead, he clenched his fists until they hurt.

Calling the police was what a normal person would do, but the police probably did this. Even if they didn't, they wouldn't care about helping the rat Andy Destra.

"Be careful with that gun."

Andy started at the voice and turned, pistol aimed and ready. The old pickpocket stood in the bathroom doorway. Now in a suit and fedora, the man held his hands palms up to show he was unarmed. With his pencil mustache, he looked like a retired magician in a Philip Marlowe costume.

"Who the hell are you? Where is all my stuff?"

"What's with the shoes?" The man nodded to the pair of shoes. "Were you bowling?"

"What's happening?" Andy asked.

"You ignored our previous warnings. Making a dramatic statement necessary," the man said. "This is your last warning."

Andy did a turn of his apartment. "You took all my stuff."

"There are things happening you can't see. Important things. You think you're doing some kind of good, which is admirable, but you're causing problems. We need you on the sidelines. For your safety," the man said. "We debated what to do about you. The vote was close. I fought for you. This was what was decided. Instead of killing you."

"We? Who is we?" Andy checked the open door behind him. "Who are you?"

"It doesn't matter, son."

"It does matter. It's really the only thing that matters. Who are you, and what did you do with my possessions?"

"I took them."

"Why did you leave the phone? Just the phone?"

"To call you."

"I have a gun in my hands," Andy shouted. "That means that you're supposed to answer my questions. How do you not know that?"

"Your investigation of the deputy commissioner drew our attention. It led down some interesting avenues. You did impressive work. But it grew from nuisance to threat. There has already been an attempt on your life. This is the compromise that could keep you alive but declawed. Without your files, you are impotent."

"You think this is going to stop me?" Andy said.

The man smiled. "Personally, no. But if you keep going, someone will kill you. You have no idea the thinness of the razor you're on. I've done what I can."

"What's stopping me from taking you down?"

"I'm on your side," he said. "But more relevant, the red dot on your chest."

Andy looked down. A red laser dot marked his shirt, center mass. It came from somewhere outside his windows, but he couldn't track the angle.

"You've got to stop all investigations of the police and Deputy Commissioner Gray. Find a new hobby. Macramé, maybe. Model railroading. Ventriloquism."

"Did Gray send that man to kill me?"

The old man didn't answer or move.

Andy stared at his empty apartment. "You took everything."

"Not everything. Not your life. Not your phone," he said, reaching into his jacket pocket. Andy tightened his grip. The old man shook his head.

He tossed something underhanded to Andy, who caught it out of reflex, his feet rooted to the ground. He stared down at the watch—his stolen watch—in his hand.

"What is it with you and my watch?" Andy asked.

"Leave Gray alone."

The phone rang. Andy jumped at the sound and accidentally fired his revolver. The bullet missed the old man and lodged itself into the wall behind him. The old man drew a pistol of his own, aiming it at Andy.

"Sorry, sorry, sorry," Andy said. "An accident. I flinched."

"Christ, son," the old man said, exhaling loudly. "It's like you're trying to get yourself killed."

The phone rang again. They both looked at it. Andy glanced at the red dot still on his chest. The phone rang again.

"I'm going to answer that," Andy said.

The man shook his head. "Don't."

"It could be important."

"Don't answer it."

They stared at each other. The old man's face had become familiar to him quickly, as though he had known him longer than he had.

"Yeah, Pops," Andy said, "I'm done listening to you."

Andy walked to the phone and picked it up, expecting to get shot. He didn't.

"Hello?" Andy said.

"I'm looking for Mrs. Destra. A Mrs. Andrea Destra."

"I am Andrea. Andy. It's a man's name in Italy."

Andy glanced at the old man, who did little more than fume. Andy's minor act of defiance had taken away most of his fear of the man.

"You are listed as the emergency contact for a Claudia Destra?"

"What happened?"

"Is Mrs. Destra with you?"

"No. She's—what happened?"

"I don't know how to say this, but we can't find her. Mrs. Destra is no longer at the facility. We think she left an hour ago. Maybe with someone. A policeman was here earlier."

"She wouldn't. There's no—what policeman?"

Andy looked at the old man, wanting some sympathy from the man who'd taken all his possessions and threatened his life. No such luck. The old man walked to the wall where the phone jack was and pulled it from the wall. The line went dead.

"Gray," Andy said.

"Hold on, son," the old man said. "You need to listen to me."

But Andy didn't. He turned and sprinted to the front door, expecting his heart to get exploded from the unseen sniper. When he reached the hall, shocked he was alive, he continued his frantic run to the back stairs. He never looked to see if the old man followed. After throwing the stairwell door open, he hit the stairs and climbed to the roof.

When he reached the roof door, he stopped and listened. He heard footsteps, but the sound receded. He quietly opened the door and then set it closed behind him.

Staying low, he made his way to the edge of the roof and found the board that he'd hidden months before. He dropped it over the gap to the building next door. Looking down to the alley six stories below, he crawled the ten feet between the buildings on his hands and knees. His whole body shook. The board bowed in the middle. He had always hated heights. Halfway across, he froze, his body refusing to move. A deep breath, a small prayer, and a fart later he was on the move again.

On the neighboring roof, he pulled the board to him. He entered the pigeon coop, feeling the birdshit squeeze between his bare toes. He woke a few sleeping birds. They did little more than coo. Andy opened the trapdoor that he'd built and got inside the space with just enough room to lie down. Closing the door, it felt like a casket, but Andy knew it was the opposite. Lying among the feces and feathers, he was safe.

In the cramped and smelly place, he had time to reflect on recent events, but they only confused him more. The parts didn't connect. Nothing added up. The only thing he knew for sure was that Gray was his enemy. And that Champ was in danger. He would stop guessing and focus on the facts.

An hour later by his oft-stolen watch, he exited the coop and took a peek at the street below. Nothing and nobody as far as he could tell. It didn't really matter, though. He was tired of running.

CHAPTER 11

What I'm going to tell you is crazy. The fuzz, the suits, the rackets, the whole thing. Sister, it's big. Meet me at the Southside at seven.

—*The last known words of Nat Turner Shabazz from a phone recording made by* Auction City Echo *reporter Kate Malmon. An hour later, Shabazz was found dead from multiple gunshot wounds. The case remains unsolved (1966).*

From the shadows of the alley across the street, Andy observed the front entrance of the senior living facility. Three police cars sat parked out front, red lights painting the buildings around them. Through the glass doors, Andy watched the nurse talk to a uniformed Thornton.

There was no way to get inside. No way to get past the cops. No way to get answers of his own. Not that he could find anything there. If Champ was missing, this was the only place he didn't need to look.

There was a five percent chance that Champ had wandered off on her own, but with all the weirdness going on the last few days, it would have been too much of a coincidence. He faced the facts. Champ had been abducted, and only one person could have done it. He knew only one supervillain. He had only one archenemy.

It was time Andy Destra and the deputy commissioner had their showdown.

◆ ◆ ◆

The walk to Gallows Terrace took longer than his previous barefoot promenade had. The plus side was that as he got closer to the moneyed neighborhood, the sidewalks got cleaner. Maybe rich people didn't chew gum. Or they didn't spit it on the ground when it lost its flavor. Or more likely, they had minimum-wage employees power wash it off regularly. Andy cooled his cut and swollen feet on the wet lawns until he stubbed his toe on a sprinkler head. After that he kept to the sidewalks.

Gallows Terrace was the only neighborhood in Auction City with buildings more than sixty years old. The destruction of the Flood never made it up the hill. When the fighting had broken out in 1929, the rich industrialists and politicians who made the Terrace their home pooled their staffs to create a makeshift militia. Standing in formation at the single road that led up the hill, valets and butlers and maids and chauffeurs, armed with guns and wood, protected the people they despised against their own. Revolt was discussed but dismissed. Paychecks came from somewhere. And there weren't going to be a lot of jobs after the city was in ashes.

Walking that historic path, Andy knew his appearance would raise eyebrows. Bloody, bare feet. Covered in pigeonshit and loose feathers. A busted-up face with an eye that was bruised black. And an expression that would register between befuddled and infuriated. If the neighborhood watch or rent-a-cops were on the ball, they would stop him before he reached his destination. Or at least try.

They had taken everything. His belongings, his life, and worst of all, Champ. The only family he knew. If she was hurt in any way, people would pay. There was no one more dangerous than a man with nothing left to lose.

◆ ◆ ◆

He'd been to the deputy commissioner's house on one previous occasion back when he'd been on the force. Andy never forgot the opulence of the mansion. All the cops he knew lived in sad brick structures out in Merseyside or East Salop. Identical drab boxes with toy-littered porches and clotheslines out back.

Andy had wondered how a deputy commissioner could afford such a lavish estate. Gray wasn't hiding it, so he figured it had to be legit: inherited, rich wife, or Irish Sweepstakes. On the Terrace it was mostly old, old money, last names that went back to the city's founding. Captains of industry, city royalty, and prominent political figures. However, on deeper inspection of the residents' pasts, one could find just as many bootleggers, slave traders, and gangsters.

The wrought iron gate to Gray's estate was decorative, not for security. The gate of a man who wasn't afraid of other men. Andy easily squeezed through the bars and headed up the almost vertical, winding driveway. The steep incline forced him to take a break every twenty strides. At one point, Andy thought he might puke, squatting with his head between his knees to quell the sick.

The old elms that lined the drive reached their bony limbs overhead in an eerie arch. Small lights illuminated the drive. Gallows Terrace— while still in the city—had the quiet of deep country, rowdy insects and rustling leaves.

Reaching the edge of the circular drive in front of the house, the ground leveled off. Andy caught movement and ducked into a crouch. The raccoon that spooked him scurried into the brush, another thief in the night.

Now that he was at Gray's mansion, he realized that he hadn't really thought everything through. He knew the *why*, but it hadn't occurred to him to figure out the *how* of the thing. He wouldn't let that slow him, though. Andy had momentum.

Andy made his way around the building toward the back. He glanced into the windows as he passed. In the few lit rooms, he saw no one. No life. But the size of the house only offered a small view. There could be a party going on at the other end, and he would never know it.

The backyard was expansive, lit near the house, but fading into the dim light of morning. At least the size of a football field, he imagined croquet and even polo had been played on that manicured grass.

He tried a window into what looked like a pantry. It opened with a loud creak, but no alarm bells rang. Andy froze for a moment and waited for the hounds to be released. Nothing.

Andy pulled the pistol from his pocket and climbed inside with neither stealth nor agility. A brief panic set in when Andy thought he'd gotten stuck. He eventually freed his bulk, knocking over a stack of canned goods. He landed hard on the linoleum, the thud quieter than expected. The upside of natural padding. He thanked fate that he hadn't accidentally discharged his firearm. Small victories.

Andy moved through the house, pistol to the floor. Nobody in the kitchen. The dining room, empty. Quiet to the point of distraction, not even house sounds. It had the smell of people, though, not stale like an abandoned building.

He stopped at the door to the library. He heard Gray's voice.

"Your objections are noted, Ashley. Wrong-minded and weak, but noted. You're in the minority. If this was a democracy—and it is not—you would be outvoted. Never forget that you can be replaced or removed." Silence for a moment. Gray listening. "A moot point. The thing is in motion. All that's left is to read this week's obituaries." Gray hung up with a slam.

Andy used that as his cue, kicking the big door wide and walking into the expansive library like a cowboy into a saloon. With a pistol in his hand and hate in his heart.

Gray stood up, surprised. The surprise turned to exhaustion. "Of course it's you, Destra. How did you get in my house?"

"An innocent man would ask me why I'm here," Andy said.

Books lined the walls floor to ceiling. There was a piano, a large globe, and a taxidermy mountain lion. A man's room. It smelled like aftershave, pipe smoke, and leather.

"I haven't been innocent since I stole a kiss from Mary Hopkins in the back pew of Saint Jude's. I hope this isn't going to take long," Gray said. "I've only been awake an hour, trying to get an early start on my day. It's a difficult job keeping the people of this city safe. Even more difficult with unnecessary distractions."

"Where's Champ?" Andy asked.

"What is that all over your clothes? Is that birdshit? And where are your shoes, man? You look a mess."

Andy didn't answer. The two men stared at each other silently.

Like a boiling pot, Gray started laughing. Small chuckles transformed into chortles. He laughed so hard that he had to put a hand on the desk for balance. "You have no idea what you're doing, do you? You don't know what to do next."

Andy stared at him, fuming. Just because the man was right, it didn't mean he had to agree with the son of a bitch.

CHAPTER 12

the wealthy sit at their rococo tables
the poor with nigh to buy or to sell
lo, the hungry shall feast in heaven resplendent
as the fed and the fat count gold in God's hell

*—From the three-part poetry cycle "A Treatise
of Man (Opalescence)" by Auction City poet
Manfred Darwood (1977)*

With the gun aimed at Gray, Andy plopped down in an oversize leather chair. He did his best to appear menacing, but he had lost his momentum. He had come to the man's house, expecting what? Answers. Surrender. Revenge. For a man who prided himself on his analytical reasoning, Andy could be a real idiot.

"Tell me where Champ is. That's all I want to know. I get sending someone after me, but she's an innocent woman."

"Champ Destra is many things, but an innocent woman is not one of them."

"You know what I mean."

"I am sure I don't," Gray said. "What do I have to do with that old drunk?"

Andy cocked the hammer back on his revolver.

Gray held up both hands slowly. "I know you got a hard-on for me, but you got some wrong information on this one. If something happened to Champ, I had nothing to do with it."

"You have your hand in everything."

"I can't help you," Gray said, sitting down in his big desk chair. "And to be honest, I'm tired of wasting my time. Why should I?"

"This gun," Andy said, jabbing his pistol at the air between them. "I have the gun."

"Sorry, Destra." Gray laughed. "Do you know how many barrels I've looked down? How many people have been in your shoes? Guns don't shake me. It's the man at the trigger that might make me nervous. You aren't that man."

"What's this world coming to?" Andy said. "Used to be you pointed a gun at someone, they did what you said."

"Progress."

"Is there a nutcracker?" Andy asked.

"What does that mean? Is that street slang for something?"

Andy pointed with his chin at the bowl of nuts on the table next to him. He was starving.

"Oh," Gray said. "It should be on the table. Unless Imelda moved it when she cleaned. Then it's anybody's guess. Dig around in the bowl."

Andy stuck his hand in the bowl, keeping his eyes on Gray. When he glanced down, he saw Gray drop his hands out of view.

"Hands on the table," Andy shouted, accidentally knocking the bowl onto the floor.

"Perfect," Gray said. "When I step on a loose filbert in my socks, I'll have you to blame."

"Even if you deny having anything to do with Champ, you hired a man to murder me. Admit that much," Andy said, his voice raising. "I am a credible threat here. You need to start treating me like one."

"I suppose," Gray said. "I'm just not buying it."

Andy fired a round into the ceiling. Plaster powder drifted down. Gray didn't flinch.

"I don't know what that demonstrated. Other than a complete lack of manners," Gray said. "What kind of man shoots another man's house?"

"I'll shoot your car next," Andy said, meaning it, even though he knew how stupid it sounded. "What do you know about Kate Girard, a bald African woman, a Japanese kid, and an old pickpocket?"

"Is that a riddle? You're all over the place, Destra," Gray said. "Let me call a few people. Professionals. Get you the help you need. I was wrong about you. You're not a threat. Just mixed up in the head."

"Why would those people save me?" Andy asked. "I get you trying to have me killed. That makes sense. I can't figure out why anyone would risk their own lives to help me. Sort of help me. They also assaulted me."

"You're really lost, aren't you?" Gray's eyes went up to the hole in the ceiling. "That's going to be a pain in the ass to spackle."

Andy stood and paced in front of the old man's desk. Gray reclined in his chair, hands behind his head.

"I've said it before, Destra. I respect your tenacity. I do. You've been a thorn in my side for a long while. You ain't got no quit in you. Every time I knock you down, there you are, back on your feet. Wish half the men under me had your grit."

"I was one of those men, but you framed me, forced me out," Andy said. "Now you're left with men like the Thorntons."

"Different animals. Different skill set. They serve their purpose. Keep the status very quo," Gray said. "This city functions only when the citizens—the taxpayers—are focused on their lives and not the people that run the city. The problem is, you kept trying to turn the spotlight toward the police, other entities. I can't have that."

"There are rules."

"Not really," Gray said. "Not in real life among grown-ups. This city went rotten long ago. From the bottom up. No reason the criminals should get all the profit."

"That's your rationalization?"

"I sleep well. Sometimes after some intimate time with a professional, but always on my side with a pillow between my knees, if you're interested."

"You're one evil son of a bitch," Andy said.

"Evil. That's cute." Gray laughed. "You've painted yourself in a corner, but I'm a fair man. If you leave right now, I'll give you a head start. Five minutes before I call my men. Best I can offer. Six, if I'm feeling generous. You have no plan, no teeth, and no chance."

Andy considered it. Probably the best offer he would get all day. He never had to make the decision, though. Gray made it for him.

Gray's gun appeared from nowhere, attached to the back of the chair, ready for a moment like this. The corrupt stayed as prepared as the paranoid.

When Andy saw the glint of steel, his instincts kicked in. If you would have asked him, he wouldn't have remembered pulling the trigger. He held a gun on a man. The man made a move. Simple math. Cop training. Human instinct. Andy shot Gray in the chest before Gray got off a shot. The old man shifted to the right and fell out of the chair, a red blossom forming on his white shirt, his hand still clutching the gun.

"No. Damn it. No." Andy ran to Gray. The old man gulped air. Andy pulled a small tablecloth off an end table, wadded it, and pressed it against Gray's chest wound.

"You killed me, boy," Gray said, his voice thin, surprised. "Bigger stones than I gave you credit."

"Why'd you pull?" Andy said. "You had the advantage."

"I'll kill you yet."

Aloysius Gray died, the man's last exhale unencumbered by any answers.

Andy took the pressure off the chest wound. He stared at the man's lifeless body. He didn't know what to do. Nobody ever taught him what happened after you killed your enemy. It was the first time he'd taken a man's life. He felt sick and exhilarated and scared. It didn't matter how much he'd hated the man. Gray had been a living person with friends and family and a past. No longer a future. Andy would have to consider his own fate, but in that moment it felt right to consider the dead man's.

The library door slammed open behind him. The bald African woman from Naga rushed into the room. Andy turned, pointing his pistol in her direction. She stopped just past the doorway, staring blankly at his revolver.

"I shot him," Andy said.

"Is he dead?"

Andy nodded. He slowly rose to his feet, keeping the gun on the bald woman. Behind her four more people entered the room. Four people that he recognized. Four people that he'd met in the last few days.

"What the hell, Destra?" Kate Girard said, her eyes on Gray's dead body. "Did you shoot him? Did you kill Al Gray?"

Andy nodded. "I shot him. Never killed no one. I shot him."

"This is bad. Very bad," she said. "Do you know what you've done? What this means?"

"I don't think any of us do," the bald woman said. "Leave him be. Be kind. He's in shock."

Kate Girard turned to the old pickpocket. "This is on you. Your fault."

"Let's blame each other later," the old man said. "No time now. This is a mess. That's for damn sure. We have to act quickly."

The one-armed woman from the Castles took in the scene. "Damage control. Stage the scene," she said, moving quickly to the window and looking into the darkness of the front yard. "We've got to move. Ben, grab all the papers. Suicide or burglary, what's the best way to frame it? Or do we throw Andy here to the lions?"

"Andy comes with us," the old man said. "Anonymous burglary. Chest shot won't play for suicide."

The Japanese kid walked casually to Gray's desk. Looking bored, he opened drawers and sifted through files and papers. He haphazardly covered the surface of the desk with the contents of the drawers. "I don't even know what I'm looking for."

Andy watched them in amazement. They were ignoring the murderer. Had he died in the gunfight? Was he a ghost?

"There's probably a safe," the old man said. "We should get on that, too."

"Didn't know you had it in you, Andy." The one-armed woman winked and smiled at Andy. She walked to the bald woman and patted her on the shoulder. "At least it wasn't you doing the killing this time, Agnes."

"I'm as surprised as you," the bald woman said.

"Will you people act like I have a gun?" Andy shouted. "Because I have a gun. It's not invisible. At least I don't think it is." He backed toward the library doors. They all turned to him.

"Seriously, Destra. What the hell happened?" Kate Girard said, moving to Gray's body, checking his pulse and then his pockets.

"Gray reached. I reacted," Andy said. "It was an accident."

"Oh, it was an accident. I'm sure you'll be fine, then. Just tell the judge it was an accident," the Japanese kid said. "The jury will understand. You shot him by accident after breaking into his house. Probably a fine. Community service. Picking up trash in an orange vest on the side of the highway."

"Shut up, Ben," the old man said.

"I'm going to leave now," Andy said. "I don't know what I'm going to do, but I'm not doing it here in this weird Benetton ad."

Andy waved the bald woman and the Latina away from the door. They shrugged and moved to either side.

"Did Gray say anything before he died?" Kate Girard asked.

Andy continued to back toward the door.

"Did he, Andy?" the old man seconded, becoming more interested.

"Not really."

The bald woman and the Latina stood only a few yards from Andy. They took a step closer. Subtle but definitely a threat, spreading his attention. Andy waved the gun between the two of them.

"Stop moving. All of you," Andy said, but the two women kept creeping forward.

"We should talk about Gray," Kate Girard said. "Sit down and figure this out."

"I don't think so." Andy took another step back. "I don't need to do anything you want me to. I don't know who you are, how you got here so quick, or what you want from me. I want nothing to do with whatever you have to do with."

"You're stuck with us now," the old man said. "We can help you."

"He is? We can?" the Japanese kid asked.

"Shut up, Ben," Kate Girard said. "Rocky decides this."

The bald woman and the one-armed woman continued their slow steps toward Andy.

"Put the gun down. If it helps, son," the old man said, "the city is not worse off with Gray gone. Maybe a little safer. He was a bad man. Although some other greedy bastard is going to rise to take his place."

"Hank Robinson. He's always been the muscle behind Gray's plans," Kate Girard said. "Although Mac might have a chance in the chaos to push Ashley forward."

Andy's head spun. "Quit talking. All of you. I'll shoot everyone for the silence. Can't you see I'm a killer now? I'm tired of your weird game. Quit pushing."

"Believe it or not, we're your only option," Kate Girard said. "We've been trying to protect you. Warn you."

"That's why you kept seeing us everywhere, dumbass," the Japanese kid said. "If we were out to get you, you'd be gotten. We're that kind of bad."

"It's like *The Wizard of Oz*," the bald woman said. "'You were there. And you.' That movie has flying monkeys, but they're not real flying monkeys. Just people in flying monkey costumes. Monkeys can't fly. I know that now."

"Champ," Andy said, coming back to reality. "I need to find what he did with her."

"I got good news and bad news, son," the old man said. "The good news is that Champ is fine. I was worried about her safety, so I flashed a fake badge and took her out of that place. She's in another facility."

"What are you talking about?" Andy asked, still backing out of the room. "You don't know her. Even if you did, why would you do that?"

"You didn't ask about the bad news," the Japanese kid said. "The bad news is that you killed the deputy police commissioner."

"Shut up, Ben," the old man said. "I know Champ. I know her well, son."

"Quit calling me son," Andy said.

The room got quiet. Nobody said a word. For a brief moment, everything stopped but the thoughts of the people in the room.

"I can't take it. Tell him already," the Japanese kid said, breaking the silence. "He's calling you son because he's your damn father. Andy Destra, meet Rocco Colombo, your long-lost daddy."

"What?" Andy asked. Definitely not what he'd expected to hear.

The old man shrugged. "It's true. I'm your father."

"Well," Andy said. "That's just fucking great."

1929

LONG PAST DAYS

I couldn't tell if the red-haired girl knew the sewers, but she moved with confidence. Short legs darting through the water. No hesitation. No second-guessing. She trusted her choices. She didn't trust me. No reason to.

We heard others. Voices. Splashing water. Running. Insane screaming. Laughing. Butchery. Muted crying.

The girl found good shadows. Narrow fissures. Hidden doors. We squeezed into a tight nook. Her freckled face close to mine. Our bodies close. Her clothes wet. Her body warm.

"Don't get any ideas." Her knife against my crotch. The gun close, too.

"Never had an idea before. Ain't gonna start now."

We could've went separate. But without a single word. Without any accord. We had taken to run together. Our plan to survive the day.

"What's at the Turkish baths?" she asked.

"My people."

"They aren't mine."

"Got anywhere else to go?"

No answer. A gunshot rang out. Dull thuds against wet bricks.

"Pipes are getting crowded," she said.

"Never been this far. Don't know where we're at."

"Let's find out."

❖ ❖ ❖

Pushed up on the manhole with my head and shoulder. Heavy. An inch at a time. Scraping against the road. Darkness above. Strange darkness. A truck was parked overhead. On top of us. Lucky for the cover. I crawled up. Scoped the street from behind a tire. The girl followed.

The fires had grown. Spread like waves. The air twenty degrees hotter. No longer winter. Smoke everywhere. Not a damned soul in the hell of it. A few scattered bodies littered the road and walk. Bloody, burnt, or beaten. A dog ran past.

"The closer we are to the fires," I said, "the safer we are from people."

"It's still fire."

"We're close. A dozen blocks. A few more."

"Watch it," she said. Made her body flat.

A group of men rounded the corner. All in uniform. Not military. Not coppers. Baseball players. I recognized them from afternoons sneaking into Charbonneau Field. Honus Harrow. Jack Brighton. Maxie Monroe. The Auction City Terrapins. Every man had a bat. Some with nails driven through them. All bloodstained.

They marched past. Ducky DePaoli juggled three baseballs. Backlit by the burning buildings. A few smiled. Demons at play.

Ducky dropped a ball. Rolled toward us. I held my breath. It stopped a foot from my leg. He moved to retrieve it. I reached for my cleaver.

I felt the girl's hand on my shoulder. Turned. She nodded, pistol in hand. We would fight together. Die together.

"Leave it," Maxie Monroe said, tossing Ducky a fresh ball. He caught it, shrugged, and joined the rest of the Terrapins.

They passed. We breathed again. The girl pulled me in the opposite direction. "There's a police station near here."

The thought of the Negro boys. Their death. The last act of brutal men. "I don't want nothing to do with the coppers."

"Their horses might still be in the stable."

❖ ❖ ❖

Heard the wild animal screams from a block away. Sharp. Unnatural. Monstrous. The sound of a woman holding her dead child.

The police station turned to burning embers. Torched first, no doubt. Abandoned. Flames licking at the stable next door. Posts abandoned. The horses forgotten. Left to die a horrible death.

The girl opened the stable door. I stood ten yards behind in the middle of the street. Three crazed animals bolted toward me. No time to move. I closed my eyes. Waited to be trampled. Felt their air, strands of mane. They ran past.

Smoke filled the stable. Horses kicked at stalls. Whinnying. Crying. The roof on fire. Dripping flame onto hay.

"No way we can ride them," I said. "Spooked to hell."

She wasn't listening. I had no vote. She braved the haze. Breathed through her hand. Opened stall after stall. Horses fled. Hit the street to find more fire. Running where it wasn't. Nowhere to go. Running in circles.

"We have to go," I screamed. The roof beginning its slow collapse.

She opened the last stall. No horse exited. She stared into the space. Pulled the pistol. Fired. Twice. Walked past me to the street. Eyes red, watering. Smoke and pain.

"Broke its leg. Panicked. Fell on its foal," she said. "Mother and child."

"You saved most of them."

"I doubt it."

One horse remained in the street. Confused. Trapped or resigned to death. Grazed on asphalt. Another orphan trying to survive.

The girl approached. Spoke softly. Cooed. The horse bucked, front legs kicking. Reflex. She stood her ground. Unflinching. The beast's heart wasn't in it. She stroked its side.

Behind us, the roof of the stable gave. Sparks and flames billowed from the door. The horse jumped. Retreated. The girl started over.

Soaking horse blankets in a trough, I watched. Admired her patience. With chaos all around, she gave the animal her calm. Won its trust.

❖ ❖ ❖

The crow's flight to the Turkish baths was a street on fire. A frightened boy and a frightened girl on a frightened horse. Our destination four blocks away. Buildings burning on both sides. Windows exploded. Flames danced. Tires of cars melted to asphalt. Waves of heat.

My first time on a horse. A city kid. As scared of the ride as the fire. A regular Tom Mix. I grabbed the girl's waist. She gave the horse a smack on the ass. We flew into the inferno.

Wrapped in the wet blankets. Scarves at our noses and mouths. We rode through the corridor of fire. Full gallop. Heat singed the hair off the backs of my exposed hands. Skin bubbled. Only four blocks. Might as well have been four miles. One minute of torture. I never felt pain like that pain.

Foam flew from the crazed horse's mouth. Running true, straight. For us. For her.

Past the fires. A street at peace. Slowing. Turning the corner.

Greeted by an army. Twenty men stood ready. Rifle barrels behind beer barrels. Angry eyes behind stacked debris. Overturned carts. Burnt-out shells of cars. The horse stopped too quick. Both thrown. Over the top. I sprawled on the stones. Lips, nose, face torn. The girl on top of me. The horse fled. Its duty done. Deserved a reward. Roses or a quick death.

The girl was quick to rise. Reached for the gun. In a daze, but I knew it wasn't the play. I put a hand on hers. Shook my head. She got the message.

The girl helped me up. One hand in hers, I held up the other to the militia. "It's Rocky. Rocky Colombo."

A long silence. A muffled discussion. Then a laugh.

"Nobody shoot. I know that kid." Sal walked from behind the barricade.

The girl and I held hands. Facing an army.

"The stones on this one," Sal said. "The kid brought a goddamn date to Armageddon."

1986

CHAPTER 13

Andy had no idea how long he had slept, but he hadn't felt that well rested in months. For one thing, the bed in the holding cell was a thousand times more comfortable than his sleeping bag. Also, they shot him up with that same magic formula that made everything slippery, then brightly colored, then gone. He would have to get the recipe. Being sedated twice in one day couldn't be good for his body, but counting sheep had nothing on quality narcotics.

◆ ◆ ◆

Back at Gray's mansion, the standoff hadn't lasted long. Andy's arm grew tired from holding the gun, a symbol of impotence he didn't want to dwell on.

The old pickpocket's claim to be his father confused a confusing situation. With everything else going on—the whole murdering-the-deputy-police-commissioner thing—he chose to let that little piece of bullshit hang in the air.

With his gun dipping from strain, he stopped listening to whatever nonsense the old man and Kate Girard were saying. He couldn't care. He had more pressing matters, like choosing between Mexico and Canada for his lam years. Was Spanish or French easier to learn?

Andy stood at the murder scene in the house that he had broken into and held the murder weapon covered with fingerprints that came from his fingers. A first-year law student could get the death penalty. On top of the overwhelming physical evidence, he had motive and a history of strange behavior. And let's not forget, the cops hated him. He was guilty, friendless, and completely screwed.

The thought of the electric chair entered his brain. An execution was wishful thinking, though. He wouldn't live to see a trial. You don't kill a cop in Auction City and not get suicided in your jail cell. If he made it into custody, he'd be hanging from a knotted sheet by day's end. But not before he was beaten mercilessly.

Andy reacted to the situation with dignity and poise. He swore all the swears he knew, fired three shots in the air, and made a run for it. He didn't make it far. Into the next room and down a hall. Maybe thirty yards. The bald woman chucked something heavy at his legs. It turned out to be a big Bible that she'd picked up. Tripping on the word of God was an ignoble way to be stopped. And a painful one. Literally falling from grace.

The bald woman and the one-armed woman took his gun and dragged him back into the library by his feet. He struggled ineffectively, a fish by its tail. With little effort, they bound his hands and blindfolded him. It was easy to make out the voices, each accent and tone distinct.

"What happens now? Do we keep him tied up forever?" Kate Girard asked. "Mac's going to be livid. What do we do with him?"

"Dump him in the river?" the Japanese kid said.

"Handing him over to the cops would be the smartest thing," Kate Girard said. "Salvage our deal."

"I won't let that happen," the old man said. "Take him to the factory. I'll talk to Mac. We'll figure it out."

With one firm hand on each elbow, they guided Andy through the house and outside. He was loaded into a van or truck or some other big, open vehicle. It was cold and smelled like artificial strawberry.

It occurred to Andy that he hadn't been gagged. He considered screaming, but his throat was scratchy and the manses in Gallows Terrace were too far apart to make it productive. The rich liked their privacy. He worked instead on loosening his restraints.

"That ain't a granny knot, boss," the Japanese kid said. "You try too hard, you'll mess up your wrists."

Andy stopped fiddling with the knot. "Where are you taking me?"

"Why do people always ask that? Like you expect me to answer, 'We're driving you to the abandoned candy factory at 1487 Riverfront Drive. And if you require any other details about your abduction, please don't hesitate to ask.'"

"More like 6243 Holt."

"That was good work." Kate Girard's voice from somewhere behind him. "Most people don't see an omission as a clue, follow a trail that's not there."

"But I don't know what I found. I have no idea who you people are."

"You don't know anything about Floodgate? Never asked anyone about it?" Kate Girard asked.

"Never heard that name before," Andy said. "What's a Floodgate?"

"You're an awful liar," she said. "You asked me about it."

"A word I heard. That's it."

"You don't know how lucky you are to have Rocco as a father," Kate Girard said.

"Are you crazy people? Is that it? Are you escaped lunatics?"

"Aren't we all a little bit crazy?" The Japanese kid again.

"Was that a joke? You're making goddamn jokes?" Andy said, furious. "The list of shit that I've gone through tonight. I got punched, drugged, had my shoes stolen—my shoes!—Champ disappeared—now apparently you have her, which doesn't calm me—a sniper held me at gunpoint, I killed a guy, all my stuff was robbed, I hid in a pigeon coop for hours."

"You're going to be pissed off about this," the Japanese kid said, "but if you're talking about the sniper at your apartment, that was a RadioShack laser pointer. No gun."

The van started, and they were on the move. Andy couldn't gauge any sense of direction or speed. He was on a flat surface, sliding around a little, often caught by a hand on the arm or just allowed to smack into the side.

"We're not the bad guys," Kate Girard said.

"I have to assume you said that with a straight face. I don't know because I'm blindfolded and bound in a van."

"I didn't say we were the good guys either," she said. "Gray was a homicidal sociopath. Leader of the most bloodthirsty gang in the city. The ACPD are vicious and dangerous. Vicious and dangerous people need to be neutralized."

"Was that supposed to sound ominous?" Andy asked. "Because it did."

"Sorry."

"Again, and I can't stress this enough, I'm tied up in the back of a van. Pretty much anything you say is scary. If you said, 'Do you like cotton candy?' I might shit myself."

"Do you like cotton candy?" the Japanese kid asked.

"The police are even worse than you imagine," Kate Girard said, "but even a corrupt organization can get more corrupted. Hell, look at Congress."

The van took a few more sharp turns. Andy slid against the side.

"You really have to stop believing what you think you know and start seeing what you don't know but think you might," she said.

And on that bullshit line of reasoning, their conversation was over.

◆ ◆ ◆

Andy didn't think he'd been out more than a few hours, but that was only a best guess considering how foggy the world remained. For all he knew, it could be the distant future. If it was 1999 or some other strange, futuristic time, he would have thought that the toilets would look different. More streamlined. Sleeker. Made of advanced alloys. Radio controlled. Something.

Toilets were on his mind because that's the first thing he saw. Prone on a cot, he had opened his eyes to a spotless metal commode. The only other piece of furniture in the room. The dent on the seat rim was disconcerting. There was a story behind that dent, one that Andy hoped he never heard.

He turned his head to find the door. A dull throb pounded behind his eyes. The door wasn't futuristic either—a regular door with a small, wire-meshed window. The face peering in disappeared when Andy turned. He sat up and gave himself a visual tour of the eight-foot-square room.

The only way in or out was the door. The vents were too small for any duct shenanigans. He could maybe fit one leg up to the thigh but didn't really see where that got him. He scraped at the wall with his fingernail, but it was solid something. He was trapped. No material to construct a weapon. A metal toilet made for an awkward bludgeon even if he figured out how to detach it. A thin blanket on the bed. A roll of toilet paper on the ground. No pillow, toothbrush, mirror, or sink. They could have at least left him a magazine. Even his barber, Walker Deloach, who was kind of a jerk, had the courtesy to leave a stack of *Easyrider*s to thumb through while waiting for his crew cut and shave.

He allowed himself a brief moment to be frightened. He felt his heart race, his legs tingle, and an intense fatalism rise. He acknowledged it and then pushed it down. The fear was real, but he could control it. He didn't want to have a heart attack and die before they had a chance to kill him.

When the door opened, it was the one-armed woman. She wore a fresh tank top, Dickies, and combat boots. Her tattoos erupted from under her shirt, hints to more beneath. Butterflies, birds, vines. A bandana rested low on her forehead, just above her penciled-on eyebrows. She wore no prosthetic on the stump.

"Your acting sucks," she said. "Your eyes are open and you're looking right at me."

Andy felt awful attacking a woman. And an amputee on top of it. A new low. But illegal abduction and imprisonment brought out the gender equality in a person's violent limits. He sat up quickly, tried to toss the blanket over her head and lunge forward.

The blanket fell short, drifted to the ground between them. He made it to his feet but never got to the lunge part. The woman gave Andy a straight jab to the nose. It sunk his battleship. He tasted blood and breathed pain as he lost his footing and landed on his butt.

"Easy," she said, incredibly calm. A woman who didn't get mad when attacked was a woman to fear. "I don't want to hurt you."

Andy gave a snort of a laugh, some blood bubbling in his right nostril. "Of course you don't."

"If you can't take a punch, don't start fights," she said. "No more stupid."

Andy nodded, grabbed some toilet paper from the roll, and shoved wads in each nostril.

"You know why I hit you?" she asked.

Andy nodded.

"And it's not going to happen again?"

Andy shook his head.

"Then we're good. I'm Pilar," she said. "Follow me."

Pilar turned her back to him and walked out the room, leaving the door open. He followed, entering a long hallway that led past a series of doors. Looking into the small windows, Andy saw more small rooms. In the only other occupied room, a bloodied man sat on a cot with the back of his head against the wall and his eyes closed. Despite the discoloration of his face from bruising, he recognized the man right away.

"That's the guy that tried to kill me," Andy said, stopping at the door.

"Yeah."

"What is this place?"

Pilar didn't answer, holding open a door at the end of the hall. He gave the man in the cell one last look. He opened his eyes and turned just as Andy ducked out of view.

He walked past Pilar into a conference room, a long table in the center. A half-dozen chairs. She pointed to one end of the table. Andy sat. A sixteen-millimeter projector sat behind him.

"Should I list my questions alphabetically or by order of importance?" Andy said. "I don't know where to start. Maybe with, where am I? Who are you people? Is there coffee? Why am I here? What was that *Empire Strikes Back* 'I am your father' bullshit? Where is Champ? We can start with those, but I have more."

"You're going to watch a movie." She walked to the opposite end of the room. "I'll get you some water. Coffee if it's already made, but I ain't brewing no fresh pot."

"That answers one of my questions. The least important one."

"That's what the movie is for."

"Is this for real? You're going to show me a movie?"

The woman pulled down a screen. "Only a few people have seen this. Consider yourself special. Shut up and watch."

She walked behind him, turned on the projector, and cut the lights. The SMPTE leader counted down. Five. Four. Three. Two. Pop.

◆ ◆ ◆

FLOODGATE: THE LAST LINE OF DEFENSE

EXT. AUCTION CITY SKYLINE - NIGHT

The lights of the city shine over the Thief
River. The King Olaf Bridge glows. The title
(no production credits) appears over the
image. Followed by the Floodgate symbol and
the following message:

PENALTIES FOR UNAUTHORIZED VIEWING WILL
BE SEVERE. VERY SEVERE. IF YOU ARE UNSURE
WHETHER YOU ARE AUTHORIZED OR NOT, YOU ARE
NOT. STOP WATCHING IMMEDIATELY. YOU HAVE
TWENTY SECONDS.

BLACK SCREEN

Twenty seconds of black leader. Accompanied
by pleasant music, possibly Monteverdi.

EXT. UNDER A BRIDGE - NIGHT

A HOBO (46) roasts a hot dog over an open
campfire, his bindle on the ground next to
him. He takes a pull from a jug marked XXX.
He looks up, double-taking as if seeing the
camera for the first time.

                    HOBO
    Oh, hey there, young pup. If you're
    watching this, then you're who and
    where you're supposed to be. If not,
    may God have mercy on your soul. Well,
    get yourself warm by the fire. This
    railrider has a tale to tell. And
    from the look on your face, you're

a-searchin' for answers. It's a
winding story, so get cozy and I'll
cover the whats, hows, wheres, and
whys. Oh, and the whens. It all starts
in nineteen and twenty-nine, a year
filled with turmoil and strife.

EXT. CITY STREET 1929 - DAY (SEPIA)

Cars and carriages compete for space on the
busy street. The sidewalks are filled with
people. Businesses bustle with activity. A
streetcar crawls past. A beat cop twirls his
baton.

> HOBO (V.O.)
> For most citizens of Auction City,
> life was simple. Work and family.
> Industry and trade thrived, and
> whether you made your buck honestly or
> otherwise, there was a place at the
> table. The Great Gateway, America's
> Gibraltar, Auction City welcomed all.
> Enough for everybody. Until the world
> changed. And not for the better.

A series of SPINNING NEWSPAPERS reveal the
headlines: WALL ST. PANIC AS STOCKS CRASH;
BILLIONS LOST; UNEMPLOYMENT TRIPLES; STREET
VIOLENCE ON THE RISE.

> HOBO (V.O.)
> It didn't take long for the muckety-
> mucks and waistcoats to screw it
> up for everyone. Greed hit like a
> grenade. Started big and got bigger.
> Those who once shared a dollar now
> fought over a dime.

The NEWSPAPER headlines read: GANG WAR
ERUPTS; AUCTION CITY BURNS; THOUSANDS DEAD;
POLICE HAVE LOST CONTROL; US ARMY REFUSES TO
ENTER CITY.

                    HOBO (V.O.)
    Everyone in Auction City knows about
    the riots and the fires. Thousands
    died. The city burned. The Great Gang
    War. What came to be known as the
    Flood. When it was over, the city had
    changed. The aftermath still felt
    today.

The NEWSPAPER catches on fire, flames filling
the screen.

CHAPTER 14

Criminality is the best and often only way for the powerless to experience power. Sometimes the only way to be heard is to shout.

—From Dr. James Ebb's introduction to his controversial bestseller Criminal Utopia: A World without the Burden of Law (1976)

"Are you kidding me?" Andy said, turning to the one-armed woman. "Is this a joke?"

Using some tape, she spliced the reel together where it had snapped.

"What do you expect? *Ghostbusters?*" Pilar said. "You're lucky it's in color. It's ancient, like twenty years old."

"Why the hell am I watching this?"

"You'll see. The second part is in your wheelhouse," Pilar said. "You know all the history, but it's about to get to the real stuff. The fun stuff."

"Your evil cabal—or whatever you are—has an industrial training film?" Andy asked.

"Cut me some slack. I ain't wanting to remember all that history and whatnot. Movie does the job."

"If it's as effective as the one they showed in fifth grade about the reproductive system, I'm still going to have to learn from my mistakes."

She pointed at the screen. "This next part is important."

"Why is the actor playing a hobo?"

"Shut up and watch the movie."

◆ ◆ ◆

EXT. UNDER A BRIDGE - NIGHT

The HOBO takes another pull from his jug. He belches.

Images flash on the screen, illustrating his monologue. Photos from the past. Illustrations. Old film footage, if available.

>   HOBO
> Back in those days, four organizations
> ran the criminal rackets in Auction
> City. The Trust, the Wretches, the
> Tongs, and the police. You heard me, the
> cops themselves. Turf wars over illegal
> alcohol rose. Smuggling and gambling,
> too. Never more than a few bodies at
> first. Disagreements are a part of
> business. Until the Flood. That's when
> the pot boiled over. Speaking of which,
> my beans are burning.

The HOBO quickly grabs a smoking pot off the fire.

QUICK SERIES OF SHOTS, BOTH STILL & ARCHIVAL FILM FOOTAGE

The city burns. Bodies in the street. Men fighting. A crying child. People fleeing.

Buildings looted. Chaos. The aftermath. Whole
city blocks in ashes.

> HOBO (V.O.)
> Thousands died that day. Eighty percent
> of the city burned to the ground. The
> war lasted a day, but the violence
> continued for weeks. The US Army could
> only contain it, never breeching the
> city limits. Like all wars, only the
> men who started the conflict could end
> it.

On the word END, the film FREEZES, holding on
a fuzzy photograph taken from a distance of
a group of men meeting in the middle of an
intersection.

> HOBO (V.O.)
> The leaders of the Trust, Wretches,
> Tongs, and the chief of police were
> summoned by the only organization
> with enough power to command it.
> The Church. But it was money, not
> God, that made them obey. Over hours
> of tense negotiations, a truce was
> finally reached.

MAP OF AUCTION CITY

Borders drawn by neighborhood and district
with symbols for each organization. A plate
of spaghetti and meatballs labeled TRUST, a
pair of brass knuckles labeled WRETCHES, a
Chinese take-out container labeled TONGS,
a badge labeled ACPD, and a cross labeled
CHURCH. The FLOODGATE symbol slowly fading
over the middle of everything.

HOBO (V.O.)
The city was divided by territory among the three exclusively criminal organizations. The ACPD held power through the legitimacy of law. The Church as the bank, controlling all monetary exchanges: banking, laundering, and transactions. Just enough power to keep the peace. And as peace was profitable, the leaders complied. Over time, the Church's tax-exempt status proved to be even more suitable for moving illegally obtained moneys.

EXT. UNDER A BRIDGE - NIGHT

The HOBO laughs until he coughs, spits on the ground, and takes another drink.

HOBO
God really does work in mysterious ways. Even with the leaders in agreement, they still needed some way to enforce the truce. To make sure that everyone played fair. And to communicate to the people on the street that the war was over.

A PHOTO OF A GROUP OF MEN

The only known photo of the first Floodgate: members of the Trust, Wretches, Tongs, ACPD, and Church stand side by side. Armed and frightening. (Contact the Auction City Historical Society for image.)

                    HOBO (V.O.)
While they got their name later, the
solution was Floodgate. Representatives
from each organization. A united army.
Each soldier temporarily severed their
ties with their respective groups and
created an autonomous organization to
ensure the city's violence ceased.
They took orders from the Church.

ANIMATED SEQUENCE

On the screen, the plate of spaghetti and
meatballs, pair of brass knuckles, Chinese
take-out container, badge, and cross appear
over the map.

                    HOBO (V.O.)
Floodgate proved effective. In the
rebuilding and peacekeeping after the
Flood they became folk legends. The
tales told not nearly as tall as the
truth. And that's where the story
ends. As far as the world knows, once
there was peace, Floodgate disbanded.

The HOBO motions to lean in, as the camera
tracks closer.

                    HOBO (V.O.)
But the last chapter hasn't been
written. When Auction's rebuilding
was complete, the truce remained.
Cooperation proved more profitable.
Floodgate went underground. Their
usefulness applied in new capacities.
To this day, Floodgate acts as the
investigative unit of the city's

combined criminal organizations.
Working in the shadows fit the
changing world.

The animation coincides with the changes that
the HOBO recites.

HOBO (V.O.)
The Trust grew out of its street
roots and expanded to form an almost-
legitimate multinational conglomerate.
The Tongs were absorbed by the Triads.

The badge flashes on the screen.

HOBO (V.O.)
In 1966, the ACPD left the group. They
had simply become too corrupt for the
criminals. A cold war between the ACPD
and the organizations began. Although
the two groups are often forced to
work together when similar interests
are at stake.

The badge fades on the screen.

HOBO (V.O.)
There is little doubt that the next
Flood will come from the divide between
the police and the organizations.
Unless the Church and Floodgate can
maintain the balance.

Replacing the badge, a fifth icon, a lunch
box labeled CITIZEN appears.

HOBO (V.O.)
Floodgate worked best with five
members. A replacement for the police
was chosen. To provide a different

```
     perspective and to represent the
     people of the city, a member of the
     general public was recruited to join.
     To act as ballast.

The image turns into two hands shaking and a
group photograph. In the 1967 photograph (see
Gamma File #67-gp888), five people stand side
by side: Kate Girard, Rocco Colombo, Father
Sean O'Shea, Jerome Jefferson, and Wang Lei.

                    HOBO (V.O.)
     Floodgate. Criminal justice by criminals
     and for criminals. Protecting secrets.
     Protecting business. Protecting Auction
     City. Truly, the last line of defense.

FADE TO BLACK
```

◆ ◆ ◆

The screen flashed to a yellowish white, a hair dancing in the corner of the frame. The film reel turned in the projector, loose end flapping in a rhythmic slap. The lights flicked back on. Pilar turned off the projector, leaving only the buzz of the fluorescents.

Andy stared at the screen, processing what he had seen. He turned to Pilar, who nodded her head. Andy turned back to the blank screen. He drummed his fingers on the table, caught himself doing it, and stopped.

Andy stood up and pointed at the screen, shaking his finger.

"I fucking knew it," he said, turning to Pilar. "I knew something was going on. A big thing under the surface. I knew it. I was so close to finding all this out. I wasn't crazy. Now that I see it, I can see it. I knew it."

"Yeah," she said. "You weren't even close."

"But I would've. I would've found out," Andy said. "I got even more questions. Tons of questions. New questions. Oh, man, I knew it."

"I got no idea what's next for you," she said. "Rocco told me to show you the movie. I showed you the movie."

"Rocco? That's the guy that said he was my father."

"He saved your ass," she said. "He's the only reason you're here and not next to Gray in the morgue. We wouldn't've been helping you out."

"Helping me out?" Andy stage-laughed.

"You got no idea the shit you stirred," she said. "There are a lot of people—most of them—that want you dead."

"It's all making sense," Andy said. "What the hobo said. That Floodgate never went away. That the mobs are aligned under some super-secret pact. Under the radar."

"I thought you'd take more convincing," Pilar said. "Most people would find it outrageous."

"One last time. To get it straight. To make sure I'm not completely bananas," Andy said. "You and Hobo Joe are telling me that three mobs, the cops, and the effing Church run the city and have since 1929. On top of that there's a group called Floodgate—you guys, my kidnappers—that act as a—what?—police for this group."

"CliffsNotes version, yeah. We don't throw around the name Floodgate anymore. Even if some old-timers still do. The cop brass know we exist, can't shut us down, but constantly threaten," Pilar said. "We're not above the law—we're below it."

Andy counted on his fingers. "The cops police criminals. You're criminals that police criminals. But also police the police."

Pilar nodded.

"What do you want with me?" Andy asked. "Why was I allowed to watch that?"

"Rocco. It's his deal."

Andy stared hard into the woman's eyes. "What happens if I don't cooperate?"

"You get one chance to do what you're told. If you don't," Pilar said, "best case, you go down for Gray's murder. You left loads of evidence at the scene."

"If that's the best case, what's the worst case?"

"We're criminals, dumbass. If you don't play along, somebody—maybe me—will torture you, chop you into pieces, burn your dead bits, and then bury the ashes all over the city. Standard TCBB—torture, chop, burn, bury."

Andy stared at the one-armed woman, trying to look strong.

"I'm just kidding." She laughed, a small snort.

It took a moment. Andy exhaled, feeling sick. "You got me."

"If you were a threat, you'd get shot in the head and dumped in the river. We're not show-offy."

Andy didn't find it as funny as she did.

Pilar stood up, walked to the screen, and pulled the cord. The screen shot up into its canister with a loud bang. "I know this all sounds scary and shit. Like a deal with the devil. It's not like that. The cops and politicians, they're as worse as us. You worked for them. You know. If you want to do good in Auction, you got to join the outlaws."

"Who will kill me if I don't."

"I didn't say it was a perfect arrangement."

CHAPTER 15

During a city council meeting, a large rat ran through the
hall. It scurried from one corner to another searching for a
means of egress. Each council member casually ignored
the large rodent. No one said a word, their silence implying
that no one wanted to potentially insult the relative of one
of their colleagues.

—*Attributed to* Auction City Intelligencer *newspaperman*
Sam Faulk (1964)

Pilar left the room. Andy counted to ten and tried the door. Locked,
of course.

He paced, looking for anything that might help him. He grabbed
some chalk from the chalkboard and put it in his pocket. Andy didn't
have any plans for it, but having chalk was better than not having chalk.
He found it comforting to have more than lint in his pockets. Mess with
Andy Destra and you might get chalked.

He had no options. The one-armed woman was right about
that. He'd murdered a man. Maybe one option. Running for his life.
Escaping. He was desperate, but that didn't mean he was going to

blindly trust a bunch of criminals, a fake hobo, or a stranger claiming to be his father.

He flipped over a chair and kicked at one of the metal legs, thinking he could forge some kind of crude weapon from it. He managed to bend it, but for all the working back and forth, he couldn't detach it. Sweaty and angry, he ceded and torqued it as close to its original shape as he could.

Andy picked up the film can next to the projector. The edges of the metal were rusted. More time and he could file it down to make a Frisbee-type throwing star. Andy noted his level of desperation.

A faded sticker on the outside had the Floodgate symbol and a handwritten message that read:

Floodgate: The Last Line of Defense ©1969—
If Lost Return to 6243 Holt Ave., Auction City—
$5,000 Reward, if left unwatched. Unwatched.
We Will Know.

Andy took the film from the projector, put it in the film can, and shoved the saucer-size disc down the front of his pants. If he got out, he wanted hard evidence.

He paced the room. Andy was concerned for his own life, but his worry was for Champ. Not knowing where she was or if she understood what was going on did not sit well. The thought of her being scared made him want to fight. He needed to get out of there.

Andy wasn't ready to address the issue of this man, Rocco, claiming to be his father. What kind of name was Rocco for a real person? The kind of person who might name his son Andrea.

He would wait for hard evidence, but it bothered him how empty it felt. Even the possibility that it was true and he had met his father generated nothing. He had always imagined a heartfelt reunion or a fistfight to work out their differences. All he saw was the man who had abandoned a baby that turned out to be him. To be fair, the murder scene dampened the moment a bit.

He didn't usually trust cinematic hobos for historical fact, but he accepted that everything in the movie was true. He knew it. Andy could slot the scenario into his knowledge of the city and see how neatly it fit. He wished he had his files. They would confirm the concept of the syndicates' alignment and Floodgate's existence. By applying the existence of collusion to Auction City's criminal history, he could authenticate the hobo's veracity. Now there's a phrase you didn't hear every day.

Everything about Auction City's crime statistics suggested a puppet master running the show. Drops in street violence that made no sense. The strange migration of crime. Plenty of small drug arrests, but only big busts for operators based outside the city. It made the strange plausible. An outsider might call it coincidence, but most Auctioneers accustomed to the idiosyncrasies of the city would give a knowing nod.

The appearance of competition by rival organizations that were actually allies created an effective model for an oligarchy. It operated with the illusion of choice. Hell, it was how the US government worked. Everybody knew that criminals existed, but we expected them to be at war with each other, not just with society. Knowing that they weren't made it unseemly. How dare the bad guys cheat.

Andy sat down, forgetting that he had the film can in his pants. It jammed him in the beans, smarting his nethers. He took the film can out and slid it along the long table. Andy exhaled and let his head fall back. He stared at the cottage cheese ceiling.

What else could he do? He was locked in a room with no shoes and only chalk to defend himself.

◆ ◆ ◆

A half hour later, Cardinal Macklin strolled into the conference room. The archbishop of the city wore a simple collar and a smile. He placed a cup of coffee in front of Andy and opened a briefcase.

"Your holiness," Andy said.

"Call me Mac."

"I take cream and sugar."

"Well, today you become a man," the Cardinal said, sitting in the closest chair. It collapsed underneath him. Macklin sprawled on the ground. He winced, sat up, and angrily grabbed the chair. The broken leg rolled away from him. "Did you try to break off this leg and forge a weapon out of it?"

"Maybe," Andy said.

Macklin stood up and gave Andy a long stare. He threw the chair to the side, grabbed another, examined the bottom of it, and sat down.

Andy smelled the coffee. "You slip me another mickey? Knocking me unconscious seems to be your guys' MO."

"The coffee is unsullied," Macklin said. "In regard to the other incidents, I prefer not to micromanage the decisions of the team."

"Is there a box for comments? I have a few."

"You murdered Al Gray," Macklin said. "The deputy police commissioner. The team has spent hours on damage control. Rocky's insistence on your usefulness has created an option for you. The only option you have."

"Thanks, but I know my options. I go to jail. Or I go on the run," Andy said. "No matter who you people are, you don't have power over those choices."

"Of course we do." Macklin laughed. "Pilar showed you the film."

"Criminals control the city. The Church keeps them marginally honest. Floodgate is their army or police or whatever," Andy said. "Gray's still dead. Doesn't change anything."

"Weren't you a cop? You only killed the man if there is evidence that shows that you did. Without evidence, you didn't kill anyone.

That's the way truth works," Macklin said. "After you left, the team created a credible crime scene. Burglary gone bad. A few false leads. A credible suspect. Some interesting documents complicating Gray's reputation were leaked to cooperative press. That should create a diversion. We've made the narrative work to our advantage. And to yours. Nothing points the police toward you.

"The team started going through your files. Interesting stuff, they tell me. Your knowledge of the city and its players could be valuable. Some of your theories are barmy, as wrong as they are right, but there's good work in there, too."

"Thanks, I guess." Andy said. "Why do you need me?"

"We don't. Lord God, nobody here wants you around but Rocky, but he's earned the favor."

Andy tried to remember what his life was like a week before: getting up, visiting Champ, investigating leads that he knew would lead nowhere, putting up flyers that were well-intentioned litter. It seemed as if all that had happened to a different person in a different country on a different planet in a different dimension.

"And not to put too fine a point on it," Macklin said. "You don't have a choice."

"What if I don't want to be a part of any of this whatever-the-hell-it-is?"

"Your decision. Say the word. We'll turn over the evidence we have—the murder weapon, surveillance tape, et cetera—and you'll be indicted for the murder of a police officer."

"You put it that way, I guess I'm in."

"Give it time. You'll get to the point when you no longer feel like a prisoner, but a coworker. An ally, not a cog in the wheel."

"Or a fly in a web," Andy said.

"Exactly."

Andy took a drink from his coffee. Bitter and cold. Fitting. "Your team, the group, the five from last night. That's everybody? That's Floodgate, right?"

"They don't like that name. Say that a secret organization doesn't need a name, because it's a secret. That it sounds too much like a comic book. I still think it has a great ring to it."

"One person representing each group, that's what the hobo said."

Macklin nodded. He turned the giant ring on his pinky.

"Let me guess. Rocco, my"—Andy made air quotes—"'father,' he's with the mobsters, the Trust?"

"The quotes and tone aren't necessary. The man is most certainly your father," Macklin said. "He represents the Trust, but they haven't been mobsters for a long time. Not in the traditional sense. Suits in buildings now."

"And my one-armed best friend, Pilar—the gangs, obviously. But why is there a Japanese kid if the Chinese are involved? He's 893, all the way."

"Yes, Pilar is with Consolidated. Ben is 893. Good eye. The movie you watched is from the late sixties, outdated. Three years ago, the Japanese bought out the Triads. The yakuza now hold the seat."

"That leaves the bald woman and Kate Girard."

"Agnes is with us, the Church. She is special."

"She assaulted me with a Bible."

Macklin laughed. "Her sense of humor is odd. She's only recently started flexing that muscle. I hope you like knock-knock jokes."

"And Kate's the citizen," Andy said.

"When the police broke off twenty years ago, she came aboard."

"It's crazy-sounding. All of it. The whole thing. You know that, right?"

"Of course. Why it's a good secret. Who'd believe it?"

Andy took a big swig of coffee, winced at the still-awful taste, and spit half of it back in the cup.

Macklin stood. "Let me give you an example of how things work. Recently there was a theft of some stolen goods. Details aren't important. The victims can't go to the police to complain that the stuff they stole got stolen. However, they have a right to the loot. While there might not be honor among thieves, there are rules. At least here in Auction. That's where the team comes in. You can't stop crime from happening, but you can sure as hell organize it.

"The Flood woke up this city. Changed it. Most people have a vague idea of the Flood as a part of the past. Don't ever believe for a second that kind of violence can't happen again. Outside threats, government interference, necessary removals. You wouldn't believe the number of times when all-out war came close to happening.

"Do you know who stopped it? We did. Not the police, not the politicians, not the US Army, us. We keep this city safe. By keeping the dishonest honest."

Macklin popped open the briefcase and pulled out two thick files. "You think your knowledge of the city is extensive—wait until you see what we know. Dirt going back decades. Scandals that never surfaced. These are the notes from a few cases. You'll recognize them. Only fair, now that you're on the other side of the curtain."

◆ ◆ ◆

Macklin left Andy in the room with the case files, a fresh cup of coffee, and a stale egg salad sandwich that had the taste and consistency of a stuffed animal left in the rain. He'd eaten worse.

Having case files in front of him again, eyes on the day-to-day of an investigation, it made him antsy to work a case. Interview witnesses. Work alongside other investigators. Stay up late, stare at a big board, and piece together the menu of a giant meal from the scraps left on the table. It could have been the sense memory of the bad coffee and awful sandwich, but he realized how much he missed being a cop. How much had been taken away from him when he'd been forced out of the ACPD.

He shook his head, dismissing the thought. "Stockholm Syndrome," he said to himself.

The two thick files were labeled: "Jesus 'Chucho' Montoya ACPD Investigation" and "The DC Gray Problem—Ongoing." The files revealed the shadow world that he had speculated existed. They answered dozens of questions that he had asked during his investigations on the force and off it. They told the real story. One where conspiracy theories became conspiracy facts.

FILE #031285-002-KG

JESUS "CHUCHO" MONTOYA ACPD INVESTIGATION

BACKGROUND

MARCH 12, 1985—During the investigation of the burglary of the Gallows Terrace home of Horace Mycroft (see attached ACPD report), several pieces of jewelry were discovered at Lost & Found Exchange, a pawnshop owned by Montoya. Not directly affiliated with any organization, Montoya works closely with the Trust, Consolidated, and the ACPD. Fencing stolen goods or impounded evidence. A go-between with organizations in New York, Chicago, and Atlantic City. He banks with the Church.

ACPD investigator Det. Andrea Destra discovered discrepancies and opened a larger case. He sat on Montoya and followed the money trail. With a warrant for bank records and other financials, he is piecing together hidden financial systems that could threaten the Church and other members of our concern, as well as the ACPD.

As the Church's financial system affects the ACPD, as well, DC Gray was contacted and briefed. In response, Gray ordered a transfer for Destra to another division within the department. He put his own man on the case, limiting the damage. As of this date, no further action is required.

APRIL 30, 1985—According to sources, Andrea Destra continued his investigation of Montoya and his financial history. While obtained through inadmissible means, the information could still jeopardize many operations. The Church is at the greatest risk, any suggestion of their involvement catastrophic. The flow of money could be crippled. (Handwritten note in margin: You don't bomb Switzerland.)

Gray went big on his solution. He arrested Destra on bribery charges, along with a handful of officers that posed a threat to Gray (see attached list of officers and background). A bold move. Gray earns political points. It looks like he's cleaning house, transparent, cracking down on bad cops. Three birds, one stone.

NOTE: The Church needs to shore up their banking protocols and security. It shouldn't have gotten this far. How a low-level affiliate could jeopardize anything is a problem. If Destra's knowledge is the only threat, is his removal the simplest solution? Upon his incarceration, an accident in custody seems like it would solve the problem. He'd be both discredited and neutralized.

According to RC, Andrea Destra has value. He should for no reason be terminated. Suggest that Gray drop the charges. Discrediting and ostracizing him should quash his threat.

Per our request, Gray released Destra. He should be monitored, his future function determined at a later date.

Chucho Montoya should be neutralized immediately.

It was like seeing his life from the other side of the mirror. Said the White Rabbit.

The thirty-plus pages of supporting materials rounded the spine of the manila folder, including police reports and internal memos.

Confidential information. Surveillance photographs. The whole package detailed the elaborate scheme used to implicate him in the corruption charges. And the similar frames of the other officers doing time. Even though he hadn't ratted them out, he had felt bad for those men. Gray had railroaded them for the simple reason that they were good police.

He guessed that the RC stood for Rocco Colombo. His would-be father had been looking out for him. Not enough to get him out of the mess, but enough to not make it worse. Andy didn't know what to do with that information, considering that the organization that Rocco worked for caused the initial problem to begin with.

The second file was even thicker, the entire professional and criminal life of Deputy Commissioner Aloysius Gray. Ostensibly a biography documenting his long history as a police officer and as the leader of its various rackets, including his involvement with the criminal organizations before the ACPD left that group.

It appeared that after Gray had ordered the death of Nat Turner Shabazz in 1966, the criminal organizations believed that Gray had overstepped. The police and the criminals parted ways, their visions of the future and distribution of power no longer aligned. The reluctant working relationship that formed was dysfunctional, only used when extreme necessity dictated. The Church's role as bank to both sides helped maintain the tentative truce. Mostly, each operated as if the other didn't exist. A cold war with a trade agreement. Gray's knowledge of the collusion gave him ambitions. The militarization of the force and their autonomy grew under Gray's guidance. Nothing happened without his red stamp.

At the time of his death, Gray had been pushing for more profit, creating alliances, and attempting to expand his reach beyond the current agreed-on boundaries. He had tried to create instability by meeting with 893 at Ikejime to convince them that the Trust was becoming too powerful. Macklin found out about the meeting and decided to attend, as well, angering Gray. Andy had inadvertently walked in on that meeting on his last trip to Little Nagasaki.

In Gray's own words gained from surveillance recordings: "I want a piece of the pie from those thugs, not just table scraps. We're the goddamn police, goddamn it. They start treating us like it or we burn them down."

Included as one of the appendices was a list of Gray's most loyal ACPD officers, with cross-referenced file numbers for each of them. Andy knew dozens of the cops on the list, including the whole page devoted to the Thorntons. The scale of Gray's and the ACPD's corruption was far greater than what he had imagined. And Andy's imagination had it as the most corrupt in the nation. The laundry list of crimes committed by the ACPD included the suggestion that Gray had his predecessor, Deputy Commissioner Jordan, killed in 1958. One of many funerals catered by Gray.

Andy had never liked Gray, had not meant to kill him, but he was warming to the idea of his death. It wasn't a good feeling, just a new one.

◆ ◆ ◆

An hour later, Andy had finished reading and rereading the files. He wanted to spend a week in their records department. So many cross-referenced files that were cited but not included. And no doubt, stacks of data about other events in the city's history that told stories different from the ones he and the rest of the world knew. Floodgate held the true history of the city. He had to read it all. That information was his Ark of the Covenant, and it was jammed into that damn warehouse. Andy reminded himself to watch *Raiders* again. It was really a good movie.

He let the possibilities bounce around his brain. The crime and malfeasance had been going on for decades without him. He figured it could wait another hour or two. Some things were more important than the unchecked corruption of a major American city.

When Rocco Colombo and Kate Girard walked into the conference room, Andy only had one thing to say, only one thing on his mind.

"I don't know what you have planned for me, but I'm not doing a goddamn thing until I see Champ," Andy said. "And I get some shoes. I also need shoes."

CHAPTER 16

I HAVE ARRIVED STOP MY FORTUNE AWAITS STOP

> —*Final telegram message of Pádraig Collins. His body was found three days later with six pennies in his pockets and six toes missing. The crime remains unsolved. The toes were never recovered (1933).*

Andy and Rocco faced each other in the conference room. They'd been staring at each other for the better part of five minutes. Andy got a good look at the man claiming to be his father. He maybe saw a resemblance, but like hell would he admit it.

"So you're my old man?"

"Yeah."

Andy waited for more but didn't get it. "Too busy fighting crime to raise a son? Or fighting for crime, I suppose."

"It was more complicated than that."

"Was it?"

"Yeah."

Rocco started to say more, but he stopped himself.

"It's a sad situation," Andy said, "that I immediately believed all the crazy Floodgate conspiracy stuff, but I still haven't signed off on the whole son thing."

"I don't know what to tell you, son," Rocco said. "I never thought we would ever meet."

Kate Girard poked her head in the door and held up a pair of tennis shoes. "Finally found a pair. Time to go."

◆ ◆ ◆

Rocco and Kate walked Andy through Floodgate HQ. The hallway of holding cells opened up into a massive factory. The Japanese kid had been telling the truth when he joked about the location during Andy's abduction. They'd taken him to the abandoned candy factory on Riverfront in the industrial area along the Thief River. Sometimes the best lies are truths that no one believes. The old Bradford Confections & Novelties sign rusted on its side against the far wall. The fat turtle mascot held a lollipop and stared creepily, one eye scratched white. Strange machinery stood dormant. Taffy-pullers? Gumdrop-droppers? Large gears and metal arms covered in dust and webs. They looked like medieval torture devices. Closed for ten years, a faint sugary smell still lingered in the air.

The factory floor had been converted into an open work area. A half-dozen desks, each with a phone. Couches and tables scattered about. A stack of unopened computer boxes. A foosball table, air hockey, and a "Nugent!" pinball game created a makeshift game area. The bald woman, Agnes, played pinball, contorting her body as though attempting to psychically control the movement of the steel ball. She repeated the words *Wango Tango* like an incantation.

"There's a certain amount of downtime," Kate said. "I was opposed to the games at first, but I came around after I got the high score. Agnes is on a crusade to beat it."

Pilar talked in Spanish on the telephone. She doodled on a pad, mostly drawings of tigers.

Cardinal Macklin approached Rocco, Kate, and Andy. "Take him to see Champ. Then I'm going to need you two. We got work to do. Gray's death created a power vacuum in the ACPD. Hank Robinson has filled it. I got a feeling he's got notions."

"Robinson is a dumber, meaner version of Gray," Andy said. "Never had an idea of his own. He'll push whatever Gray started."

"What about Randall Ashley?" Rocco asked. "If we can find a way to put him in charge, that would be optimal. He's the only brass that we might be able to work with."

"I'll reach out to him, but Robinson has rank," Macklin said. "Maybe we can harvest a mutiny."

"Make it personal for Ashley. There's bad blood between him and Robinson," Andy said. "My gut says most of the men would prefer Randall Ashley in charge."

"Moot point right now. Robinson's got the reins and he's refusing a sit-down with us. We need to be prepared for any backlash over Gray's murder."

"They didn't buy the whole burglary-gone-wrong thing?" Kate asked.

"Would you? They think it was us. Pilar's telling everyone on the street to be careful," the Cardinal said. "It could be a shitstorm heading our way."

"What's Ben doing? Where is he?"

"No idea." Macklin shook his head walking to a desk and picking up a phone. "That damn kid."

Andy spotted his banged-up filing cabinets, along with boxes that he assumed contained his stuff. The file cabinets stood alongside newer cabinets and a wall-mounted bank of shotguns and assault rifles. The arsenal looked as if it could outfit an army platoon.

"We threw away your furniture," Kate said. "All your other stuff is here."

"This," Andy said, "all this Hall of Justice stuff. It's like kids playing superheroes. You realize that, right? It's hard to take seriously."

"There's a difference between a soldier in the barracks and one on the battlefield," Rocco said. "The details aren't as important as the big picture."

"Don't get me wrong," Andy said. "I'm lost. Completely directionless. Life ruined. Mission accomplished. It just feels slapdash. We're in a candy factory. And there's pinball."

"Does that mean you're not going to want to do karaoke later?" Kate said.

Andy, Rocco, and Kate walked to the makeshift auto pool. Cars, motorcycles, vans, and other vehicles sat parked in one corner of the gigantic factory. Most of them functional and nondescript, although Andy spotted a few luxury cars, an ambulance, and an ice cream truck. They headed straight for the Chrysler Town & Country Andy had seen the other day. Rocco got in the backseat. Kate opened the front passenger door to the wood-paneled station wagon for Andy.

"Nice car," Andy said. "We going to a six-year-old's T-ball game?"

"What did you expect, the Batmobile? It seats eight. And nobody gives a station wagon a second look."

◆ ◆ ◆

Andy's final escape attempt was an abortion from the word *go*. He wasn't even sure why he did it. Something about the principle of the thing. Not being told what to do. Idiocy in the name of controlling one's destiny.

The plan was simple. At a stoplight, make a run for it. No frills. A classic.

As Kate drove through an odds-defying number of green lights, Andy sweated through his clothes. One arm casually rested on the armrest, fingers poised to grab the door lever. He turned to get a gauge of Rocco's position behind him. The man stared straight back at him, surprising Andy a little.

"I got a question for you," Andy said, trying to be casual. "Why tell me now? That you're my father?"

"I didn't tell you. Ben did," Rocco said. "Circumstances led to it."

"I can understand not showing up when I was a kid. You abandoned me, after all. Might as well stick by your cowardice. But once I was an adult, seems like the worst you could expect was a punch in the jaw. Which I owe you, by the way."

"Try it, son. I might let you. I might not. I ain't your average old man," Rocco said. "You joined the police. That complicated things."

"I left the force two years ago. As you know. You have a file on me."

"I sat next to you a few times at the counter of Hartshorn's. Watched you eat your chicken-fried steak. Never found the right time. Never knew what to say. How to start the conversation. You're right—I'm a bit of a coward."

"Until events forced your hand?"

"Something like that," Rocco said.

"What about my mother?" Andy turned to Kate, examining her profile.

She caught him watching. "Are you suggesting—? No damn way." She laughed.

"You're the right age."

She stopped laughing. "Careful."

"Champ, then? Is she my mother?"

"Champ is not your biological mother, but she is your mom."

"Then who is my mother?"

"One parent at a time," Rocco said. "Get used to having me around first."

When Kate finally stopped at a yellow light on Jacoby Boulevard, Andy almost forgot his plan to escape. He hesitated and then popped the door open. Before he could swing his legs around, a cab trying to beat the yellow slammed into the open car door, bending it back until it crunched into the front fender. The cab didn't even slow down.

Andy was too embarrassed to run. He sat and stared at what could have been his death.

"That's coming out of your first paycheck," Kate said.

"You people get paid?" Andy asked, looking back at the busted door.

"What do you think this is, an internship?" Rocco said.

Andy attempted to pull the door back, but it came off and crashed onto the boulevard.

"The damn cabbies in this town," Kate said. "They act like laws don't mean anything."

◆ ◆ ◆

Andy remained compliant for the rest of the drive. He looked out at his beloved Auction City. It looked the same but felt like a piece of bad fruit. From the outside, you couldn't tell, but once you took a bite, you couldn't look at it the same way knowing it was rotten inside.

That was disingenuous, a weak attempt to romanticize. The city had spoiled long ago. A better analogy would be that looking at the city was like looking at rotten fruit under a microscope. Seeing it closer and in more detail, one could identify the strange shapes of its disease. Or maybe it wasn't like fruit. Maybe it was a vegetable. Or a tomato or avocado, which were kind of both. Andy decided that good metaphors were hard to come up with, and he wasn't the one to do it, but that the city was a metaphor for something. And so was fruit.

◆ ◆ ◆

"This is where we're going?" Andy said. "You're kidding me?"

They pulled in front of 6243 Holt Avenue. The three of them got out of the station wagon and walked to the front door.

"I'll meet you at Hartshorn's," Rocco said. "I got calls to make."

Kate opened the door for Andy, and they entered the building together. Andy stopped in the foyer, looking at the flowers in the vase. "Were you the whistler the night I came here?"

"Or was it a ghost?" Kate smiled and walked past him down the long hallway, turning into the fifth small room. Andy followed. Even in the day, the place was creepy. Dark and noticeably vacant.

Kate pulled at a bookcase. On a hinge, it opened to reveal a staircase that led down into darkness.

"This is getting a little too *Scooby-Doo* for my taste," Andy said.

"Do you ever stop talking?"

Andy followed Kate down the steps and through a dimly lit basement that spanned the length of the block. The percussion of their footsteps echoed around them. There didn't appear to be any outlets, until Kate pulled open a false wall.

"What is this place?" Andy asked.

"We call it the Fortress. It's the safest place in Auction. A series of interconnected buildings. The only entrance is on Holt Avenue. If you don't know the layout, the doors, you'll never reach certain sections. I only know how to get to a few places."

They climbed three flights of stairs, walked down a narrow hallway, used a foldable ladder to go up one more level, crawled through an oversize duct, and finally down a fire pole to another hallway.

"How long you worked with Rocco?" Andy asked on their journey.

"Twenty years," she said, "but if you think you're getting any secrets from me, you're an idiot. I'm still miffed you thought I was your mother."

"It wasn't completely out of the realm of possibility."

"I won't forget it," she said.

"You were the first Floodgater that wasn't a crook. From a lawyer to this?"

"It suited me. Lawyering isn't exactly God's work. I was more interested in justice than law," she said. "It's not like it incorporates all criminals in the city. It's not a union of wife beaters and rapists and child molesters. This is a group of businessmen that choose to work outside legal means. Infighting cuts into their margins. No reason for crime to be uncivil."

"What about the people they sell drugs to? The poor they exploit? Aren't they hurt by 'business'?"

"That's really a larger discussion about libertarianism. I'm willing to have that conversation, but another time." Kate stopped in front of a door, knocked three times, and waited. "We're here."

◆ ◆ ◆

Champ sat back in a recliner, thumbing through one of her photo albums. Andy was glad to see that they'd brought them with her. When she looked up and saw Andy, her eyes got teary. She set the album to the side, stood, and went to him. She hugged him for the first time he could remember. Held him close, crushing his ribs. When she released him, she held his face in both hands, staring into his eyes.

"I wanted to tell you," she said. "I wanted to tell you everything. For so long."

"It's okay, Champ. I understand," Andy said. "Are they treating you right?"

"Better than ever," she said.

Andy glanced over his shoulder. Kate stayed by the door, talking to Russell, the male nurse who opened the door for them. He was a big man who could have easily been a bouncer on his day off.

Champ sat down on the recliner. Andy took a seat across from her on the leather couch. The place was bigger and nicer than the senior living facility. The furniture, as well.

Kate and Russell headed into one of the back rooms.

"So. Rocco. He's really my father?"

"He is. My late Manny and him, they ran together. Going way back. Before the war. One day soon after Manny passed, Rocco, he came to me, asked me to look after you. For a little while. That little while lasted until now. You saved my life."

"I don't understand."

"Without Manny, I didn't know what to do. Was completely lost. We had our lives planned together, and then he was gone. I tried to kill myself. Drank even more than what you seen me. I was dying alive.

"Maybe Rocco knew it. Knew I needed something—someone—to care for. When he handed you to me. This thing that weighed maybe fifteen pounds. This living thing with eyes and hands and feet. I had a reason to be. Someone that needed me. A reason to be better than I was. I ain't never called myself your mother, because that's not what I am. I was your protector. Your Champ. You were my salvation."

"What about my real mother?"

"Can't help you there. Rocco never told me. You'll have to ask him."

Kate came back in the room twenty minutes later. Champ's soap operas had started, so their conversation had ended except for brief moments during the commercial breaks.

Andy had more questions for her, but they could wait. He had the gist. Rocco had brought Andy to Champ, and without a second's hesitation she had taken him in and raised him as her own. How much more did he need to know? Despite the fact that Champ drank too much, was prone to anger, had been in more fights than Larry Holmes, and spent plenty an evening in a jail cell, she had stepped up and been the perfect person to raise him.

Forgiving Champ was the easy part, because she had nothing to apologize for. She had kept a friend's secret. The hard part was learning how to deal with having a father. There was only one place to start. With pie.

CHAPTER 17

I don't forgive. I don't forget. I hold a grudge. I remember
everything. Hell, I took notes. The bastards might get angry,
but they're bastards. They don't get to win.

—From the introduction to the memoir Assistant to the
Mayor's Assistant *by former Auction City politico Erica
"Boop" Neubauer (1985)*

Rocco and Andy sat at the counter in Hartshorn's Diner, each with a
cup of coffee and a piece of pie in front of them. Rocco got apple
with melted cheese. Andy went with lemon meringue. The awkwardness
didn't stop either of them from eating. Max Hartshorn made good pie.
Kate smoked on the sidewalk, leaving the two of them on their own.

"You seem a little old to be running around crime fighting,"
Andy said.

"Probably," Rocco said. "I'm seventy-two, but I don't feel a day
over seventy-one."

"Aren't you afraid you're going to get hurt?"

"Old people aren't the only ones that can get hurt. I hold my own,"
Rocco said.

Andy filled his mouth with delicious pie.

"Champ is like a sister to me. I couldn't go up. See her like that." Rocco shook his head. "When I picked her up last night. She knew who I was. Then she didn't. It's hard to see."

"But that's what real people do," Andy said. "They stay. Even when it gets hard."

Rocco took a sip of his coffee and wiped his mustache with a napkin. "It isn't always the things we do that damn us. Sometimes it's the things we don't do. The fights we walk away from. The words left unsaid. The people we leave behind."

"You said you came here," Andy said, "sat next to me. How many times without saying anything?"

"Couple dozen," Rocco said.

"What do you want from me? Expect from me?"

"Nothing. You're not the one in debt," Rocco said. "When you went after Gray, the flyers, all that, there was going to be a day that he'd get tired of it. Do something bad. I thought I could warn you off, protect you by threatening you."

"How did that work out?"

"Dumb plan," Rocco laughed. "But I'm a half-full kind of guy."

"I ended up killing the deputy police commissioner," Andy whispered.

"Didn't see that coming, to be sure," Rocco said. "But I probably wouldn't have spoken to you if you hadn't. I'd still just be an idea, a dead man to you."

Max refilled their coffee cups, shutting up Rocco for the moment. He picked at the melted cheese on the plate. When Max was at the other end of the counter, Andy spoke up.

"Floodgate the reason you left me with Champ?"

"Part of it." Rocco stroked the veins on the back of his hand. "I wish I could tell you that I left out of a sense of duty. Or they forced me. That it was beyond my control. But if I'm going to talk with you,

I'm going to talk straight. I left because I was better at the job than I'd ever be at being a father. Mostly, I left because I could."

"You're not exactly endearing yourself," Andy said.

"I'd been back from my time in the army for two, three years. I worked for Fat Jimmy Furgele before the war. After, I worked for his son. His old man gave him the nickname Tony Cajones, but it was forced. Tony's nothing like Fat Jimmy, different generation, runs the operation like a Fortune 500. Calls himself Anthony. Which is his name, but that's not the point. Bottom-line thinking. Political power, media control, beyond making a buck.

"Not the Trust I knew. Speaking another language. I understood the rackets. Loyalty still had meaning, though. They found a place for me. They called me a liaison, but I was a fixer. I kept the peace. I settled scores. I refereed street business. I knew everyone and everything that was going on in the city, but I quickly learned I didn't know a goddamn thing."

"I know the feeling," Andy said.

"I held court in Stogie's. One day, three men walked into the bar. A Chinese, a Negro, and a priest. I expected Stogie to hop the bar, toss them. He never cottoned to Negroes in his joint. Didn't know where he stood with Chinamen. Never seen one brave enough to walk north of Quarry Road.

"Stogie didn't do nothing. As much nothing as he could muster. Never saw no one exert so much effort to not doing a thing. Acted like they weren't there. Cleaned clean glasses. Scraped at an imaginary stain with his thumbnail. I thought maybe I was hallucinating. Either way, the mirage drifted toward me. When the Negro spoke, he told me that Sal Carrelli wanted to talk to me. It didn't get more real than that."

"I know that name. He was one of the original Floodgate members. I thought the kid's book just made up names. He's real?"

Rocco nodded. "They took me to him. Back of a plumbing supply warehouse. He didn't look good. That's what a gut shot does to a man.

Tough got you far, but it couldn't make a bullet not kill you. I didn't ask why we weren't in a hospital.

"The same doc had taken a slug out of my leg the year before. Doctor .45, we called him. A whiz at backroom surgery and pharmaceutical relaxation. When he said he couldn't do anything for Sal, nobody needed a second opinion. The only thing the doc needed to know was whether Sal preferred laudanum or poppy tea, and what song he wanted played at his funeral.

"Dying, Sal asked me to do two things. Punish the person who killed him. And take his place in Floodgate. At the time, I didn't know what that meant, but I agreed to both. Those two requests amounted to Sal's last words."

Andy glanced outside at Kate, who threw her cigarette onto the sidewalk and crushed it. She pulled out a pager, looked at it, and crossed the street to a payphone.

"He'd been in the group since the Flood?"

"All the way back. Like you, I thought Floodgate had dissolved," Rocco said. "The work suited me. I missed the action, the war. Nothing worse than a bored thug. Floodgate gave me the chance to bust some heads and feel good about it. I kept my promise to Sal."

"What about the man who shot him?"

"You want anything else to eat, Andrea?" Rocco said.

"Was it your choice to give me a girl's name?"

"A man's name in Italy. You said it yourself."

"Do you see the Pantheon outside?" Andy said. "You know how much hell I caught in school?"

"It was your grandfather's name," Rocco said. "Tradition is important."

"It's traditional to not abandon your son."

Across the street, Kate hung up the phone, threw some more change into the machine, and made another call. The speed with which she dialed told Andy that it wasn't good news.

"Al Gray's death was a long time coming," Rocco said, after making sure Max was out of earshot.

"I'm starting to get that sense, but it don't make the medicine go down any easier."

"Gray made Stalin look like Jimmy Carter. A lot of bodies on him. Ruined what the police could be. The few good cops, like you were, can't pick up that slack. End up getting done by the bad ones."

"I can't see you wanting to clean up the ACPD. Keeping it corrupt would be to your advantage."

"It's not about what we want. The ACPD is going to be corrupt no matter what we do," Rocco said. "It just needs to be the right kind of corrupt."

"There are plenty of uncorrupted police departments," Andy said.

When Rocco stopped laughing, he said, "If dogs could talk, they'd still eat their own vomit."

"How do I fit in to all this? To Floodgate?" Andy asked. "I literally have no idea what I'm going to be doing an hour from now, let alone tomorrow or in a month."

"I'm developing a loose plan for you. The whole concept is about twelve hours old. Seat of my pants here."

"That makes me feel better."

"Your skills have use," Rocco said. "I grew up a hood. I killed in the Flood, in the war, and before and after. Everyone's a soldier for something, even if it's themselves. And every day is a war. I killed soldiers on the other side, just as they would've killed me."

"We're talking about criminal mobs, not soldiers."

"Grow up, son," Rocco said. "You're looking for good guys and bad guys. We're the effective guys. If there's a problem, Floodgate has the power to fix it. You want to stop tourist muggings on Exposition? Of course you do, because if tourists are afraid to go there, businesses both legal and otherwise are hurt. The police can't stop it. Instead, Floodgate coordinates with Consolidated to spread the word and punish the morons who break the rules. Hospital time instead of jail time. Shift the more talented strong-arm men to a more suitable job. No reason to put someone out of work. Let the pickpockets know that tourists are still fair game, so long as no one gets hurt."

"People are still getting robbed."

"But not hurt. Part of the Auction City tourist experience. A small price to pay for a good story to bring home to your neighbors in Wichita."

"What if the problem Auction City has is that a cadre of criminal organizations is conspiring to control the entire city? Can Floodgate solve that problem?"

"No," Rocco said with a wide grin, "because it's the solution."

The bell tied to the door rang loudly. Andy and Rocco turned. Kate rushed inside, breathing hard. She walked quickly to them. "We need to go. It's all gone to hell."

CHAPTER 18

We're gonna need a bigger ark.

—*Graffiti under the King Olaf Bridge (1975)*

Kate threw a portable cherry top beacon on the roof of the station wagon, ran the siren, and hit the gas. Andy didn't even know the car had a siren. Maybe they *were* in the Batmobile, instead of a station wagon with a missing door. The cigarette lighter probably triggered a hidden ejector seat.

The station wagon darted in and out of traffic, two tires over the curb getting around a slow-moving cab. Screeches and metal scraping. Without a passenger-side door, wind and gravel spit in Andy's face and against his right arm. Red lights, stop signs, and pedestrians no longer mattered in Kate Girard's world.

"Whoa, whoa, whoa," Andy said. He turned to Rocco.

"Hold on to something," Rocco said calmly from the backseat. "That seat belt is broken."

Andy reached for the seat belt around his waist. It came apart without pressing the button. He glanced up at the quickly approaching ass end of a moving van and tied the two ends in a granny knot. Kate juked around the van with a quick jerk of the wheel.

"You can't just put a light on a car and blare a siren," Andy said to get his mind off dying in a hulk of flaming metal. "If you could, everyone would do it."

"They just haven't thought to try," Kate said, giving Andy a look that was usually reserved for a mother who'd just caught her toddler eating kitty litter. You're stupid, but I'm not going to give up on you.

"Nun," Andy yelled, pointing forward.

Kate caught the pedestrian out of the corner of her eye. She glided around the woman, missing by inches. The hem of the nun's windswept scapular grazed Andy's face.

Kate glanced over her shoulder. "I contacted our people. I'll have access. Not you, of course. Find a phone. Get everyone ready. Moving."

Rocco nodded, pulling out a small address book and flipping through it.

Kate turned to Andy. "This is serious, where we're going, what's happening. We're going to need your help. You better be ready."

"What's going on?" Andy asked.

"The cops just declared war."

◆ ◆ ◆

The Town & Country screeched to a halt in front of a three-story brownstone. The tenements of the Ruins loomed just blocks away, but the corrosion of the slums didn't carry over onto this street. The trees were healthy. The leaves raked. None of the buildings had bars on their windows. No graffiti on the walls. The street itself appeared freshly paved, which was a miracle in Auction City. With most of the city coffers siphoned directly into politicians' and contractors' pockets, the pothole stood as the city's lovable mascot. It took serious weight to get one filled.

Four patrol cars, two unmarked cars, and a crime scene van sat scattered in front of one building. Police tape cordoned off the building and sidewalk from the growing crowd. Through the nonexistent passenger-side door, Andy heard the neighborhood folk launching questions, speaking loudly, for now peaceful but a cough away from chaos. A couple of nervous cops eyed the curious and angry.

"Keep your mouth shut. Play Watson," Kate said before getting out of the car.

"What does that mean?" Andy turned back to Rocco. "Does that make her Sherlock?"

"It makes her boss," Rocco said.

Kate ducked under the police tape and joined a detective. She looked behind her, didn't find Andy there, and motioned disappointedly with one hand for him to come. Andy hurried over, got caught and uncaught in the police tape, and joined the huddle. The moment the plainclothes detective spotted Andy, his face changed.

"What's he doing here?" the detective said. "You know who he is?"

"He's with me. Consulting work," Kate said. "Is there going to be a problem?"

The cop gave Andy a one-eyed stare, spit on the ground in the opposite direction. "Don't raise a stink. Don't get noticed. Don't touch nothing. Don't get in no one's way. My ass is on the line. You can look, but it's not an open invite."

Kate walked toward the front door, Andy following. When they were out of earshot, Kate said, "We got a few friends on the force. Here's the thing. Odds are, cops did this. If that's the case, the evidence is already lost or compromised. Their investigation will be a joke. This is our only shot to maybe learn something."

Kate handed Andy two rubber gloves, then put a pair on herself.

"I never worked homicide, which I'm assuming is what this is. You really think the cops killed someone?" Andy said.

"Payback for Gray."

"Holy Christ. Who did they pay back? I'm right here," Andy said. "This is my fault."

"See what you see," Kate said. "Not just the crime scene, but watch the cops."

"Whose house is this?"

Kate ignored the question. "Are you okay with blood?"

"Not great," Andy said. "Why I preferred a desk."

"I've got smelling salts in my purse just in case."

◆ ◆ ◆

The front room was simply decorated, a middle-class home. A girl's bicycle leaned against a wall, pink tassels draped from the glittery handlebars. One of the more ominous items to find at a crime scene. A photo of a Latino couple with a young daughter hung on the wall next to an image of Our Lady of Guadalupe.

A crime scene tech with a clipboard and a few evidence bags walked past Kate and Andy to the front door. He gave them a puzzled look but didn't say anything.

"Who's the primary?" Kate asked as he passed.

"Sean Thornton," the man said and left.

Andy leaned in and stared at the family photo. "Is that—"

"Hector Costales," Kate said.

"Oh, shit. Is this because—he's dead?" Andy said. "Because of Gray? That's bad."

Kate nodded.

Andy shook his head. "Not just bad. It's bad bad. In the poor neighborhoods, the gangs, even regular folk, they treat him like the Second Coming. The city will riot."

Kate nodded.

Andy leaned in, keeping his voice to a whisper. "If the cops had anything to do with this and it gets out, it'll—I have no idea what it'll do."

"Now you know what we do and why," Kate said, moving through the house.

"No, I don't."

Turning a corner into the living room, the first thing Andy saw was the blood. It was impossible to miss. It was everywhere. Which made sense, considering the four shot-up bodies littering the room. The man closest to the sliding glass door that led to the back door had been practically cut in half, the carpet saturated black underneath him.

There were too many people in the room. Cops and technicians stayed on the perimeter, taking notes and talking to each other, but he could see blood on their shoes and smears where they'd tracked it. One of them laughed at the end of someone's joke. They were casual amid the carnage. A couple of cops smoked, using an ashtray that already had some butts in it. They weren't concerned about contamination. Or cancer.

A photographer tiptoed around the bloodstains, snapping each body at multiple angles, the flash popping and humming. For balance, the photog leaned against the wall and a table, his fingerprints joining any others.

But Andy's eyes kept returning to the blood. So much blood. He grew light-headed. An elbow on the wall, he took a deep breath, but the thick, meaty smell made it worse. His stomach turned. The world grew yellow. He closed his eyes and counted slowly backward from ten. He got to seven.

◆ ◆ ◆

Andy woke to an acrid and painful sear in his nostrils. He snapped away his head, banging it on the door frame. Kate pulled the smelling salts away, her expression somewhere between disappointment and amusement. He'd fainted, splayed on the ground, legs at odd angles. All the cops in the room looked his way, cruel smiles on their faces. Most shook their heads in disgust.

Andy pushed himself up. His hand sank into bloody carpet, the liquid squeezing to the surface, between his fingers. His head got foggy again. He decided that he was fine where he was.

"Give me a sec," he said.

"An inauspicious beginning," Kate said.

"You get what you pay for."

"While you're down there. Tell me what you see."

"Blood. Mostly blood." He looked at his hand stained with someone else's blood. Kate handed him a handkerchief. He scrubbed at it, but it left a stain and dark red around his fingernails.

Andy handed the used handkerchief to Kate, but she didn't take it. He shoved it in his pocket and took in the room, starting with the banner that read **HAPPY BIRTHDAY** taped to the ceiling and coming off at one corner. A blood-spattered birthday cake lie on the ground, a clear boot print in the frosting.

Andy sat up quickly. "Where's the kid? Were there kids?"

Kate put a hand on his shoulder. "Just the daughter. She's okay. They left the girl unhurt. Cops and social services have her."

"They get anything from her?"

Kate shook her head. "Only that her mommy and daddy are dead."

Andy nodded. A stupid, insensitive question.

"Let's talk about the obvious," Andy said. "It's the work of a group of people. Organized. Maybe military. The man on the couch doesn't look like he had a chance to move."

"That's Hector Costales. His wife next to him."

"Whatever happened, happened fast. Probably three men. Maybe more, but they would have bottlenecked at the back door. I would guess professional violence," Andy said. "That boot print could be something. But the cops trampled most of it. I see a few different shell casings from here. There won't be any usable prints. Looks like someone took a bite out of that piece of cake. One of the shooters getting cute, maybe."

Andy rose to his feet, keeping a hand on the door frame. Sweat poured from his face, but he felt his legs beneath him, his blood pressure adjusting.

"Know anything about the other bodies?" he asked.

"Could be friends. Or a couple of Hector's lieutenants."

"What in the hell?" Sean Thornton stomped straight through the crime scene, contaminating it and tracking bloody boot prints in his wake. "How did this rat-faced prick get in here?"

"The mayor asked us to poke our head in," Kate said. "See if we could assist."

"He's with you, Girard?" the Thornton asked. Veins in his neck bulged. His face red. "Then I want both of you gone."

"Any suspects?" Kate asked, calm.

"No, but there could always be a couple more bodies."

❖ ❖ ❖

In the short time Kate and Andy had spent at the crime scene, the crowd outside had doubled. And gotten louder. Word had spread. People shouted questions at the cops. Two television news vans had found the site, reporters and camera operators jostling for the best spot to get the shot. Andy recognized four different sets of gang colors, including the Voodoo Posse, Cash Money Brothers, T-Birds, and a large contingent from the Wretches. They were all Consolidated.

Hector Costales had originally been the leader of the Wretches, the oldest and largest gang in Auction City. Until he found a way to unite the ten largest gangs, forming Consolidated. At first feared, the community quickly embraced the idea once they saw the street violence all but disappear. They even made a movie about it, but in typical Hollywood fashion, the story got changed in development. A good movie, just not historically accurate.

"What happened to Hector?" someone shouted.

"Cops finally kilt him," another yelled in response.

Kate and Andy stood inside the police tape but away from the growing army of cops. It didn't take a tarot reading to see where this was headed.

"A lot has to happen fast," Kate said. "We've got to coordinate with Consolidated leadership. Without Hector, there's nobody in charge. The whole thing could all fall apart today. We can't have that kind of chaos on top of this. This city loves a riot."

Andy looked back to the crowd, now chanting, "Pigs kill. Kill the pigs." He spotted Rebane waddling through the mob, a corn dog in one hand, a microphone in another. A cord ran from the mike to a recorder in his pocket. He and Andy made eye contact. Rebane gave Andy a questioning smile, then wagged his eyebrows, looking toward Kate. Andy pretended he hadn't seen him.

"This is all about revenge for Gray's murder. They know the burglary story is bullshit," Kate said. "Hank Robinson and Gray weren't just colleagues. They were friends. With Robinson in charge now, he's going to come at us. Costales was the wrong target for Gray's shooter, but Robinson won't stop there. Not how the cops work."

"It could be Gray himself," Andy said.

Kate laughed. "From beyond the grave? Is he a zombie or a ghost?"

Andy shook his head. "Robinson isn't smart enough for something this well planned. He could be finishing what Gray started. Someone tried to kill me before Gray died. What if Gray set this in motion? Gray is making his move to take over the city. Except he's dead."

Kate thought about that for a second. "It definitely has Gray's handwriting on it. He kills two birds. Costales's death creates chaos within Consolidated—plus he gets some riots. Nothing like riots to remind the deeper pockets that they need a strong police force to keep the barbarians at the gate." Kate stepped away from Andy, looking at the crowd. "Gray or Robinson or both, someone's coming for us."

"We need to talk to the guy you got locked up. The one that tried to kill me."

"We have to warn the others," Kate said. "Consider ourselves targets, as well."

A bottle smashed against the side of the building. The cops turned, one pulling his weapon but keeping it trained at the ground.

A group of young men started to rock one of the police cars back and forth in an effort to flip it. Down the street, more and more people arrived from the direction of the Ruins. A police van crept through the crowd, palms slapping its side. When the back opened, SWAT in riot gear exited and created a line in front of the building.

This was just the beginning. It was going to get worse. A lot worse.

1929

LONG PAST DAYS

Sal took me and the girl into the warmth of the Turkish baths. Safe for the moment, I would never feel secure. For the rest of my life, I would always be ready to run.

My clothes, rags. Burnt, torn, filthy. Raiding the closets of the baths. Lost and found. Abandoned remnants. Shirts. Pants. Socks. Shoes. I gussied up. Pieced together a fresh suit. It almost fit. Even grabbed a tie. Not to wear. To kill quietly. My thinking perverted. All objects now murder devices.

The girl came in. Wearing a fresh dress. Small. Wet red hair. Freckled face clean of sewer grime and ash. Bruised and cut. Blushing at my wide eyes. Looking down at the floor made her prettier. Modesty turned to anger. Eyes fire.

"Don't make me clobber you." Punched my arm and walked away.

I was in love.

❖ ❖ ❖

Twenty men gathered around the tiled pools. Sweating in the steam. Winter outside. August in there. I regretted choosing tweed. Me and the girl, we stayed against the wall. Bystanders, not participants.

A few eyed the girl. Said nothing. I didn't like how they looked at her. No different from the men in the sewer. Confusing beauty and youth with something weak. Something they could take. I wouldn't let them. When they saw the murder in my eyes, they looked away.

Fat Jimmy plotted, planned, ordered. His men leaned close. Whispers back and forth. Getting a message and leaving to carry it out. Bathhouse turned war room.

A line of men waited for orders. Standing at attention. Tommy guns. Pistols. Knives. Bloody faces and bodies. Jaws clenched. If they were afraid, it didn't show.

Sal spotted me. Walked over. A slight limp. Some burns and bruises. A long slice across his cheek and lip.

"Who is she?" Like the girl wasn't there.

"A friend. My friend."

He took a look at her. Shook his head. Turned back to me. "You try to take care of her, she'll get you killed."

"I can take care of myself, you guinea prick." The girl's hand on the butt of her pistol.

Sal slapped her and took her pistol away. A half second. All it took. She held her face. Not scared. Embarrassed.

My hand was on my cleaver. Don't remember moving it there. Didn't know until later that I was ready to kill Sal. If his hand rose to her again, I would have tried.

Guido Rattone ran in. Arrow in his shoulder like in a cowboy movie. Yelling for everyone to come out to the street. To grab their weapons.

"Don't shoot me, gal." Sal handed the pistol back to her. Turned to me, glanced at my hand on the cleaver. "She might get you killed, Rocky, but people have died for worse reasons."

Sal and the other men hurried outside.

"You okay?" I asked the girl. She wouldn't make eye contact. Her cheek bright red.

"I've been hit before."

❖ ❖ ❖

"There are hundreds of them."

"Thousands."

"I've never seen so many goddamn Chinamen in all my life."

The girl and I stood in the bathhouse doorway. Glimpses between heads and shoulders. Everyone taller, on toes to see for themselves. All eyes on the street. Fat Jimmy's men peeked past the wood and metal. At the deliverers of their demise.

Rows and rows of Chinese. An army in bloodstained white. Torches in some hands. Weapons in others. Few guns, mostly sharpened steel. Swords, axes, knives, and diabolical weapons with strange oriental names that I would never know. Twisted, deadly shapes.

The city burnt behind them. Black smoke and heat. A phantasmagoria. Demons rising from the flames.

They chanted. Mongol words vibrated in my chest. Strange and foreign and hate filled. Metal weapons on metal as chorus. Shrill and sour sounds.

Fat Jimmy pushed me aside, taking a look from the door. "Like a dago Alamo," he said. A big smile.

"What do we do?" Marco Ronda asked.

"What do you think?" Fat Jimmy said. "Kill 'em all."

❖ ❖ ❖

"Let's get out of here. We'll find somewhere safe," the girl said, pulling me inside. "Everyone here is going to die."

"These are my people," I said. "I owe them."

"I don't," she said. "Whatever you said yesterday don't mean nothing today. Look at the city. That place is gone."

I stared at the fire that had replaced the city that I grew up in. The only place I knew. I had never even stepped outside the county.

"Even more reason. I can't leave. But you can." I gently pushed her shoulder. Pushed her inside. "Find a back window. Something. Get out. Try to make it to the river. To the Terrace. Or out of the city."

She gave me a long stare. Then checked the cartridges in her pistol and handed the gun to me. Frowned. Shook her head.

"Try to stay alive," she said. Turned and went into the building.

Knew she would have a better chance. Not a good one but a better one. It was disappointing, though. Not how our adventure was supposed to end. No such thing as happily ever after. Not on a battlefield.

I joined the men and their wait to be massacred by a horde of Chinese crime soldiers.

❖ ❖ ❖

The standoff was tense. The fight would happen. But nobody in a hurry to die. Steeled for one last battle but not impatient.

The Chinese chanted on. Swayed to the rhythm of the words. I wished I knew what they meant. Why they sounded so calm. Not like Fat Jimmy's men who shouted, angry. No aggression from the Chinese. Disciplined. True soldiers.

The chanting stopped. Dead silence. A motionless army. Unblinking. Unwavering.

"What the hell is going on?"

"Nothing good."

"Get ready for anything."

"They blink before they strike."

A sound like a growl. Heavy wheels on stones. The army parted.

"Maybe they got a dragon," someone joked halfheartedly. He wasn't far off.

The Chinese rolled out a cannon.

1986

CHAPTER 19

I took the steaks. I sure did. Prime T-bone. But I left four dollars. Honest. Can't help it if someone stole the damn cash register.

—Accused looter during the Midnight Riots testifying
in court (1968)

Riding back to the candy factory, Andy looked for signs of rising discord. Among the regular pedestrian traffic, he spotted people heading toward the Ruins. Walking with purpose, with attitude, with anger. Mostly black and brown. The men in suits walking in the opposite direction, casual and oblivious. Shoulders bumped without either side pausing to acknowledge.

The street would spread news faster than any media outlet. The death of Hector Costales and his wife would be all over the city within an hour. By phone, by whisper, and by shout. When the massacre led the evening news, the information would be stale to anyone without a 401(k). And when it found the front page the next day, only the trust-funded on Gallows Terrace would learn something new.

Among the lower classes, Costales was as close to a folk hero as the city had. He was more than a gang leader, knowing how to earn goodwill. Everyone loved Robin Hood. His after-school programs, food banks, work-training programs, and nonstop advocacy for the poor cemented his slum sainthood. Hated and loved, like any true martyr. A reminder that ruthlessness and compassion weren't mutually exclusive. Even if the compassion was a facade, his actions spoke louder than the politicians' empty words.

The crowds would grow. Some in peaceful grief. Some in nonviolent protest. Others with the intent to destroy. To unleash their frustration. To illustrate their anger. To exploit the chaos. A riot was little more than a community gone mad. It was a good thing that the weather was cold. If Costales had been killed in the summer, the city would already be ablaze.

That's not to say that fires hadn't been set. As they arrived at the waterfront factory, smoke rose from the Ruins and the eastern part of Exposition Boulevard. According to the radio, people were starting to gather. No incidents. A few burning couches. No mention of the police response, although one cop had to be taken to the hospital after getting hit in the head with a toaster flung from someone's window. But that could happen on a regular day in Auction.

The day would be a cakewalk compared with the night. Looters got braver as it got darker. The wrong people took command. The anger would boil over. Poor people were going to die tonight.

◆ ◆ ◆

Walking into Floodgate HQ, Andy, Kate, and Rocco were greeted with the sound of breaking glass, furniture knocked over, and a steady rant in English and Spanish. Pilar had not taken the news of Hector Costales's murder well. Three coffee mugs, a potted plant, and a six-pack of Bubble Up bottles appeared to be the victims of her reaction. A trash can got a good kicking. She wore a prosthetic arm, perhaps to do more damage. The metal hook on the end showed wear, dull and scuffed.

180

"Slaughtered him. And Anna. *Cómo podrían? Hector Costales era*—never going to be anyone like him. *Él ayudó a.* Did more for me, my girls, than anyone. I'd be dead, a slave, worse. *El Roto lo debemos. Inocente* Anna, never hurt no one. Motherfuckers will pay. Going to hurt them. I am going to kill."

Rocco sat down at a desk. He dialed a phone and pressed his ear to the receiver, a finger in the other ear. He shouted his name over Pilar's rant and asked for Cardinal Macklin. He glanced at Pilar but made no attempt to quiet her.

Andy turned to Kate. "What do we do now?"

"That's the spirit, Destra. *We* have a lot to do," Kate said. "After Pilar winds down—she will. If she doesn't let off some steam, the wrong people get hurt. We need her to hurt the right people. She's got to figure out Consolidated. Until they have a new leader, it's a snake without a head, whipping its tail around, breaking everything in sight."

"We need to confirm that it is Gray and/or Robinson responsible for the murders. That it's the cops," Andy said. "If it is them, they're not done. This is the beginning."

"Mac will make contact with the rest of the leadership, make sure they are warned and safe. They got to Costales. We have to assume the other leaders are targets. I don't think we're safe either," Kate said.

Pilar had found a hammer and beat holy hell out of one of the filing cabinets. Andy was relieved it wasn't one of his. They had sentimental value.

"You up for talking to your would-be assassin?" Kate asked. "The guy tried to kill you the day before Costales's murder. If he's part of the same plot, he's our best shot at confirming Gray's or Robinson's role. Maybe even some insight into what the overall plan is."

"You think he's going to talk to us?"

"Probably not."

"What then?"

"Agnes."

"Is that an answer?" Andy asked.

Kate shrugged and found a seat at one of the desks. She motioned for Andy to sit. He picked up the loose pages of the day's newspaper and folded them back together as best he could. The headline read, "Top Cop Death Shocker." Written by Kurt Rebane.

> AUCTION CITY—When the police arrived at the Gallows Terrace home of Deputy Commissioner Aloysius Gray, it was obvious that something was amiss. The door was ajar, wood splintered at the latch. Guns drawn, they entered the home and found the body of the deputy commissioner shot in the chest.
>
> But it doesn't end with a simple burglary gone wrong. As shocking as the peace officer's death, a mountain of evidence was discovered that implicates the late Gray in a world of corruption, backroom dealings, and even murder. An overwhelming amount of evidence to crimes committed during his tenure, including the fabrication of evidence to disgrace a number of his own men.
>
> When the city should be mourning one of its leaders, instead we are forced to see the lie that Aloysius Gray told even the people closest to him.

The newspaper article continued, detailing the specifics of Gray's illegal activities. The list was long.

"How?" Andy said, after reading the article twice.

"We used Gray's journals, ledgers, notes, and even trash. The man was so corrupt, we had to manufacture very little. It was just a matter of sneaking it to Rebane before the cops could bury it. Not only does it publicly steer attention away from the crime but a dead crooked cop is investigated differently. Once the allegations exist, they have a harder time creating their own narrative. We included evidence on how you and the others were railroaded. No harm in clearing your name while we were at it."

"Am I supposed to say thank you?" Andy asked.

"We still hold all the evidence that incriminates you as the real murderer," Kate said.

"So probably not."

Pilar's rant had turned into a low mumble. She paced in a tighter and tighter circle, until she dropped onto the couch and stared daggers at the wall across from her. She breathed heavily, her metal prosthetic hook opening and closing, clicking with the rhythm of her breathing. She hated everything about that wall.

Rocco hung up and turned to Kate and Andy. "Mac's going to do his thing. The Trust will control the message on the news, radio, and tomorrow's papers. The murder they have to report, but any looting will be backpaged. Slow the momentum. Although tonight will tell. Mac was still trying to salvage some sort of peace with Robinson, but if we're assuming that he had Costales killed, that needs to be shitcanned. I advised that he move on to Randall Ashley. Set mutiny in motion."

"Are the leaders safe, at least?" Kate asked.

"They've been warned. Each organization is taking necessary precautions. Left the Fortress as an option. The Trust, 893, and the—"

"Where the hell have you been?" Pilar yelled, interrupting Rocco.

Everyone turned to see Ben Jigo at the entrance, Agnes standing behind him. The fifth member of Floodgate had been noticeably absent since Andy's abduction.

Ben held out his hands defensively. "What? What's going on?"

"I paged you an hour ago," Rocco said.

"I found him at that massage place again," Agnes said.

"My rubdown ran long. Left my pager in the cubby. It's about full relaxation. If it's any consolation, the massage made me collected and ready to work."

Pilar jumped off the couch and charged him. Her shoulder dug into his midsection and drove him against the wall.

"Get her off me!" Ben screamed, before his voice was cut off by her hand around his throat.

"Hector Costales is dead," Pilar said.

"I didn't kill him," Ben gurgled. He punched Pilar in the stomach. A decent uppercut but not much behind it. From Pilar's nonexistent reaction, his fist might've hit steel. He tried again, but the blow was weaker from his loss of air. Still no reaction. He gave up, choosing to get choked instead.

Agnes put a gentle hand on Pilar's shoulder. Ben spit sounds, his arms flailing at his side. Rocco and Kate didn't move to intervene. Andy watched the drama play out.

"Let him go, Pili," Agnes said, her voice gentle. "We are a team. We must act like one."

Pilar's eyes never left Ben. "You hear that, Jigo? We're a team. That means if you don't take this murder seriously. If you screw around on this. I will hurt you. Genitally." She let go brusquely, shoving him to the side. Ben fell to the ground, sucking in air and massaging his bruised throat.

Pilar stomped over to Kate. "Tantrum done. I'm ready to work."

CHAPTER 20

You're not looking at the facts. If they'd've been alive,
they'd've voted for me for sure. That's a fact. Try to refute it.
Prove me wrong. You can't. So what's the problem?

—*Attributed to Jefferson Stringer after being indicted for*
voter fraud after it had been revealed that more than a
thousand Civil War dead had helped elect him into his
city council seat (circa 1957)

"You ready for this?" Kate asked Andy. "We do things a little differently here."

They stood outside the door of an interrogation room. Andy stared at the man inside through the small window.

"The son of a bitch tried to kill me," Andy said. "Walked up to me on the street with a shotgun."

"You can't take things like that personally."

"Of course you can," Andy said. "How do you not take attempted murder personally?"

"He was just doing his job," Kate said.

She opened the door and entered the room. The man sat handcuffed to the table in front of him. The blood had been cleaned from his face, but both eyes were bruised black and his nose took a sharp left in the middle. Andy didn't think he looked that bad for a brick to the face. He didn't look up when they sat across from him.

"What's your name?" Kate asked.

"Lawyer," the man said.

Kate laughed. "You think we're the police? Are you kidding me? Oh, man. You're either dumb or stupid."

The man looked up, his eyes scanning past Kate to Andy. "I remember you."

"Who hired you?" Andy asked.

"You know, for a chubby fuck, you're faster than you look."

"Fear of dying improves one's forty," Andy said. "Who are you working for? Who else are you working with? Are there other targets?"

"Is that all you want to know? How about the secret to pleasing a woman, while I'm at it?" The man put his head back down. "You ain't getting nothing from me."

"We figured, but it was worth a try," Kate said. "Some people like to do it the hard way."

"Go fuck yourself."

"I'll get Agnes," Kate said.

He peeked up from the table. "Some other bitch ain't going to scare me more than you. Still a woman."

"I'm not trying to scare you," Kate said.

◆ ◆ ◆

Andy and Kate waited in the open area on the couch. Agnes had been in the interrogation room for fifteen minutes. She had come out twice. Once to grab a staple remover and a phone book. The second time she asked Kate if they had an ice cream scoop.

"Why would we have an ice cream scoop?" Kate asked.

"For scooping ice cream," Agnes said. "No matter. I'll improvise. There's a three-hole punch somewhere around here."

Andy didn't think he could feel any sympathy for someone who'd tried to kill him. Not until that moment.

Rocco, Pilar, and Ben had all left on various errands and missions. When Agnes returned to the interrogation room with the three-hole punch, Andy stood up and paced. "Isn't there something we can be doing?"

"Mac's wrangling the generals. We're soldiers waiting for orders. Not much to do until we got something to do."

"What the hell's she doing to him?" Andy asked.

"I've never asked," Kate said. "Never wanted to watch. She's effective, though. He'll talk."

"Your torturer is with the Church? Is she, like, a nun?"

"Does she look like a nun?"

"Then what is she?"

"She's Agnes," Kate said. "That's about as much as any of us know."

"How'd they get you to switch from one side of the law?" Andy asked. "Have something on you, too? A crime to hang over your head like me?"

"They asked. Pretty much it. I've always had larceny in my heart." Kate laughed. "I hit a ceiling because I was a woman. That sat poorly with me. When they asked, I saw an opportunity."

"An opportunity?"

"Take a look at the group. Really take a look. We're all outsiders," Kate said. "Forgotten. Ignored. Underestimated. Assaulted.

"Rocco was a crook going back to the Flood.

"Pilar? When was the last time you saw one of the Broken in a position of power? With a job at all? Plenty of sympathy for those kids. Led to nothing but talk from the people of this city. They were beggars, after all. Once the headlines died, they were abandoned. The Church and Consolidated took them in. Hector Costales led that charge. Pilar still takes care of most of those girls.

"Ben's uncle is the head of 893. They didn't know what to do with him, a spoiled, rich kid. I get the feeling 893 is unhappy, bought some bad fish off the Chinese. They certainly don't take Floodgate seriously. Sent Ben to us to kill two birds, get rid of him and not waste a good man on us. He feels disrespected, disowned. Not exactly a motivator. He's smart, but he has no incentive to work hard.

"And Agnes is Agnes."

◆ ◆ ◆

Andy got all three of the Cat Scratch Fever drop targets and almost completed the Gonzo board. Ten thousand points shy of Kate's high score on the "Nugent!" pinball game, he watched his second ball roll down a side lane.

"Are you sure you've never played this before?" Kate asked.

Andy launched his last ball. It bounced around.

"Careful," Kate said. "Don't get nervous."

Three thousand points shy of the high score, Andy got overzealous. He banged the side in an effort to save the ball. But Ted Nugent didn't like to play rough (although he probably did). The game tilted, and Andy watched the ball slowly bounce its way down the dead machine, impotent to do anything about it.

"Tough luck, Destra. You got close," Kate said. She kept her smile in her pocket. She had won. No reason to rub it in.

Andy stared at the Nuge wailing on his guitar, but the Motor City Madman had been nothing more than a quiet observer to his massive choke (also something that Ted Nugent would probably do).

"I'm out of quarters," Andy said.

"Joe Sullivan."

They both turned. Agnes had left the interrogation room. She was drying her hands with a dish towel. There was a speck of blood on her shirt collar.

"His name is 'Cemetery Joe' Sullivan. Which is a funny name, because he's dead."

CHAPTER 21

People that think violence is bad have no understanding of
what violence is. They live in a nonviolent world, no different
than a child that hates the spinach he's never tasted.

—*From Talbot Cantrell's written statement. Cantrell, an aikido
instructor, put four members of a college fraternity in the
hospital after they jumped him outside the Auction City
homosexual bar Salted Nuts. No charges were filed against
the men. Cantrell served eight years in prison (1971).*

"Agnes, where's your restraint?" Kate Girard shouted. "Killing him
was the exact opposite of what we need."

"Does this happen a lot?" Andy asked. "Her killing people? You
people killing people?"

Agnes laughed. Or what Andy assumed was a laugh, a quick exhale
out her nose and a hand covering her teeth. Her eyes were definitely
laughing, and not in a not-insane way.

"It's not funny," Kate said. "We've talked about this."

"I see what I said. Why you think . . ." Agnes said, still laughing.
"The man is alive. In the room, he is living. But also he is dead."

"What is he? Schrödinger's cat?" Andy said.

Kate stared at her. "Is this one of your riddles?"

"No, but I learned a new one. It was written in a bathroom for men," Agnes said. "What's the difference between a Peeping Tom and a pickpocket?"

Kate blinked and took in a deep breath. "We're on a schedule, Agnes. What do you mean by 'but also he is dead'?"

Agnes looked confused. "You don't want to know the answer to the riddle?"

"No," Kate said. "This is considerably more important."

"It feels undone." Agnes shrugged, looking disappointed. "Mr. Cemetery Joe was serving a life sentence for murder in the Sweetbriar State Penitentiary. Convicted of one murder, but he admitted to killing a dozen other people to me. A freelance gunman. Eight years into his sentence, he died in a prison fire."

"I remember that fire," Andy said. "From a couple months ago. He used the fire to escape?"

"In a way," she said. "Before the fire, a deal had been struck. He would be released from the prison, evidence would be manufactured to suggest his death, and he would gain safe passage out of the country."

"In exchange, he kills me?" Andy said. "Seems like a lot of work to hire one assassin. Especially in this city."

"If you were the only target, it would be ridiculous," Agnes said. "He was given a list. Each with individual bounties."

"People do like complicated plans," Andy said. "'Here's some money, shoot a guy' feels plain."

"Why not cut and run?" Kate said. "The man's free."

"Greed and fear," Agnes said. "Each name on the list had a monetary value for him. Retirement in Argentina costs money."

"Who hired him to kill me?" Andy asked.

"Mr. Cemetery Joe didn't know who orchestrated the escape or gave him the list," Agnes said. "He might have lied about not knowing, but that's not realistic in terms of the experience that we went through together just now."

"It's Gray or Robinson," Andy said.

"However the arrangement was presented to him," Agnes said, "he feared his employer enough to go through with the plan and trusted them enough to hold up their end of the deal."

"How do we find out who was on that list?" Kate asked.

"The man is not bright," she said. "His memory shaken. I struck him with a brick. It may be lost. He did remember my picture. And the archbishop's."

"If he didn't know who hired him," Andy asked, "how did they communicate? Pass notes in home ec class?"

"He made contact through two guards. I have their names."

"We need to talk to them," Kate said.

"Wait a minute," Andy said. "He couldn't have killed Hector Costales. He's been here all day."

"Oh, hell." Kate turned to Agnes.

"I was getting to that," Agnes said. "He was not the only convict that died in that fire."

◆ ◆ ◆

Kate dug through one of the Floodgate file cabinets. Andy thumbed through his own. He wondered if their system was better than his. He doubted it. It was a strange thing to be competitive about, but Andy had to take his wins where he could get them.

Agnes watched them both, humming softly to herself. It made Andy uncomfortable, but there wasn't anything Agnes could do that wouldn't make him nervous.

"You never told us, Agnes," Andy said. "What's the difference between a pickpocket and a Peeping Tom?"

Kate exhaled and shook her head.

Agnes smiled broadly. "A pickpocket snatches watches. It's funny, yes?"

Andy chuckled. He'd heard the joke before, but he wanted to do everything he could to make friends with the scary lady.

"Can you explain the joke to me? I do not understand it," she said. "Is it why Rocco taking your watch was funny? Explain, please."

Andy gave Kate a desperate look. She shrugged.

Luckily, Andy found the file and didn't have to answer. "Here it is!" he shouted triumphantly, pulling out the newspaper report of the Sweetbriar prison fire. He spread the paper out on a table. Extensive coverage with photos.

Andy read aloud, blah-blah-blahing through the details of the fire. They weren't important. An entire cellblock had to be evacuated. Six men died in the fire. The six men's names read like a psychopath's Christmas card list. Pictures accompanied the short bios of the dead men. Mean faces and dumb mugs. Not one of them looked like someone you would want to meet in a dark anything.

> RONALD MARK HENRY, also known as the "Thief River Killer." For three years, he terrorized the Castles and the surrounding area. Serving consecutive life sentences for the murders of seven women and three men. The subject of the movie *Thief River*, starring Harrison Monroe.

> NORMAN HOPEWELL, former marine. Received Purple Heart and Silver Star medals from the conflicts in Korea and Vietnam. Serving a life sentence for the for-hire murders of three union officials.

> IPO KAHULAMU, former army munitions expert. Radical member of the short-lived Hawaiian Secessionist Movement. Serving multiple life sentences for the Lourey Station bombing of 1972 that killed seven people and injured fifty-eight.

JOSEPH SULLIVAN, also known as Cemetery Joe, a self-described freelance enforcer. Serving a life sentence for the murder of off-duty FBI agent Martin Gonzalez.

LOUIS WELLS, career criminal and half of the team responsible for the six-day siege of the downtown branch of the Auction Savings & Loan in 1981. Serving thirty years for assault, attempted murder, kidnapping, and armed robbery.

STUART WELLS, twin brother of Louis Wells. Serving thirty years for the same crimes as his brother. The siblings had been at separate prisons, but Louis had recently been transferred to Sweetbriar.

"Other than the Hawaiian, I know these people," Kate said. "They are bad men. Hopewell the marine ran mercenaries overseas for the CIA. Settled in Auction and pretty much ran a mini-army. He will be the leader. Considering the precision of the Hector Costales hit, Hopewell most likely ran that operation. Probably with Stu and Lou Wells as his second and third guns."

"Ronald Mark Henry doesn't make sense," Andy said. "He's not a pro. He's a serial killer."

"Unless the whole plan is to create chaos," Kate said. "Who knows what Gray was doing?"

"Great, I killed the Bond villain, but all his henchmen are running around doing his bidding," Andy said. "So how do we find Oddjob, Nick Nack, Jaws, and the others?"

◆ ◆ ◆

Andy peered into the small window of the holding cell. Cemetery Joe Sullivan faced the wall, standing an inch from it, his nose almost touching. His body shook as he wept. He didn't look hurt. The trauma something deeper.

Agnes walked behind Andy.

"The man tried to kill you," she said.

"What did you do to him?"

"Kate calls it 'the old-time religion.'"

"Can I talk to him?"

"He's in no condition," Agnes said.

"I want to know why he went after me," Andy said. "If he had a list of targets, why me?"

"All the other ones had higher bounties," Agnes said. "He figured he'd work from the bottom up."

"Trying to kill me is one thing," Andy said. "That's just insulting."

CHAPTER 22

It ain't about the law, Scooters. Or the police or the lawyers or the judges. It's about that blind broad in front of the courthouse. All said and done, everyone gets theirs. Lady Justice, she's the one we answer to. The wrong don't got no rights.

—From the comic strip character Hawk Shaw to his faithful boy sidekick, Scooters MacGregor, after defeating arch-villain Bang Pow, the "Oriental Moriarty of Auction City." Written by Carter Stanz. Art by Fisk (1947).

One phone call to the Sweetbriar State Penitentiary for Men quickly revealed that Connor Beauchamp and Frank Whittle, the two prison guards Cemetery Joe had named as the men who'd carried out his escape, hadn't shown up for their scheduled shifts that morning. The likelihood that they'd both caught the flu on the same day seemed remote.

The two men lived a convenient three blocks from each other in Blackstreet Hollow, an upper-middle-class neighborhood slightly too upper and too middle for a prison guard. It suggested crooked money in the same way that Gallows Terrace suggested dump trucks full of crooked money. The commute to the prison was at least an hour each way, although plenty of people drove farther for a good school district and a larger-than-average backyard.

Kate coordinated with Rocco. He would grab Ben and hit Beauchamp's house, while Kate and Andy braced Whittle. The guards were only pawns in the whole scheme. Agnes's presence would be overkill. She went to help Pilar tamp down the gangs' response to the Costales hit and oversee their selection for a new leader of Consolidated.

Frank Whittle lived in a one-story ranch house on a cul-de-sac. The kind of neighborhood with tire swings and kids riding their bikes in the summer. Wind chimes hung from the eave near the front door, tinkling in the breeze. A late-model Trans Am sat in the driveway, black with a gold eagle on the hood, a pine air freshener hanging from its rearview. It was the kind of a car a man loved and always described as "cherry" or "boss."

Andy and Kate sat in a town car across the street, watching the front door. It continued to do its job of being a front door. Quietly and solidly efficient in its doorlike qualities.

"Are we going to go in there? Talk to him?" Andy said. "Or are we going to sit here?"

"You're anxious to get going?"

"There's a group of convicts on the loose in Auction. They got a list of targets that my name's on. Not going to sleep too well knowing that," Andy said. "I might've got brought in without asking, but I'm in it now."

Kate reached for the door handle.

"I need a weapon," Andy said. "I can't go in there with nothing to defend myself."

Kate thought about it for a moment and then shook her head. "Not yet."

"Okay," Andy said, "but every time I don't shoot someone, that's on your conscience."

◆ ◆ ◆

They kept it casual. No reason to go SWAT team on the situation. Up the walkway and to the front door, two normal people visiting a friend.

With one hand on the butt of the pistol beneath her jacket, Kate gave the door three hard raps. A loud thud echoed from inside. A muffled voice. Glass breaking.

Kate drew her weapon, shot the doorknob twice, and kicked in the door. Andy would have rushed in right behind her, but he was so impressed by the fluidity of her actions and the badassery of it all that he found himself staring in awe for a few extra seconds.

In the living room, a heavyset man hung from a ceiling beam, an extension cord wrapped around his neck. The man clawed at the cord, his face dark red, fat tongue sticking out of his gasping mouth. His eyes bulged with fear and asphyxiation.

"Help him," Kate said, heading in the direction of the garage.

Andy grabbed the man around the knees and lifted. He felt something pop in his back and an electric shock down his left leg that couldn't have been good. He held on through the pain. Spit rained down on Andy as Frank Whittle frantically took in air.

"Help me," Whittle croaked. "Help."

"What the hell do you think I'm doing, you fat bastard?"

Two gunshots echoed through the house, coming from the garage.

Both men got quiet. Though he needed air, Andy felt Whittle hold his breath. They both had a clear view of the door to the garage. Whittle rested his butt on Andy's shoulder, essentially sitting on him. The position didn't hold the most dignity, but it made it easier for Andy to keep him aloft.

"If anyone but the woman I came with walks through that door," Andy said, "I'm going to let go of you and run like hell."

"No, no, no," Whittle said.

"I will," Andy said. "I thought you should know, so it wasn't a surprise."

"Please don't."

They stared at the door and waited. Nothing else to do. Andy scanned the room for a weapon. He would try for the front door, but in a pinch the fireplace poker would have to do. Maybe he could knock the bullets out of the air.

Both men exhaled audibly when Kate walked through the door.

"What happened? Are you okay?" Andy asked, his words stumbling into each other.

She nodded, but the hand with her pistol in it shook. "He drew on me."

"Dead?"

She shook her head. "Slipped under the garage door. I winged him."

"You need to help me here," Andy said. "This guy is made out of whatever happens when you mix doughnuts and Burgie."

"Hey," Whittle said. "I have a slow metabolism."

Kate grabbed a chair from the dining room. She worked on the cord around Whittle's neck. Two cracked fingernails later, she got it off. Without the cord doing the work, Andy's balance got thrown off. Whittle fell off his shoulder, landing on the coffee table and collapsing it like a cartoon, the table's legs splayed to the side.

Whittle sat up, one hand rubbing his bruised throat, the other holding his lower back.

"Frank Whittle," Kate said. "You're not safe here."

"No kidding, lady," Whittle said. "What is this about?"

"The Sweetbriar Prison fire," Kate said. "The hangman was a police officer. More will be coming. To finish what they started."

"You recognize the cop?"

"Hamish Thornton," she said. "Confirms Gray or Robinson as the mastermind behind this. The Thorntons are loyalists."

"Of course it was a Thornton," Andy said.

"Connor," Whittle said to himself, scrambling to his feet but falling back down. "If this is about Sweetbriar, they'll come after Connor, too."

◆ ◆ ◆

It was less than a minute's drive to Connor Beauchamp's split-level. They could hear sirens in the distance. No doubt responding to the gunfire at Whittle's house.

The ice cream truck that Andy had seen at the candy factory was parked out front. Two ten-year-old girls knocked on the window and tried to peer inside.

Whittle was out of the car first, surprisingly fast for a fat man.

"Damn it," Kate said. "Grab him."

The front door opened before they got to him. Kate reached for her gun. Rocco walked out, holding the doorknob and shaking his head. Whittle stopped in his tracks.

"You don't want to go in there," Rocco said.

"Who are you?" Whittle asked, trying to look past him.

"I'm the guy who didn't get here in time."

Whittle fell to his knees. He turned to Andy and Kate as if he didn't understand, but he understood all too well. His eyes filled with tears, a low moan bubbling in the back of his throat.

Rocco walked to Whittle and helped him up by one elbow. He put an arm around his shoulder. The fat man dug his face into Rocco's chest. Rocco let him.

"I need to see him," Whittle said, but there was no fight left in him. He made no effort to move closer to the house.

"No," Rocco said. "No, you don't. No good would come of that."

Rocco walked the lost man past Andy and Kate to the ice cream truck. He opened the back and helped the big man inside. Andy and Kate moved closer but kept their distance. The two girls watched with interest but said nothing.

"Connor," Whittle said. "He was a gentle man. Not what people thought. Gentle."

"I'm sure he was," Rocco said.

"Was," the man said, rolling the past tense over his tongue.

"We're going to take care of you," Rocco said. "You're safe."

"Doesn't really matter, does it?"

"You need to tell us where the prisoners from the Sweetbriar fire are. What you know."

"The fire. Connor tried to talk me out of it. Should have listened. It's my fault," Whittle said.

"We want to get the men who did this."

"He said that it was one of those things that's too big to stay secret. That it would blow up in our face. No such thing as easy money. I got Connor killed."

"Hey, mister," one of the girls yelled.

Rocco ignored her. "Do you know who hired you?"

"We got messages and money. Third-party threats and cash. I left the convicts at a warehouse down past Cedarville. That's where our part ended. Don't know where they went. Figured the less I knew, the better."

Rocco stared up at the sky for a moment, then back at the man. "I believe you, but we're going to need to talk more. If you get cold, there's a blanket in there." Rocco shut the back of the truck.

The two girls walked to Rocco, both holding up money.

"Hey, mister," the braver one said again.

"I'm closed," Rocco said.

"Give us ice cream," the girl demanded. "It's your job."

Rocco started to say something that began with the letter *F* but stopped himself. He threw open the back of the van, reached past the crying fat man, and grabbed two ice cream sandwiches. He handed them to the girls.

"I wanted a Bomb Pop," the girl said, pouting and holding the ice cream sandwich with two fingers like it stank. A foot stomp and downcast eyes, practiced moves that probably worked on her parents, didn't have the same impact on a former street thug turned covert criminal investigator.

Rocco took the ice cream sandwich from the girl's hand, dropped it on the ground, and stepped on it. Really ground it into the asphalt. He smiled at the other girl, reached into his pocket, and gave her twenty dollars.

"That's for not being an asshole."

CHAPTER 23

Street Gangs Consolidate: What's Next? A Trade Union
for Loan Sharks? The Arsonists & Kidnappers Guild?
Amalgamated Rapists?

—*Op-ed headline by Herbert Farr in the* Auction City
Intelligencer *(1978)*

Andy rode with Frank Whittle in the back of the ice cream truck.
The man spilled his story, eyes and mind somewhere else. He told
Andy how he'd been approached to bring messages to the prisoners,
followed by small gifts. The money was generous. He didn't question
it. The other guards had something on the side. Why shouldn't he get
his? He brought Connor into the scheme.

When they were told—not asked—to play their part in the fire,
escape, and cover-up, they initially refused. Threats to parents, siblings,
and random acquaintances eventually changed their minds. They knew
they were in over their heads when a van brought six corpses and a bag
of teeth to the prison. Every detail of the plan had been drawn out,
timed, and coordinated. After they dropped the men off, they never
heard from their benefactor again. Aruba, here they come. Or so they
thought.

Andy wrote down the Cedarville address where Whittle and Connor had delivered the convict all-star team, but that trail would be ice-cold. With a ticking clock, they needed tracks, not crumbs. They needed to know where the men were now, not months ago.

The ice cream truck pulled into the parking lot of Bruce Reiss Memorial High School. The campus had remained abandoned since a rendering plant accident that flooded the area with pig fat and blood. Three years had passed, but it still smelled like pork rinds aged in a vat of tar.

Andy got out of the back of the truck, a Choco Taco in hand. Whittle stayed in the back, staring into space. Rocco locked the door.

"Surprised you keep it stocked," Andy said, an ice cream headache hitting him fast and hard.

"It's all in the details," Rocco said.

"I didn't get much more from him."

"I heard," Rocco said. "What do you expect? The guy's in shock."

"You treated him with compassion," Andy said. "It's all you can really do."

"The man is hurting," Rocco said. "I understand pain."

Kate pulled up in the town car, got out, and joined them.

"Rocco," she said, "it didn't occur to me with everything going on. Where's Ben? Weren't you going to grab him on your way to the prison guard's place?"

"Couldn't find him. Didn't answer my pages," Rocco said. "Don't tell Pilar. She'll kill him."

"Let's hope it's Ben being Ben and not any more than that," she said.

◆ ◆ ◆

Consolidated was supposed to be meeting to formulate their response to the Costales assassination. When Andy, Kate, and Rocco walked into the school gymnasium, they were treated to a medieval melee. In the center of the basketball court, more than twenty people were beating the bejesus out of each other. A few men remained on their feet, fists ready, looking for their next opponent. Most of the others rolled on the ground, swinging, grasping, kneeing, biting. No weapons. A couple of women participated in the scrap, holding their own. Put a cage around them and you could charge five bucks a head.

The hardwood court was slick with sweat and blood. Combatants slipped, opponents taking advantage. Loose teeth crunched underfoot. A couple of participants lay unconscious, tired, or beaten, no longer fighting. It didn't save them from getting an insurance head stomp or a revenge groin kick. Old rivalries and layaway vengeance.

Pilar and Agnes leaned against the wall next to the entrance, stoically watching the rumpus play out. Agnes held an eight-pound dumbbell in a lazy hand. Pilar had settled for a Louisville Slugger. Two duffel bags sat at Agnes's feet. Kate walked to the two women. Andy stayed with Rocco by the door, lost in the spectacle of the violence. He couldn't tear his eyes away. Once one bout ended, another took its place. There was an illogical and emotional part of him that wanted to jump into the middle of it all.

Kate gave the bag a light kick, clacking metal inside.

"If we hadn't taken their guns, knives, and assorteds," Pilar said, "this could have gotten violent. Someone might have gotten hurt."

"I know how much you abhor violence," Kate said.

"It is good they fight," Agnes said. "Emotions are difficult for such people. They have a lot of anger and sadness and childlike confusion."

"They'll get tired. Most of them are in shitty shape," Pilar said. "Once they call winners and losers, all they'll have left in them is talking."

Kate motioned to a stack of folding chairs against the wall. "Good thing you hadn't set those up yet, or this could've gone George 'The Animal' Steele."

"Would've made it faster," Pilar said. "This is taking forever."

◆ ◆ ◆

Fifteen violent minutes later, the leaders of the ten gangs that made up Consolidated sat in a circle in the middle of the basketball court. Their seconds stood behind them, a little wobbly. The ones who couldn't sit or stand sprawled in the bleachers, staring at the ceiling or napping. Nobody had survived the fracas unscathed. Bruised faces, black eyes, cut lips, weird swells, bloody knuckles, torn clothes, missing teeth. Every color in the injury rainbow was represented. A chorus of heavy breathing with a few groans, the whole room sounded like a steam engine. Nobody bothered to clean the floor, all their blood pooling together.

Part of being a cop in Auction City was learning to identify the different criminal organizations—particularly the street gangs—by sight. Jackets emblazoned with names made it easy, but most wore simple additions that identified their affiliation: colorful bandanas, black armbands, tattoos. Hector Costales had consolidated the gangs, but that didn't mean they had given up their individual identities. Andy performed the roll call in his head. Lords of Death, Voodoo Posse, Cash Money Brothers, Ghetto Ghouls, Ghost Shadows, T-Birds, Crucifiers, Los Locos, Rogues, and, of course, Wretches.

Pilar stood in the center, a school principal scolding a bunch of middle-school students who'd just pantsed a substitute teacher.

"Now that the fronting is over, you ready to act like men?" She turned to the female leader of Los Locos. "And women?"

"He started it," someone said. A few of them laughed.

"Nothing funny about what's going on, *estúpido*," Pilar barked. "If you let Consolidated fall apart, you're pissing on Hector's grave. Out of respect, you'll put the bullshit aside and figure this out. You got no other choice. Apart you are weak."

"Who you calling weak?" someone said.

"You. All of you. Consolidated is the bottom of the ladder together. Apart, you'll disappear." Pilar put two fingers in her mouth and whistled loudly.

Twenty women marched into the gymnasium. All around the same age as Pilar. Mostly black and Hispanic, but a few white girls, too. They wore evening gowns, miniskirts with black fishnets, tank tops over long shorts and high socks—no consistency in their costumes. A few of the girls had disfigured faces: liar's scars, acid burns, worse. The others were missing at least one limb. Some wore prosthetics. They all carried weapons. At least the way they held the items in their hands made the ordinary implements look like weapons. Hammers, lug wrenches, gardening shears, a thick tree branch with some leaves still attached, a cast iron skillet, a bowling ball bag.

The women created a circle around everyone, saying nothing, bored eyes staring at Pilar. Waiting for their next order. Andy was glad to be outside the circle.

"You know who I am. What I am. What we are." Pilar held up her prosthetic arm as a reminder. "Tortured by bad men. Then abandoned by the people that found it too hard to look at us. Hector Costales gave me a chance. He gave all of us a chance. On Hector's orders, you were told to cooperate with me and my people in the event of his death."

"Just 'cause you want me to come out and play, don't mean I got to," the Rogues' leader said. A skittish, rodentlike man with crazy eyes. "Hector's gone. I don't take orders from a dead man."

"You weren't listening. You take orders from me. Until you—all of you—choose a new leader," Pilar said. "Someone to carry on what Hector started. I don't care who, so long as everyone agrees and there's no bad blood."

The leader of the Voodoo Posse—a tall Jamaican with clumpy, graying dreadlocks—stood up. "How you telling us what to do? Hector dead, mahn. No Hector, no Consolidated. Believe it."

"You really want that?" Pilar asked everyone. "For the gangs to split back up? Go back to turf wars, stupid grudges, fighting for scraps? Children instead of men? Some of you are that stupid, to be sure. But I ain't. Hector died for Consolidated. I won't let his death be the end of it."

"Who kill Hector?" the Jamaican said. "Everyone say the pigs."

"Could be someone in this gym, yo," the Ghetto Ghoul rep shouted. "Shit. Could be someone in his own crew." He pointed at the recently crowned leader of the Wretches.

The accusation didn't go over well. The Wretches leader jumped from his seat and ran at the thick black man, tackling him in the mid-section as he rose. "Hector was my brother!" he yelled. With a second wind, everyone stood to begin round two.

"No!" the twenty women shouted in unison, taking one step forward, a boom on the hardwood. The sound shook Andy's bones, more threat than warning. He wasn't the only one.

The men froze. They brushed themselves off and sat back down without a word.

"That shit don't get us nowhere, Javier," Pilar said. "Russel, you, too."

Javier spoke first. "Hector was my crime partner from all the way back."

"Your neighborhoods are burning," Pilar said. "While you sit here and circle jerk, your people are getting hurt. Business suffers. You're losing money. Someone needs to keep the streets from getting out of control. Not the cops—they want the city to burn. If there's too much violence, looting, the National Guard, the damn army comes in. You'll lose control of your blocks for good. Buildings burn, you got nothing but empty streets to do business. Nobody wins, that happens. Hector Costales dies for nothing."

"We vote," the Chinese leader of the Lords of Death said. "Nominations and votes. Like politicians but fair. Still United States. We're still Americans. Democracy."

"That's right," Pilar said.

"Fuck this," the stringy-haired biker from the Crucifiers said, standing and walking out of the circle until he was face-to-face with one of the women. "You going to get out of my way, *chica*?"

The one-legged woman stared blankly at the man. She turned slowly to Pilar.

"I got no problem hitting a bitch," the biker said. "Wouldn't be the first time."

Agnes walked behind the seemingly disinterested woman and tapped her on the shoulder. Agnes said, "I will take care of this, Monique." The woman stepped to the side, letting Agnes take her position. Agnes smiled at the Crucifier. "It is important that everyone participates in the democratic process. Voting is a privilege."

"I know who you are. I'm supposed to be scared of you, right?"

Agnes looked down at the dumbbell in her hand. "Would the world be a better place without you in it? If God took you, would your family cry or cheer?"

He breathed hard, a slight nose whistle. "What?"

"I will answer the question for you. As a member of Consolidated, maybe yes. You might serve a purpose. Outside Consolidated, I doubt your usefulness."

"Make your move, you black dyke."

The silence in the big room was deafening for that brief moment. Andy could feel the tension. Someone quietly said to themselves, "Oh, shit."

Agnes smiled.

"I seen her done it," the Cash Money Brother blurted out. "Messed this other brother up. Twice as big as you, dog. Did it with nothing but a coffee mug and a spoon. Motherfucker's in a wheelchair. Shits in a bag. Everyone knows you don't mess with Lady Luthor."

Agnes said, "I get the feeling you already defecate in bags. But as recreation, not necessity."

The biker threw a punch that never landed. Andy couldn't tell exactly what knocked the man unconscious. Probably the dumbbell, but he didn't see the impact. One second later, Agnes walked away and the biker hit the ground, unconscious before he landed.

"Damn," someone said.

Agnes turned to the Crucifier's second. "You've been promoted to interim leader. Do you want to leave as well?"

The biker looked at his former boss. He took a seat in the prone man's chair. "Let's vote on this sumbitch. Ain't nothing more American than democracy, right?"

"*Gracias*, Agnes," Pilar said. She scanned the crowd. "Choose a leader. I don't care how. Vote on it. Fight it out again. Leg wrestle. Measure your dicks. Do it. Make it unanimous. I'm going to leave you in the company of these fine young ladies. When you're done, everyone walks out friends. No bitching or complaining. Get back to making money. The city gets back to its regular screwed-up self."

❖ ❖ ❖

While they were inside the gymnasium, Frank Whittle had attempted to slash his wrists with the serrated edge of a saran wrap box. He only managed to make a mess, blood and melted ice cream covering the back of the truck. The cuts were so shallow he wouldn't even need stitches.

Rocco taped up the man's wrists. Whittle apologized the whole time, repeating "I'm sorry" until it became a mantra. Rocco finished, gave him a squeeze on the shoulder, and told him that everything was going to be okay.

Rocco walked to the others. "I'm going to take him to the Fortress. Make sure someone keeps an eye on him. Maybe get someone up there to talk to him. I'll catch up with you."

He drove the suicidal man away, playing the ice cream truck music. Maybe to try to cheer Whittle up. It was happy music.

Andy leaned on the front panel of the town car and listened to the radio. The gangs had been in the gym for fifteen minutes. Waiting for a group of thugs to choose a new leader was apparently an involved process. No roshambo or one-potato-two-potato for these guys.

Peaceful protests and not-so-peaceful ones had popped up all over the city. The news reader gave updates on which streets were closed because of crowd activity. All bus lines into the Ruins had been canceled. The subway still ran. A curfew had been issued for the entirety of the Ruins—referred to by its "real" name, Hampshire Court. In contrast, they made a point to tell the public that the Auction City Yacht Club Winter Cotillion would go on as scheduled regardless of any unrest.

The three women huddled around a bank of payphones. Andy turned off the radio and joined them. Kate doled out change.

"This is all I have left," she said. "Someone's going to have to make a run to the Laundromat on Capital and get more quarters."

"The guy gets mad when you use the change machine and leave. Like you're stealing," Pilar said.

"Well, if he does," Kate said, "have Agnes knock him unconscious with a dumbbell or a sock full of quarters."

"If I had quarters, we would not need change," Agnes said.

"It was a fair fight," Pilar said.

"It wasn't a fight," Kate said with a laugh.

"What are we doing?" Andy asked, to no one in particular.

"Trying to track down Ben," Kate said. "He doesn't know that he might be a target."

"Probably getting his *culo* waxed," Pilar said.

"After that," Kate said, "I don't know. Whittle was a dead end, and Beauchamp's just dead. We know we're looking for the escaped-convict hit squad, but no clue where they are. We can guess who their potential targets are—the leaders of the Trust and 893, Mac, Floodgate—but where does that get us?"

"What about the Thorntons?" Andy asked. "They're involved. We grab one. Give Agnes a pizza cutter and some tweezers and let her ask some questions."

"What would I do with the tweezers?" Agnes asked.

"Thorntons wouldn't talk," Pilar said. "Too dumb to understand pain."

"Hopewell and the other convicts have to make a move eventually," Kate said. "We concentrate on slowing the rioting. They'll stick their heads out at some point."

"That's seriously what you people consider a plan?" Andy said. "There's a small army of psychopaths hired by the police roaming the streets of Auction, and your plan is to wait?"

"Didn't think of it as a plan," Kate said. "More of a reality."

"They've been out of prison a couple months," Andy said. "That means they've been staying somewhere. Where? There's got to be a safe house. We check real estate under Gray, Robinson, his associates. That's off the top of my head. Haven't you run a real investigation? If they're armed, then they got the guns—and a lot of them, from the looks of the Costales crime scene—from someone. Could be supplied by the police themselves, but that could involve them being traced back. What if they got weapons somewhere else? Legally or illegally, there are only so many people that would deal in that kind of firepower. Where would you go to get a battalion's worth of artillery?"

Kate and Pilar looked at each other and said, "The Chief."

CHAPTER 24

The army psychiatrists wouldn't take me. Said I was too ready to kill. I suppose those head doctors know their business, but you'd've thought sending me to Germany would have been better. Can't see why they wanted me to kill Americans instead.

—From an interview with Macon Crouch, two days before his execution for killing ten people in the course of a three-day murder spree throughout Auction City and its suburbs (1945)

The industrial neighborhood had no foot traffic. Scattered vehicles lined the streets, trucks and panel vans. An anonymous area where work got done. Machinists, tap and die, and fabricators. A Greek diner offered blue plates on the corners, a raw egg in every beer.

The military surplus store and firing range fit the location, a concrete brick bunker with three layers of barbed wire circling the flat roof. A hand-painted sign read **CAMO & AMMO: FOR YOUR RECREATIONAL AND SURVIVAL NEEDS**. Steel trash cans and bags of garbage sat on the sidewalk in front of the store. Auction City garbage collectors weren't known for their regularity. Or their hygiene.

Kate got out of the car. Andy grabbed the door handle.

"You wait in the car," she said.

"I'm not a German shepherd. I thought I was on the team now." Andy caught the whine in his voice and adjusted. "I'm part of this, aren't I?"

"The Chief is—" Kate searched for the right word. "Let's say cautious. He's a gun trafficker that believes in the imminent collapse of the Zionist government. Meetings with the Chief are—for lack of a better word—delicate. They require a deft hand. Usually there's a month-long negotiation just to determine a meeting place and time. Walking straight in, asking questions, he's going to be vexed. And he's not going to forget last time."

"What happened last time?" Andy asked.

"Nothing much," Kate said. "I'm sure he's healed by now."

She removed all the weapons on her person, handing Andy two pistols, a throwing knife, a fighting knife, another knife, a small can of Mace, and a beavertail sap.

"You sure this is everything?" Andy asked. "No surface-to-air missile in your garter?"

◆ ◆ ◆

Waiting again. Andy hated waiting.

There was nothing visual to distract him. He tried to daydream, but it only brought him back to where he was. He considered leaving. Keys sat in the ignition. He could drive away, head in any direction. Out of the city, out of the state, away from everything. He could start over, leave Auction City behind him.

He still had Champ and wanted to spend as much time with her as he could before she no longer knew who he was. Then there was Rocco. What did he even do with that? What did you do when you'd been searching for something most of your life, and when you got it, it just was. He wished he was more angry or more happy to see the man.

Instead it felt as if he'd met some old guy. A new person in his life with the strange title of Dad.

Andy owed Auction City nothing. Based on his scorecard, it hadn't treated him all too well. Yet despite its awfulness and darkness and slime, it was the place he knew. It was his home. No other place would sit quite right. He knew what he hated about Auction. He'd have to learn all new things to complain about in a new city.

He didn't drive away because he was where he was meant to be. When you were a little bit crazy, a little bit crazy is the kind of life you were meant to lead.

Staying didn't mean that sitting in a car for twenty minutes worked for him. He needed to know what was going on. Curiosity was definitely going to be his undoing. They couldn't reveal part of a mystery, give him a peek into a strange new world, and then relegate him to the sidelines. Alice was going to catch that damn rabbit.

◆ ◆ ◆

Entering the alley next to Camo & Ammo, Andy kept to the shadows. The barred windows were blackened out from the inside and covered in razor wire. The back of the store abutted another building. No back door. He bet on a series of secret tunnels winding underneath the city like an ant farm.

Lines of barbed wire ran the perimeter of the roof. Andy put his shoulder to a dumpster, rolling it flush against the building. No stealth to the maneuver, louder than a dancing hunchback.

He attempted to climb on top of the lid, slipping and hitting his chin. He missed biting off the tip of his tongue but managed to chomp a little cheek. The taste of blood had become so familiar the last couple of days, he barely noticed.

On the next try, he clumsily scrambled onto the dumpster, dragging his gut over the edge. He stood on top of it and grabbed the eave of the building's roof and proceeded to not do a chin-up. Almost half of one, for anyone keeping score. He dropped back down, gave himself a pep talk, and tried again, arms shaking in spasms of failure. Unfortunately, pep talks didn't magically give one upper body strength. A good plan thwarted by a bad diet, no exercise, and moronic optimism.

Andy awkwardly hopped off the dumpster, skidding on the ground and landing on his back. He sat up, now convinced that the roof was a waste of time. Why try to get inside? He would disrupt the meeting, which was probably going well. Somewhere, the skeleton of Aesop laughed.

He walked back through the dark alley to the car, feeling like an idiot. Leave the cloak-and-dagger stuff to the professionals. He was a desk jockey, pure and simple.

But even an idiot can feel dumber.

He saw the man's gun before he saw the man. It took a few seconds to figure out what he was looking at, as the man wore a camouflage bodysuit and face paint. In a marvel of intricate detail, his body was painted exactly like the brick wall. To Andy it appeared as though the man had stepped out of the wall itself.

"You been there the whole time?" Andy asked.

The man said nothing, waving him toward the mouth of the alley.

"Did you watch me try to get on the roof?"

The man nodded.

"Don't tell anyone about that, okay? Kind of embarrassing."

Andy walked toward the man, the gun at his midsection.

"I'm here to talk to the Chief. I'm not a threat."

Brick Camo waved him toward the front entrance of the store.

Andy nodded. He looked up and down the street, hoping for a witness. No one. Nothing. He would have settled for a tumbleweed, just for the company.

He spotted movement from the corner of his eye. Agnes on the roof of the store. A blink of an eye, but he was sure it was her.

Things were about to get weird. Well, weirder.

Andy stopped when he reached the sidewalk. Brick Camo motioned him toward the door more aggressively.

"Sorry, man," Andy said. "I'm going to stand here and see what happens next."

Brick Camo never got the chance to respond. Agnes took him out. Nothing high-tech or fancy. No blow darts or stun guns for that scary lady. She threw something. Some metal cylinder. Whatever it was, she had a closer's cannon. Strike three, the man was out. It plonked off his head, knees spaghettied, and he dropped like a ton of camouflage bricks. Barely a sound.

The projectile rolled near Andy's feet. A can of soup. The woman had weaponized Campbell's Cream of Mushroom. Take that, Andy Warhol.

Andy grabbed the pistol from the unconscious man's hand. The trash in front of the store shifted. Brick Camo wasn't the Chief's only line of stealth defense. If not for the slight movement, Andy might have missed the man in a ghillie suit made out of garbage sitting among the trash cans near the entrance.

Before Garbage Suit could form a battle plan, Agnes went Wile E. Coyote on him. Higher ground appeared to be the advantage everyone claimed. She dropped something square and heavy directly on his head. A car battery. The sound made Andy queasy. If Garbage Suit was alive, his days of advanced calculus were behind him.

Andy waited for whatever came next. For the trash cans to become some kind of Gobot or the building itself to turn into an army of ninjas. He felt surrounded but couldn't detect the threat.

Nothing happened. Absolutely nothing. A whole rectum-loosening load of nothing.

Andy stood frozen. That was his plan. He was going to stand where he was and wait for someone to tell him what to do. He didn't care who it was. The next person he saw, he was going to do what that person said. Probably how Jehovah's Witnesses recruited.

After a minute, Agnes walked toward him, dragging a third man behind her. He was missing a foot, his leg wrapped in a tourniquet. The man left a wet trail in the dirty alley. Agnes leaned down to the one-footed man and spoke softly. She crossed herself and whispered in his ear.

"What did you do to him?" Andy asked.

Agnes looked up, her finger at her pursed lips. Andy shut up. She finished giving the man his last rites.

When she was done, she walked past Andy toward the town car.

"Where is that guy's foot?" Andy asked.

"The roof was covered in bear traps. He slipped."

She opened the trunk and lifted the spare tire. An organized arsenal rested underneath: pistol-grip shotguns, rifles, automatics. Agnes grabbed a handful of throwing knives.

"Firearms are for people that do not know how to fight," she said. "They are for the weak."

Andy watched her walk toward the store. He looked down at the pistol that he'd taken from Brick Camo, thinking about what Agnes had said. He shrugged and followed her. Because what the hell else was he supposed to do?

◆ ◆ ◆

The guy working the counter didn't reach. His hands were in the air the moment Agnes walked inside. Arms stretched so high, he probably pulled his latissimus dorsi.

The store was jam-packed with narrow aisles of camouflage gear, camping supplies, and military surplus. Everywhere Andy looked he found something that could kill, maim, or keep you alive in the event of Armageddon. Crossbows, throwing stars, knives, and swords. More swords than seemed practical. For all the potential destruction, it felt like a toy store.

Jesus Christ and God were represented, as well. Posters, Bible quotes, a staggering number of crucifixes, and what looked like life-size faux-stone Ten Commandments with an eleventh commandment scrawled into it: "Thou Shalt Not Trust the Government." Amen, brother.

"Heavy on the God stuff," Andy said.

Agnes gave him a look.

"Oh, yeah," he said. "Sorry."

She motioned to the door behind Counter Guy. A mounted sign over the door read SHOOTING RANGE—LOYALISTS WELCOME handwritten in a scrawl with a childlike drawing of a stick figure on a staircase. The frightened counterman found a key, unlocked the door, and threw it open. Without any prompting, he dropped to the ground facedown and spread his arms and legs.

A set of stairs led to the basement. Two gunshots echoed from below. Muffled and distant.

"What's the plan?" Andy whispered.

She pointed at the man on the ground and headed into the basement without answering. Andy assumed that he was meant to guard him.

"Don't worry about me, man," Counter Guy said. "I ain't moving. That's Lady Luthor, for sure. No joke. She'll ghost you."

More gunfire erupted from the basement.

CHAPTER 25

Aggression is the wise man's diplomacy. Rather than wasting time in compromise, empathy, or forgiveness, all one has to do is slap a face. Beautiful in its simplicity. There are millions of faces that would benefit from that slap. The slap of true awakening.

—*From the seven-volume* My Life on Seven out of Nine Planets: A Chronology of the Divine, *by Milt Walsh (aka Kinsman Titus), former leader of the Auction City–based Chosen Children of Ch'lil. Died by self-immolation minutes before the FBI raided his yurt (1975).*

Andy took aim at the open door to the basement. Hands steady, old instincts coming back. Ready to shoot someone. It wouldn't be the first time. Hell, it wouldn't be the first time in the last twenty-four hours.

Agnes's voice rose from the basement. "Tie the man up and then come down here."

Andy's knot skills proved seriously wanting. Gigantic mounds of rope, all quantity, no quality. The man he was trying to restrain talked him through a trucker's hitch, but Andy assed it up.

Andy slowly descended the stairs. In the narrow shooting range, an old man sat in the corner on a stool, holding his bleeding arm. A knife protruded from the wound. A pistol on the ground. Agnes stood near him, a throwing knife cocked. She'd caught a graze across her leg, some blood staining a tear in her pants.

"You didn't have to get violent, Agnes," the Chief said. "I wasn't going to hurt Girard none. Making a point about a thing is all. Making liars honest is what. There's a way I do things."

Kate sat tied to a chair at the far end of the shooting range. The target behind her had holes in it. The old man had shot around her. Some were inches from her. Andy did his best to undo the knots, but he was as bad at untying ropes as tying them. Fingernails bitten to nubs long ago, he couldn't get a good grip. After some clawing and biting, Andy ran upstairs and grabbed a survival knife that John Rambo would have called overkill. It sliced through the ropes like—well, like a knife through rope.

Feeling her red wrists, Kate walked with Andy to the Chief and Agnes. She leaned down, taking a look at Agnes's wound, but Agnes pushed her away.

"The pain keeps me sharp," Agnes said.

"You're ridiculous," Kate said.

The Chief looked closer to annoyed than scared. He wore a Hawaiian shirt, yellow shooting glasses, and a blue veterans' cap that read: USS TANGIER—PEARL HARBOR SURVIVOR. He was about sixty-five, a trim white beard and chest hair meeting at his throat. Loose skin revealed toned muscle underneath.

Kate put a finger in the Chief's face. "What the hell, Chief? How long have we known each other? Didn't give me a chance to tell you why I was here. Went right to shooting at me."

"I wasn't shooting at you. I was shooting around you," he said. "I have to assume that people—especially you people—are here to kill me. Best offense, you know."

Kate shook her head and turned to Agnes. "How did you know I was in trouble?"

"You were in trouble the moment you walked inside. The Chief is mad."

"How many bodies?" Kate asked.

Agnes looked down at her feet. Kate turned to Andy.

"One dead, one alive, one maybe," he said.

"You killed one of my boys?" the Chief said.

"He had trouble negotiating your own defenses. The roof is dangerous," Agnes said.

"They're still outside?" Kate asked.

"In the alley. In a pile," Agnes said.

Kate shook her head. "Take Destra. Clean up whatever mess you made. The Chief and I are going to chat."

"You want me to talk to him?" Agnes winked at the Chief.

"That won't be necessary, you bald psychotic," the Chief said. "I'm a survivalist. And survival is all about adapting to the environment."

◆ ◆ ◆

"You sure this is the guy we should be talking to?" Andy said. "The Chief looks to me like any other end-of-the-world whackjob. All Jesus and guns."

"Jesus is our Lord and Savior."

"Right," Andy said. "I knew that."

"Do not underestimate the Chief," Agnes said. "He's a decorated war veteran. Auction City's main source of third-party guns, information, and, on occasion, he brokers paramilitary activity in town."

"Is there a big need?"

"These are troubling times," Agnes said. "Now grab the garbage-covered man's feet."

Andy reached down and picked up his half of Garbage Suit. A slight groan told him that the man was alive. Andy was relieved that the ghillie suit covered his face. He never wanted to know what kind of damage the car battery had done to the man's head.

Agnes slapped Brick Camo hard. He came out of his daze, staring glassy-eyed at Andy and Agnes. Sweat streaked some of the greasepaint from his face. He tried to focus.

"You could've killed me, Agnes," the man said.

"But I didn't. Did I, Steve?"

"You two know each other?" Andy asked.

"We train at the same dojo," Agnes said. "Master Hong would never forgive me if I'd killed him. Teacher's pet."

Andy helped up the man and walked him toward the store.

"How long did it take to put on that paint?" Andy asked.

◆ ◆ ◆

Walking into the store from the basement, Kate wiped the blood on her hands onto a handkerchief. The cuts on her knuckles looked red and raw.

"There's more than violence, you know? Other ways to get answers. Subtler ways," Andy said. "The man said he would talk."

"This?" Kate looked at her hands. "This is from after he talked. For tying me up and shooting at me. You let things like that go, people do it again. The Chief actually asked to be hit one extra time to ensure there was no grudge. Although I'm thinking now, he may be into that kind of thing."

"It's your world, not mine," Andy said.

"He supplied weapons to the convicts we're looking for," Kate said. "At least he's pretty sure it was our guys. And the timeline makes sense. The same kind of deal as the guards. A blind drop. Money in one place. Weapons in another. Never had direct contact. Third-party contacts. A truckload of firearms and explosives."

"Another dead end," Agnes said.

"He gave us what he knows," Kate said.

"Are you kidding me?" Andy said.

"If you've got a better way of doing this, feel free," Kate said.

"All I've seen you guys do is bust heads. Lazy shortcuts. Beating confessions. Have you ever actually run an investigation? A real one? One that requires work?"

"Our success rate is impeccable," Kate said.

"Because everyone is dead, I bet. Unnecessary killing." Andy shook his head. "It's not about what he knows. It's what he doesn't know he knows."

Andy walked past Kate and headed down the stairs. In the basement, the Chief looked comfortable in his restraints. He watched Andy curiously. The Chief looked like Kate had tuned him up good, but that didn't stop him from smiling through bloody teeth.

"I prefer to be hit by women," the Chief said. "It's a proclivity. There's an intimacy to a woman punishing me that I find arousing."

"I did not need to know that," Andy said.

"I don't believe I know you."

"I'm a prisoner slash consultant. Call me Andy."

"Not the most intimidating name. The name of a ventriloquist's dummy."

"Did you hear about Hector Costales?" Andy asked, looking for somewhere to sit but settling on leaning against the wall.

"Bit of a massacre is what I heard."

"Do you know Norman Hopewell?"

"Knew, not know. Hopewell is dead. Prison fire. What does one got to do with the other?"

"But you knew him?"

"Our paths crossed. Similar lines of work. Parallel interests. A good customer."

"Tell me what you know about him. Whatever comes to mind."

Andy heard footsteps behind him—Kate descending the staircase. Arms crossed over her chest as she leaned against the doorjamb, she looked unimpressed.

"I'm guessing he's not as dead as everyone says." The Chief stared at the ceiling. "He could've took out Costales. Military, brutal, organized. Left the kid alive, right? Yeah, he might be the guy. If he was alive."

"What is Hopewell like?"

"Norman sees himself as a leader of men, prefers to give orders not take them. Loves talking military history, but I don't think he understands most of it. One of those dangerous muttonheads that thinks he's smart. Considers himself a legendary pussyhound, but all his stories were about hookers from around the world. Doesn't seem like it counts as a triumph if all you had to do was pay. Charm, not money, should get you in a broad's pants. Ain't that right, Kate?"

"It's why you turn me on so much," Kate said.

The Chief gave her a wink as best he could through his swollen eye.

"Shut up. Both of you," Andy said. He turned to Kate. "How long were these men in prison?"

❖ ❖ ❖

Using the store phone, Kate called Rocco and told him to meet her and Andy at Madame LaFleur's brothel.

Agnes would stay and make restitution with the Chief. He was still a powerful man within the community. Penance was due for the loss of his men. They would negotiate the cost. The apologetic healing power of cash, a long-standing Church tradition.

Andy waited by the front door, thumbing through a stack of Jack Chick tracts.

Resting on the ground and looking only slightly healthier, Steve, the man in the brick camo, said, "Hey, buddy."

Andy nodded. "How you feeling?"

"I'm centered in mind and body," he said. "But it'll be a time before I go down the canned soup aisle again."

Kate hung up and joined Andy at the front door.

Steve reached into his shirt and held out a thin paperback book to Andy. He took it and looked at the cover. *The Royal Canadian Mounted Police 12-Week Exercise Program.*

"Changed my life," Steve said. "Next time, you'll be able to make it onto the roof. Be able to do a chin-up."

Andy looked at Kate. She shook her head.

"Thanks, pal," Andy said. "I thought that was between you and me."

"You're going to have to suck in your gut until then," Kate said, patting his belly. "That is, if you want to impress the girls at the whorehouse."

CHAPTER 26

Let me get this straight. It's legal to do for free. But if I get paid for the same thing, it's a crime? The action isn't illegal. It's the transaction that's against the law? That's not only ridiculous, it's downright un-American.

> —From Geraldine Fossett's court statement defending
> herself against a felony charge of pandering. She was
> convicted but served no time. One year later, she married
> the judge (1985).

Rocco had arrived before them, waiting in front of a nondescript brownstone in the quiet neighborhood. He leaned against the fender of a car, smoking a cigarette and feeding some pigeons torn-off crusts of bread.

"I didn't know you smoked," Andy said as he and Kate approached.

"A person doing something is less conspicuous," Rocco said, handing the cigarette to Kate and dumping the rest of the bread crumbs. "What took so long?"

"Streets are closed. More people out," Kate said, taking a drag of the cigarette. "Less in this neighborhood, but in the areas where people don't own washer/dryers, it's getting worse."

The smell of smoke had begun to fill the city. Faint, but enough to put a tickle in the back of Andy's throat.

"You ain't going to believe it." Rocco pointed at a Ford Ranchero across the street. Tricked out. Bright red with flames painted on the side.

"I am going to kill that son of a bitch," Kate said.

"What? Who?" Andy said.

◆ ◆ ◆

Ben Jigo was surprised to see his coworkers. That's what happened when you were handcuffed to a bed with two naked prostitutes doing things to you with a candle and its wax, and said coworkers kick in the door to find you in that compromising position. He didn't appear that put out, although his carnal interest visibly waned.

Andy and Kate followed Rocco into the room. They took in the tableau. Andy had never been to New Orleans, but the red velvet walls and satin sheet made him think of the baroque. The nude women made him think of nude women.

"Hey, guys," Ben said, grinning. "I was working, but I got a little tied up."

Nobody laughed.

"Ladies," Rocco said, "your services are no longer needed. Madame LaFleur is aware of the matter."

"They haven't been paid, so if you could toss them a few bucks," Ben said. "I'm a lot of things, but a cheapskate isn't one of them. They worked their butts off."

"Not quite off," Kate said, admiring their young bodies.

Rocco looked around the room, found Ben's pants on the ground, and dug through the pockets for his wallet. He pulled out all the money and handed it to the girls.

"Are you crazy? I'm not that generous. That was like a grand," Ben said.

"Just the tip," Rocco said with a wink. "Thank you, ladies."

The two naked women took their time picking up their clothes. Andy realized that it had been a while since he'd been with a woman. He'd been so focused on his investigation that his libido had shut down beyond necessity. The last time he'd masturbated, he'd fantasized about a previous time that he'd masturbated.

One of the girls touched Andy's shoulder and winked as she passed through the doorway. Unflappable. That was professionalism. True salesmanship. He felt a stirring, a slight motion down there.

"Shut the door, son," Rocco said.

Nothing like a father's voice to ruin the mood. Andy closed the door, getting a last look at their bare behinds.

"This is a low for you, Jigo," Rocco said. "We got a genuine god-damn crisis. City's burning. People fighting. Thorntons running rough-shod. One dead leader. Killers with targets on the loose. Hell, you got a bullseye on you. And we find you here. Like this."

"You going to uncuff me, Rocky?" Ben asked. "The keys are on the nightstand. Unless Kate wants to explore her curiosity. There's still some wax, and this nipple was severely neglected."

Kate sat on the corner of the bed. "Pretty cocky for someone in handcuffs. Although cocky would be an overstatement considering the tackle you're sporting."

"They blast the air-conditioning in here," Ben said, then turned to Rocco. "Look, I get it. The thing is, I don't care about all that stuff. About Floodgate or 893 or any of it. I wanted to be a ska guitarist. My uncle made me part of this group, but nothing says I got to be good at it. Or even try. All this shit is happening. Riots, that's crazy. I figured, hole up somewhere safe. From there, I decided to just hole up. You see what I did? Hole?"

"Yes, we got the subtlety of your quip," Kate said.

"I'm not good at any of this stuff. On the street or at a desk, it bores me stupid. Can't excel at something you hate."

Rocco shook his head, picked up the key, and undid the handcuffs. Ben sat up, putting a pillow over his crotch.

"Don't tell Pilar, okay?" Ben said. "She'll kill me. Seriously, she'll fake-arm-crush my larynx. You know she will."

"Get dressed," Kate said. "We're going to have a long talk about how the rest of this day is going to go."

Ben opened his mouth to say something, but he saw something in Kate's demeanor. He nodded. "Yes, ma'am."

◆ ◆ ◆

Madame LaFleur looked and sounded the part of a whorehouse madam—pillowy cleavage squeezing out of a tight black corset, and a light French accent. She walked Andy and Rocco through the front room and past three tired, scantily clad women and one wide-eyed sailor in a crackerjack uniform.

"We can talk in my office," the madam said.

Her office shattered the facade. Andy expected Bourbon Street but got Conglomerated Amalgam Industries. All business. An industrial-strength steel desk that would have looked appropriate in a construction site trailer acted as the room's centerpiece. Filing cabinets, stacks of papers, a bulletin board with notes. Fax machine and a home computer. There was a "Hang in There" poster with a kitten hanging from a tree, for Christ's sake.

Rocco and Andy took a seat as Madame LaFleur parked herself behind her desk. She took off her beehive wig and rested it on a mannequin head.

"Thing weighs forty pounds, I swear," she said, squeezing the back of her neck.

"How's tricks, Sheila?" Rocco said.

"Same joke every time, Rocky," she said. "You know how it is. Between the twenty houses, I got upward of four hundred on staff.

Always a fire to put out. A boiler out in one place—then we're out of lube in another. Price of doing business. Priorities met, though. I keep their pensions stable, their medical insurance up-to-date, and the daycare people happy. It's a logistical nightmare. But as much as I complain, I can't complain."

"Paperwork. No matter what you do, there's always paperwork," Andy said, more to himself.

"Who is this?" she said.

"Andrea Destra," Rocco said. "He's working with us."

"Andy. Nobody calls me Andrea."

"You two related?" she asked. "He could be your grandson."

"How old do you think I am?" Rocco said.

"How old is dirt?" She laughed. "You wouldn't be the first grandfather bringing his grandson to a whorehouse to make him a man. It's a tradition in some families."

"Families have weird traditions."

"You don't even know the half of it. Some of them are downright immoral." The woman stood and held out her hand. "I'm Sheila McCormick. Madame LaFleur is for the customers."

Andy stood and shook her hand. A firm handshake. "Nice to meet you, Madame—Sheila."

"You look familiar," she said. "Did you used to have a regular Thursday appointment at Panda Massage on Exposition? With Kiki?"

Andy shook his head, sweat forming on his brow. "Nope. Not me. I have one of those faces."

"We need information about some clients you may have had," Rocco cut in. "Maybe came to one of your shops. More likely a call out, house call."

"You know my policy about confidentiality," she said, bristling a little.

"You exploit women," Andy said, "but you draw the line at giving up a john?"

Rocco put his face in his hand.

Sheila gave Andy a hard stare. "While I can see why you would assume my girls are exploited—there's a history in this profession—I assure you they are not. There is no coercion. No one forced to do anything they don't want to. I can't control what brought them here, but all—all of them—are in a better circumstance. When laws are stupid, I find no reason to obey them. The girls are well compensated, protected, and beyond normal problems, happy. It's just sex. Leave your Sunday morning morality in your other pants."

Andy nodded and looked at his shoes, not knowing what to say.

"All of this is new to Andrea."

"Andy," Andy said instinctively.

"He used to be a cop," Rocco said. "They put ideas in his head."

"Some of our best customers."

"We need to know about these clients," Rocco said, "but don't worry. We're not going to make the information public. We aren't going to blackmail anyone. Or hurt them. They're already dead."

◆ ◆ ◆

Sheila McCormick hung up the phone, made some notes on the pad in front of her, and flipped through her Rolodex. Rocco set down the book he'd picked up, *The Winner's Guide to Time Management*. Andy had spent his time thinking, although he couldn't remember what he'd been thinking about. He essentially stared into space the whole time. His brain had probably been so confused that it just needed to shut down for a bit.

"That's all of them," Sheila said. "There's a couple independent outfits, but they don't keep records, and there's a chance in hell they'll talk to me. Got one that fits what you're describing from Hands On Exotic. They have delivery service. A new regular. Nice neighborhood. Always asked for four women—one of them black or Asian. Every three or four days. Nothing too weird. Five guys, then four. I talked to one of the girls, she said it may have been a hideout, but it could have been roommates who were slobs. Take-out containers and pizza boxes, the window shades always down. They were polite and paid. One of them was Hawaiian or Samoan, if that means anything."

"That's them," Rocco said. "The address?"

"You didn't get this information from me. You weren't here." She tore off the piece of paper from her notepad and slid it across the table. Rocco took a look at it.

"You've got to be kidding me. We were just there," Rocco said. "It's in the same damn neighborhood as those two guards. Is everyone in the Hollow in on this whole scheme?"

◆ ◆ ◆

Outside the brothel, Andy huddled with Rocco, Kate, and Ben.

"Are we on the same page?" Kate said, directed at Ben.

He nodded. "No guarantees I'll be any help, but I'll try. I get it, I guess."

"Ben and I will head back to the factory, get all the gear and weapons we need," Rocco said. "You and Andy coordinate with Agnes and Pilar. We'll need a few of her girls."

Everyone looked at each other. Nothing else to say. Rocco and Ben walked away in opposite directions to their cars.

Kate gave Andy a light punch on the arm. "How you holding up, sport?"

"When the ocean rages around you and you don't even have a set of arm floaties, you don't have to think. You just have to swim."

"When I picture you in water, I picture you in arm floaties," she said.

"Manly arm floaties," he said. "Sexy, manly arm floaties."

"Very sex—"

But the explosion interrupted Kate. The explosion that knocked both Andy and Kate back into the brick building. The explosion that sent a burst of flame and charred metal in their direction. The explosion that blew out their eardrums and singed their eyebrows. The explosion that killed Ben Jigo instantly.

1929

LONG PAST DAYS

Who brought a cannon to a respectable fight? This was an Auction City street corner, not the Gettysburg Address. There were no limits to a Chinaman's savagery.

Like everyone else, I looked to Fat Jimmy. He was our boss. He must have a plan. Know what our next move was. But he wasn't looking at the cannon. Or the Chinese. He was looking down the street. At his own pace, a collared priest in one of those priest dresses strolled between the two warring parties.

The priest was short. The size of a boy. But I knew plenty of sturdy bantams. Runts needed to be tougher. Little legs, big balls, what my pal Yodels Tooley used to say. Yodels looked like a racetrack jockey but fought like a drunk gorilla.

The priest wasn't Yodels. But must've had matching testicles. Two armies watched. A thousand men. On the brink of large-scale murder. The small man walking into no man's land. Fat Jimmy's barricade on one side. A Chinese mob with a damn cannon on the other. The priest, no weapons. Not even a Bible. Smiling as if he just got cake.

The shouted swears of Fat Jimmy's boys stopped. A few crossed themselves. Glanced around confused. Stared out at the mad monk.

I'd always known priests were crazy. Too many commandments. All these things you can't do. No touching girls. Heaven ain't worth it. No wonder priests drank.

A long-haired Chinaman stepped forward from the mob. A foot taller than the men next to him. Their leader. His wispy beard sideways in the breeze. He reached back to one of his men. A sword appeared in his hand. Long and curved, oriental steel stained with blood.

Voices called out from among Jimmy's men.

"The Chink's going to kill the father."

"Should we shoot?"

"Don't worry. He's got God on his side."

"Right now, I'd rather have the devil."

The Chinaman took two steps forward. The priest reached into his shirt and pulled out some sheets of paper. Held them in the air. Waved them like a white flag. He would probably say what he did next was beseech. He beseeched. Shouted strange words in the direction of the Chinese. A white man talking in that crazy oriental felt wrong. The Chinaman answered back. The priest responded.

"What the hell are they saying?" someone asked no one.

They fell silent. The Chinaman nodded and lowered his weapon. The tip of the sword clanging on the road.

The priest turned to Fat Jimmy. "The Church has a solution. A plan to broker a deal between the conflicting parties. The fighting, it is about money, territory, power. All of that can be returned to you and more. A lot more. We believe that agreeable terms would be reason for the violence to stop. No more death. No more destruction."

"I lost a lot of men," Fat Jimmy said.

"So did they. So did everyone in this city," the priest responded. "No matter what set the war in motion, you aren't fighting for that anymore. This morning is the past. I'm talking about the future."

"We all going to pray together?" Fat Jimmy said. "Can't trust these heathens."

"They need not believe in God. As long as they believe in the Church. Our particular skills and financial acumen. Money can be made, Mr.

Furgele. For everyone. For you. For Chou Han. For all. More than before. The city can rise again. And you can rule it."

"More than before?" Fat Jimmy repeated. "I'm coming out there, padre. It sounds like we should talk."

"In the spirit of peace," the priest said. "No arms."

"My fists don't come off, but I promise not to use them," Fat Jimmy said. Dropped the ax handle and the pistol. Opened his jacket, turned. Walked into the open.

The Chinaman watched. Grunted strange orders to his men. Jammed the sword into the mortar on the street. Joined the holy man and Fat Jimmy Furgele.

❖ ❖ ❖

An hour later, I felt a hand on my elbow. Small, intimate. Not the way a friend touches you. I turned.

The girl stood in the door. Looked up at me.

"What do you think they're talking about?" the girl asked. Not explaining why she was still there. Why she hadn't run. What she'd been doing the last hour. She kept one hand on my elbow. The crowd dense. Her body pushed into mine.

"They're talking," I said. "That's the thing."

The three men had been out there so long chairs had been brought to them. And a table. And wine. They whispered. They yelled. Twice, Fat Jimmy stood to walk away. Rejoined. At one point, the Chinaman laughed. I didn't know they could. The world was a queer and perplexing place.

"Do you think the fighting is over?" she asked. "That things will go back to the way they were?"

"The way they were ain't no more."

"I wouldn't trust a Chinaman. Or the Church. Or your boss. Low types, the lot of them."

"And who are you? Miss Lady Farthington?" I said, mad at her for the first time. Calling Fat Jimmy low was calling me low. "I thought you left."

She looked hurt. "I still can."

"No," I said. "Just take it easy with the smart talk. We, none of us, are better than any of anyone else."

"All men know is fighting," she said.

"Wars end. Not when everyone's dead, but in the middle. When there's still people alive to sign a treaty."

The city still burnt. Heat from the fires trapped by the inky smoke that filled the sky. My lungs burnt. My eyes watered. Blew my nose. The snot, what wasn't bloody, was gritty and black.

I looked down at the girl. Small. Tough. Pretty as found money. I didn't know where she came from. Who she was. Only knew that moment. Because moments were all we had.

Three gunshots cut the silence. I jumped, used to the false peace. Gunfire had continued but from a distance. This was close. Next to us.

Spines tensed. Hearts skipped. Breathing stopped. Everyone shifted, got ready. Weapons clanged. Guns raised.

The men in the center all stood. Fat Jimmy dropped his wine glass and turned to us. Held his hands up to his men. The long-haired Chinese warrior to his.

"It's okay," Fat Jimmy said. "Don't do nothing."

One of Fat Jimmy's men pointed and shouted. "What the hell are they doing here?"

In an ersatz military march, a hundred men and women in torn and tattered clothes approached. Negro, Irish, Gypsy, South American, Finn, Persian, and from places I had never heard. The Wretches. Immigrant gangs and alley thugs. Feared and loathed. Different and other. They held crude weapons fashioned from metal and wood. Handmade. Indescribable. Heavy and wrong. Sharp edges. Red with rust and blood.

"I was wrong," I said. "We should go."

"Can't leave now," the girl said. "It just got interesting."

And then it got more interesting. The coppers arrived.

1986

CHAPTER 27

The building was there. Right there. Then boom. It was gone. And there was fire. All kinds of fire. It burned in colors I ain't never seen. Flames like hot rainbows. The man died in something beautiful.

—Eyewitness description of the Chedda Brothers Painting Supply fire. Rahul Chedda perished in the fire. An insurance investigation led to charges against the victim's brother, Akshat Chedda. He served fifteen years. Three hours after his release, he killed himself by jumping off the King Olaf Bridge (1969).

Andy tried to snap out of his daze. Shook his head, confused. The world had capsized, erupting in brightness and sound. His pupils were pinholes, the world grainier and grayer. The only thing that registered was the burning car. Not a car anymore, but twisted metal, flames, and black smoke. He swam in muffled silence, a ringing approaching from deep underwater.

Kate sagged on the ground, her back against the brick wall that they had been thrown against by the force of the explosion. Andy crawled to her and checked her pulse. A heartbeat and shallow breath, but alive. A rough inhale turned into slow gasping. A jagged piece of metal jutted from her shoulder, blood boiling at the edges of the wound. Instinctively, Andy reached to pull it out, but withdrew his hand when it burned him. The skin on his fingertips stuck to the hot metal and peeled off.

Andy's face stung. He reached up, cutting his hand on a piece of glass jutting from his cheek. A body check revealed no more visible wounds, but he ached all over. No consolation, considering the genuine possibility of internal injuries.

He stood, but his legs gave underneath him, knee hitting the curb. With his hands against the wall for balance, like a kid afraid to let go of the pool edge, he found his feet. The heat from the burning car was almost unbearable. If not for the rest of his pain, he wouldn't have been able to stand it.

He leaned down and took hold of Kate's upper body, dragging her toward the front door of the brothel.

Rocco reached them and took the other side of Kate. The brothel door opened. Sheila McCormick stood with a double-barrel shotgun. The sailor ran outside to help carry Kate inside.

"Call an ambulance!" Andy yelled. "She's hurt bad."

They carried her up the front stairs, Andy and the sailor on either side of her, Rocco carrying her legs. Kate mumbled a few words but didn't wake. The sound of gunfire erupted, and the sailor spun and fell. Andy shifted to keep from dropping Kate.

"Inside, inside!" Sheila yelled. "Someone's shooting."

As Andy reached the door, he looked down to the sailor. The dead man stared back, one lifeless eye, the other shot out. That's what he got for trying to help.

They rushed inside, a few more shots. Brick chipped near the entrance. Sheila closed the door and set a series of locks. Closed a vault-like steel door behind it. Andy and Rocco set Kate on the divan.

Andy went to the window and cautiously peeked from behind the curtain. No movement. Only the burning car. The shape of Ben's head and shoulders still visible in the rising flames, one hand on the steering wheel. Andy watched him burn.

A hole appeared in the window. He didn't hear the shot.

"Get away from there!" Rocco yelled. Advice Andy didn't need. He moved next to Kate. Rocco inspected her wound.

Phone receiver cradled in the crook of her neck, Sheila said, "All hell's broken loose. Riots and demonstrations. Streets too full to get cars through. Nine-one-one put me on hold. I'm listening to Night Ranger."

"On a good day, ambulance takes more than an hour," Rocco said.

Sheila hung up the phone. "Doesn't matter. The phone went dead."

"How strong is that front door?" Rocco asked.

"Cops raided the place last week," Sheila said. "Door broke their battering ram."

"First aid kit?" Rocco asked.

Sheila left and returned with medical supplies. She kneeled next to Kate, touching the metal with the tip of her finger. She withdrew her hand and put on a pair of leather gloves.

"I need your help," she said to Andy.

Andy kneeled next to her.

"We pull this hunk of metal out, Kate's going to bleed like Niagara," Sheila said.

"If we leave it in?" Andy asked.

"Won't be able to stop the seep she's got going. Never good to have foreign objects protruding out of a person."

Kate's eyes popped open and darted around, unfocused and wild. She looked from Sheila to Andy to Rocco. Putting her weight on her bad shoulder, she tried to stand. When the pain hit, she screamed. Sheila and Andy did their best to hold her down.

"Get off me. Let me go!" Kate shouted.

Rocco grabbed Kate's face in her hands. Held her until her eyes focused on his. Rocco spoke slowly. "Car explosion. You're wounded. Ben is dead. You're safe, but we got no time. This is going to hurt. A lot." He pulled a leather knife sheath from his jacket and placed it between Kate's teeth.

Rocco turned to Sheila. "Do it."

Sheila wrenched the shard of metal from Kate's shoulder. It made a fizzing sound that Andy wanted to forget. Dark-red blood oozed from the wound. Kate moaned and squeezed Andy's wrist, veins bulging and hand turning white. Andy didn't make any effort to break her grip even though it hurt like hell. Kate's eyes were wild with pain, darting back and forth, and then she mercifully passed out.

Sheila poured styptic powder into the wound, followed by a handful of gauze, putting as much pressure on it as she could. Red blossomed from its center. Holding the gauze in place, she tightly wrapped the wound with bandages and tape. "Edges cauterized from the heat already. The chitosan will stop the bleeding. Not the worst I've seen. But nothing clean about that wound. Field dressing will do for now, but she needs a doctor."

A volley of shots shattered the window, pockmarking the wall above their head. They ducked, Rocco laying his body over Kate.

Andy peeled Kate's fingers from his wrist one at a time, her grip not giving, even unconscious. He looked down at his hands. Kate's blood. Some of his own. He grew dizzy. "Back door?"

Sheila pointed over her shoulder, her gloved hands bloodier than Andy's.

Rocco stared at Andy for a moment and then reached for his face. Andy flinched and then felt immediate warmth. Rocco held a small piece of glass when Andy backed away.

"Bleeding's not bad. We'll patch you up later," Rocco said.

Andy nodded and made his way to the back of the brothel. Behind him, he heard Rocco say, "Do you have a police scanner? Something monitoring their calls?"

"Who do you think I am? An amateur?" Sheila said.

◆ ◆ ◆

There were no windows near the solid-looking back door. Good for security, but no way of seeing what was behind it. Peering through the vertical mail slot into the alley behind the brothel, Andy saw nothing at first. Until he caught movement behind a stack of pallets. The man wasn't trying to hide, using the wood as cover.

Andy recognized Stu or Lou Wells from the newspaper article about the supposedly deceased convicts. His Uzi looked like a ukulele from a distance, a big man with a small instrument. Small but deadly.

"One of the Wells boys is out back," Andy said, returning to the main room.

"Figures," Rocco said. "The other one'll be out front."

"Do we try to take them?" Andy asked. "Two against two."

"No promise there ain't no backup. And we got no idea what explosives they're packing," Rocco said. "If Agnes were here, I'd like our odds. But just me and you, I don't know."

"You better listen to this," Sheila said.

A police scanner could be like listening to the news in Polish. If you spoke Polish, it made sense. You could sit back and enjoy the weather (bleak), sports (How can both teams lose?), local news (Invaded again?). But if you don't know the language, it's impenetrable.

Andy and Rocco spoke the language fluently. And the scanner informed them that a lot had happened in the last ten minutes.

The bomb that had killed Ben Jigo wasn't the only explosion that had gone off in the city. A restaurant in Little Nagasaki had been hit. The narthex of the Church of the Seven Martyrs had been destroyed. The fifth floor of an office building near downtown had caught fire, raining glass on pedestrians below. Riots and looting had grown in the Ruins. Buildings burned as firefighters got spread thin. Gunfire had been reported throughout the city. The bridges were backed up with car and pedestrian traffic as people fled.

For all that mayhem, the dispatcher repeated the same orders to the officers on the street. Stand down. Stay back. Assist firefighters. Protect the precinct buildings. Certain other buildings. Protect specific neighborhoods. An idiot could guess which ones. Stay out of harm's way. Close streets. Cordon off areas. Let the slums burn. Let the people fight. Let the opportunists loot. The official order was to do nothing. Let history happen.

"These had to be coordinated explosions," Andy said. "It's the kind of thing Gray could conceive of, using the unrest on the streets to sneak in some violence of his own. Blow up some buildings. Blame it on the rabble."

"We need to put an end to this," Rocco said.

"And how do we do that?"

"I don't know. First we have to get out of here alive," Rocco said. "Didn't mean to bring this to your doorstep."

"Cost of doing business, but you're on your own now. I got to keep my girls safe," she said. "We're going to hole up. Wait this out. I would suggest you join us, make it a party, but Katie needs a doc."

"Any adjoining roofs?" Andy asked. "Some other way to get Kate out of here? Get around the shooters?"

"The roofs won't work. Too much space between. Different heights," Sheila said. "There's another possibility, but I don't know if it's a better option or just a different one."

"Tell us," Rocco said. "We need to move."

"Follow me to the dungeon."

CHAPTER 28

We all lost friends. We lost family. Our possessions. And
our homes. We almost lost our city. But we're still here, and
so is our city. And by God, we have each other. We have the
great people of Auction City. What we rebuild will be better
and stronger and stable, because we are united. We are
one. We are Auction.

—From a speech given by Mayor Homer Maxwell, cutting
the ribbon at the groundbreaking for the new city hall to
replace the original destroyed in the Flood (1931)

With an arm around her waist, Andy half walked, half dragged
the semiconscious Kate down the low-ceilinged corridor. Rocco
led the way, ten yards ahead. The beam of his flashlight cut through
the blackness. The ground grew damp. The passage sloped down. The
spiderwebs that missed Rocco enveloped Andy's face. He inhaled
web—and probably spider and spider eggs—gagging but continuing
his trudge forward, the taste of dusty cotton candy.

Kate groaned and mumbled something. Andy stopped to get a
better grip.

"I could use a little help!" Andy shouted.

"You're fine," Rocco said. "Keep your damn voice down. I get the feeling a loud enough noise will collapse this bastard."

Andy glanced at the wooden braces, crude and damaged. The walls seeped water, pooling at the edges. If it hadn't collapsed in the hundred years it had been there, what were the odds it would collapse today? Right?

Kate stared wide-eyed at Andy, taking a second to figure out what was happening. In the faint light, her face shifted from confusion to something harder.

After a moment, she asked, "Who did this? And how do I kill them?"

◆ ◆ ◆

Andy had postulated that the Chief had a secret tunnel, but, in fact, it was Sheila McCormick, nee Madame LaFleur, who had led them to her basement, through a series of cardboard brick dungeons that looked like children's playhouses, and into a storeroom filled with everything from toilet paper and Post-it Notes to bulk prophylactics and giant rubber penises. Moving a cabinet of body butter to the side, she revealed an ancient wooden door. More apt in a castle than a supply closet.

"Where does it go?" Rocco asked.

"Don't know," she said. "Old Shanghai tunnel? Smuggler's path? Mistress burrow?"

Using a crowbar, Rocco pried off the door, revealing the dank, creepy passage that led into deep blackness. Banging sounds erupted from upstairs. Someone trying to get inside.

"Put your back against a wall and protect your girls," Rocco said to Sheila. He handed her a slip of paper. "If you can get a message out, call this number. Tell whoever answers to find a doctor. Bring him to the factory. Plan for battle."

"Here's some extra gear." She handed each of them a flashlight and a heavy rucksack.

"Stay safe," Rocco said.

"Don't worry about me, you old bastard." She gave Rocco a kiss, smearing lipstick across his mouth. "Nobody messes with me in my house."

◆ ◆ ◆

The old man had continued so far ahead in the tunnel that Andy lost sight of his flashlight beam. Kate felt less heavy in his arms. She seemed to be gaining some strength.

"It's like your stories," Kate said. "Running through the sewers. All that bullshit hero stuff in the Flood. You and Mac with your stories."

"Are you talking to me?" Andy asked.

"Of course she isn't." Rocco reappeared out of the darkness.

"Back in those olden times, old man. You and Beth riding the horse and all of it," Kate said, her voice slurring from the painkillers Sheila had given her. "Away from the mobs and the fires."

"You were in the Flood?" Andy asked. "Who is Beth?"

Rocco shined the light directly into Kate's eyes. She flinched. He reached and held her face in his hand. "You done goldbricking, Girard?"

"I don't need help." Kate shoved Andy aside, standing on her own. Her body shook, but her eyes grew more focused. "Whatever Sheila gave me, I would do on weekends. I'm higher than a castrato. Feeling no pain and floating on marshmallow rainbows."

"I need you to act like you're not hurt. Just for a bit," Rocco said. "Until we get you somewhere safe."

Kate took the flashlight from Andy's hand and headed down the corridor. Rocco and Andy looked at each other.

"She's tougher than both of us combined," Rocco said.

"I don't doubt that."

They followed, the slope more pronounced.

"Where does this lead?" Andy asked.

"Down," Rocco said.

"Oh, hell," Andy said.

They had reached the end of the passage. A dead end. Rough-cut stone, sparkles of granite shining in the flashlight beam. Debris from the tunnel's construction stacked in the corner: bricks, wood, and stone.

"This can't be right," Andy said. "There has to be a way out."

"There doesn't have to be anything," Rocco said. "Sometimes you're screwed."

Kate put one hand against the damp wall, her eyes closing for a long blink. She snapped out of it, checking to see if either of the men noticed. Rocco didn't. Andy didn't say a word.

"Maybe we passed it," Andy said. "No reason a door or other tunnel or whatever has to be here at the end."

Leaving Kate at the tunnel's end, Rocco and Andy made their way back up the passage. They ran the flashlight over the damp walls and ceiling, looking for any exit.

"Nothing here," Andy said. "You?"

"Nothing."

A shotgun echoed from the direction of the brothel. A woman's scream. Andy and Rocco froze, looking into the darkness. Waiting for what was next. Faint splashes of water. A man's voice, but Andy couldn't make out the words. Rocco drew his pistol and motioned for Andy to head back to the end of the tunnel.

"What are we going to do?" Andy whispered.

"We're going to fight. Probably die," he said. "Not much to plan when you're in a goddamn tunnel."

They turned and ran the thirty yards back to the dead end, the voices and splashing behind them distant, but growing closer.

When they reached the dead end, Kate had vanished.

"Where the hell?" Rocco said. He reached out his hands to feel where she had last been.

"There," Andy said.

He pointed to a hole, low on the wall. The bricks stacked in the corner had blocked its view. A person could easily fit. Andy poked his flashlight into the hole. It opened into the top of a very large exposed pipe, low water moving at a downward angle. It was difficult to focus on the water, but it didn't smell clean.

Rocco looked over his shoulder. He pulled out a grenade from his coat.

"What is that?" Andy said, which he immediately thought strange, as he knew exactly what it was. Maybe that's just the thing a person said when he actually saw a real, live grenade in the hand of someone about to use it in a ramshackle tunnel.

"Sheila's duffel has a mess of goodies," Rocco said.

"We don't know who is coming down the tunnel," Andy said.

"At this point it doesn't really matter."

"We don't know where that pipe leads," Andy pointed out. "We could get trapped. Drown. Who knows?"

"We are already trapped," Rocco said, pulling the pin and throwing the grenade down the long passage. He slid through the hole and jumped into the open pipe. The water pushed him into the darkness.

Andy's eyes followed the arc of the grenade until it disappeared. Dim flashlight beams came into view. The splashing close.

A man with a very deep voice clearly said, "You hear something, Stu?"

Andy realized he wasn't moving. That he stood completely still. He didn't know for how long. He couldn't calculate how many seconds had passed, but that grenade was about to pop. He stopped thinking and dove into the open pipe.

❖ ❖ ❖

Andy slid at what felt like fifty miles an hour through the slick, mossy pipe. The viscous water hadn't looked as though it was moving quickly, but that had obviously been an illusion. The flashlight wanged around, giving a disco-ball effect with little sense of the space. Like being inside a kaleidoscope. A kaleidoscope rapidly sluicing sewage. Not the most requested toy come Christmastime.

He thought he heard the explosion behind him, but it was more likely manufactured in his imagination. It wasn't a tree falling in the woods. He didn't have to hear the damn thing to know what had happened. He knew how grenades worked, and Sheila McCormick didn't seem like the kind of person who provided duds.

Andy made himself as streamlined as he could and prayed that he didn't crash into a grate or any of a number of things that could kill you underground. Were the rumors about alligators true? The water slide might have been fun if not for that looming dread. And, of course, the voluminous amounts of sewage that he'd accidentally swallowed.

Without any warning, Andy was airborne. He had reached the end of the line, and it had shot him past the flow of water. The brief moment of weightlessness was both exhilarating and horrifying. He belly flopped into a pool of thick water, sinking, swallowing more water, and then clawing his way to the surface.

It smelled like the inside of a dog fart.

There were a few built-in lights illuminating the space in a dull glow, buzzing and blinking. Which was important, as he'd lost his flashlight on impact.

Andy treaded water in a big open pool, the confluence of a number of pipes flowing into it. Old and brick with a few modern additions. He caught sight of a figure swimming with a flashlight. Rocco.

"Where are we?" Andy shouted, getting more of the mephitic water in his mouth. He swam in the same direction toward a ladder that led up to a landing.

"Sewers," Rocco said.

"No shit."

"Actually."

Rocco was already halfway up the ladder when Andy reached it. His hand slid on the sludgy metal, but he managed to climb up after him. He lay on his back on the brick bank, catching his breath, turning every so often to hock out globs of the ick he'd ingested. He tried to remember his last tetanus shot and made a mental note to get ten of them very soon.

Rocco kicked the bottom of his foot. "Get up, son. We got to find Kate." He shined his flashlight into the sludgy water, running the beam across the surface.

"She might've made it out. She had a head start," Andy said, getting up. "She's confused but still a badass."

Rocco shined his light through the chamber. The space was large, with pipes delivering water and sewage from above. The bank they stood on branched out in two directions, tunnels on both sides receding into darkness.

"I know this place," Rocco said.

Before they developed any kind of plan, a wet, filthy Kate ran into view from one of the arching passages. She ran along the bank toward them, arms flailing like a madwoman.

"Thank God," Rocco said. "We got to clean out that wound."

Without answering, she ran past Rocco and Andy toward the passage on the other end. Not a word. Her eyes wild with fear.

"Kate, you're hurt!" Rocco shouted, following after her. "Where are you going?"

"Away from the monsters!" she yelled without turning back.

Rocco and Andy followed after her. She was fast for an injured middle-aged woman.

"Did she say monsters?" Andy asked.

Weird groans, growls, and roars echoed from where Kate had entered the chamber. The sound of movement, wet and menacing. Just when things couldn't get any weirder.

Andy shrugged. "Monsters, it is."

◆ ◆ ◆

They caught up to Kate in the next chamber. She was frantic, a cornered animal, but she stayed with them. If they kept moving, she remained calm. Whenever Rocco stopped, even for a second, to get his bearings, she freaked out. The drugs had messed with her head, brave one moment, terrified the next.

They moved through an underground river system with space to walk on either side. Rivers of sewage opened up into larger chambers. Andy guessed that they were a couple of stories underground, no manholes or indications that the street was directly above. The weight of the city rested on top of them.

"If I can find some landmark, I can maybe get us out of here," Rocco said. "Fifty years, but some places never leave your memory."

"During the Flood?" Andy said. "With Beth?"

"More happened in one day than in most lifetimes," Rocco said.

Rocco guided them through the labyrinth of tunnels and passages. He moved with a confidence that made Andy optimistic. Rocco might not have known where they were going, but he sure as hell thought he did.

Forward momentum, that was the kind of strategy that you needed when monstrous sounds followed you no matter which way you turned. At times they grew closer and weirder. It was certain that whatever made those sounds knew the layout of the place better than they did. Andy

256

regretted having ever read H. P. Lovecraft. He wondered if he would go mad and his hair would turn white when he finally witnessed the indescribable, preternatural horror.

"Here. Finally. Here." Rocco pointed at a crack in the wall. Not an official passage but a geological fissure. One just wide enough for them to squeeze into.

"You sure?" Andy asked. "It doesn't exactly look safe."

"There's an old subway line on the other side. I'd bet you any amount." Rocco slipped into the narrow opening. Andy helped Kate, following her.

The passage ran at a strange angle. They could walk upright but had to lean against one jagged wall to maintain balance. More than once, Andy cut his hand on something. Small but painful. Considering the catalog of injuries that he'd inventoried, it bothered him that something could add to the pain. Pain should be finite. No such luck. Life could always get more painful.

The passage opened into a chamber three times the size of the one they'd arrived in. No more water. And other than the smell coming off their bodies, the air was stale but clean. Rocco fanned his flashlight, revealing the room to be an abandoned train platform that predated the current subway and had been abandoned for some time. The tiling and architectural flair were of a different era. Probably one of the failed pre-Flood attempts at underground transportation. Something that ran on steam or springs.

"I told you I knew where I was," Rocco said. He leaned back toward the passage. "I don't hear anything following."

"That's because they're already here," Kate said. "The monsters are here."

Rocco brought his flashlight beam around in a wide arc. A congregation of thirty men and women descended a staircase opposite them onto the platform. Their clothes appeared gray in the dim light. No consistency to their costuming other than its drabness. Some in suits and dresses. Others in primitive rags. One man was naked, his body covered in caked gray mud. The familiar sounds rose from the silence as they approached. Hums, chest beats, clapping, haunting sustained notes. Together creating an inhuman and ghostly chorus.

Rocco turned back to where they'd come from, but his flashlight revealed more gray men and women sliding through the fissure. Oozing from the darkness and joining their brethren.

"The people of the Underneath," Rocco said with a sigh.

CHAPTER 29

Didn't know him. Met him that day. Sometimes you have to trust a stranger. Especially when that stranger has a three-year-old's smile and bright-blue eyes. And fourteen guns in the trunk of his Impala. Talk about being ready for anything.

—*In a jailhouse interview with Molly Dasho, the waitress who joined Hark Turkus in an eight-hour robbery spree that left four dead in Auction City (1961)*

"Things are going to get weird," Rocco whispered. He stood completely still, keeping his hands away from his body. "Play along. Don't fight it. And whatever you do, don't punch holes in the masquerade."

Andy nodded but had one hand on the gun in his waistband. He watched the strange group of underground dwellers approach them. They moved like ghosts, eyes never quite focused, looking around more than at them. They circled Andy, Kate, and Rocco. Their hums and moans vibrated in Andy's chest. His rapid heartbeat supplied the percussion.

Kate balled her fists, ready to fight. Her eyes darted around as the group grew closer.

"Are they really cannibals?" Andy asked.

"They can hear you," Rocco whispered.

In a fluid motion, the crowd surged forward. Play along, Rocco had said. Andy used every ounce of effort to not fight it. He felt their hands run along his back, his arms, his legs.

"Stay still," Rocco said. "Let them."

Andy felt the pistol lift from his waist. Hands reach into his pockets. Watched Kate and Rocco get the same treatment, a dozen hands searching their bodies. Weapons removed, disappearing into the rags of the ashen crowd.

Kate shoved one of the men away. "Get your hands off me."

"Kate," Rocco said. "Careful."

"He grabbed my tit!" she yelled.

The coordinated moan of the crowd grew in volume, increasingly high-pitched. Andy's ears rang, still sensitive from the explosion. In a quick motion six members of the crowd scooped up Kate and lifted her over their heads as if she were crowd surfing. Kate twisted but got nowhere.

"You want to fight, you got yourself a goddamn fight!" Kate yelled, kicking at the heads of the people near her feet.

"Stop it, Kate!" Rocco shouted. "You're going to reopen your wound. Stop it, damn it."

Andy held out his hands. "She's injured. Hurt," he called to the crowd. "Whacked out on pain medication. Hallucinating. She thinks you're monsters."

"They're monsters," Kate said. "The monsters have me."

For a brief moment, nothing happened beyond Kate's kicking. The collective sound of the crowd dropped in volume. They spoke in unison. It sounded as though they were saying *mermen* over and over again. Just what Andy needed, some half-man/half-fish creatures to emerge from somewhere.

The mob set Kate back down. She dizzily swayed, but Rocco pulled her toward him as soon as her feet hit the ground.

"You're okay," Rocco said. "Take it easy."

"I don't know what's happening. Where the hell are we?" Kate asked, looking around.

"We're in the Underneath," Rocco said. "I need you to stay calm."

The crowd noise had died to a creepy harmony, soft hisses and moans. What the Eagles would sound like if they were ghosts haunting an abandoned house.

"What do we do?" Andy said. "What happens now?"

"They're dangerous. But only if you call them on their act," Rocco whispered to Andy. He made his thumb and forefingers into a circle and announced, "I am an ally of Saint Agnes. Honor my presence. I request a parlay with the great one, Merlin."

From *C.H.U.D.* to Renaissance Faire in one sentence. At least "Merlin" made a fraction more sense than *merman*. The crowd fell silent when Rocco spoke the wizard's name. One person coughed, but that was accidental.

"I guess Merlin beats Larry as the name for the king of the mole people," Andy said.

"That's exactly the kind of shit that will get us killed," Rocco said. "It's all about the theater of the thing."

"Who asks for an audience with Merlin?" a voice proclaimed.

The crowd parted, giving Andy, Kate, and Rocco a view of the platform stairs and the man descending them.

If your name was Merlin, you should embrace it. Especially if you were the leader of a community that lived in the sewer system. Whether Gandalf or Doctor Strange, go the extra mile. An eye patch or face tattoos or a raven on your shoulder.

Merlin did not disappoint. He had a pointy goatee, had combed the ends of his eyebrows up into a curl, and wore a red cowl. Without it, the small man would have looked like a junior college accounting teacher. Short and pudgy with a gut. The ensemble was costume-shop quality. The only giveaway to the modern world were his cowboy boots.

They had snake heads on the toes that probably looked cool in the catalog.

"I am Rocco Colombo. I am Floodgate," Rocco said.

"Merlin knows who you are," Merlin said. "Merlin follows the Overneath."

Andy leaned toward Rocco. "Is this guy kidding?"

"Shut it," Rocco said, giving Andy a hard look.

"State your business to Merlin," Merlin said, continuing to approach.

"We are not here by choice. We mean no insult," Rocco said. "We were chased down here. Our friend is hurt."

"We are all chased down here," Merlin said, "by one way or t'other. That does not change the fact that your presence violates the Treaty of the Immiscible that Merlin drafted with Saint Agnes. And your weapons nullify any beseeching of sanctuary."

"They've been distributed among your people. Used only to defend against those that pursued us," Rocco said. "We would never use them on your people."

"Merlin's progeny are powerful." Merlin glanced at Andy. "Merlin recognizes Colombo and the woman, Kate Girard. Who is this one? Who is the stranger you've brought among us?"

"I can speak for myself," Andy said.

"And yet Merlin wants not to hear from you," Merlin said.

Andy took a step forward. The sounds of the ragged crowd grew as they threw their arms forward, wiggling their fingers in front of them. The sun-starved skin of their gray hands like dying earthworms.

Rocco put a hand on Andy's shoulder. "Safe passage back to the surface. We want nothing more," Rocco said. "To disturb you no more. What will that cost us?"

"As Merlin has little use for your Terran dollars," Merlin said, "you must conform to the traditions of the Underneath. The universal currency of information. Floodgate's greatest commodity has historically been the hidden knowledge that you possess about the people of the city. Merlin requires a secret. Give Merlin a wonderful secret, and my flock will take you back to the Overneath."

"You've got to quit calling it that," Andy said.

Rocco ignored Andy and nodded. "One secret."

"As is the way of our kind," Merlin said. "A very special secret."

Rocco thought for a moment.

Merlin leaned toward Andy, not quite whispering, "For clarification, only half of Merlin's children are cannibals. It's a personal choice and an acquired taste."

"I got it," Rocco said. "I will tell you something that nobody but a select group knows."

"That sounds like a very special secret," Merlin said.

"Andy is my son."

Merlin stared at him for a moment. "Who gives a shit?" he said, dropping character and then catching himself. "I mean, Merlin does not accept this inconsequential secret in exchange for safe passage. Merlin will have the hungry prepare the stewing cauldron."

Rocco pointed at Andy. "He is also the man that killed Aloysius Gray."

Andy looked to Rocco quickly. He hadn't forgotten. He just wasn't prepared to have one of his co-conspirators confess his crime to a complete stranger and his human ant farm. Especially his father.

"If true, that stands as very special." Merlin turned to Andy and leaned in close. His breath stank, a combination of sardines and more sardines. "How does Merlin know the veracity of this statement? The gazettes above claimed some manner of sneak thief orchestrated Gray's demise. You appear not as one prone to the burgle."

"That's the thing about secrets," Rocco said. "They're different than the story everyone else hears. It's what makes them secrets."

JOHNNY SHAW

Merlin turned to him and nodded, and then back to Andy. "How did the late policeman die? Did you plunge a stake through the old man's heart?"

"Shot him," Andy coughed out. "I shot him."

"The banality of powder weapons," Merlin said. "Such an unremarkable way to vacate this plane."

"It was an accident. There was a confrontation."

"Do not do that," Merlin said. "Do not minimize it. You killed a man. An irreparable act. Yet a solemn one. Respect the man—your victim—enough to make his end an apologue. One with a moral and a lesson and worth. Every death deserves to be a parable of sorts."

"Does it?" Andy asked.

"Good enough secret?" Rocco asked, anxiousness in his voice. "Does that get us out of here?"

Merlin gave Andy a final stare. Very deliberately, he touched Andy, Rocco, and Kate on both shoulders, holding his hand on each for a full second. He stated with formal authority, "Merlin commands safe passage."

The crowd hummed agreement. Merlin walked back in the direction he had come. "I bid you all a fond valediction."

"How do we get back?" Rocco asked.

"My flock will take you. Merlin has spoken."

One by one, the crowd broke the circle and jumped onto the train tracks, heading into the dark tunnel.

◆ ◆ ◆

In the short time they had been in the Underneath, the streets above had grown thicker with pedestrian traffic. Fires and looting had broken out along Benchley Boulevard and the rest of downtown. Broken glass littered the sidewalk where store windows had been shattered. Looters ran in and out of stores carrying all manner of goods.

The only visible police presence were three cops who did their best to clear a gang of looters out of a stereo store. At gunpoint, they forced the men and women to leave empty-handed. With the looters rousted, the policemen got their shopping done, loading turntables and equalizers into the trunk of their squad car. When the store owner rushed out and tried to stop them, he was severely beaten.

The sun had set. The few working streetlights gave little illumination. Scattered fires provided additional light, giving the urban landscape a hellish patina. Even with the fires, most of the city lived in shadow.

The strange underground mob had led Rocco, Andy, and Kate along the tracks and up a series of ladders, and finally they loaded them into a sidewalk lift. The small elevator surfaced in a downtown alley. Two tall brick buildings on either side, walls tagged with graffiti that spoke a secret language.

Kate sat on a milk crate, catching her breath. She pulled out her cigarettes, squeezing the water out of them and throwing the pack to the ground. Andy and Rocco eyed the street from the alley.

"So," Andy said. "Are we going to talk about Merlin and everything that happened down there?"

"He developed a shtick. It's an effective defense," Rocco said. "Crazy gets left alone. The more people think they're cannibals or monsters or ghouls, the safer they are."

Kate's head dipped. She caught it and sat back.

"She looks rough," Andy said. "Saint Vitus is the closest hospital, but it's a dozen blocks."

"Hospitals are going to be overloaded. We set Kate up with a bed in the candy factory. Pull a croaker. Get the biggest guns we got. Hit that safe house. End this."

"That's a hell of a to-do list. I don't even know what 'pull a croaker' means," Andy said. "None of that stops the rioting."

"Nothing stops rioting, son. Consolidated will guard certain assets, friends, but the city's going to burn a little."

"That's depressing," Andy said.

Kate tried to stand but fell forward. Andy caught her before she hit the ground.

"How you doing, Katie?" Rocco said.

"I'm fine," she mumbled with a grin. "Never better."

"Time to get back to work." Rocco marched to the street and smashed the window of the first parked vehicle he came across. Andy helped Kate to the Chevy Suburban and set her down in the backseat. He brushed the broken glass off the front seat and got in himself.

Rocco fiddled with the ignition. He glanced up at Andy. "Those subterranean weirdoes left us unarmed. Check the glove box for a gun."

"Are you serious?"

"How long have you lived in Auction City?" Rocco said.

Andy opened the glove compartment. Sure enough, a small snub-nosed revolver sat among registration and insurance papers and about ten thousand ballpoint pens.

"It'll do," Rocco said.

He pulled the wide ride onto the street. The density of the traffic and crowd kept them to a crawl. The Suburban crept through the mass of people moving at a snail's pace with the rest of the cars.

Angry drivers honked. Heads stuck out windows, swearing and yelling. A cabbie got out of his taxi to have a debate with the car behind him. The debate included a tire iron to the hood. Andy gave the cabbie an edge in that argument.

"This isn't working," Rocco said, turning the wheel and hopping onto the sidewalk. Pedestrians jumped out of the way as he barreled past the stalled cars. At the first intersection, he slowed and turned hard right, clipping a newspaper rack but staying on the sidewalk. Pedestrians turned wide-eyed as the Suburban accelerated toward them.

"What is it with you guys and driving on the sidewalk?" Andy asked, stiff-arming the dashboard and waiting for some kind of inevitable impact.

"It's a nice night for a drive through the park," Rocco said. He was having a little too much fun. Andy saw Redling Park four blocks ahead. How many people could they run over in that short distance?

He was about to find out. Two men carried a couch out of a shattered department store window. Rocco rode the horn to warn them. The men turned in time for one of them to get hit and the other pushed against the wall by the spinning couch. Rocco didn't even slow down.

"You just hit that guy," Andy said.

"He can sleep it off on his new couch."

The Suburban reached the park without driving through another person, but not for lack of trying.

"Slow down," Andy said, seeing the concrete stairs that led down to the bike paths.

The grade was steep. They were going too fast. A second later they were airborne. The roughness of the road gave way to a feeling of weightlessness.

Rocco turned to Andy. "See. That wasn't so bad."

Then they landed. The Suburban hit the center of the staircase, bucking and tipping to the side. Andy and Rocco banged their heads on the ceiling. Kate bounced and slid around in the backseat, but luckily she was out.

On two wheels and an angle, the Suburban violently thumped down the slope. Rocco turned the steering wheel in a ridiculous effort to gain control, but that's not how science worked. It did about as much good as a kid yanking one of those steering wheels on a shopping cart.

At the bottom, the truck landed on its tires, bounced twice, and came to a stop. Andy and Rocco stared straight ahead.

Rocco smiled. "You were right. I'm going to admit it. When you're right, you're right. I took that grade too fast. You live, you learn. Next time, it'll be smoother."

"Right," Andy said. "Next time."

Rocco stepped on the gas and drove down the bike path, heading for the riverfront and their secret candy factory criminal consortium headquarters.

CHAPTER 30

A man's got to have morals. A code of ethics. Without 'em, we're nothing but animals. I might be a hood, but I ain't no traitor.

—«John "Jackie Bazooka" Benini, suspected capo of the Furgele criminal family on his role in assisting federal investigators in the apprehension of a group of fraudsters selling counterfeit war bonds (1943)

Rocco slowly drove past a woman wearing what looked like a prom dress. Her black hair stood at sharp angles, hair-sprayed into a fan at the front. Old knife wounds scarred her face in a crisscross. She held a shotgun in plain view. Between the hair, the dress, and the shotgun, there was no doubt she was ready to party.

The woman squinted into the windshield of the Suburban. Rocco gave her a nod. She nodded back. One block later, they passed another of Pilar's army. The serene confidence of the women gave Andy chills.

The rollup gate into the factory opened as they approached. Agnes held the chain and waved them inside. Before they'd rolled to a stop, Agnes had the Suburban's back door open.

"It's a nice surprise to see that you're not dead," Agnes said. "Sheila said the building next to her brothel collapsed. That you were in a tunnel beneath it."

"Is Sheila okay?" Rocco asked.

"She took a bullet from one of the Wells brothers, but will be fine."

"You get a doctor?" Rocco asked.

Agnes gently picked up the unconscious Kate from the backseat and carried her through the factory toward the back rooms. Rocco and Andy followed close behind.

"Borrowed one," Agnes said over her shoulder.

She carried Kate into the long hallway and past the room where Andy had been held when he'd first arrived. It was hard to believe that it had been only that morning.

"Come on," Rocco said, giving Andy a light slap on the back and then steering him toward the open factory floor. "Agnes and the doc will make sure she's okay. We got a raid to prep for."

Pilar had organized an arsenal of weapons displayed on the long table in front of her, from knives to guns and back again. Next to her a stocky woman with a liar's scar running from the side of her mouth to almost her ear pumped shells into a pump-action shotgun.

"You're alive," Pilar said. "I owe Agnes ten bucks."

"You should know by now," Rocco said. "It'll take more than a collapsing building to kill me."

"This is Mirna," Pilar said. "Soon as the bombs went off, I got all the girls together. They're ready for battle. Just point us in the right direction."

Rocco gave her the rundown. Ben's death and Kate's injury. The brothel siege, the tunnels, and the Underneath. Finally the location of the safe house where the remaining escaped convicts were hopefully still holed up.

"What was the damage from the bombs and fires?" Rocco asked.

"Church got blown to hell, but Mac is safe. A bunch got killed, though. Some lieutenants in 893. CFO of the Trust. Everyone got hit hard. The leaders themselves got out. Should be at the Fortress by now."

"Time we hit back," Rocco said.

"If six men died in the prison fire," Andy said, counting on his fingers, "you got one, Cemetery Joe, locked up here. Pretty sure that grenade took out the Wells brothers in the tunnel. Leaves us three: Hopewell, the Hawaiian bomber, and the Thief River Killer."

"And the Thorntons. That clan is a whole 'nother ball of shit," Rocco said, picking up a revolver and checking the cartridges.

"Can't I live with the fantasy for five minutes that we're just after three psychopaths instead of a whole army of them?" Andy said. "The safe house is still the primary target, right?"

"Listen to him," Pilar said, smiling. "'Primary target.'"

"It is, right?" Andy asked. "Those three convicts want me dead. The sooner we stop them, the sooner this day is over and I get a good night's sleep. So someone, give me a goddamn gun and let me shoot some people."

"While I like the enthusiasm," Pilar said, "I ain't going nowhere with you two until you take a shower and change your clothes. You both smell like shit."

Andy smelled his shirt. "That's probably from the shit."

◆ ◆ ◆

Of course they had a room devoted to costumes and disguises. What self-respecting criminal organization wouldn't? Although Andy was hard-pressed to figure out what the pirate costume could be used for, beyond normal pirating applications.

Andy and Rocco flipped through the hangers, looking at the dark suits and holding them up against themselves. He felt like a kid getting fitted to be a ring bearer at a wedding.

"Some of these suits go all the way back to the Flood," Rocco said. He held up a baggy pinstripe suit that looked like every movie gangster's outfit. Andy was tempted to take it from him and try it on, but it looked as though it was for someone who was four feet tall and five feet wide.

"I'd be interested in hearing about the Flood," Andy said. "I've read most of the personal accounts I could find. History books."

"Thousands were there. Millions have stories. And all of them were heroes," Rocco said.

"Not many telling stories of how they looted or killed."

"If you survived it, you did horrible things," Rocco said. "That's how you know if someone's telling the truth. If they admit that. Or if they say nothing. Sometimes the only way to tell the truth is to keep your mouth shut."

Andy studied Rocco's face.

"I ain't what you expected, am I?" Rocco said.

"I wasn't expecting anything," Andy said, jamming a velvet suit back in the rack. "I've been fatherless for more than thirty-five years. I don't barely know you. Apart from the insanity of this Floodgate stuff, you're just some guy."

"Okay," Rocco said.

"That's all you have to say? 'Okay'?"

"A speech, some words, they ain't going to change nothing. An apology would be insulting."

Andy turned to him. "I spent so much time. Did so many things. It was all about finding you, figuring out who you were. Or rebelling against who I thought you were. What happens when you spend your life searching for something—someone—but when you find it, you don't care anymore? I'm not disappointed in you. I'm numb to the idea."

"I don't know, son," Rocco said, still thumbing through the suits.

"You won't even tell me about my mother. Is she alive? In the city?" Andy said. "I guess I probably feel the same about her as you, but that's for me and her to figure out. You show back up, but you set the rules.

And you won't tell me the one last thing that I need to know. To close the damn book and put it on the shelf."

"Elizabeth McIntyre," Rocco said. "Beth."

"The Beth that Kate mentioned," Andy said. "Something about running around in the sewers during the Flood?"

"We had an adventure."

"If you knew her then," Andy asked, "how come I wasn't born until twenty years later?"

"Life is strange."

"And?" Andy asked. "That's really all you're going to say?"

"You know her name," Rocco said. "Be happy about that."

"I'm elated."

Rocco took a breath, and then looked back up at Andy. "Christ on a crutch. We aren't dressing for a fashion show. Grab whatever fits."

Andy nodded and pulled a disco-era suit off the rack. It was unnecessarily orange with lapels the size of aircraft carriers.

"Okay," Rocco said, "not whatever fits. Find a black suit."

"You got it, Pops," Andy said, putting as much snide as he could into it.

Rocco gave him a look. "You're seriously going to go with Pops?"

"It was either that or Daddy-O."

◆ ◆ ◆

In their matching black suits, they looked like father-and-son federal agents. They poked their heads into the small room where a nervous doctor worked on Kate's shoulder. She wore only a red bra from the waist up. Her eyes had lost some of the glaze from the medication. Agnes stood in the corner.

"Not much more I can do," the doctor said to her. "As long as you get rest, you'll heal fine. Too much activity could open that wound back up."

"This ain't my first demolition derby, Doc." Kate gave him a hard slap on the ass with her good arm. He jumped.

"Good to see you back to your old self," Rocco said.

"What kind of real woman would let something like a car bomb stop her?"

"Uh," Andy said, "pretty much all of them."

"Not the ones I know," Kate said. She held up her hand and Agnes gave her a soft high five.

"Did you say car bomb?" the doctor asked. "Were you ever unconscious?"

"I'll rub some butter on it."

"There's a difference between tough and stupid," the doctor said. "They're going to need me back at County. The ER was stacking up when you—when I left."

"Don't interrupt when the criminals are talking," Agnes said.

The doctor nodded and sat down.

"Did I dream about being chased by monsters, or did that really happen?" Kate asked.

"A little bit of both," Andy said.

"They killed Ben."

"Not the monsters," Rocco said. "But, yeah. He's dead."

"He was worthless at a job he didn't want to do," she said, "but he didn't deserve that."

"No, he didn't," Rocco said.

"Give me ten minutes to get some new civvies. I got some vengeance to burn," Kate said. "And, Andy, quit staring at my tits."

◆ ◆ ◆

"The Japanese need to be told about Ben. It's delicate," Rocco said as he and Andy walked into the long hallway. "Something that needs to be done in person. We'll go through Naga on the way to the safe house."

Cemetery Joe Sullivan walked out of his holding cell ten feet in front of them. In his hand was a crushed ballpoint pen wrapped in wet toilet paper, some kind of poor man's lock pick. He turned and saw Rocco and Andy.

"Well, this is embarrassing," Cemetery Joe said.

Rocco went for his weapon. Cemetery Joe charged him. It was close, but Cemetery Joe won the race and got his shoulder under Rocco's arm, forcing it up. Rocco fired into the air. The bullet disappeared into the plaster ceiling, leaving a small divot. The two men fell backward, slamming into Andy. Knocked off balance, he fell and slid along the hall floor.

By the time Andy got to his feet, Rocco and Cemetery Joe were wrestling on the ground, all arms and legs, Rocco's gun pointing willy-nilly. They punched and grappled with their free hands. For a man in his seventies, Rocco had some fight in him, but he couldn't keep it up against the younger man. Andy drew his weapon, but he had no clear target.

Agnes stepped into the hallway behind Andy. She held a scalpel in each hand. Not many people would respond to a gunshot with such inadequate weapons. After what Andy had seen from Agnes, he wouldn't bet against her.

As Rocco pounded Cemetery Joe's thighs and side with his knee, Cemetery Joe brought an elbow down onto Rocco's neck that took most of the old man's strength. The fight was over.

Before Agnes or Andy could intervene, Cemetery Joe had wrenched the gun away from Rocco and put it to the side of the old man's head. They rose together, Cemetery Joe keeping an arm around Rocco's neck.

"Don't move," Cemetery Joe said.

"You can live," Agnes said. "If you put down the gun, you can live."

"Especially you, you bald bitch. I don't want to see a muscle twitch. You stay the hell away from me." He looked as if he was going to cry.

"What did she do to you, Joe?" Rocco asked. "She must've really got to you."

"Shut up!" he yelled. "Tell her to stay away. I'll shoot your head off your body."

"Stay put, Agnes," Rocco said.

Pilar entered the hall behind Rocco and Cemetery Joe. She remained silent, moving stealthily, a knife in one hand.

"You know what, Pops? I've had it," Andy said. "For an elite criminal organization, you people sure screw up a lot. The unprofessionalism is hard to bear."

"Not really the time, son," Rocco said.

"Do whatever you're going to do, Joe. I'm sick of it. Yesterday I was living a normal life. Well, not normal, but you know." Andy walked forward, keeping his gun aimed at Cemetery Joe. "And now I'm a deputy to the moron police. They never have a plan. And the endgame is to let assholes continue to control the city."

"The preferable assholes," Rocco said. "It's relative."

"Shut the hell up!" Cemetery Joe yelled. "Both of you."

Andy kept walking forward. "Here's the thing, Joe. I don't care if you shoot him. Yesterday, he didn't exist. I won't miss him. So unless you have another threat, I'm going to do whatever the hell I want."

"You people are crazy," Cemetery Joe said. "I could shoot you, too."

"You could try," Andy said.

Pilar motioned with her hand for Andy to keep talking. She crept closer.

"Let me tell you something about your hostage."

"I don't want to hear it. I don't want to hear any of it. I want a car or a boat. I want—"

Andy interrupted. "That's my long-lost father. He abandoned me when I was born. We lived in the same city the whole time, and he didn't contact me until he had to."

Cemetery Joe's eyes closed in resignation. He sighed. "There's someone right behind me, isn't there?"

Pilar plunged the knife into the back of Cemetery Joe's neck, severing vertebrae and spine. The pistol fired. Rocco had leaned at enough of an angle for the shot to miss his head. His ears would ring like the aftermath of a Quiet Riot concert, but he was alive. The same could not be said for Cemetery Joe Sullivan.

Rocco slid out from under the dead man, holding one hand to the side of his face. "Thanks, son. Great job distracting him. Even I believed you didn't care if he shot me."

"The lies we tell," Andy said. He stepped over the dead man and walked out the hallway.

CHAPTER 31

He dangled the bespectacled scientist off the edge of the roof. "You tell those other turkeys who put this jive bionic heart into my fine African body that Black Robot is coming for them. They gonna feel the funkadelic power of one angry cyborg brother. Can you dig it?"

—Excerpt from the men's adventure novel Auction City Assassin, *the first book in the Black Robot series by Brace Godfrey (1971)*

"You know what?" Andy said. "I'm sitting the rest of this out."

"What?" Rocco shouted. Andy couldn't tell if Rocco's volume was out of anger or if the old man couldn't hear him.

Andy sat on the couch in the factory's open area. Rocco loaded the weapons on the table into three large duffels. By the sheer volume of weaponry, it looked as if they were invading South America.

"I watched a guy get spine-stabbed," Andy yelled. "I hurt all over. And while there was a part of me that actually cared if you got shot—and definitely if I got shot—you know what? I don't want to play anymore."

Rocco shook his head and pointed at his ear. "Nothing. Just ringing. Sorry. Be ready in five to hit the road."

Kate sat down next to Andy. Her arm rested in a sling. She still didn't have all the color back in her face, but she had plenty of fire in her eyes.

"If you want to sit this one out, we can't stop you."

"You're not going to turn me over to the cops for killing Gray?" Andy asked. "You still have that hanging over my head."

"This doesn't work if you don't want to be here."

"I don't."

"Yes, you do," Kate said. "This gig is perfect for you. You're built for it. We're offering you a great opportunity. Unlimited resources, no oversight, and access to information that you can't even imagine."

"Can't enjoy any of that if I'm dead," Andy said.

"Some danger comes with the deal," Kate said. "I want to show you something."

◆ ◆ ◆

"Holy crap," Andy said. "This place is massive."

Overhead fluorescents lit the basement storage area, enveloping the room in a sickly glow. Dusty file boxes on steel shelves. Rows and rows that stretched the length of the factory. Everything labeled with numbers and codes, it resembled the records room in the basement of the ACPD's Central Records, only three times the size.

"These are past cases, old news, ancient history," Kate said. "The files upstairs, those are our active files. We end up down here a lot, though. You'd be surprised how many things in the present have roots in the past. Auction is embroiled in its history. The people of this town love their feuds."

"I'll admit it. I'm a little turned on. I can see myself down here," Andy said, opening a random box and looking at the multicolored sheets of paper and files inside. "But running around the streets, getting shot at. We were in the sewer with Merlin, the Cannibal King. That was bananas."

"You go where the work takes you. It's never boring." Kate tapped a file box on a top shelf. "I stumbled on this when I was looking for something else."

The box was labeled, "1949–1962—Melungeon Hayte River Smuggling Trade." Andy pulled the heavy box down. He set it on the wheeled footstool in the aisle and popped off the lid.

Photographs filled the box. A picture of a young Rocco holding a swaddled baby. An older photo of Rocco, Champ, and Champ's husband, Manny, in their twenties. The rest of the photos were of Andy. Him and Champ building a snowman. Little League games. The school play where he played Benjamin Franklin. His high school graduation. Police Academy graduation. With another cop, Hanley Woronov, at a sidewalk crime scene. The photos spanned his entire life.

While the graduation and sports photos were taken from the crowd, the others were shot from far away. Telephoto. Across the street. Behind bushes. Around corners. His life surveilled.

At the bottom was a crayon drawing that Andy knew he must have drawn but didn't remember. A frowning, stick-figure Andy stood in front of a purple house. There was a green dog and a person who looked like a potato with legs. The only words on the paper were a scrawl that read *Dad and Mom* next to two potato-people floating above the rest of the scene.

"He never stopped caring about you," Kate said.

"He never started," Andy said. "You stay with the people you care about."

"Not all people know how to do that," Kate said. "Rocky's life has been all death and loss. He wanted one piece of it to survive."

"Since I met him, I've been in constant danger."

"Proves the point," she said. "He didn't want you in this life, but now it's the best place for you. Even with a few bullets flying over your head."

Andy looked at a picture of him and Champ at Splash Gardens. He remembered that trip to the water slides vividly. The surge of water from one of those vertical pipes had jammed his shorts straight up his ass. You didn't forget a thing like that.

"Doesn't change a thing," Andy said, flipping through the images in the box.

"It's not what it changes. Not meant to change anything," she said. "It's what it reveals. It's just information. Data. Do with it what you will."

"He's a guy I met yesterday," Andy said.

"You might not know him, but he's known you his whole life," she said. "He's your father. You've given him a day. And a crazy day at that. Maybe he deserves more."

Andy picked up a photo of Champ pretending to hit a young Andy, him pretending to get hit. He tossed it back in the box, replaced the lid, and lifted it up onto the high shelf.

"He didn't regret his decision," Kate said, "but that didn't make it easier on him. You were in better hands with Champ."

"I don't doubt that."

"If you're happy not having a father, then keep your distance."

"You act like we should make plans to go fishing on Sucker Lake. Or have him teach me how to ride a bike. Toss a ball around. But his idea of a good time is running a raid on a safe house harboring dangerous escaped felons."

"It's his way of bonding."

◆ ◆ ◆

Andy got in the ice cream truck. His brief moment of rebellion had passed. The shock of seeing Cemetery Joe stabbed—while still in his mind—was tempered with the reminder that the man had tried to kill both him and Rocco.

He was ready to do battle, but he wasn't doing it for Rocco. Or for Floodgate. Or for the city. He was doing it for himself. To learn who he was. Time to see how insane his world could get.

Andy watched Rocco drift into walls as he walked to the ice cream truck. He blamed it on the weight of the weapons bag, but Andy knew that was an excuse. His balance might have still been suspect because of his ear injury, but there wasn't a chance in hell he was going to miss this fight.

Andy drove with Rocco navigating from the passenger seat. Pilar and Mirna took the Town & Country. Agnes followed on her motorcycle, because of course she rode a motorcycle. They would reconnoiter in Blackstreet Hollow and case the safe house.

While they attempted to neutralize the threat of the escaped convicts, Kate remained at the candy factory with the rest of Pilar's girls. She would coordinate with Cardinal Macklin, and track the progress of his efforts to oust Hank Robinson as the new deputy commissioner and put Randall Ashley in his place. Wars weren't always won on the battlefield. For this to end well, boardroom treaties needed to be made, and that was Macklin's job. Until the generals negotiated the end of the war, the soldiers wouldn't have peace.

If they could stop the three remaining guns-for-hire and Mac could work out some deal with the ACPD, they could all eat cake at the end of the day.

Driving to Naga, Andy noticed that the streets had grown emptier. With the darkness, the earnest protestors had gone indoors. Aside from a candlelight vigil they passed, the rest of the shadows were filled with the opportunists, rioters, and the angry. Both the innocent and the guilty outside on that night should expect trouble.

The good news was that Pilar's diplomatic efforts within Consolidated seemed to work. The Wretches and other gangs had become a visible presence, policing the streets block by block and spreading the word that they were the law for the night. The process would be a slow one, but should prove effective in avoiding a citywide riot. The unrest had started with the death of the gangs' leader. Without their endorsement, the mob would lose steam.

The news that played out in the papers and on television would tell a different story than the one Andy was seeing from behind the scenes. No matter how the day ended, the public would never know about Andy's role in the day. It was fascinating to see the conspiracy from the inside.

◆ ◆ ◆

The ice cream truck stopped on the edge of Naga. A line of Japanese gangsters blocked their way. A quick glance to the rooftops revealed sniper rifles and even more soldiers. Rioting wasn't going to reach this neighborhood. Little Nagasaki was fortified.

"I'll do the talking," Rocco said.

"I wouldn't know what to say anyway," Andy replied.

Rocco got out, visibly disarmed himself of all his weapons, held his arms to the side, and approached the row of men. Andy took his cue and did the same.

The 893 crew looked more like the backup dancers for a New Wave band than a deadly army, but Andy had no desire to test them. The bright colors of their suits, the strange sunglasses, and their spiked and coifed hair were offset by the very real guns they all carried.

"Floodgate," Rocco said.

The men kept their eyes straight ahead. They never looked in Rocco's direction. A man stepped forward through the line of soldiers. Andy recognized him as the bouncer in lime from Ikejime. He gave Rocco a nod. The shoulders of the soldiers relaxed by a quarter-inch.

"Come with me," the bouncer said.

The bouncer guided them through the maze of streets. Andy lost north, but he thought he could probably find his way back. He had counted seven lefts and three rights. Next time, he would bring bread crumbs.

When they had reached their destination, the bouncer opened the door to a building with no sign in a row of buildings with doors and no signs. Andy gave Rocco a questioning look. Rocco shrugged, giving him no confidence. Andy and Rocco walked inside. The door closed behind them, and they stood together in the pitch dark.

"I think I prefer monsters chasing us through the sewers to this," Andy said. "Not even a nightlight."

"These are our allies. There's nothing to be worried about."

When the lights turned on, Rocco's words proved to be absolute, one hundred percent bullshit. After their eyes adjusted, they were greeted by the realization that they were surrounded by a dozen armed men. Guns pointed directly at them, some barrels only inches away. Usually something to be worried about.

Rocco spoke slowly. "The man that you entrusted into our organization, Ben Jigo, has been assassinated. For that I am sorry. The impact of one of the recent explosions. We are also aware that you suffered losses from a simultaneous attack. Our condolences to your fallen. We are on our way to stop those responsible. The war continues, and we have no desire to operate without a representative from 893. With the loss of Jigo, we request a new recruit to take his place in Floodgate."

Nobody moved or spoke for a moment. A space formed and an old man walked into the center of the circle. Andy recognized him from the back table at Ikejime.

"My nephew? Did he die well?" the old man asked.

"Benjamin Jigo was a credit to Floodgate. His death was honorable," Rocco said.

"It's 1986, Colombo. We're gangsters, not samurai. And for a criminal, you've got to be the worst liar I know," the old man said. "But the lie is appreciated. I will give you a soldier. Someone more suitable to your needs. I'm beginning to see the usefulness of your team."

"Has Macklin contacted you?"

"We will be meeting within the hour."

Andy and Rocco left with a Japanese man in a New Orleans Saints jersey named Hiro, who the old man promised was one of their best. The guy had a permanent smile and a thick Cajun accent, and he seemed to be ready for anything.

"Are you going to show him the hobo movie?" Andy asked as the three walked back to the ice cream truck.

"You kidding me? I get to watch movies on this gig? With hobos in them? Like *Emperor of the North*? Love Lee Marvin," Hiro said.

"Going to toss you in the fire," Rocco said. "You'll have to pick up most of it on the fly. Right now, best we can do is point you at the bad guys."

"Throw me in the water. I swim like an eel," Hiro said. "Boys in 893, they ain't never known what to do with this Casian. Been their utility infielder mostly. A little bit of this. A little bit of that. I'm ready for some straight-up action. Point me toward the front line, hoss. You find me a fight, and I'll stay busier than a one-armed monkey with two peckers."

"Oh, man," Rocco said. "You're going to fit right in."

CHAPTER 32

When our eyes met, I was sure we had made a connection.
That we understood each other. I've always believed that the
eyes never lie. Maybe that only applies to humans.

—From apprentice zookeeper David Downing's statement
after being asked why he had entered the tiger cage at
the Auction City Zoo. His injuries required three surgeries
and more than one hundred stitches (1972).

The safe house was a dozen blocks from where Frank Whittle lived.
They had driven past the building on their last outing to Blackstreet
Hollow.

From the outside the house appeared abandoned, what a real estate
agent would generously call a fixer-upper. Dead lawn, peeling paint,
missing roof shingles. A sore thumb in the otherwise well-kept, middle-
class neighborhood. A bank foreclosure or a death in the family.

Pilar, Mirna, and Agnes posted up a block away. Andy pulled the
ice cream truck to the curb, and he, Rocco, and Hiro joined the women.

"No movement. Nobody's gone in or out. Nothing," Pilar said.

"Could be booby-trapped," Rocco said.

"This is where they've been holing up," Andy said. "I don't think they expected us to find this place."

"Don't matter when you got a bomb guy," Hiro said.

"You're Ben's replacement? New 893?" Pilar held out her prosthetic arm to Hiro. "I'm Pilar. This is Agnes. She's part of the gang. Mirna's just helping out for the day."

He shook the hook end of her prosthetic without losing a step or making it awkward. "Hey, y'all. I'm Hiro. Rocky and Andy here, they gave me the thirty-second version. I was just saying that if you got a bomber, some shit's going to explode."

"Look for tripwires, careful opening doors. Not all of us should go," Rocco said, looking around at them. "We could wait, but a second salvo is coming."

"You guys are the pros. I'm the new guy," Hiro said, still smiling. "But if I get blown to bits, I'm going to want a couple days' paid vacation."

◆ ◆ ◆

Rocco and Andy found a hiding place behind the building. A tall row of junipers against the back fence created excellent cover. They would take the back door. Pilar and Mirna would hit the front. Agnes and Hiro stayed on the street as backup. As simple as simple got. Elaborate plans had more working parts to screw up. In an effort to make it more official, they synchronized their watches.

Norman Hopewell was a mercenary, and by reputation a good one. Ipo Kahulamu dealt explosions, and there were few as unpredictable as a munitions man. He had killed Ben. The Thief River Killer, that psycho, was a whole different story. Andy couldn't figure out the madness of Gray's plan where letting that guy back into society was a good idea. They were about to crash a wild party. There would be casualties.

Five minutes to get into position at the back door.

"No hurry," Rocco said. "The less we're exposed, the less chance of losing surprise."

Andy nodded.

"I appreciate you coming along, son," Rocco said.

"I would've been bored back at the candy factory."

"This won't be boring. That's for damn sure."

They sat in silence. The sounds of a quiet neighborhood: sprinklers and barking dogs.

"You ever go fishing?" Andy asked.

Rocco gave him a funny look. "Used to drop a line off the rocks under TKO. Near the concrete pillars. The fish we caught always smelled like gasoline from the rubber factory runoff. Three eyes, no scales, and a huge dick. What made you think of fishing?"

"Making conversation."

"This father-son outing is going to be a little more intense." Rocco looked at his watch again. "Let's set up at the back door, son."

◆ ◆ ◆

Andy spotted the doghouse when his feet hit the dirt patch of the backyard. Rocco landed next to him, holding his lower back as he rose.

"Getting old is like having the flu all the time," Rocco whispered.

Andy pointed at the doghouse. Rocco drew his pistol and crept to it. He looked inside and shook his head. He waved Andy toward the back door.

Andy pulled his own weapon and crept low. He hadn't been on an honest-to-goodness raid since he'd been in uniform. He felt the adrenaline rise, heart beating quickly, vision sharp, everything moving in fast motion and slow motion simultaneously. He silently prayed that he didn't accidentally shoot himself or someone on his side.

Rocco kneeled at the back door. He pulled out a lock pick set and went to work. The lock was nothing fancy. Andy could open it in a half minute. He wondered if his old man had better lock skills. Question answered. It took Rocco less than twenty seconds. The old man glanced at his watch, turned the knob, and slowly opened the back door.

The two of them froze. Waited. Andy's leg shook. He had to piss. A pigeon landed on a wire that ran from the house to the alley. It looked bored. The smoke that rose from the city looked like nimbus clouds. Peaceful from the backyard of a gang of escaped convicts' safe house.

The pigeon flew away when the front door crashed open. A loud bang. Shouting and breaking things. Their cue. Rocco threw the door open and rushed inside, Andy right behind him.

One corner of the mudroom held shrink-wrapped boxes on a pallet: canned chili and bottled water. Lots of Spam, as well. A washing machine and dryer on the other side. A pile of dirty laundry on the ground. A pungent smell filled the room, like food left out.

Rocco rushed into the next room. Andy stopped. Protruding from the laundry, he spotted a foot. With the memory of the Chief's camouflaged men, Andy trained his gun on it. He kicked at the clothes where he guessed the head was.

The dry eyes of a long-haired dead man stared back at him. Wispy goatee, flaking skin. The man hadn't died recently. A bullet hole dotted his forehead. An ant crawled from the dead man's nostril.

"Don't move," Rocco yelled from another room.

"Hands! Hands!" Pilar shouted.

Andy grabbed a Members Only jacket from the floor and covered the dead man's face.

◆ ◆ ◆

In the living room, a large man sat at a long folding table. He looked like a Buddha, rooted and unyielding. With long wavy hair, the Hawaiian wore a disarming, beatific grin. The giant man did not look surprised or afraid of the guns pointed at him.

On the table sat all the makings of serious physical destruction—an array of components, tools, timers, and bricks of plastic explosives. Everything connected by a weave of wires. It might or might not be a completed device. From a layman's perspective, it was difficult to tell which did what. No one was impatient to find out.

Directly in front of the Hawaiian goliath lay photographs in a row: images of Kate, Rocco, Agnes, Pilar, and Ben. The members of Floodgate. A big X blacked out Ben Jigo's face.

"Ipo Kahulamu," Rocco said. "We expected Hopewell and Henry, too. Wanted to say hello to all of you."

"I am Ipo," the man said. He picked up Rocco's photo, held it up, and nodded.

"You murdered a friend of mine," Rocco said.

"The man in the car," Kahulamu said. He held up Pilar's photographs. "Not my best work. Rushed. Effective but lacking nuance."

"Bombs have nuance?" Pilar asked.

"In the right hands."

"Why are explosives guys always bananas?" Rocco said.

"Bananas? Is that a slight to my Hawaiian heritage?"

Rocco shook his head, seemingly worried that he had been inadvertently racist to the bomber.

"I know you." Kahulamu pointed at Andy. He reached to a separate stack of papers, pulling out Andy's picture.

"Are those all the targets?" Andy said.

"Who is she?" Kahulamu motioned with his chin toward Mirna. "I would remember that scarred face."

"I'm your worst nightmare," Mirna said.

"You are beautiful." He turned back to Rocco. "The black one outside should join us. And the one that wears red. Did she die from her injuries?"

Pilar took a step forward. He turned to her and shook his head. She stopped.

"She's alive," Pilar said.

"Is there a chance she will not survive?"

"She'll live," Rocco said.

"Too bad. I was hoping to be done."

"You are. It's over," Rocco said.

"You think you've caught me?" he said. Laughter followed. "I've been waiting for you."

The big Hawaiian lifted a hand from beneath the table. He held a grip detonator with wires leading both onto the table and somewhere below him. A dead man's switch.

"Be careful with those guns," Kahulamu said. "The moment I let go, a dog-choking amount of explosives will detonate. You, me, Mrs. Macintosh, and all her cats across the street, we all go boom. *Ua Mau ke Ea o ka ʻĀina i ka Pono*."

The calm Hawaiian bomber showed no nervousness. Andy couldn't say the same for himself or the others.

"As everyone is deciding what to do next, do you mind me asking a question?" Andy said. "Who is the dead man in the laundry room?"

Rocco turned to Andy, one eyebrow arched.

"Ronald?" Ipo said. "He never fit in. Annoyed Hopewell from the start. Two different personalities. The gecko and the bat. Ronald was a sadist, which can often be overlooked in this profession, but he got mouthy. Hopewell made a decision. I did not argue."

"Ronald Mark Henry," Andy said. "The Thief River Killer."

Ipo nodded. "You cannot trust a man with three first names."

"If you detonate the bomb," Rocco said, "you would be killing yourself."

"I hadn't thought of that."

"Really?" Andy asked.

Kahulamu ignored Andy. "I made a different arrangement than the others. Hopewell fights for himself. I fight for a cause. The money I earn will finance my people's movement, regardless of my survival.

Sometimes the most selfish actions prove selfless. I would rather die on my terms knowing that I died for what is good."

"What if I told you that you would be safe?" Rocco said. "Left unhurt."

"Then I would know that you are someone I cannot trust."

"So we have ourselves a standoff," Rocco said.

"A Mexican standoff," Kahulamu said, giving Pilar a wink.

"I'm Puerto Rican, *que gran hijo de la puta*," Pilar said, and leapt at the man who held their lives in his hands.

1929

LONG PAST DAYS

The priest, the Chinaman, the Wretch, the copper, and Fat Jimmy talked for hours in the middle of that street. Leaving us to stand and wait. Life and death in their hands. The Chinese sat on the ground. The Wretches remained on their feet. The coppers stood at attention. Eyeballing the criminals around them. Wanting to open fire on the scum of society.

Fat Jimmy's men let nervousness get the better of them. In the shadow of the gibbet, a good joke was welcome. Or hell, a bad one.

"I loaned a Chinaman money once. After two weeks, I raised the vig. He asked why. I said 'fluctuations.' He answered, 'Well, fluck you wops.'"

The other men laughed nervously. A few glanced at the Chinese. Out of earshot. Didn't mean they couldn't hear. The Chinese had their mystical ways.

"You think it's over? The fighting?" the girl asked me.

We had moved away from the others. Huddled in a corner. Their nerves gave me nerves. I still didn't like the way the other men looked at her. As if she was the last chance for something. Something from before.

I thought about Ma. About our room. Our life. Our home was gone. The impact of war. The crater of a bomb. Most of the city looked burnt up.

The fleeing filled the bridge, sagging in the middle. Peace on a battlefield only meant clearing the bodies.

Didn't mean there wasn't hope. That there wasn't a future. As uncertain as what that could mean.

"They wouldn't talk this long unless something was being worked out," I said. "They got to listen to a priest. He talks to God."

"The Chinese have different gods."

"Maybe those gods know the priest's God. Maybe they golf together. They can talk it over on the back nine."

Her smile made me feel like I had done something good.

"I'm glad I met you today," she said. "Even if it was in the sewer."

"Wouldn't never have met otherwise."

"Maybe it was fate."

A whistle blared from the center of the street. Everybody reacted. Bodies shifting. Sounds of surprise. I turned with everyone else.

Fat Jimmy gestured toward his men. Yelled. "Sal, I need you and three men. Men you trust. Men that can fight. Men you are sure of. Grab them and join the party." The other leaders delivered the same message to their men. Multiple languages. Variations on the idea.

Sal nodded. Turned to the men. Scanned their faces. Walked among them. He put a hand on Giorgio Alfieri's shoulder. I knew Giorgio. Ironically named Jolly George. A man you would want in a fight. But nowhere else. The humorless man said, "Tell me how you want me to die."

Sal pointed at Marco Lupo. Nobody questioned that choice. The Red Wolf was feared in every corner of the city. Marco nodded and stepped forward.

And then Sal turned to me. A nod. I pointed at myself. He nodded again and said, "Rocky." Why would he pick me? I didn't even have a good nickname, just a Y on the end of my name.

The others stared at me. Angry. Jealous. Insulted. But grateful it wasn't them.

I turned to the girl. "I'll be right back. I think."

❖ ❖ ❖

Sal, Giorgio, Marco, and me. Three men and a boy. Walking across the street to our fate.

We joined the men from the other groups. Enemies united. Four Chinese from their camp. Four Wretches, all different shades of brown. Four uniformed cops, hands on their clubs. We all were surprised when four priests armed with tommy guns walked out of an alley.

To say that the moment was tense would be like saying the Great War was a bit of a dustup. Murder and fear hung in the air. Were we about to gladiator it out?

The Chinese leader pointed at me. Shouted in his crazy language. The priest translated. Said to Fat Jimmy, "He thinks that one's too young."

"He's a kid, Sal," Fat Jimmy said. "What about Carlo?"

Sal shook his head. "Maybe a kid this morning. Not no more. Not after today. Stood with me. Made it from the park to here. Survived the fire and them slants to get here. He's my pick."

I felt as if I should say something. Then that I shouldn't. I didn't.

Fat Jimmy shrugged and turned to the priest. "You heard the man."

The priest said some Chinese. Probably didn't use the word *slant*. The leader grunted, or it may have been a word. Weird language. Whatever it was, I passed the test.

"The war is over," the priest said, translating as he went.

My body relaxed a little. No longer holding my breath. Hands peeled from the curl of a fist.

"We still have an important battle," the priest said. "To win it, you're going to work together."

❖ ❖ ❖

They were going to divide us into four groups. One of each of us in each group. Me, a Chinaman, a priest, a Wretch, and a copper. Enemies, now men-at-arms. We were to walk the streets and deliver the message of peace. If that didn't work, we would force it on them.

It sounded crazy, but I was ready to do what I was told. Being on my own had been too damn scary.

Everyone was going to work together for a while. The Trust would work with the Wretches and Chinese. Put out the fires, search for survivors, grab power. Businesses on hold. The cops would be cops, but leave the gangs alone. Together we would rebuild the city. Our way.

❖ ❖ ❖

In a back room of the baths, Fat Jimmy kept an arsenal. The others had already found their weapons. I stared, overwhelmed. All new to me. Never used more than what was lying around or what someone handed me. Rows of guns, blades, and bludgeons. Fat Jimmy collected destruction. Firearms of kinds I had never seen. A collection of pipes, both steel and lead. If not for the other weapons, a hardware store display. Well maintained but not unused. Scuffs on every club. Stains on knives. Notches on guns.

"You must have made an impression," the girl said, walking into the room behind me.

"It feels like history," I said. "With me in the middle."

"You made an impression on me. That's for sure."

"I'm not going to do anything until I know you're safe."

She looked at a revolver on the table. Picked it up. Felt its weight. Held it toward me. "Take this one. It'll fit your hand. I have a good feeling about it. That it might save your life."

I took it. Our hands brushed for an instant.

"You've got it all wrong," she said. "I kept you safe. And now it's over. You don't need me anymore."

"I'm not joking. It's still dangerous out there. Fighting is only done for those that know it's done. Let me get you home."

"I don't know if I'm going home."

Sal poked his head into the room. About to say something. Saw us together. Paused. Then, "A minute to say your good-byes, Romeo." He left.

"Maybe we were only meant to know each other today," she said. "Today was our day."

"That's not how it works."

"It's exactly how it works."

We stood there. Our minute passing. Looking at each other. Words failing.

"I'll find you," I said.

"I bet you will."

She reached up to my face. Still holding the pistol, I put my hands around her waist. We held each other. We kissed. One last look. One last kiss. That was it.

I joined the other men. We spread the word of the truce. I got more bruises than sleep. We pulled people from fire and rubble. We brought water and food to the desperate. We fought. Punished looters and con men. Killed those who exploited the chaos. We brought the city back from the dead.

It would be almost twenty years until I saw the girl again. I hadn't even known her name until all those years later.

Beth.

1986

CHAPTER 33

Are you a complete ignoramus? How could I possibly have a good reason for such madness?

> —*Statement of Nicholas Slosser after being asked why he stripped nude, painted his body silver, stole a helicopter, and landed it in the middle of Charbonneau Field during the fifth inning of an Auction City Terrapins home game (1980)*

The big Hawaiian screamed as the split hook of Pilar's prosthetic arm pinched his hand tighter onto the detonator. With her free hand, she threw wild punches at the man's face. He grabbed her hair and pulled her over the table, but she remained latched to him.

"Get this Mexican off me!" Kahulamu yelled.

"I told you. I'm Puerto Rican, *mamabicho*," Pilar said.

Mirna jumped the table and joined the fray. She got an arm around his neck and attempted to choke him out, but the man was huge. The line where his neck began and his shoulders started proved vague, his throat protected by thickness. Kahulamu didn't look bothered by the woman around his neck, but Pilar was like a ferret on a finger. As hard as he shook, she wasn't coming off.

Rocco moved to line up a shot. With Mirna behind the man, he couldn't risk it.

"You should not have done that," the big man said. "Pele is unforgiving."

Kahulamu reached for the device in front of him with his free hand.

"No!" Andy shouted as he leapt forward to stop him. Too late.

The good news was that they didn't explode. The bad news was a loud and sustained beep sounded and a digital timer lit up in the center of the mass of wire and metal. The timer was set to three minutes. It counted down.

"Damn it," Kahulamu said. "I forgot I attached that timer."

"Shut it down," Andy said.

"Sorry for the delay." The Hawaiian laughed. "You're done, Venus de Mexico. If you let go, we explode. If you hold on, we explode. Only a few minutes later."

He said all that despite Pilar and Mirna hurling fists in his face. Kahulamu threw an elbow behind him that clipped Mirna in the temple. She tumbled to the ground.

"Fuck that," Mirna said. She stood up, pulled her gun, and shot Kahulamu in the head. No fanfare. His thick hair flew to the side, but it caught whatever escaped the inside of his skull. The matted hair dripped thick red. Kahulamu sagged but moved surprisingly little. His center of gravity already settled.

"Two minutes, forty-five!" Andy yelled.

"Everyone out," Pilar said. "Get out."

"Unhook your arm," Rocco said.

"Not how this one works. I have to maintain the pressure," she said. "It's time to haul ass."

"I won't," Mirna said.

"What good does that do?" Pilar yelled. "Go."

"Find some duct tape, some string, something to keep that detonator closed," Andy said to Rocco and Mirna. "I'm going to disarm this son of a bitch."

"You don't know how to do that," Rocco said.

"Just because I haven't doesn't mean I can't. I was dealing with a similar device earlier this week," Andy said. Although he remembered that he hadn't been overly successful then, and it had been a television, not a bomb.

"You can't disarm a bomb based on a delusional belief in your abilities."

"Find something to keep that detonator closed, and we won't have to find out," Andy said. "We're running out of time."

◆ ◆ ◆

A minute later, they hadn't found anything that would work. There weren't many choices in the house. They tried the laundry, but it couldn't get tight. Nor could Rocco's belt or shoelaces. Some peeling duct tape had lost its stickiness. Pilar held on, her face red and sweating.

Andy had opened the side of Kahulamu's device and stared at the very complex system of wires. A good chunk of it made no sense to him.

"Way more complicated than a television set," Andy said.

"What did you say?" Pilar said.

"Nothing."

When the clock ticked past two minutes, a thimbleful of urine leaked from Andy's body. So much for clean underwear in case of an accident.

"It's time for you two to go," Andy said to Rocco and Mirna. They continued to search drawers and shelves, looking for anything helpful.

Rocco threw a drawer across the room and kicked a wall. Mirna crossed her arms and shook her head.

"Por favor, mi hermana," Pilar said. "Someone has to protect the others."

Her wet eyes locked on Pilar, Mirna ran a finger along the scar on her face. Pilar nodded. Mirna walked out the front door.

Rocco put a hand on Andy's shoulder. "Let's go."

"I can do this," Andy said. "I know I can."

"It's a losing bet."

"You can go, Destra," Pilar said. "This isn't on you. I'll hold on until you're clear."

"Come on," Rocco said.

"No," Andy said. "Now quit wasting my time, and let me defuse this bomb."

"Then I guess I'm staying, too," Rocco said. "Wouldn't be much of a father if I didn't have faith in my son."

"Don't be stupid," Pilar said. "Both you *estúpidos* need to go."

Rocco and Andy looked at each other and smiled.

"Like father, like son," Andy said.

Andy, Rocco, and Pilar laughed. Jokes didn't have to be particularly funny when you were in a safe house with a bomb and a dead Hawaiian giant. They laughed because it was probably their last. The punch line a minute away.

"I know you're lying about knowing about this thing, but tell me you know what you're doing," Pilar said. "Even if you don't."

"I wouldn't be here if I didn't think I could do this," Andy said. "I'm not suicidal."

"Don't fuck this up," she said. His new mantra. He could see her straining to hold her grip, the veins in her arms bulging from the effort. She did her part. Now it was time to do his.

"You can do this," Rocco said.

Sweat ran off Andy's forehead into his eyes. He blinked it away, wiped his face with his shirtsleeve.

Multicolored wires ran from the timer into various parts of the mechanism. For all its seeming complexity, a bomb was a simple device: a trigger, a timer, a power supply, and initiator, and an explosive. He was looking for the power supply and the primary trigger system. With a pair of pliers he'd found on the table, he carefully pushed some wires out of the way. Within the maze, he found what he was looking for.

In high school, Andy had gone through a phase where he sought out the books that nobody was supposed to read. The ones that you couldn't get in bookstores, but some guy knew some other guy. Mail-order from back pages of leaflets. That reading list included books like *The Anarchist Cookbook* and *The Militant's Formulary*, books with—among other things—detailed information about bomb making. He hoped he remembered the basics.

Five colored wires ran from the primary power source. One of the wires would be coming from the timer, others going out to the trigger mechanism and the initiator. There could also be dummy wires. He needed to clip the one that distributed the trigger message to the rest of the mechanism, essentially the fuse. Ignore the timer and kill its brain.

"How much time left?" Andy said, following each of the wires' paths with his eyes.

"Forty-eight seconds," Pilar said, interrupting her recitation of the Lord's Prayer in Spanish.

"I understand what's going on in here, but I'm still going to have to guess."

"Get out of here," Pilar said, resigned. "I appreciate the try."

"I didn't say I gave up," Andy said. "What's your favorite color?"

"Uh," Rocco said.

"No way," Pilar said. "Ain't going to be on me if this thing goes."

"I'm going to clip the red wire."

"You had much luck with red wires in the past?" Rocco asked. "Seems like red is obvious. The one that everyone clips first. Like red cars get more speeding tickets."

307

"Which wire is the ugliest?" Pilar asked.

Andy looked at the mechanism, never having really considered the relative beauty of a wire. "I suppose the gray one."

"Cut the gray one," she said.

"Timer?"

"Twenty seconds," Rocco said. "Cut the gray one."

Andy reached into the device with the wire cutters. He squeezed the wire cutters to clip the gray wire, but they slipped in his sweaty hands. With an audible snip, he accidentally cut the red wire.

They didn't explode.

"The clock is still going," Pilar said.

"I wasn't cutting the timer. It will still run down. It should hit zero and then nothing should happen."

"Should?"

"Theoretically. But don't let go," Andy said. "That detonator is attached separately."

Andy, Rocco, and Pilar watched the clock as it counted down.

"Do you want to hold my hand?" Andy asked Pilar.

She shook her head.

"Will you please hold my hand?" he asked her.

She grinned, reached out, and grabbed Andy's sweaty hand. Rocco put his hand on Andy's shoulder. Nothing more to say.

Five. Four. Three. Two.

"I cut the red wire," Andy blurted out.

"You dick," Pilar said.

One.

◆ ◆ ◆

It took Andy and Rocco ten more minutes to find something to keep the detonator closed. Finally, Rocco caught sight of the shrink-wrap around the boxes of chili and Spam in the mudroom. They pulled it all off and cut it in strips. It took a while, but they got it wrapped tightly around the detonator, the prosthetic hook, and the dead man's hand.

"Sorry about having to leave your arm," Rocco said.

"No big deal. It's like losing a pair of sunglasses," Pilar said. "I got another one in the car."

Andy collected all the paperwork that Kahulamu had in front of him. Each of the pictures on the desk. Some scattered notes and scraps of paper. Whatever he could find.

Five convicts down. Only Hopewell remained.

"Let's get out of here," Pilar said, examining their slapdash effort on the detonator. "I don't trust this thing one bit."

When the two of them reached the front door, Pilar turned to Andy. "Thanks. I don't know if I would've stayed." She gave him a hard punch on the arm and walked outside.

Mirna, Agnes, and Hiro waited three blocks away. They sat on the curb, big smiles when they saw Andy, Rocco, and Pilar approaching. Mirna ran over and gave Pilar a bear hug, lifting her off the ground. Agnes kissed the palm of her hand and placed it on Pilar's cheek.

"What took you so long?" Hiro asked. "When it didn't explode, we figured that was a good thing. But none of us were going to look down the barrel of that bazooka."

"Great job in there, son," Rocco said, slapping him on the back.

Maybe for Rocco and Andy it was bombs, not fishing trips. Sewer cannibals, not ball games. Lost time was lost, but Andy could see that their future was going to be an interesting one. That they were going to be in each other's lives in their own weird way.

"I grabbed all the Hawaiian's stuff," Andy said, holding up the fistful of papers. But nobody heard him.

The house exploding drowned him out. A burst of fire and black smoke erupted from the roof. The windows and walls blew out onto the street, fire following. It was beautiful and then gone, bits of house drifting to the ground.

Saran wrap was a great invention, but it wasn't designed to hold a dead man's hand and a prosthetic arm over a grip detonator. No fault to the product. That's just a really specialized function.

CHAPTER 34

Why I want all my eggs in one basket? They all in one basket, I drop the basket, I ain't got no eggs. And I like eggs.
Better I keep them all over the damn place.

—*From the stage play* Super Barrio Mothers, *by Gilberto
Moreno, which premiered at Auction City's historic Cocteau
Theatre (1986)*

A few minutes later, Kate pulled up in a van with the image of Red
Sonja riding a surfboard and fighting a bear airbrushed on the side.
Full Molly Hatchet–era Frazetta. Majestic.

"I thought we weren't using the Shaggin' Wagon anymore," Rocco
said.

"It's a classic. Besides, it was the only vehicle left that wasn't a stick,"
she said, lifting the elbow of her arm in its sling.

"Any word on Hopewell?" Rocco asked. "He's the last convict we
got to track down."

Kate shook her head. "But there's good news on the ACPD front.
Mac's worked out a deal with Randall Ashley and the other cop brass.
They were all scared of Gray, but Hank Robinson is just a bad Xerox of
Gray to them. He'll be done on the same day he got crowned."

"The other cops will switch that easy to Ashley?" Andy asked. "He's got clout, but Robinson practically has his own militia."

"Ashley claims to have the majority of the brass and the rank and file. The loyalists will have to be convinced."

"They can talk politics all day, but Hank Robinson isn't going away without a fight," Andy said. "He's got the Thorntons. And Hopewell is out there planning some mayhem. If Robinson gets pushed against the ropes, he's going to swing wild."

◆ ◆ ◆

They huddled around the bank of payphones. Andy never realized how much spare change was necessary to run a criminal operation. They needed to reach Macklin and the other leaders to coordinate their next move.

"All I'm getting is the 'This number is no longer in service' message," Kate said. "Tried three different numbers."

"The phone lines at the Fortress are independent. The whole network would have to be down," Rocco said.

"Mac is at the Fortress?" Andy asked.

"It could be the riots. One of the fires impacting the lines," Kate said.

"Doubtful. Mostly underground," Pilar said.

"Who else is at the Fortress?" Andy cut in.

"After the bombings, Mac insisted on bringing all the leaders there, including the new leader of Consolidated," Kate said. "It's the safest place in the city."

"Champ is there, too," Andy said. "Does Robinson know about the Fortress?"

"Gray did," Rocco said. "So I have to assume that Robinson knows, as well."

Andy made a sound of frustration that sounded like *whaaa-jaaavaaa*. He looked up at the sky, took a deep breath, and said, "So, you're telling me Robinson knows where all the leaders are congregated? Thus it could be concluded that Hopewell might know where they are, as well. The man that was hired to kill them all? And the phone is dead at that location?"

"When you put it that way," Kate said.

"The phones didn't just happen to go out. Hopewell is going to attack. If it hasn't already begun."

"Then we—" Rocco said.

"I'm not done," Andy said. "You put pretty much the only person I care about there, too. Great job."

"We don't know if—" Rocco said.

"Sometimes I wonder how you people managed to maintain this thing for so long. How the city is still standing. Hell, you've done jackshit about the riots," Andy said. "You seemed so nefarious at first, but it's really a seat-of-your-pants, shit-for-brains kind of operation up close. It's all facade. Professional talent with amateur brains."

"Now is not the time," Rocco said.

"Or maybe it's overconfidence. You've been at it so long that you haven't faced an actual threat. So removed from the day-to-day that the delusion of invulnerability set in."

"Maybe you can write a scathing op-ed for the *Intelligencer*," Rocco said. "Right now, we have to figure this out."

"A hobo revealed your secrets to me. A damn hobo. And now I'm going to take an ice cream truck to an ambush. It's ridiculous. You people are frigging ridiculous." Andy stomped toward the ice cream truck. He stopped and turned. "Well, are you all coming, or do I got to stop the bad guys from killing the other bad guys all by my damn self?"

In movies the heroes showed up in the nick of time. In movies the heroes won. In movies there were such things as heroes. Movies were full of shit.

Andy doubted there were any heroes in this scenario, but nick of time be damned. They were definitely late to the party.

The first thing that Andy saw when the ice cream truck turned onto Holt Avenue was a Japanese man with a gigantic sword chasing a uniformed police officer down the street. Not the strangest thing he saw, just the first thing.

Violence filled Holt Avenue. Three blocks of fighting men and women. Not a riot but a melee. This wasn't a protest or an angry mob. These were soldiers in a combat zone. Andy heard a couple gunshots, mostly in the distance. The men and women fighting in front of him battled with bare hands and bludgeons, brawling in quarters too close for firearms, too much of a chance of shooting an ally. If not for the cracking bones and spraying blood, it looked as though the combatants were dancing. Dancing each other to death.

It appeared to be everyone against the police. Either that or an attack on men with mustaches. Members of 893, Consolidated, and suited bodyguard types that Andy took for Trust stood toe-to-toe with uniformed officers and plainclothes detectives in short-sleeve shirts and ties. Nothing pretty. Nothing choreographed. Sloppy forearms to the ears, kicked shins, throat punching, and a whole lot of rolling on the ground.

There were scattered bodies, too. Dead or unconscious. Most likely both. It was the most insane thing Andy had ever seen in Auction City, and he had just been chased through the sewers by mole people.

"Ashley might have overestimated Robinson's influence," Rocco said. "If these are the cops loyal to Robinson, he's got more support than I thought. And I got no idea what he's trying to accomplish here, except maybe kill as many of his enemies as he can."

"If it looks for a second like Robinson is going to win this fight," Andy said, "the cops sitting this out will turn on Ashley."

"But if they think Robinson will lose," Rocco said, "they'll turn. They ain't got no loyalty."

"Except the Thorntons."

"Not much we can do," Rocco said. "This will play out how it plays out. Hopewell is our concern. Five convicts down, one to go. We have to stop him from whatever he's about to do. Or what he's already done."

"How do we stop someone from doing what they've already done?"

"You know what I mean."

"Whoa," Andy said, reacting to a bald man in an Armani suit who leapt off a parked car and landed on two police officers, knocking them to the ground.

"We can't just sit here and watch," Rocco said.

"I don't ever want to get used to killing people," Andy said. "More people are going to die, aren't they?"

"God, I hope so," Rocco said.

Andy stopped the ice cream truck in the middle of the street. They stepped into the back. Rocco found a four-way lug wrench and handed it to Andy. He got a long piece of pipe for himself.

"The front door to the Holt building is the only way in," Rocco said. "Follow me." He laughed to himself and flicked on the ice cream truck music.

Without another word, father and son joined the fray to their own demented soundtrack.

It took Andy a couple of tries to get used to his new weapon. The crosslike shape wasn't great for swinging, but it was effective for poking. A jab in the eye dropped a rotten cop he used to know to his knees. It didn't stop him completely, but enough for Andy to give him a kick to the face. Punishing bad cops could become addictive.

He turned to find Rocco and get his father's approval, only to get a punch to the side of the head from a gigantic fist. He kept his feet, but only just.

"I was hoping I would see you," the Thornton said. Andy had no idea which one. One of the younger ones.

"You Thorntons are everywhere," Andy said.

"There's a lot of love in my family," he said.

"Any daughters? Or just gorillas?"

"You don't want to mess with a Thornton lass. Even I'm scared of them."

"Are we going to do this?" Andy asked.

The Thornton charged forward. Andy kicked his knee with a straight foot. The Thornton's leg bent back in the wrong direction with a nauseating, meaty snap. The man fell. Andy threw up all over him. He felt worse for the vomit than the broken knee.

Not sticking around to gloat, he caught sight of Rocco fifteen yards closer to the door, making quick work of some cop half his age. He didn't bother to use the pipe, taking down the kid with one hand. What Rocco lacked in speed, he made up for in power. For an old guy, he still had some pop in his punch.

As Andy ran to the front door, someone pushed him on the back, making him stumble forward and eat it on the sidewalk. He turned to see Brandon Carver, a cop with a reputation for taking advantage of women in custody. A real piece of shit.

"Hey, ratfuck," Carver said. "You've had a beating coming for a long time."

Then the man collapsed. A soup can rolled away from his prone form. Andy looked for Agnes, but he didn't spot her in the crowd. He thanked the statue across the street. The church had a blackened hole from the explosion earlier in the day, but that scary angel still stood. Watching over him, protecting him.

❖ ❖ ❖

The vase in the center of the table had been broken, shards scattered over the back of a dead man. There had been a hell of a battle. The strewn bodies of men in suits and police decorated the room. Quiet as a tomb, the fighting was over for these men. Probably never knew what they were fighting for. Soldiers following orders. Paid to take a side.

"All I care about is Champ," Andy said.

Rocco thought for a moment. He nodded. "I caught sight of Hopewell on the roof of the building next door."

"Kate took me to Champ's before, but it was twisty and turny," Andy said.

"No time to write it down, so listen."

❖ ❖ ❖

Andy walked down the dark hallway and into the sixth sitting room. He pulled at the bookcase, realized that Rocco had said the fifth sitting room when he tweaked his back, and went into the right room. A dubious start to his journey. Andy moved the correct bookcase and headed down the passage into the basement and across into the building next door.

Through hallways and passages, up and down staircases, behind fake walls. It didn't take long for Andy to get lost. He retraced his steps and found a stairwell that looked familiar. The sounds of fighting played out in the distance. One flight up without incident. When he stopped to catch his breath, he heard a door close. Above him, footsteps descended the stairs.

There was nowhere to go. No place to hide. Andy considered calling out. It could be an ally, one of the Trust bodyguards. Unfortunately, none of his supposed allies knew who the hell he was. He didn't know the password or the secret handshake. And he looked like a cop, having not abandoned the cop look from his time as a cop. His flattop could get him killed.

He felt hypocritical about the lecture that he had given Kate and Rocco regarding their slapdash operation. Every plan he had ever devised consisted of him running at a thing. Or waiting for a thing. Or hiding from a thing.

He pulled his pistol and held it in front of him, ready for whatever appeared on the landing above him. He saw the red hair first.

"You've got to be kidding me," Andy said. "Another one?"

"Destra?" the Thornton said, surprised. "What the hell are you doing here?"

"You got to start wearing name tags," Andy said. "Keep your hands away from your weapon."

The Thornton's eyes fell to the pistol in Andy's hand.

"You are pointing a gun at an officer of the law," the Thornton said, now angry.

"I'm pointing a gun at a thug."

"You're interfering with official police business. We have warrants. Charges. Taking down a major criminal conspiracy." The Thornton took the first step down toward Andy.

"I don't want a fight. I need to get past you. That's all," Andy said. "You can go this way. I'll go that way. Deal?"

"Nope." The Thornton pushed off the step and flew toward Andy, both hands in front of him like Superman. Andy fired, but that didn't stop the Thornton from landing on top of him.

Andy never went completely unconscious, but for a few seconds everything went swirly. The back of his head had plonked against the landing. He now knew how Rowdy Roddy Piper felt after Jimmy Snuka performed the Superfly Splash. That's the image that filled his head. The Thornton's head on Snuka's body. The best finishing move in wrestling. The weirdest things popped into the mind of the semiconscious.

Decreasingly less painful hooks to the midsection pulled him from his WWF daydream. The Thornton—under duress, Andy would have guessed Seamus—punched at him, but the flurry felt like a machine running out of batteries. In fifteen seconds, the Thornton stopped fighting.

Andy rolled the man off him and stood. Andy's clothes were covered in blood. He got immediately dizzy and fell on his ass. He counted to ten. Deep breathing slowed his heart rate. He tried and succeeded in standing. Seamus looked dead. He kicked the Thornton with a toe like you would to check if a dog was alive. This hound wasn't.

Andy limped up the stairs, using the bar for support. On the next floor, he found the fire pole he had slid down with Kate. It brought him to what he was pretty sure was Champ's floor. The hallway was clear. No noise. No movement. No people. The faint smell of smoke, but that could have been in his nostrils from the street.

He found the door, luckily remembering the number. Although in this Escher-inspired series of structures, the apartment numbers were probably changed daily. He had to start somewhere. Andy thanked the air and tried the knob. Of course, it was locked.

Andy gave the door a shave and a haircut and waited. Light-headed from the fight and his short journey, Andy took a knee to avoid passing out. The moment his knee hit the ground, the top of the door exploded, shards of wood flying into the hallway. Right where his head had been.

Why couldn't anything be easy?

CHAPTER 35

Mayhem will not be tolerated.

*—Hand-painted sign attributed to the vigilante group known
as "Floodgate" (circa 1929)*

A ndy sat on the ground, clutching his pistol in two hands. He waited a count of three for the next shot, but it didn't come.

"Sons of bitches shot Russell!" Champ yelled from inside.

"Champ," Andy shouted, "if that's you shooting, it's me. It's Andy."

"Who's there?" Champ asked. "Is someone out there?"

"It's Andy. You know me."

She fired again. The new hole exploded below the previous one. Champ appeared to be attempting to draw a snowman on the door with a shotgun.

"You have to remember me. You have to try. I know it's hard," Andy said. "I'm going to stand up. Don't shoot me. I want you to see my face. Once you see me, you'll know who I am."

Andy holstered his pistol and took a deep breath. He didn't want to give himself enough time to realize how stupid this move was. He stood and stuck his face in the upper hole in the door.

"It's me," he said. "Try to remember."

"Andy," Champ said nonchalantly. She pointed a shotgun from a defensive position behind the sofa. "What are you doing here?"

"I came to make sure you're okay."

"Couldn't be better," she said. "Did you bring any food? I've been hankering for a slice."

"Can I come in?" Andy asked.

"You don't have to ask. You know that," she said. "We're family. Do you want some tea?"

Andy reached through the shotgun-forged breach in the door and let himself inside.

"Thorntons running around all flibbertigibbety," Champ said. "One of them shot Russell. I drove the bastard off with my persuader here."

"How hurt is Russell? Where is he?"

"Not too bad. Tried to call an ambulance. Phone is dead. I field-dressed the wound. He's napping in the bedroom."

"Who gave you a shotgun?" Andy asked.

"There were four of them in the closet when I moved in. I suppose for mice."

"Do you mind if I take it?" Andy asked, approaching with his hand out.

Champ clutched it to her body. "I might be losing my mind—don't mean I shouldn't be armed."

❖ ❖ ❖

From Champ's living room window, Andy caught a bird's-eye view of the chaos on the street. From that height, it was impossible to tell who was fighting whom. A blur of bodies moving in waves, the uniformed police the only identifiable team. He wished the others had worn jerseys or very large name tags. Fighting in shirts and skins would have really helped out Andy.

Champ sat on the couch with the shotgun between her knees. She thumbed through the *TV Guide*. "Probably something good on Channel 6. Maybe an old movie? Or *Rockford Files*? Can't beat Rockfish."

Gunfire erupted from the hallway. Andy looked to the ridiculously ineffective front door. Nothing more than a hinged wooden hole.

"Get back behind here, Champ." Andy led her behind the couch. "Stay down."

"Tell whoever it is to make it snappy. The answering machine message at the beginning is the best part," she said.

Andy had his pistol out as he walked slowly toward the door. This wasn't the kind of battle that he could hide from. More gunfire stopped him halfway to the door. Footsteps approached. He crouched and aimed his weapon. The door flew open. Andy came within a breath of shooting Agnes and Cardinal Macklin.

Agnes pulled Macklin behind her, practically dragging him into the apartment. She closed the door, looked at it, and started moving an armoire.

"Help me," she said.

The archbishop held a small derringer on Andy but lowered it when he recognized him. Andy helped Agnes block the door with the armoire and get a table behind it for support. It wasn't going to stop anyone who really wanted to get inside, but it would be enough of a hassle to make entry dangerous.

"Are you hurt? Are either of you hurt?" Andy asked.

Agnes shrugged and moved to the window.

"What's happening out there?" Andy asked.

"That Hopewell is one determined bastard," Macklin said. "I don't know what Gray promised him, but he's playing this out to the end. The man raided our meeting. Came through the ceiling, for Christ's sake. The chandelier hit the ground with him and an army of Thorntons right behind. Guns a-blazin'. It got worse from there. Agnes pulled me out."

"Leader of the Trust fell," Agnes said. "Some 893 soldiers. Hopewell has little fear, fights well."

"Who are these people?" Champ said, waving the shotgun wildly between Agnes and Macklin.

Macklin turned, frightened, his small gun aimed at Champ.

"No, no, no," Andy said. "Stress confuses her. Just be nice, and she'll be nice to you. We're all friends here."

Champ squinted at Macklin. "You dirty son of a bitch."

"It's okay, Champ," Andy said. "That's Cardinal Macklin."

She kept the shotgun trained on Macklin. "I know who he is. He owes me money."

"You have him mixed up with someone else," Andy said. "His Holiness is the archbishop of Auction."

"Champ Destra? It is you." Macklin laughed and lowered his derringer. "She's not mistaken. The lady is right. I do believe I owe her. Fourteen dollars, wasn't it?"

"Are you kidding me?" Andy said.

"It was years ago," Macklin said. "But a momentous evening. Dick's Dock, if memory serves me. Champ challenged me to some form of drinking competition. Right in my wheelhouse. I was overconfident."

"You welched."

"Not entirely my fault, my dear. If I recall, a doozie of a brawl broke out, and I became embroiled in ministering to some heathens with my fists." Macklin reached into a hidden pocket, found a money clip, and peeled off a couple of twenties. "With interest."

Champ lowered the shotgun and took the money.

"Okay," Champ said. "We're square."

Macklin shook his head. "Dick's had the best degenerates. So many souls to save."

"We need to get the two of you into the safe room," Agnes said. "Away from the windows and the doors."

"There's a safe room?" Andy asked.

"Why do you think I came here?" Agnes said. "They're scattered throughout the complex."

"Russell, her nurse, is in the back. He's hurt. I don't know how bad."

"I'll take care of this young lady and her nurse." Macklin held out his elbow to Champ, as if asking her to the dance floor. "Shall we?"

She took his elbow, still clutching the shotgun.

"Keep her safe, Mac," Andy said.

"The big sissy has always been a sentimental sap," Champ said.

"You can see why she's so special to me," Andy said.

They went into the back bedroom, closing the door behind them.

Agnes grabbed Andy's arm, her fingers digging into his bicep. She walked him to the armoire.

"Hopewell and the Thorntons," Agnes said. "They are the most dangerous. They are the active threats. They need to be stopped."

"What about the other police, Robinson, all the fighting in the street?"

"If you know another way for a good end, then by all means," she said, "but I am lost for a different strategy."

"There were supposed to be all sorts of backroom dealings. Ashley was taking over the police." Andy found himself yelling. "I thought you people had a plan. Or at least knew what was going on."

"I've never tried to understood what happens between those that are really in charge. I am a soldier."

"So I got to see behind the curtain, but apparently there's just another curtain behind that one. And we have no idea what's going on back there?"

"Hopewell and the Thorntons are making Gray's loyalists—now Robinson's loyalists—brave. We take away their champions, we make them rethink their alliances—that will benefit our efforts."

"So all that fighting on the street? That's what? A distraction?"

"Essentially. We take care of our side of things," Agnes said. "I have already facilitated three journeys to the afterlife in my efforts to keep the Cardinal alive."

"So what do we do?" Andy said. "And don't sugarcoat it."

"We find Hopewell, the remaining Thorntons, and we kill them," Agnes said and handed him a pistol machine gun. "We kill them all."

"I was kidding. I wanted you to sugarcoat it."

◆ ◆ ◆

The two of them pulled the armoire crashing to the ground. Agnes opened the door and looked down the hall. She waved Andy to follow.

"I am going to find Pilar and her girls," she said. "Are you going to be okay on your own?"

Apparently that was a rhetorical question, as Agnes was gone before Andy had a chance to answer. He considered turning around and joining Champ and Macklin in the safe room. He headed down the hall instead.

Andy had no idea where he was headed and not a strong idea of what he was going to do when he got there. At this point it was easier for Andy to react to whatever happened than plan for something that would never happen. The equivalent of running blindly with his hands over his ears and no sense of smell. Standard operating procedure for Andy.

At the end of the hall, there was a large window. Andy's view was exclusively of the adjoining building's roof, one floor below. The roof was flat but covered in vents, ductwork, and other utility units. Stacks of construction material crowded the already dense space.

On the roof, Rocco was pinned down by rifle fire. He hunched behind a large air-conditioning vent. A tall man in full camouflage poked out from behind cover and fired shots from an assault rifle that pinged off the metal above Rocco's head. Norman Hopewell. It had to be. Only an asshole wore forest camouflage in the city.

Andy may have only known Rocco for a short amount of time, but he wasn't going to let an asshole shoot at his father.

Andy looked down at the machine-gun pistol in his hand, making sure that he knew how to operate it. The window didn't open, so he aimed the weapon at the camouflaged man through the glass. When he opened fire, two things happened: glass shards went everywhere, and he missed horribly. If he was being honest, he came closer to hitting Rocco.

Both Hopewell and Rocco looked up in his direction. Nerves and window refraction out of the way, Andy fired again, missing but not embarrassingly so. Hopewell hadn't even bothered to dive for cover. Hopewell brought his rifle to his shoulder.

Andy dove backward down the hall. Gunfire ripped through the ceiling above him, raining ceiling tile debris on his head. Hopewell was a much better shot than he was.

Once the gunfire ceased, Andy crawled through the broken glass to the window. Hopewell moved along the edge of the roof. A glance to the window, but back to concentrating on Rocco's position. If Hopewell made it to the corner and around some ductwork, he would flank Rocco.

Andy yelled Rocco's name. Rocco gave Andy a thumbs-up, followed by a bunch of hand gestures that Andy didn't understand.

"I have no idea what that means!" Andy shouted and pointed. "Hopewell is coming around to your right. To your right."

Rocco pointed at his ear and shook his head. He shouted what was probably "I can't hear you," but it sounded like "My man mere moo."

Andy checked Hopewell's position and threw one leg over the edge of the window, then the other. Cutting his hands, he lowered his body down the side of the building. When he was fully extended, hanging from his hands, he knew he needed to let go. He glanced down, realizing he'd miscalculated. What he thought would only be a few feet was more like ten. He would have to get his eyes checked if he survived the day. He tried to do a chin-up and pull himself back up, but we all know how that went.

Bullets flying in one's direction were a great motivator. The moment he heard the first shot, his fingers released. His feet landed on the pebbled roof, knees buckling beneath him and pain shooting up his thighs. He fell onto his side, protected from any more gunfire by a large generator.

Using the air-conditioning ducts for cover, he crawled in Rocco's direction, kicking with his legs like swimming on the ground.

Andy peeked over the edge of the ductwork. Rocco was only ten yards away, looking right in Andy's direction.

"Hopewell is somewhere to the right," Andy said. "He's flanking you."

Andy's message arrived too late. Hopewell stepped out from the stairwell structure at the corner of the roof. Rocco's back might as well have had a bullseye painted on it.

The camouflaged military man smiled.

Andy rose, screamed gibberish, and fired his machine-gun pistol. Which was empty. Which was bad.

Hopewell shifted his rifle away from Rocco and pointed it at Andy's head.

CHAPTER 36

I don't find any of it funny anymore.

—Reported last words of Auction City seamstress Candy
Maxwell right before she stepped off the O'Donoghue
Street railway platform. She was killed a second later
by the oncoming H train (1956).

In the moment before his imminent demise, Andy's world went quiet. He didn't hear the fighting on the street, the chaos of the city, or Hopewell's cruel laughter. A peaceful second of contemplation that could have been spent on philosophy and the nature of man. The only thing that went through his head was his acknowledgment of the pathetic metaphor of an empty gun. Why did there have to be so many symbols for impotence? If Andy survived, he would get back on the dating circuit. It couldn't be that much more painful or frightening than getting shot at.

Hopewell fired his weapon, but the bullets never reached Andy.

When Andy opened his eyes, he saw Rocco holding a heavy piece of sheet metal in front of him. Hopewell's bullets were pinging off it, the ricochet sound as loud as the rifle. The steel dimpled, but the bullets didn't puncture it.

Andy ducked for cover. He chucked the empty machine-gun pistol and pulled his revolver. He crawled along the edge of the ductwork, trying to get a better angle at Hopewell from the side.

Hopewell marched forward toward Rocco. A volley of his shots tore into the exposed fingers of Rocco's left hand, spraying blood and flaying them to the bone. Rocco winced and fell to a knee, but he held on to the heavy sheet of metal. It must have weighed close to eighty pounds. Hopewell reached Rocco, standing over the shielded man.

Andy rose from behind his cover and fired his pistol. All three shots hit their mark. The hand, the shoulder, and the neck. Hopewell fell a few feet from Rocco, one hand clutching his neck.

Andy jumped the ductwork and ran to the two men. He kicked Hopewell's gun away. Andy pulled Rocco's handkerchief out of his pocket and wrapped his father's fingers, the white fabric immediately saturated by blood.

"Nice shootin'," Rocco said.

"Thanks," Andy said. He started lifting the metal sheet to pull it off Rocco.

Rocco nodded his head toward Hopewell. "Make sure."

Hopewell was alive, fingers reaching for his rifle a foot away. More instinct than purpose. Andy kicked the rifle farther across the roof.

Hopewell laughed. "Well, ain't that a pisser."

"Why didn't you run?"

"No better way to go than doing the thing you love."

"There's still time to get help," Andy said.

"People don't survive grenades."

"What do you—"

Andy dove back. He pulled the sheet of metal off Rocco and flipped it on its end on top of Hopewell, then shielded Rocco's body with his own, arms around the old man's head. Nothing happened for exactly two seconds. Like the awkward moment holding a smile waiting for someone to take a photo.

The sheet of metal only slightly contained the grenade blast. Andy felt the heat and shock wave on his legs and the bottoms of his feet. Pebbles from the roof sandblasted his exposed skin. Small projectiles, but nothing big enough to kill him. Scratches on his scratches. Bruises on his bruises.

When Andy looked, a hole had replaced Hopewell on the roof. No sign of the military man. The sheet of steel flew in the air thirty feet above like a piece of cardboard caught in the wind. It reached the apex of its ascent, arced, and plummeted. Rocco and Andy lay directly in its flight path. Andy picked up Rocco by the armpits and push-dragged him toward the edge of the roof.

The bent sheet of metal stabbed through the roof like a knife. It cut through multiple floors, slicing its way through the center of the building.

Andy held his father. "This is where you say you're too old for this shit."

"You're only as young as you feel," Rocco said. "And frankly, right now I feel two thousand years old."

◆ ◆ ◆

Leaning heavily into Andy, Rocco guided them through the maze of the building. Andy's body hurt like hell, but he was past complaining. He imagined himself in a full body cast. His idea of a vacation.

Smoke filled the hallways, a fire burning somewhere in the building. Turning a corner, they almost ran into Frank Whittle, the prison guard. Armed with two kitchen knives, he looked crazed.

"I got one of them to admit it," Whittle said. "It was police that killed Connor."

"Not all of them," Rocco said. "Gray, Robinson, the Thorntons."

Whittle shrugged. "Cops are cops." He ran in the opposite direction reciting "This Little Piggy" in an eerie, singsong falsetto.

◆ ◆ ◆

Back in the foyer of 6243 Holt Avenue, Andy and Rocco walked over the bodies to the front door.

"Hold on a second," Andy said. He scoped the ground and found a revolver. He checked to make sure it was loaded and rejoined Rocco. "Feels ghoulish, but mine's empty."

"He's not going to need it," Rocco said.

"You should wait it out in here."

"And miss all the fun?" Rocco said. "I've never shied away from a fight in my life."

"You should listen to yourself sometime," Andy said. "I'm going to get you somewhere safe. Then I'm going to get Champ and Mac out of here. I got enough fight for that."

Andy opened the door, and the two men walked out onto Holt Avenue.

The chaos had ended but not the threat. Instead of the expected bedlam, the police and their opponents had divided into two clear fronts. A row of police cars blocked one side of the street. On the other side, everyone else: Trust, 893, Consolidated, a few priests, and most surprisingly, some police officers.

Police helicopters flew overhead. It appeared that they were corralling the TV helicopters, keeping them from getting a shot of the action.

Behind a Crown Vic barricade, Hank Robinson stood with a bullhorn in one hand and a revolver in the other. The cops around him looked mostly like Thorntons with a few scattered loyalists. Not many left. Robinson was done. His Alamo.

With Rocco on his arm, Andy made his way through the crowd. Pilar and a few of her girls found them.

"What is this?" Andy asked.

"Good. You're here."

"What the hell does that mean?" Andy said. "Here for what?"

Pilar walked into the no man's land between the two groups, facing Robinson and his men.

"I can make it on my own," Rocco said. Andy let go of him. Rocco gingerly limped next to Pilar. Andy didn't understand, but he knew what he was supposed to do. He joined them, standing next to his father.

Out of the crowd, Agnes and Hiro emerged and joined the line. Floodgate stood strong. The five of them faced the police. Kate was going to be upset that she missed this moment, Andy acting as her proxy. The affiliated men and women behind them stood quiet and ready.

One of Robinson's men swore, took off his badge, set it on the hood, and walked toward them. They let him pass. Another did the same and followed. Robinson shouted into the bullhorn. In his frustration, he had forgotten to turn it on. He threw it on the ground, plastic shards scattering against the asphalt.

"It's over, Hank," Rocco said. "You can't win this."

"I'm not trying to win anything."

"What are you trying to do?" Rocco said. "What do you want?"

"Satisfaction," Robinson said. "Boys, you ready to show them?"

The five remaining Thorntons shouted, "Hooah!" They tossed their weapons to the side, balled their fists, and formed a row of their own. Three generations of goons represented, donnybrook ready. Raised on corned beef and John Wayne.

High noon at midnight.

"Oh, screw this," a voice said from behind Andy. He turned slightly to see the current head of the ACPD Fiscal Division, Randall Ashley, walk from the crowd, past Floodgate, and into the street between. He stripped off his dress blues as he walked, shedding both jacket and shirt.

Down to his tank top, Ashley stopped in the middle of the street and struck a barehanded boxer's pose, left held high. "You want satisfaction, Hank? Step up and take your beating. This has been a long time coming."

"Like hell!" Robinson yelled, tearing off his coat and walking past the Thorntons. They looked at each other, confused, but that was nothing new. "You've never been anything but a chicken-livered suck-up."

The two old men circled each other, pumping their arms, throwing jabs, and yelling insults at each other.

"Skulker."

"Poltroon."

"Bully."

"Wimp."

Rocco put a hand on Andy's shoulder for balance. Andy gave him a look. Rocco shrugged.

With the police and gangs of criminals as their audience, two old men beat the hell out of each other in the middle of the street. A war reduced to name-calling and a playground scuffle.

"What can you do?" Rocco said. "It's Auction City."

1929-1986

LONG PAST DAYS

According to the history books, the Flood lasted one day. The truce, hours. But it took almost two years to pull the city from anarchy. To establish peace and balance. To rebuild enough to live. For those two years, I worked ceaselessly with Floodgate. Not a single day off. They treated me with respect. I was embraced by men I admired. The work felt important. I felt important.

Between crises and injuries, I thought of her every day. At the time I didn't even know her name.

When I could, I looked, asked, tried to find her. With only a description. In a town scattered and surviving. No one could help me. They couldn't help themselves.

❖ ❖ ❖

When Floodgate disbanded—or so I thought—I went back to working for Fat Jimmy and the Trust. Back to being a hoodlum. More time to look for the girl, but every day my drive faded a little. I hadn't forgotten her. Only stopped looking. Out there somewhere. A nice memory, but she was lost to me.

I worked the rackets until December 1941. Pearl Harbor. Fat Jimmy was a patriotic man. Encouraged those of age to do their duty. I joined the marines. Had always liked boats. Never been on one but fancied how they looked.

The USS *San Juan* wasn't like the sailboats or barges in the river. It was the vessel that chauffeured me to battle. Guadalcanal. The Solomons. Unlike the young soldiers I fought alongside, the Flood had prepared me for the horrors of war. The only soldier in a foxhole having flashbacks to an even more violent time.

The war ended. I returned to Auction. Fat Jimmy had succumbed to his vices, and his son, Tony, had taken his place. Out of respect, he gave me a managerial position, but the organization was changing. Until Sal made his deathbed pitch, and I was back in a Floodgate.

❖ ❖ ❖

A case I had been working took me to Gallows Terrace. Something about stolen art or art forgery. The Chinese had some gripes about national treasures. It was all very complicated.

I had expected the maid or butler, but the woman of the house opened the door. It was her. It was the girl. Standing in the doorway of a Gallows Terrace mansion. The red-haired girl I had met in the sewers under the city. Twenty years older. A woman. More beautiful. Radiant. Real.

She gave me a bored look, then recognition. A hand to her mouth. Eyes big. She looked over my shoulder and made her face neutral. My partner, Father Mickey, was with me, in civvies, not his collar. He joined us. Formally, she introduced herself as Mrs. Elizabeth McIntyre. The first time I heard her name, but all I heard was the Mrs. part.

In what I guessed was the parlor, the three of us sat. Elizabeth and I traded glances. Mickey had questions about the art thing. The reason for our visit. She provided answers. Yes, her husband was overseas. Yes, he spent a lot of time in Asia. Yes, he had an import-export business. We already knew all that. He was a Trust man, working with the Triads. I had no idea what she knew about that, under the impression that we were insurance investigators.

When we were done, I reached for my business card, acted like I didn't have any, and asked Mickey to get them from the glove box. Gave us a minute.

"I looked for you," I said.

"I didn't want to come home. I couldn't stay in Auction. Spent six months in New York. My parents found me, shipped me to Europe," she said. "Boarding school."

"You're from the Terrace?"

"That day, I had run away from home. Why I was in the city when the Flood began. It wasn't important where I was from, because I had no plans to return."

"Yet here you are," I said. "Back in Gallows Terrace."

She didn't say anything. Studied my face. Smiled.

"I want to see you," I said.

"That's a bad idea," she said.

"Some of the best ideas I've ever had have been the worst ones."

Mickey walked back into the parlor. Business cards in hand.

It didn't matter. I knew where she was. Who she was. How to find her. If I could wait twenty years, I could wait however much longer.

❖ ❖ ❖

I used the art-smuggling investigation as an excuse to drop by. Often. Damn near every day. Using my imagination to fabricate reasons.

It took some asking. Some persistence. A lot of begging. She finally agreed to have dinner with me.

Her resistance wasn't that she was uninterested. She told me she was. But she was married. We hadn't seen each other in twenty years. And didn't know each other then or now. But we had shared something important. Only one day, maybe. But when your one day is the Flood, how many more do you need? How much more are you going to learn about a person?

We went to dinner at a roadhouse out past Cedarville. No cloth napkins or two forks for them. Lucky to get your food on a plate. Even in the rustic environs, I wore my funeral suit. Looked sharp. She stunned in green.

She looked over her shoulder through dinner. Worried she'd get recognized. But the three drunks and the working girl at the bar weren't interested in a couple of city folk unless they were buying the next round.

We talked nonstop. Relived that day. All the thoughts that were never words. Tried to fill the two-decade gap. My life so full of secrets that I kept to the war. Stories I didn't like telling. I let her do the talking.

I had known nothing in '29. My picture of her constructed from that day and my imagination had all been wrong. She was from a different world. She ran among people I didn't understand. But I knew her better than she thought. Because I knew her strength. Her courage. Her laugh and her smile.

We both knew we weren't meant for more than that day. Two refugees who had learned how to survive. Forced together by circumstances. Not by fate.

But in that moment. In a country dive. The lighting making everyone but her look like a ghoul. Red hair cascading over green satin. She was irresistible.

The food was horrible. Inedible. But the wine went down smooth. Three hours later, we got a room for the night in a fleabag motor court along the highway.

The next morning we said good-bye. Meant it. I felt good about it. She said she did, too. Like finding a lost toy from childhood. A prized top. That yo-yo you made yourself. Relieved because you thought it was gone, lost forever. But what do you do with it? What could you do but put it back in a box on a shelf in the closet?

❖ ❖ ❖

She contacted me ten months later. We met. She handed me a baby. A four-week-old baby. Put it in my arms. Told me I should meet my son before she took him to the orphanage.

Can't describe that moment. My son. Just like that. A boy with my eyes.

I didn't know what to do. But I couldn't send that child to an orphanage. He needed family. Some kind of family. I was almost grown when I lost my ma in the Flood, and it hurts every day. Changed me. My boy wouldn't grow up an orphan.

Elizabeth had managed to avoid her husband for the last six months. His overseas job did most of the work for her. The rest taken care of by a fabricated European vacation. There was no way she could keep an illegitimate child.

And neither could I.

That's when I thought of Champ. Her husband, Manny Destra, had died three months earlier. Felt some guilt about it. I had been there when it happened. Not my fault, but maybe I could have stopped it. So many gray areas in the life I now led.

I had done my best to keep an eye on Champ. She was devastated by the loss. Nothing worse than watching the toughest person you know crumble, quit a fight. Like a boxer tagged with an uppercut, their body no longer doing what they want. Legs giving. Body falling.

The best way to get a person to do what you want is to tell them to do it. Don't ask. Tell. If I had said, "Will you take care of this child?" she would have said no.

"I need you to take care of this child." That's all I said to Champ. She said yes.

I knew it was permanent, but told myself that I would be there on birthdays. Back with me as soon as I settled.

I never settled. Floodgate became my life. There was always a new threat. A new adventure. The city had Communists and the Benchley Street Wars and the Black Snake cult and university radicals, and soon I was immersed.

Before I realized it, my son, Andrea, was a full-grown man.

I could only watch from a distance. Protect him from threats he didn't know existed. And as I amassed enemies, the thought of any potential danger that I might bring his way kept me from exposing the truth to him. The right time to tell him hadn't just passed. It had never existed.

Sometimes it takes a death to bring a family together.

Now I have a son. Not again, but for the first time. He doesn't know me. He doesn't like me. My age and job don't bode well for a long life. But maybe we have a couple of beers, have a few laughs, and catch some ugly fish in the river under the bridge.

1986

CHAPTER 37

Do the people make the city? Or the city make its people?
Just as our bodies generate new cells every seven years,
the people that reside in this city aren't the people that
lived here a century ago. Maybe it's the city that defines
itself.

> —From an anonymous man interviewed by the Channel 6
> News on a live broadcast in answer to the question, "Who
> are you voting for in this year's mayoral race?" He later
> admitted to inhaling an enormous amount of modeling
> glue prior to the interview (1969).

There were very few things sadder than a hurriedly and unenthu-
siastically decorated grocery store sheet cake. At the same time,
there's nothing more essential to an office going-away party. It was not
a component of the party. It was what defined it.

Candles burned on the unnatural pink-and-teal frosting, topped
with the uninspired message, "Well miss you, Kale." How much effort
did it take to drop in an apostrophe or cross a *T*?

Already liquored, Kate held up a plastic cup of champagne. "We
don't get medals, but we do get paid. Here's to you guys. Some of you
are new. A few of you, I've fought alongside twenty years. Lost too many

friends in that time. But I never lost myself. So screw you guys—here's to me."

They all raised their cups and cheered. Macklin poured a round of refills, spilling as much on the floor as he got in the cups. He drank what remained directly out of the bottle.

"What are you going to do now?" Hiro asked, his face beet red.

"Whatever the hell I want," Kate said. "Florida. The beach. I can still work a two-piece. Work my wiles, while I still got wiles to work. Find some mature gentleman who can still hoist his main. Live the dream."

"There are many sea captains in the region," Agnes said.

Everyone laughed. Agnes looked confused but joined in.

"You've earned it, Katie," Macklin said, holding up the bottle and giving her a wink.

"It's not going to be the same without you," Pilar said.

"You're going to miss the city, Katie," Rocco said. "The action."

"The only shots coming my way from now on are going to have rum in them."

Andy had a sip of the champagne, but he wasn't drinking. He had plans later that evening.

Kate was going to be hard to replace, a key member of the team. At least Andy had already seen some action. He would do his best in his new position as the fifth member of Floodgate.

◆ ◆ ◆

A few hours later, the going-away party wound down. Rocco helped Kate into the passenger's seat of the station wagon. Draped over his body, boneless and beaming. Agnes waited behind the wheel.

"Everyone coming back to my place? Let's keep this party going!" Kate yelled, probably thinking she said it with a normal volume.

"That's not happening," Rocco said.

"While you're out," she said, "pick me up some Dolly Madisons."

"You're going home, Katie," Rocco said.

"That's what I said."

Rocco closed the passenger door and gave the roof two knocks. Agnes backed out of the factory. He watched her go. Andy walked up behind him.

"Thanks for understanding," Andy said.

"You don't know how many times I've thought about going back there myself," Rocco said. "Didn't work out for me. I hope it helps you find what you're looking for."

◆ ◆ ◆

The last time Andy had been to Gallows Terrace, things hadn't gone according to plan. He had gone to confront a man but ended up killing his archenemy, meeting his long-lost father, and joining a ragtag criminal constabulary. Standing in front of a new set of iron gates, he wondered what could go wrong this time. Maybe he would end up fighting a monkey army and being abducted by Martians, instead of a simple meeting with his birth mother.

He'd been standing in the same spot for the better part of a half hour. For the tenth time, he read the piece of paper that Rocco had given him. A name and an address.

Beth McIntyre 138 Pierrepont Lane

An intercom box sat mounted to the brick wall that surrounded the property. A brass placard next to it read: The McIntyres. Andy pressed the button. A sharp buzzing noise made him jump.

A voice from the other end said, "Who is it?" Through the static, it sounded like Charlie Brown's teacher. Andy could tell it was a woman's voice, but that's as far as he got.

He walked away. Away from the house. Turned off Pierrepont Lane. Down the hill. And out of Gallows Terrace.

Maybe he would come back. He didn't know. But today was not the day.

Beth was married to the same man. Their forty-year anniversary made the newspaper. Had a few kids with him. Andy's presence could do no good other than clearing a ledger, but it could do considerable harm. Thirty-seven years is yesterday when it comes to betrayal. He wasn't angry at the woman. He understood her decision. His gift to his mother would be to leave her to her life.

Besides, he knew who his real mother was.

◆ ◆ ◆

Champ set the photo album down when Andy came into the room. Her nurse, Russell, was back at work, sitting next to her and looking at the photographs with her. He wore shorts due to the bandage and brace on his leg. He was shirtless, too, displaying muscle groups that Andy didn't know people had.

"Why aren't you wearing a shirt?" Andy asked Russell.

"I told him to take it off," Champ said.

"Why?"

"Are you kidding me? Look at him," Champ said. "Make them dance, Russy."

Russell smiled and flexed his pectoral muscles individually, the muscles leaping in his chest. Champ clapped and laughed.

"Good to see you're recovering," Andy said.

Russell stood and went into the back bedroom, leaving them the room. Andy took his spot on the couch.

"Cardinal Macklin told me to tell you that he might be dropping by later," Andy said. "See how you're doing."

"Is that so?" Champ said, an eyebrow raised.

"Why? What?"

"He got a little handsy in the panic room," Champ said. "I chalked it up to the adrenaline. Getting shot at. Didn't know he had notions."

"He's a priest."

"I know," she said. "I like perverts."

"Let's see what's on TV," Andy quickly said, fumbling with the *TV Guide*.

They watched back-to-back reruns, *Switch* and *McMillan & Wife*. During a commercial break, Andy asked, "You got everything you need, Champ?

Champ put a hand on his forearm. "I do now."

◆ ◆ ◆

Driving the ice cream truck through the city, Andy could still see the aftermath of the Costales Riots. A few burned buildings. Damage to public sculpture. Specific graffiti. However, as Auction City riots went, it didn't even rank in the top ten. People on the street, but without the police escalating it, a natural calm followed. Broken glass and overturned cars, but no more bodies.

Ashley had won that fight. Bleeding and bruised, he had dragged a beaten Robinson in front of the line of Thorntons. They looked at their fallen leader, then to Ashley, and saluted. The nature of the new ACPD leadership was yet to be seen, but the Gray/Robinson era had ended. There was hope for the city. And for its criminal element.

Andy had fed a story to Rebane that explained the events in the way Macklin decided they should be reported. Peppered with truth, verified by proper sources and eyewitness accounts, it was just farfetched enough to become history. As reported, the Auction City Police Department suffered a number of casualties in its efforts to save people from a burning building. Dozens died in the Holt Avenue fire. Rebane didn't buy any of it, but he knew a front-page byline when he saw one.

Andy hadn't absolved himself from the crimes he'd committed. While wrongdoing and crime were clearly different, the act of killing a man wasn't a thing he wanted to forgive himself for doing. It carried weight. A thing he bore—if not on his back, then in his pocket, as a reminder of the repercussions of his actions.

He pulled the ice cream truck into the candy factory, knowing how silly that sounded.

◆ ◆ ◆

It was close to midnight, but Andy's new apartment was too clean and organized to feel lived in. He ended up where he felt most at home, in the bowels of Floodgate HQ.

Andy pulled the next box off the shelf. He noted the numbers on the side and checked it against his inventory. He shook his head, disappointed.

For all the information they had stored in that basement, it wasn't any good to anybody if they couldn't find anything. The system was broken. Like everything else involved in their operation, it looked impressive from the outside, but was slapdash and fraying at the edges.

The box didn't just hold the files it was supposed to. It did contain a sandwich circa the Reformation. The artifact had hardened into a fossil but somehow still held the faint smell of bologna.

The Apple IIe they had finally taken out of the box would help, but it was going to take years to inventory and reorganize their system. The thought of all that organizing made Andy smile broadly. He picked up the sandwich with two fingers and tossed it in the wastebasket with the dead mouse and Ziploc of Funyuns that he'd also unearthed.

"Thought I'd find you here," Rocco said. He strolled down the aisle. "How'd it go?"

"I went to see Champ instead."

Rocco nodded.

Andy kicked the box at his feet. "Going to be down here every day for the next ten years by the look of it."

"The whole history of the city in these boxes," Rocco said. "A walk-in closet worth of skeletons."

"Even with all this recorded history, most stories don't make it onto paper. Most of them, they stay in people's memories."

"You may be right," Rocco asked. "I got some stories, to be sure."

"I'd love to hear them," Andy said.

Rocco sat down on the small stool. "Best place to start is the Flood."

Pilar poked her head around the corner, interrupting him. "You're here. Great. I've been looking for some backup. Lords of Death are raising some kind of hell in Chinatown. It's causing a stink between Consolidated and 893."

"Sounds like big trouble," Andy said.

"Hiro's in the conference room," Rocco said. "After seeing the hobo film, he tasked himself to shoot a new intro movie. He's back there trying to figure out how to work the video camera."

"Agnes is already on her way over," Pilar said. "If we want to avoid bodies, we best get moving."

"Load up the station wagon," Rocco said. "We'll be right up."

Andy closed the box and returned it to the shelf. "I still want to hear those stories."

"We got time," Rocco said.

ACKNOWLEDGMENTS

Enormous thanks to:

Everyone at Thomas & Mercer. I couldn't ask for a smarter and more talented team working to find readers for my books. Specifically, editors Anh Schluep and Alan Turkus, who didn't blink when I told them how different this book was going to be. And, of course, Jacque Ben-Zekry. If a more loyal and stubborn champion for writers exists, I haven't met them. Every day, I'm glad that little maniac is on my side.

My developmental editor, David Downing, who has started to get used to my habits and idiosyncrasies after editing three of my books. Despite his insistence that the semicolon is a legitimate form of punctuation, the book always gets sharper and more concise in his care.

The most underrated and essential part of the process, my first reader. Since I started writing books, I've only trusted one person, author Bart Lessard, to read early drafts of my work. The insights that I walk away with from his feedback always give me new energy and great ideas. Auction City would not exist without him.

My mom, Pinkie, for being my mom.

My partner in crime, fellow adventurer, and the love of my life, Roxanne. I can't imagine where I would be without her. She makes me laugh every day and lets me make her laugh. And there ain't nothing better than that in the whole damn world.

◆ ◆ ◆

Floodgate was written at Beulahland and Rocking Frog Cafe in Portland, Oregon.

ABOUT THE AUTHOR

Illustration © 2012 Roxanne Patruznick

Johnny Shaw was born and raised on the Calexico/Mexicali border, the setting for his Jimmy Veeder Fiasco series, which includes the novels *Dove Season* and *Plaster City*. He is also the author of the Anthony Award–winning adventure novel *Big Maria*. His shorter work has appeared in *Thuglit, Crime Factory, Shotgun Honey, Plots with Guns*, and numerous anthologies. He was the creator and editor of the short-lived fiction publication *Blood & Tacos*. Johnny lives with his wife in Portland, Oregon.

You can find him online at www.johnnyshawauthor.com.

Follow him on Twitter @BloodAndTacos.